CHAPTER OF SH

CHAPTER
OF
SHADOWS

❖

AILEEN ARMITAGE

COLLINS
8 Grafton Street, London WI
1990

William Collins Sons & Co. Ltd
London · Glasgow · Sydney · Auckland
Toronto · Johannesburg

BRITISH LIBRARY CATALOGUING IN PUBLICATION DATA

Armitage, Aileen
Chapter of Shadows.
I. Title
823.914
ISBN 0-00-223537-4 ─142.

First published in 1990
© Aileen Armitage 1990

Photoset in Linotron Plantin by
Rowland Phototypesetting Ltd,
Bury St Edmunds, Suffolk
Printed and bound in Great Britain by
William Collins Sons & Co. Ltd, Glasgow

For the Women of the Year Luncheon in
recognition of their sterling work in
aid of The Greater London Fund for
the Blind

'And I will show you something different from either
Your shadow at morning striding behind you
Or your shadow at evening riding to meet you;
I will show you fear in a handful of dust.'

T. S. ELIOT, *The Waste Land*

CHAPTER ONE

Cold rain sleeted against Leah's cheek and she shivered as silent men lowered the coffin into the gaping grave. The second coffin lay ready on the sodden grass; soon Max would lie alongside his Maddie, inseparable in death as they always had been in life. Leah felt a lump constrict her throat. It must be wonderful to be so loved, totally and unreservedly.

Man that is born of woman has but a short time to live.

The words were whipped away and lost in the gusty sleet sweeping across the graveyard. The vicar's voice sounded as thin and desolate as a ghost's, his white cassock clinging damply to his spare frame. Leah grew angry.

It should have been sunny, she raged inwardly. The least a benign God could have done after robbing Maddie so cruelly of life was to give her sunlight on the day of her funeral – glorious, golden light such as she had always shed on those around her.

'*Silly of me,*' Maddie used to say, '*but I've always hated the cold and the dark. It always reminds me how my mother died, staying out all night on the moor in the middle of winter to tend a newborn lamb. Poor Mother.*'

Leah recalled watching Maddie's slim figure only three weeks ago as she boarded the boat train, how she'd bubbled with all the excitement of a ten-year-old about her first skiing holiday, but that was part of her grandmother's fascination. In her sixties she still retained an eager zest for life; she would never have grown old. In her mind's eye Leah could see her still with the tall figure of Max close behind her, leaning out of the window to wave as the train slid away and blowing a kiss. Now Maddie lay cold and still, crushed to death under foreign snow.

Leah looked across the open grave to where her mother stood. Daddy close beside her, his handsome face expressionless and Leah noted sadly how, even in grief, their bodies never touched. Mother was pale, like all redheads, her skin now showing faint, almost imperceptible lines about the full lips and clear eyes, like fine porcelain beginning to craze. But she was a beautiful and impressive woman still, the tumble of curls only slightly less defiantly red than a year or two ago. She looked stunning in black, so different from the bright colours she usually wore. Mother looked every inch the successful businesswoman and even nearing fifty she still caused heads to turn when she entered a room. It was not going to be easy telling her . . .

Maddie and Max gone. Eva could still hardly believe it. No more hugs and kisses in Maddie's warm arms, no more reassuring strength to chase away the moments of despair. Always enthusiastic for life, Maddie was now snuffed out like a candle.

Candles. A sudden mental image flashed across Eva's inward eye of Maddie's father, old man Renshaw, all those years ago.

'Turn that bloody paraffin lamp off. Don't you know there's a war on? You can use candles same as everybody else.'

How time flew, she mused. But for the war life might have turned out very differently. She would never have been evacuated from the bombed backstreets of Middlesbrough to the safety of Scapegoat Farm with Maddie and old Renshaw. She might have stayed a city kid who grew up to marry another slum kid as her own mother had done, never knowing the moors and pure, clean air, never knowing Maddie, nor seen the love that blossomed between her and the lonely Austrian refugee who came to work at Scapegoat. They had made a wonderful couple, each revelling in the other's love. Eva's eyes filled with tears.

Alongside her she could see her own husband's bowed head, his hair now dark grey like the weathered slates on the roof of Barnbeck's old village church, giving him the patriarchal air of a biblical apostle. But Alan Finch was no saint. He was an ageing roué, a man who'd never been able to come to terms with responsibility. At least he had known what to do when tragedy struck.

Eva recalled the winter sunlight streaming across the reception area in the Paris hotel while she had been settling her bill, and how she'd been looking forward to getting back home to London.

'Madame!'

The woman behind the reception desk had held up an envelope. Eva recalled putting down the suitcase and tearing open the telegram, then staring at the printed words, a feeling of clammy unease clutching her chest.

Phone immediately. Urgent. Alan.

He'd broken the news as gently as anyone could, but it was hard to credit. Maddie dead, the lovely, lively woman who'd become best friend and mother when her own mother had disowned her. And Max dead too, both at once. It just wasn't fair to those left behind.

Eva swallowed hard and looked up across the grave towards her daughter. Leah stood with her hands tightly clasped before her, blonde head bent, pale and tight-lipped while the vicar's voice droned on. Behind her the burly figure of Nathan stood watching, and for the first time it struck Eva what a handsome couple they made, her daughter and her stepbrother. Maddie and Max had been so proud of their only son. Strange, having a stepbrother only two years older than her own child.

'*Ashes to ashes, dust to dust . . .*'

They were lowering Max's coffin into the damp earth now. At least for Maddie and Max it was a blessing they had gone together. Inseparable in life, neither could have borne the suffering of living without the other. Tears stung Eva's eyes. It must be wonderful to be so loved . . .

The ritual ended. Alan Finch watched his wife with pride as she inclined her head to acknowledge the condolences of the villagers who had come to bid farewell. Her lovely face was composed as she listened. Long estranged they might be, but Eva would always be a woman he could admire and respect. And the sight of her stirred those old, familiar feelings . . . An old lady clung to Eva's arm.

'I know she become Maddie Bower when she wed that German fellow, but she'll always be Maddie Renshaw to me. There's always been Renshaws in Barnbeck. I'll never forget how kind she were – how she took you in when you was a little evacuee lass. Eh, she were a good 'un, were Maddie . . .'

Alan sighed and turned away. This was no time to go to her, to try to comfort her – she needed to be left to come to terms with grief and guilt in her own way, to overcome pain the way she always had. She was a proud woman.

He tugged Nathan by the arm and the two men strode away uphill towards Scapegoat Farm.

Nathan strode, head down against the rain, oblivious to the mud squelching over his shoes and a helpless ache burning inside him. If there was a God He was cruel and selfish, taking both Mother and

Father at one go when they had so much to live for. All the improvements they'd made to Scapegoat, all the plans they had still to carry out – all worthless and pointless now.

He tried hard to drive the anger out of his head, to replace it with happy memories, but they would only come in the briefest of snatches, dissolving before he could draw comfort from them. Instead he could see only the icy snow engulfing their beloved faces, and the anger came rushing back.

He must try to suppress it, to remember that others needed him now. Leah and Eva were just as heartbroken. He recalled how they had stood at the graveside, beautiful and composed, and he was proud of them. He was aware of Alan striding in step beside him, head bent against the sleet, and brushed the tears from his eyes with the back of his hand . . .

'Come and see this new filly I've got,' he muttered. Alan nodded and their footsteps rang on the cobblestones as they crossed the yard towards the stable.

Leah stood waiting by the lych gate, watching Eva as her footsteps crunched along the gravel path towards her. This was hardly the time or place to tell her mother what was on her mind, but some time soon she would have to speak. Her mind was made up, and Mother was not going to like it.

Neither spoke as they trudged up the muddy lane, heads bowed against the sleet and each deep in her own thoughts. Leah was biting her lip, conscious of the cold wind numbing her cheek. It had to be now or never.

I've got to break it to her sooner or later. It's only fair to let her know.

As Leah lifted the latch on the farm gate she took a deep breath and spoke, her voice gruff with unshed tears.

'I'm not coming back into the business with you, Mother. I've made my mind up.'

Her mother looked startled. 'Not coming back? Nonsense, love – of course you will. You're just upset – we all are.'

'I mean it, Mother. It's not for me.'

'Oh, for heaven's sake, Leah, not now.'

'Mother, you've got to listen. This is important to me. I can't go on working in your shadow.'

'Rubbish. You're not in my shadow.'

'I've got to get out,' Leah repeated firmly. 'I don't want to become like you – married to the job.'

Eva stared, speechless for a moment, then touched her daughter's hand. 'I loved them too, you know. I'm just as shattered as you are.'

Leah turned to her angrily. 'So why didn't you see them when you had the chance? Why weren't you there when they wanted you?'

'You haven't forgotten, have you, Mother? They're coming today, on the way to Switzerland. We said we'd have lunch with them.'

'Today? Oh no, I've got an appointment.'

'What's so vital that you can't postpone it?'

'A meeting. Trying to raise cash for the new site.'

'Can't it possibly wait?'

'You can't just drop everything at a moment's notice in a business like Urchin, you know that.'

'Urchin. That's all I ever hear.'

'Now look, Leah. I started this company and I've kept it going all these years on my own. No one else controls Urchin – it's mine.'

'OK. I'll go and meet Maddie and Max on my own.'

'Tell them I'll definitely meet them on the way back – take them for tea at Fortnum and Mason's – how's that? But business first, Leah. That's what's kept us fed all these years, remember.'

The yard lay quiet under the rain as they crossed the cobblestones towards the house. Even the horses in the stables made no sound, as if aware of the solemnity of the day. As they reached the door Eva spoke gruffly, her hand on the doorlatch . . .

'Anyway, now is not the time for decisions. You've only been in the business for a year – give it a chance.'

Leah shrugged. 'It doesn't matter what you think, Mother – I'm leaving. I've got to.'

Her tone was defiant but Eva could see only a pale-faced girl, raindrops gleaming in her hair and coat collar pulled up close around her neck. She looked so young.

Eva gave a thin smile. 'We'll see. Look, it's freezing out here – let's go in and have a nice hot cup of tea.'

Alan and Nathan were not in the farmhouse. They must have gone down to the stables together, Eva concluded. A girl from the village was singing a tuneless pop song to herself as she cut bread for sandwiches in the kitchen. Eva took off her sodden coat and stood warming herself in front of the blazing fire.

Leah sat, shoulders hunched, on a fireside chair. Eva could see the tears glistening in her eyes and touched her shoulder.

'I'd take that wet coat off if I were you, love.' Leah made no move. Eva went on gently. 'Look, love, if you've really had enough of Urchin, why not come back to Scapegoat for a while? It'd give you time to think.'

Leah's shoulder was stiff under her touch and her voice sounded strangled. 'No. The farm is Nathan's affair.'

'It's highly likely they've left it jointly to him and you, knowing how you feel about the place. You've always loved it here.'

'That was when Maddie was alive. It's different now.'

Eva's tone was soft, persuasive. 'You could take over the riding side for a bit and relieve Nathan. You're great with horses.' Seeing that Leah would not look up to meet her gaze she went on, 'Anyway, time enough to decide when you know what's in the will.'

She meant the words to sound conciliatory, to reassure her daughter that she would not bring pressure to bear, but Leah looked up sharply and she saw the sudden set of her expression.

'There's more to life than cash.'

'Don't think I didn't love them too, Leah, but money is important, believe me.'

'But not the be-all and end-all of life. That's where we differ, Mother. Can't you see – that's why I've got to get away? I don't want to become like you.'

Anger flashed in Eva. She fought back the almost overwhelming urge to grab her daughter by the scruff of the neck and tell her a thing or two, but what was the use? How could she expect a girl not long out of university to understand that life didn't always work out the way one hoped, that sometimes making money and earning prestige was the only way left to prove one's worthiness? The only way to fight back when love failed?

'It sometimes has to fill the gap,' she said quietly. 'I'll go and make that tea now.'

Leah had made no effort to hide the studied coldness in her tone and Eva's heart was heavy. As she left the room she saw her daughter rise stiffly from the chair to take off her coat, sighing deeply. It was going to take a great effort to break through Leah's grief and the barrier which had somehow suddenly sprung up between them.

Leah sat moodily on the bed in the little room which had always been hers. A lump swelled again in her throat as she fingered the patchwork bedspread Maddie had stitched for her all those years ago, and she wondered why such fierce resentment burned in her when she came near her mother.

She couldn't help it. Mother could have humoured them that last day in London. She could have been within reach when the news came through.

And on top of that Mother's words had angered her. Talking of wills and money when Maddie and Max lay newly-buried not an hour ago – it seemed somehow sacrilegious. Only Mother, businesswoman to the end, would think in terms of money at a time like this. Heartless, that's how she seemed. God forbid, thought Leah, that she should ever grow like that!

Not like Dad. Whatever his faults, he cared nothing for money so long as it was there. Poles apart Mother and Dad might be in their attitudes to life, but somehow they complemented each other. If only they had stayed together – if only they would patch up their differences now and come together again, the world would seem a happier place.

A tap at the door disturbed Leah's moody reverie. She looked up sharply. 'Yes?'

To her relief it was Nathan's dark head which peered round the door. 'You OK?'

'Fine. Come in.'

She watched him ease his great size around the door and come to stand in front of her. For a moment dark eyes searched hers. He was very serious for his twenty-four years, thought Leah, darkly handsome and solemn-eyed like his Jewish father but bigger altogether, broad-shouldered and hard-muscled like an ox. He had Max's self-control too, only his pallor indicating the shock he too must be suffering at their sudden death. He stood looking down at her, stiffly unnatural and ill-at-ease in a suit. He hadn't noticed that one shoelace was unfastened. He cocked his head to one side and smiled. 'What's up, love?'

Leah spoke quietly. 'Mother's angry with me.'

'Whatever for?'

15

'I've just told her I'm leaving, getting out of Urchin.'

'I see.' Nathan rubbed his chin, a gesture which instantly reminded her of his father. 'Is that wise? You've got a damn good future there, and it means a lot to your mother – I'd think twice about it if I were you before rushing into things.'

'I'm not. I know what I'm doing. It's not just a sudden whim. I've been thinking about it for a long time.'

'Know what you want to do instead?'

'No. Only to forge a life of my own.'

He lowered his weight on to the bed beside her. 'Well, if you've made your mind up, why not ask Eva to help you find another job? She's got loads of contacts.'

'I wouldn't ask her. Urchin is her life, not me.'

He gave her a quizzical look. 'I think I detect a note of self-pity, Leah, and what's more I don't think Eva's as hard as you make out. She cares a lot about you.'

'But I don't want her moulding my life, Nathan. She likes organizing things – I want to set my own terms.'

For a moment there was silence, then Nathan spoke softly. 'You could come back here – stay as long as you like. Take time to sort things out.'

He took hold of her hand. It was small and white between his large, work-roughened fingers. Like a dead pigeon on brown earth. She pulled her hand away quickly. 'No, Nathan – I've got to get away from the past, from here as well as from Urchin. Can't you understand? I thought that you, of all people –'

He gave a rueful smile. 'OK, don't bite my head off.' He stood up and reached down to tug gently at her hand. 'Mr Wadsworth will be here soon. Come on downstairs.'

She looked down at the great hands engulfing hers again and sighed as she gave in to their strength and stood up. 'Nathan, Mother thinks they might have left the farm to you and me. I don't want –'

He laid a finger to her lips, cutting her short. 'Whatever's in the will, Leah, is all right by me. It'll be what they wanted. OK? Come on down now.'

Leah glanced at her tear-stained face in the dressing table mirror. 'I'll be down in a minute – and Nathan, your shoelace is undone.'

★

16

Eva stood by the window and watched Nathan's broad frame descending the stairs, but Leah wasn't with him. The girl from the village, a freckle-faced blonde with a narrow waist and splayed hips, moved about the table, laying out ham and tinned salmon sandwiches and seed cake. For long moments there was silence except for the clink of cutlery as the girl laid knives alongside the plates. Then she stood back and looked inquiringly at Nathan.

'Do you want me to do owt else, Nathan? Shall I hang on a bit?' He shook his head.

'That's fine, thanks, Sandra. You can go home now.'

'What about washing up the pots though? Can you manage?'

'We'll manage fine thanks,' said Eva. 'Don't worry.'

The girl seemed reluctant to leave but eventually Nathan showed her out. When he came back Eva could hear him humming quietly to himself as he clattered cups and saucers in the kitchen.

Alan sat by the fire, picking out coals from the scuttle with a pair of tongs and laying them carefully on the dying embers. Eva had a sudden fleeting memory of old man Renshaw, all those years ago during the war, making the same slow, deliberate movements as he admonished the defiantly unpenitent little evacuee.

'How many times must I tell thee, Eva lass? Leave them bloody chickens alone else they'll not lay. There's no toffees for thee on Saturday if tha does it again, I'm telling thee.'

Alan switched on the television. Eva forgot old Renshaw. Figures moved in a wordless dance across the silent screen, and Eva took a deep breath. 'Thanks, Alan,' she muttered.

His gaze swivelled to fix on her. 'What for?'

'Seeing to the arrangements. I'm grateful.'

He waved a hand. 'No need. Someone had to do it. We did what we thought you'd have done, that's all.'

He smiled that lazy, good-natured smile of his and for a few fleeting seconds Eva felt again the intimate conspiracy they used to share. Then, just as suddenly, the feeling vanished.

'How did you find me in the end?'

'Clay Richards' office.'

Eva looked at him in surprise. It couldn't have been easy for him to ring Clay after all these years. 'Why Clay's office?' she asked.

Alan shrugged. 'I tried your office – you weren't at the hotel they'd booked. I tried everyone else. When they told me he was in Paris . . .'

Eva switched off the television, then seated herself in the chair across the hearth from him and spoke quietly. 'Alan, I think we should talk before the solicitor comes.'

Alan shook his head. 'That's nothing to do with me – it's Bower business. I ought to be on my way.'

'I'd like you to be here. It's Leah's future. She's just told me she wants to leave Urchin.'

'Well, she's twenty-two, old enough to decide for herself.'

'She's no plans, nowhere else to go. It's grief talking – you know how she adored Maddie. She needs help, Alan.'

Alan eyed her solemnly. 'She's a grown woman, Eva. Let her make up her own mind in her own time.'

'And make her own mistakes? She's all mixed up, Alan.'

'We made ours. We survived.'

Eva clicked her tongue. 'It's hopeless talking to you. We have a problem daughter in need of guidance and you can't be bothered.'

'Immature, maybe, but what do you expect? It takes two to raise a child and you robbed her of a father.'

Eva could hear the coolness that crept into his tone. 'I had no choice but to leave you, Alan.'

'And take Leah away from me?'

Eva's back stiffened. 'I gave her love and security, just like Maddie and Max gave me.'

'We could have given her that, together.'

'Not security. Not with you gadding off with your lady friends all the time.'

Alan leaned forward in his chair, dark eyes earnest. 'I loved you all the same. I still do.'

Eva snorted and turned sideways in her chair, unwilling to meet his gaze. Alan's hand touched her knee.

'I mean it. You know we still have something, Eva.'

'Crap. It's no use, Alan – the past is dead. There's nothing left between us now.'

His fingers slid along her thigh and she trembled as he looked up at her under his eyebrows. 'Isn't there?'

Nathan came in from the kitchen, wiping his hands on the teatowel. 'I can see Mr Wadsworth's car coming up the lane. I'll get Leah.'

As he climbed the stairs Eva rose to her feet. 'I'll make some more tea.'

She took down the big brown teapot from the shelf and spoke casually. 'You will have a word with Leah before you go, won't you, Alan? Try and persuade her to listen to sense. She takes notice of you, though heaven alone knows why.'

'Because she knows I care,' he murmured.

Tea was a muted affair of quiet, inconsequential conversation interspersed with awkward silences. The table cleared, Mr Wadsworth, the solicitor, pulled papers out of a crumpled briefcase and spread them before him. Leah was aware of her father making a move to leave, of her mother whispering earnestly to him by the door, and of them both then taking a seat to listen. Nathan sat by the fire, head bowed.

Mr Wadsworth's manner was tinged with embarrassment as he cleared his throat to begin the business of the reading. Leah noted absently how his left eye seemed to wander off on its own devices while the other focused on Nathan.

'But now I'm afraid I must carry out my official duty and inform you all as to the contents of Mr and Mrs Bower's will,' he announced as he settled his weight on the wooden chair and began shuffling the papers.

Apart from the crackle of the fire in the hearth it was quiet in the farmhouse kitchen, not so much with expectancy as with resignation, but not yet acceptance. The old order was dead, the two who had been the stable central force in the family gone, but none of them could quite yet believe it.

'So there it is,' concluded Mr Wadsworth. 'In essence, apart from the one bequest to Leah Finch, the farm, riding stables and the residue of the estate belong jointly to the two children of the marriage, Nathan Bower and Eva Finch.'

Leah was aware of her mother's sharp movement, of the glance in her direction, but Leah made no sign of reaction. She felt neither surprise nor disappointment. Maddie and Max had done what was right and proper.

Father and daughter stood by the five-barred gate in the yard. The rain had stopped but the wet cobblestones still gleamed under the yard lights. Outside in the lane Alan's car stood waiting, glistening and silent.

'Bit of a surprise?' he asked. Leah nodded.

19

'Mother reckoned it would come to Nathan and me. Still, I didn't want it anyway.'

'Your mother still wants you to have it. That's why she offered –'

'I want no part of it, Daddy. It's Nathan's farm – he's always loved it and it means nothing to me now.'

'It's a fair offer, darling. You love the countryside, and you'd be doing her a favour.'

'I told you – no. I want to get away from all this, as far away as possible. Abroad, anywhere away from here.'

'If that's what you want –'

'I do,' she said earnestly.

He took a slow breath. 'Well, you've got the money to do what you want now. Have you talked it over with your mother?'

Leah shook her head firmly. 'No. She'd only try and stop me.'

He covered his daughter's hand with his. 'Try her. She might surprise you. In any event, make no hasty decisions, love. Give yourself time.' He straightened his long body and unlatched the gate. 'I'd better be on my way now.'

'Do you have to go yet?' Leah looked up at him, her misty eyes pleading with him. He touched her shoulder lightly.

'I have to, sweetheart. I have no part in this family.'

As he put the key in the lock of the car door he heard her fierce whisper.

'Nor me.' Leah moved forward and put her arms about his neck. 'Goodbye, Daddy. Take care.'

He disengaged himself gently. 'Give me a ring when you're back in London and we'll go out for a meal. I'd like you to meet Christie.'

She looked up at him sharply. 'Christie? Another girl? Honestly, Daddy – why do you do it?'

'You sound like your mother.'

'Answer me – why do you?'

He shrugged, that lazy, familiar movement that endeared him so much to her. 'Who knows? To prove I'm still young, I suppose.'

'Rubbish. Mummy doesn't need to.'

He smiled. 'How do you know she doesn't?' He touched a finger to her chin. 'Do what you feel you must, sweetheart. Be happy.'

Leah watched the car glide away down the muddy lane then, with a deep sigh, she went back into the house.

★

Eva and Leah sat by the kitchen fire. Nathan had changed out of his suit and looked far more at ease in wellingtons and an old anorak straining at the seams. 'I'm going down to the stables. It's the new filly – she's only half-schooled and she's not settled at all yet.'

Leah looked up from her book. 'Shall I come with you?'

He pulled the anorak hood up over his head. 'Better not. It's raining cats and dogs out there.'

A cold wind spattered raindrops on the flagged floor as he opened the door and went out. Eva watched her daughter's fair head as she bent over her book, then yawned and glanced at the clock.

'Did your father give you any advice about the future?' she asked casually. Leah did not look up from the book.

'No. Just to be happy.'

Eva sighed. 'Chasing happiness has never got him very far. He's never found it for all his gadding about.'

'Have you?' The voice was low but the challenge was clear. Eva folded her hands and spoke quietly.

'I've found fulfilment. I've found self-respect.'

Leah lowered the book. 'And is it enough, Mother? Don't you ever wish you had more?'

Eva looked away. 'I loved him once. Now I've got a thriving business, and I've plenty of friends.'

'So has Daddy.'

Eva's eyes grew dreamy. 'Yes, he always had. It was part of his attraction in the old days, his charm. I thought he was wonderful, but I knew he was a rogue all the same.'

'Then why did you marry him? Did you think you could change him?'

'Every woman thinks she can change her man. Stupid, isn't it?'

'He's still very fond of you, I can tell.'

'He never stuck around long enough to show it. Make sure you don't make the same mistake, Leah, being taken in by charm.'

Leah snapped the book shut. 'I don't want to hear any more.'

Eva frowned. 'I can't make you out, Leah. You can't bear to hear a word against your father. You don't know what I've had to put up with –'

'You've told me often enough. You've never stopped telling me since I was fourteen.' Leah rose, looking down at her mother with coldness in her eyes. 'You've never given him credit for anything. You're so wrapped up in your career, so hell-bent on making money, can't you see why I have to get away?'

'Leah! That's enough!'

The girl tossed the book aside on a stool. 'It's no use, you'll never understand,' she muttered. 'I'm going out.'

Eva watched as her daughter sprang up and made towards the door, grabbing up her jacket from a chair. Leah did not see the hand rise in a silent gesture of appeasement as she hurried out into the night.

Eva sat staring into the fire until the sound of the doorlatch made her turn eagerly. Nathan came in, raindrops sparkling in his crisp dark hair and an anxious expression on his earnest young face. He threw back the hood of his anorak.

'Leah's gone off – she grabbed the filly off me.'

Eva rose and came quickly across to him. 'The half-schooled one? Hadn't you better go after her?'

He shook his head. 'She rides well, she'll be all right. But she looked very upset. She probably needs to be alone.'

'I worry about her, Nathan. She's so like her father . . .'

'She's got a lot of you in her too.'

Eva gave a wry smile. 'Sometimes I wish I'd done things differently, had more time. Alan thinks that's what she needs – time.'

'And space. She needs space,' said Nathan, pulling off his jacket and shaking it vigorously.

'I know. I want to try and talk to her, but it's not easy. She's a very private person. Oh, we get on fine in the office, but otherwise –'

'Don't you see much of her outside work?'

Eva shrugged. 'We share the flat.'

She was looking at her stepbrother, hoping for words of reassurance. He seemed to sense it, and smiled. 'Look, I know you want what's best for Leah – just leave her to herself for a bit. She'll come round.'

Eva gave a deep sigh. 'I like to get to grips with a problem, Nathan, not just sit and wait. But life's not always as easy as that. Sometimes it's like a roller-coaster you can't get off . . .'

She drew back the curtain to gaze out into the night. 'She's just like Maddie,' she murmured. 'And me. Alone, on the moor . . .'

For many minutes she continued to stare out into the darkness, then at last she turned away from the window and gave a sad smile. 'I wish the sun had shone today, Nathan, for their sake,' she murmured. 'Maddie would have liked that.'

Nathan smiled as he touched her arm. 'In Yorkshire, in February? You must be crazy.'

It was late and Eva was growing uneasy. She was about to look out of the window yet again when the door opened quietly. Leah stood there, her fair hair clinging damply to her face and a flush on her cheeks.

'I've decided I'm going to stay on for a week,' she announced in a low voice, 'if that's all right with you, Nathan.'

He came across to her and took her arm. 'A week, a month, for ever – whatever you want, Leah.'

Eva gave a deep sigh and came towards her. 'I'm so glad you've changed your mind. We're all a bit fraught, darling. Tell you what, instead of going back in the morning why don't I stay on for a day or two as well? Then we could go riding together – up on the moor, to Thunder Crags. It'll do us both good, and we'll have a chance to talk.'

She saw the tension begin to drain from Leah's face, easing into a tentative half-smile. 'I'd like that,' she murmured. 'I'd really like that. But what about Urchin?'

'Urchin can go hang for a day or two,' Eva replied firmly. 'It won't go bankrupt without me.'

'Then that's settled,' said Nathan. 'Now what about supper?'

At noon next day Eva and Leah swept in, their faces aglow. Leah tossed a riding whip on the chair and lifted her nose.

'Mmm. Something smells good. I'm starving.'

Nathan smiled to himself as Sandra came out of the kitchen and took in Eva's slim bottom squeezed into Leah's spare blue jeans.

'It's wonderful up on the moor,' enthused Eva. 'Snow's melting fast.'

Leah agreed. 'Good blow of fresh air in our lungs – did us a world of good.'

Sandra sniffed. 'I've taken the apple pie out, Nathan, and the meat pasties are keeping warm in the oven. I'll be back this evening. Three for supper again tonight, is it?'

'Please,' said Leah. 'What do you fancy doing this afternoon, Mother?'

'I'll take you into town for a new pair of jeans.'

23

'No need. I've got two pairs.'

'You had, till I thought I could squeeze my size twelve backside into these size tens – I think I've split the seam.'

They were just finishing off the last of the apple pie when the telephone rang. Leah was licking cream from her spoon as Nathan went to answer it.

'Hullo? Yes? Yes, she's here.' He held out the 'phone to Eva. 'It's your chief accountant.'

Eva's good humour vanished and she was frowning as she took the receiver. 'Hello? Vincent? What is it? What? Oh, for heaven's sake, you know I'm at a funeral. Can't it wait?'

Leah sighed. Her mother still frowned as she carried on talking. 'That urgent? Can't you handle it? Or put it off then? Oh, I see.' She gave a deep sigh. 'All right then. I'll come back first thing tomorrow.'

She replaced the receiver and turned to her daughter. 'I'm sorry, love,' she began, but Leah cut in quietly.

'It's all right, Mother. Go on back to London.'

Eva sat down. 'I've got to go to Rome – let me explain –'

'No need. I know. Business first, the way it always has been.'

Eva leaned across to touch her hand. 'I wouldn't miss this chance of being with you for the world, but –'

Leah pulled her hand away slowly. 'You go, Mother, but don't expect me back in the office on Monday, or ever. I won't be there.'

For a moment Eva stared, then she sat stiffly upright on her chair. When she spoke her voice was cold. 'Oh yes you will. You'll work out your notice like everyone else. On Monday you can write me a memo.'

'Like hell I will.' Leah pushed back her chair and made for the stairs, leaving her mother staring helplessly after her.

Nathan surveyed Eva thoughtfully. 'She means it, you know,' he said. 'I've never seen her more determined.'

'Disappointed,' said Eva. 'I've let her down.'

'Let her go, Eva. It'll be for the best.'

Eva gave him a bleak smile. 'My only child, and I couldn't get it right,' she murmured. After a moment she got up and came round the table to her stepbrother, a tight smile on her lips and the old familiar light of determination in her eyes. 'But even so, everything will come right, Nathan, I know it will. They say every death marks a rebirth. It'll all come out right, just you see.'

CHAPTER TWO

Memories of Maddie slithered unbidden into Leah's mind, especially at night as she lay in bed at Scapegoat Farm. The warmth of her, enveloping everyone around her, the welcoming smile and the way she used to bend her head to listen as if there was no one else in the world at that moment. Max had been a wonderful grandfather, but the world would never see again a woman like Maddie.

Nathan said little but when Leah came downstairs one morning she found him standing with head bowed, one huge hand on the mantel-piece, staring at the photograph in the silver frame. A happy, smiling Maddie in the village church doorway wearing an austerity wedding dress of white nylon looking up adoringly into her handsome bride-groom's face. Max was looking down at her with tenderness in his dark eyes. Nathan turned away quickly at the sound of Leah's footsteps, but she had seen the glistening light in his eyes.

She could feel at peace in Nathan's company. Out around the farm or inside by the fire, they talked together of everything, of the happy times rather than the cruel trick of fate which had snatched Maddie and Max away. His huge presence seemed to fill the farmhouse with protective concern and the tenderness in their talk gave her a sense of closeness and security. Here was one person she could always trust, implicitly.

They rode together that afternoon on the moor, high above Barnbeck. Below them Leah could see the farm and the church and the cluster of village cottages, some still encircled by lingering grey wreaths of snow. Beyond she could make out the shape of the lovely old house, Thorpe Gill, shrouded among skeletal trees. Nathan dismounted and, holding his horse by the reins, spoke quietly as he looked down on the village.

'Why don't you stay here with me, Leah?'

She slid down out of the saddle and went to stand by him. 'I can't, Nathan. There's a whole world out there and I haven't tasted it yet.'

'There's a life for you here. I'd make it good for you.'

She slipped an arm through his. 'I know. But it's so quiet – nothing ever happens. People are born, they marry and die. Look at Thorpe Gill – it was beautiful when I was a kid, and look at it now. Fallen into rack and ruin.'

Nathan nodded agreement. 'Since the last of the Westerley-Kents went, nobody wants to buy a huge old place like that.'

'That's just it. Nobody ever *does* anything here. I bet Barnbeck hasn't changed in centuries.'

He smiled. 'That's part of its charm. But there are changes – you just haven't noticed.'

She frowned. 'Like what?'

'Let me show you.' He re-mounted his horse and rode off along the ridge. A hundred yards further on he raised a hand and pointed. 'See the new barns?'

She followed the line of his outstretched arm. 'On Bailey's farm?'

'Not Bailey's now. We bought it from him. And the one beyond, towards Agley Bridge. I drew up the plans for all the new buildings on both – barns, stables, everything. Dad was so proud of it.'

She heard the tremor in his tone and rode close to him, laying a hand on his sleeve. 'I'm sure he was,' she said softly, 'and of you too. You've worked hard.'

He tossed his head. 'Mum was going to start training showjumpers. I'd got the plans ready for her new stables, but now – oh, I don't know . . .'

Leah felt a surge of compassion. 'You must still go on with it then, Nathan. She'd have wanted that. You'll find someone.'

He turned his dark eyes to her. 'I'd like it to be you, Leah. But I'll do it all the same.'

Rome in sunlit winter brilliance was delightful. It always gave Eva pleasure to visit her fashion shops abroad, each one varying slightly to reflect its city; the chic Urchin salon of Paris closely resembled but did not mirror exactly the one in Madrid or its elegant Roman counterpart, and each was distinctly different from the original shop in Chelsea. The only thing which was common to all was elegant fashion, tactful help and courtesy towards the customer. Eva insisted on universal perfection.

She made her way along the tree-lined avenue towards the Urchin boutique with a feeling of anticipation lightening her step. Today she would sort out the manageress whose accounts had shown a sharp dip lately and tonight Clay would be arriving on the evening flight. These few days could prove to be both enjoyable and profitable.

A frown replaced Eva's smile as she caught sight of the shop window. It did not sparkle in the sunlight as she would have wished, and a thin film of dust lay over the black velvet draped between the emerald green shirt and the basket of exotic silk scarves on display. A dead wasp sprawled on its back between the revers of the shirt. Eva pushed open the door and walked in.

A tall, olive-skinned girl stood behind the mahogany counter, her back to Eva as she pinned a purple sweater to the folds of the velvet drapes on the wall. From the office in the back an unseen voice was calling out indistinct words in Italian. The girl shrugged.

'*Scusi*,' said Eva. The girl sniffed and, ignoring her, called back shrill words in rapid Italian to the unseen voice. Eva picked up a leather handbag from the counter.

'*Scusi*,' she said again. The girl turned and glared at her.

'*Inglesa?*' she enquired.

'*Si*. May I speak to Signora Bellini please?'

'Not today. She is busy.'

'This handbag,' said Eva. 'How long have you stocked these?'

The girl shrugged. 'Gucci handbags always. They are the best.'

Without a word Eva walked to the end of the counter and marched through into the inner office, the handbag under her arm. The assistant's eyebrows rose, but she made no move to stop her. Inside the office a startled Signora Bellini turned round at her desk.

'How long has that girl been here?' demanded Eva.

The woman raised her hands in surprise. 'Signora Finch! I was not expecting you!'

'The girl,' Eva repeated. 'How long has she been here?'

'Who, signora? Anna, my niece? Three weeks, maybe four.'

'She leaves today. And who is that?' Eva pointed towards the pimply-faced youth who entered by the back door, his shirt spattered with car grease and a large carton in his hand. Signora Bellini blushed.

'He is my son, Roberto. Say good morning to the lady, Roberto.'

He grinned sheepishly, a lopsided grin which gave Eva a sudden start of alarm. Roberto was clearly not all there. She turned to the manageress.

'Your niece and your son? How many more of your family do you employ in my shop?'

27

The woman raised flustered hands. 'No more, I assure you. Only my cousin does the deliveries for me now and again, when I need help.'

'When you are busy?' The woman seemed unaware of the menace in Eva's tone. 'You are often busy?'

'Oh yes, signora. We work hard. We work late when we must. Orders come in fast.'

'Do they now? Then why are the takings so low? And since when do we sell Gucci fakes?' Eva held out the handbag and saw the woman's face pale.

'Fakes? My cousin did not tell me they were fakes . . .'

'Show me the books, signora. And tell that Anna girl to fetch us coffee before she leaves. This could take some time.'

It was the first time Leah had ventured into Maddie's room since her death. Winter sunlight slanted in under the eaves and lay across the old high bed, lighting up the brilliance of the colours in the counterpane and the dust specks dancing in the air as Leah folded back the sheets.

An exercise book lay on the bedside table. Recognizing Maddie's neat handwriting, Leah picked it up and opened it. As she seated herself on the stripped bed words leapt out at her:

Sweet summer sang once in my veins,
Filling me with hope and radiant thrill.
Now age is creaking into my bones
But life, with love, is radiant still . . .

Leah laid the book down again quickly with a strange sense of being an interloper invading Maddie's privacy. It seemed wrong to read her innermost feelings without permission.

Leah stood at the window, looking down on the sunlit farmyard. Maddie had been proud of Max, she mused, and maybe she would be glad for those she had loved to read again of the love he had inspired in her. Leah drew a finger across the dusty windowpane, tracing idly the first word that came to mind.

Love.

A movement below caught her eye. Nathan's tall figure was striding across the yard towards the barn and at the sight of him Leah felt warmed. There was a kind of quiet assurance in his step, a resoluteness in his bearing that was so much his father. Like Max, Nathan would one day give some woman the same rocklike security and love that

Maddie had known. Perhaps that girl from the village who clearly couldn't take her eyes from him . . .

The thought irritated Leah. She turned away from the window and hurried downstairs to join him.

It was late afternoon when Eva, deciding against a taxi in order to walk and think, made her way back along the city streets towards the Grand Hotel.

Signora Bellini and her family were banished forever from the world of Urchin. Now the problem was to replace her with someone of the right mettle, someone who could match Eva's exacting standards. Clay might have some suggestion when he arrived. Clay had contacts everywhere.

Suddenly she saw it, a magnificent window filled with elegant fashion, impeccably displayed in a manner calculated to catch the discerning eye. A rich profusion of colour, carefully graduated like the spectrum of a rainbow so that no clashing violence offended the eye – this was the mark of an expert. Eva could not resist going inside.

'Signora, may I help you?'

The woman's voice was as cultured and mellow as her appearance. She could have been Sophia Loren with her impeccably-cut suit and sloe-eyed, slumberous look. Eva eyed her up and down appreciatively.

'Who did that window display? she asked.

'Why, I did,' said the woman with a smile. 'You find it pleasing?'

'Very,' said Eva. 'Do you own the shop?'

'I manage it for the owner.'

'You show pride in it,' said Eva.

'As if it were my own. I used to be its best customer until my husband died. Now I want to make it the best boutique in Rome.'

'Have you been here long?'

'Two years. Now, may I help Signora to select a gown, perhaps, or a hat? I have one in just the green to match the beautiful suit madame is wearing.' She reached for a hat perched on a model's head behind her.

'How much do you earn here?'

The woman's eyes betrayed no sign of embarrassment as she gave Eva a gentle smile and held out the hat. 'What do you think of this?'

'Because I'll pay you twice as much to run my shop,' Eva went on undeterred. 'Starting on Monday.'

★

'I couldn't have made a better choice, I'm sure of it,' Eva told Clay that night as they walked through the lounge of the Grand Hotel. 'I knew Silvana was right the moment I saw her.'

They were crossing the huge, intricately-patterned carpet surrounded by potted palms towards the Maschere restaurant. 'I take it you persuaded her then?' asked Clay.

Eva gave a mischievous smile. 'Don't I usually get what I want? She starts on Monday.'

As Clay Richards pulled out a chair for her, Eva thought what an impressive man he was. Tall and slim despite his fifty or so years, he had a distinguished air about him which kept waiters hovering attentively near. His movements were spare, but lively blue eyes missed nothing. With the same apparent lack of effort he also seemed to learn or sense before anyone else what was going on behind the locked doors of board-rooms and government offices. No wonder his subordinates at Cresco International held him in such awe and reverence.

There was a teasing note in his voice as he spooned out neat slices of avocado. 'So now, Eva, tell me, do I take it you're still interested in the Venn Street site?'

Eva nodded. 'I want it, Clay, and I know what I want to do with it.'

'You know the price. Can you raise it?'

Eva laid her spoon down and leaned across towards him. 'You're asking over the top in my opinion, but I can work it out. I'm worth a hell of a lot of money, Clay.'

'I know you are, with a chain of Urchins halfway round the world.'

'It's nothing compared to your empire but it's mine and I did it on my own. Now I want to expand.'

'And you need cash.'

Eva's eyebrows rose. 'Whatever makes you think that?'

Clay shrugged. 'I know Alan's caught a cold. I hear he's sold off another two of his restaurants. Four left out of ten now.'

Eva stiffened. 'He lost the first when you did the dirty on him. I haven't forgotten. Anyway, my husband's affairs are nothing to do with me. You know we're separated.'

Clay's gaze remained fixed on his plate. 'And I saw Vincent the other day. He was looking worried. You want to sell out, or go public?'

Eva frowned. 'You saw my chief accountant? What did you do – take him to lunch and pump him because you knew I was interested in Venn Street?'

Clay shook his head. 'No need. Walls have ears. I hear things.'

Eva laughed. 'And they're not always right. Anyway, even if I wanted to raise cash, why should I sell to you? It'd be nothing to you.'

'A chain of fashion shops could form another useful cog in Cresco International. I'd be very interested.'

'Why the hell should I let everything I've built up get swallowed up by you?'

'So if you've got a new bee in your bonnet why don't we talk it over, over coffee? Up in my suite – there's a wonderful view of the city from the balcony.'

'No funny business, Clay. We settled that in Paris, remember?'

Clay pushed the dessert plate aside and smiled. 'Life's not all about work you know, Eva. OK, nothing more, unless you feel inclined.'

'Right,' said Eva, rising from her chair. 'We'll look at the view and talk about Venn Street.'

There was a companionable closeness in the farmhouse kitchen. Nathan slumped in a deep armchair with his long legs stretched out towards the fire and the dying cadences of a Vivaldi record filled the air.

As the music ended Nathan stretched his arms above his head. On an impulse Leah threw a cushion at him and with a smile he fended it off. Seizing another cushion, she rushed at him, hurling her weight so hard against him that he rolled, off-balance, on the floor. The sober atmosphere of the room gave way to laughter as one body, burly and broad, flailed on the floor with the slight figure in a tangle of long blonde hair. Over and over they rolled, giggling and shrieking, bumping at last against the corner of the highly-polished sideboard.

Nathan lay on his back, laughing as he held the struggling Leah at arm's length above him while her fingers strained to reach his hair. Then suddenly she saw the laughter in his eyes die, and followed his gaze.

'What is it?' she asked.

Letting go of her abruptly he half-sat up and reached a huge hand under the sideboard. As he pulled it out again Leah saw the blue can of hairspray between his thick fingers.

'Mother's,' he muttered. 'She searched high and low for that before she left.'

Scrambling to his feet he put the can on the table and went back to

31

put another record on the turntable. Leah sat back on her haunches. 'Funny, isn't it, I feel as if Maddie'll walk in from the kitchen any minute.'

Nathan murmured, 'She loved this place so much. She'll always be here.'

'And yet –'

'What?'

'She told me once how she used to hate it. She was dying to get out into the world. Just like me.'

Nathan sank into the armchair. 'During the war. Before Dad came.' He gave Leah a long, thoughtful look. 'Are you sure you're doing the right thing? About leaving Urchin?'

'That world out there is still waiting to be tasted.'

'Mother changed her mind about Scapegoat.'

'Because Max came into her life. She'd have been happy anywhere then.'

Nathan sat up slowly, dark eyes serious as he reached out a hand to touch Leah's shoulder. 'She found what she wanted. I hope –'

Leah shook her head firmly. 'I'm catching the first train back to London tomorrow, Nathan.'

Eva stood with Clay on the balcony of his suite. Below them the lights of Rome glittered in the darkness and Eva was feeling relaxed. The shop was now re-organized, dinner and wine had left her feeling sleepily content, and Clay was handsome and attentive company. Moreover he held the key to her dream of setting up Calico, the magnificent new shopping mall she was planning in London's dockland. The one-time cotton warehouse would know a new and glorious lease of life.

In her mind's eye Eva could already see it complete; under the shelter of the warehouse's upper floor which overhung the river customers alighted from Calico riverboats; inside, banks of suffused lights illuminated the walkways and indoor trees and fountains and a profusion of exciting new shops delighted the eye. Coffee lounges, a Finch's restaurant – Leah would love that. It couldn't be long before she came back. Eva was looking up at Clay thoughtfully when the telephone rang.

Clay went into the bedroom and picked up the receiver. 'London? Yes, put him through. Hullo? What's the news? You're sure? Oh, thank heaven. Yes, no matter what it costs. Ring me again tomorrow, will you?'

Eva turned to him as he came back out on the balcony. 'Business?' she enquired.

He shook his head. 'The vet. It's my dog – a little Westie. He got run over on Thursday but he's going to pull through, thank God.'

Eva smiled in the darkness. There was a soft side to Clay after all. An arm slid around her waist and Eva pushed it away. 'You asked me here to see the view, remember,' she murmured. 'Nothing else.'

His voice was close to her ear. 'So I did, but I'd be less than a man if I didn't react to your closeness, Eva. And you look fabulous in black chiffon. You're a very desirable woman, you know that?'

She turned away brusquely. 'Come off it, Clay. Those days are over for me.'

He laughed softly. 'Nonsense. It's just been a long time, that's all. How long is it since you and Alan split up?'

'There've been other men, but none that mattered. I'm a married woman still, remember. Come to that, you're married too.'

'We have needs, Eva. You do like me, don't you?'

Oh yes, I like you, Clay Richards. Therein lies the danger. 'That's got nothing to do with it.'

She heard his sigh in the darkness. 'Ah well, I won't give up trying.'

'You never do. That's the trouble. I want to talk business, and all you can think of is bed.'

Eva kept her tone deliberately light, teasing. They hadn't yet talked of Venn Street.

It was then she became aware of his gaze as she stood in the doorway, the glow of lamplight in the room behind her, and she heard the quiet intensity of his tone.

'What man could blame me, Eva?'

She felt the touch of his fingers on her breast and at the same moment became aware of the feeling which leapt in her, a surge of excitement she had almost forgotten. Without thinking, and with an instinct born of need, she let him draw her close, savouring the comfort of a warm body against her own. Then, turning away sharply, she walked back into the bedroom and picked up her bag from the bed.

'About Venn Street,' she said in a tight voice.

Clay followed her into the room. 'Want to tell me what you plan?'

33

'No. It's my idea and I don't want it stolen. I want to do it on my own.'

'You need cash – I've got the cash. Why not make me a partner?'

'Like hell I will!'

'Or some other mutually satisfying arrangement.'

Eva looked up quickly, trying to gauge the meaning in his eyes. 'I don't quite understand you –' she began.

'We could meet each other's needs, I'm sure.'

'And if I don't?'

He spread stubby, short-nailed fingers. 'It's for you to decide.'

She faced him squarely. 'Lay it on the line, Clay. Are you forcing my hand? Sleep with you or forget Venn Street – is that it?'

He smiled as he seated himself on the bed and patted the counterpane beside him. 'There's no need to be so melodramatic, Eva. Let's talk it over like sensible adults.'

'Like you did with Alan? If I don't play ball, you treat me the same as you did him.'

'That was different. Pure business. I called in a long-overdue debt, that's all.'

Eva gave a wry smile. 'You mean he had nothing you wanted to trade off.'

Clay cocked his head to one side. 'Still loyal, eh?'

'No, just remembering how determined you can be.'

He reached across and took hold of her hand gently. 'I'm sure we can meet half-way, come to some agreement.'

He was smiling that easy, confident smile of his. Eva flashed him an angry look and pulled her hand away. 'Trade a screw for the chance of a site? No way, Clay.'

He lay back on the bed and folded his hands behind his head. 'You're clearly not in a mood to talk reasonably tonight,' he said equably. 'No matter. I think I may have another buyer for Venn Street anyway.'

'Stuff Venn Street,' snapped Eva. 'I don't care if I never see it or you ever again.'

And with head held high, she marched angrily out of the room.

In the lift tears burned her eyelids. It wasn't Clay's overtures which had offended her so much as the thought that she might have lost Venn Street forever. The site could have been hers, and she'd thrown it away for a principle – but she wanted it on her terms, not Clay's. The dream of Calico was slipping from her reach . . .

As she stepped out of the lift a sudden fierce determination swept through her. No, damn it, she wasn't going to give up. Somebody, somewhere, must help her bring her dream to life, or by heaven she'd find a way to do it alone.

CHAPTER THREE

Not one item of Leah's clothes or belongings remained in the Chelsea flat when Eva arrived home from work. Rosary Jones, Eva's Irish housekeeper, kept apologizing as if it were her fault.

'I'm so sorry, Mrs Finch, so I am – all her stuff was gone when I got here. I didn't even catch sight of her. Ye didn't know she was going then?'

'She'll be all right, Rosary. Maybe she's gone to her father's.'

'Her room all empty and tidy – 'tis all unnatural,' Rosary grumbled to herself. 'Not a teddy bear or a bra to be seen anywhere.'

'She doesn't wear a bra,' muttered Eva absently.

The housekeeper crossed herself. 'The shame of it,' she murmured. 'But a fine girl for all that. Never a kinder nor more polite girl in the city. Please God you're right, Mrs Finch, and she's safe with her Daddy.'

Eva picked up the onyx telephone and dialled. 'Alan? Is Leah there? . . . No? Have you heard from her? . . . Well, let me know if you do.'

She put down the receiver and saw the housekeeper's eyes upon her. 'Has she just upped and off without a word to either of ye?'

'Now, now, Rosary – it's not so strange. She's not a child any more, you know.'

Rosary crossed herself again and, pulling a string of rosary beads from her apron pocket, began muttering hasty Hail Marys. Eva patted her thin arm.

'She had time to pack her things, remember. She'll be in touch,' she said reassuringly, but she wished she could feel the confidence she exuded.

Rosary went into the kitchen to retrieve the pot roast from a hot shelf with one oven-gloved hand. The other was still wreathed in rosary beads as she sprinkled more Hail Marys along with the seasoning.

After Rosary had left Eva sat disconsolately on one of the low leather settees, gazing into the glow of the log fire. The lamps were still unlit and she watched the flicker of firelight dancing on the walls. One hand fingered the brass trim of the telephone on the coffee table beside her.

But where to ring? So far as she knew Leah had no boyfriend at the moment; she was a private soul but she did have friends. There was that old college friend of hers – what was her name? Beverley, was it, or Bryony?

No point in ringing Nathan – if he knew anything about Leah's whereabouts he'd have rung and left a message. It was clear from his manner at the funeral that he too was concerned about Leah but in his usual restrained and gentle way he'd tried not to show it. It was a pity Leah hadn't stayed longer with him. He'd have been good for her in her present state of unrest.

'*I wanted Leah to share the farm with you, Nathan. I tried to tell her.*'

'*Not yet. Give her space. You can't cage a wild bird.*'

Eva smiled wryly. It was an apt term for her, wild and unpredictable, living half the time in her own private world. If only Eva knew where she was now . . .

Leah sat on the edge of the bed and stared down at the uncarpeted floor of the dingy flat, sipping Nescafé from the chipped mug she held cupped between her hands. A slim, leggy girl in blue jeans was rooting in the dilapidated fridge alongside a rusty old gas cooker. A wire-haired terrier hovered expectantly at her feet.

'I can't go back there, Beth, I've made my mind up,' Leah was saying. 'If I could just stay a night or two, just till I get somewhere . . .'

Bethany gave a bright smile. 'Course you can if you don't mind a camp bed in the spare room. And Alfred licking you to death – I promised to look after him till the Bramleys get back. He's a poppet really, but a bit too affectionate at times.'

'Once the money comes through there won't be any problem. I'll be able to rent a place then.' Leah shivered and put down the mug, then pulled her sweater up round her neck.

Bethany pulled out the vegetable tray from the bottom of the fridge. 'God, just look at this – it looks like a vegetable swamp. I must have left them too long.'

She held out a limp, greasy-looking stick of celery which drooped slowly towards the floor. Alfred looked up hopefully, his tail wagging.

'I was going to make a vegetable casserole. Did I tell you I was vegetarian? Ever since I went out with this macrobiotic freak. See if

37

you can rescue these – they might be all right if you scrape them.'

She handed over a bunch of carrots which rested slimily on Leah's palm, and began scooping handfuls of green mush out of the bottom of the fridge. Then she straightened, holding some unrecognizable object aloft.

'What the hell was this?' she said in wonder. 'I think it's breathing.' Leah looked away.

Finally they sat down to eat a rather lumpy omelette Bethany contrived out of two eggs and an assortment of tinned red kidney beans, peas and a few left-over mushrooms. Leah couldn't help noticing that even Alfred turned his nose up at the taste he was offered.

'It's nourishing anyway,' Bethany said cheerfully as she ladled the concoction onto two plates. 'Lots of protein in eggs and pulses.'

Right about now Rosary would be laying the dining table for dinner in Mother's warm and welcoming flat, Leah was thinking. And checking the oven . . . Roast duckling? Baked trout? For the first time she began to realize how spoilt she'd been up to now.

The spare bedroom turned out to be an oversize glory-hole, cluttered with a tumble of rucksacks, long-neglected college text books and plastic binliners filled with what looked like offerings for a jumble sale. Leah lay on the hard surface of the camp bed, trying to avoid the edges of the metal frame jutting into her hips.

The door wouldn't close properly, which was perhaps a blessing or she might have stifled in the tiny space between the piles of clutter Bethany had heaped around the bed. Every now and again Alfred squeezed in around the door and came to lick her face enthusiastically before wriggling out through the gap again.

It must have been around one in the morning when Leah awoke. Just beyond the wall separating the glory-hole from the flat next door voices were shouting, a man's and a woman's. And then the screaming started, a series of moans turning to shrieks which mounted to a climax and suddenly ceased. Leah shuddered, alarmed for the woman. Should she do something about it? Call Beth, do something? Half an hour later the noises began all over again, and there was no desperation in the sound.

The racket continued, on and off, until after four in the morning. Leah sat on the bed, unable to sleep, until at last she heard Bethany moving about.

'Sleep all right?' Bethany enquired. She looked bright and fresh as

38

she brushed out her long hair. 'Alfred wasn't too much of a drag, was he?'

'No, but your neighbours –' Leah began.

'Oh, Wilson and Marianne. They're West Indian, you know. Not at it again, were they?'

'They were bloody noisy. I didn't know whether they were fighting or Wilson was just the best thing since sliced bread. I don't know how you slept through it.'

Bethany shrugged. 'Oh, you get used to it. You will too.'

But a week later Leah felt dizzy and sore-eyed from lack of sleep. 'I'm sorry,' she told Bethany. 'You're very kind, but I'm afraid I'll have to try and find somewhere else for tonight.'

Bethany put a plate down on the floor for Alfred. He circled it warily before sniffing at it. Bethany looked anxiously at Leah. 'It isn't Alfred who's upset you, is it?'

'No, it wasn't Alfred,' smiled Leah. 'He's lovely.'

'It's this place, isn't it? I really must try and do something about clearing it up before Mum comes to stay.' Bethany sighed and gave a wistful smile. 'Anyway, I should be used to it. At least you stayed a week – most people only last one night.'

The secretary held out a note as Eva entered the office.

'Memo for you, Mrs Finch. Leah called in.'

Eva read the words typed on the sheet of paper. *Memo to Mrs Finch, from Miss Finch. You wanted my resignation in writing. Here it is. I resign forthwith, and I won't be working out my notice. Stuff the pay. Leah.*

The secretary was watching for her reaction. Eva laid the note aside on her desk and sat down. 'Is Vincent here yet?'

'He's waiting for you. Shall I buzz him to come on through?'

As Valerie returned to the outer office Eva drew a deep sigh. Wherever Leah was, she was clearly still as defiant as she had been in Barnbeck. Nathan was right – she'd have to be patient.

Vincent Galbraith entered, pushing his spectacles up on his thin nose and with a sheaf of papers under his arm. He seated himself on the edge of the chair opposite Eva and began talking.

'We must review the options open to us and make a choice,' he said in his precise Scottish way. Eva watched how his fingers twitched the papers nervously, how his hair fell lopsidedly over one lens, and found it hard to banish pictures of Leah which kept flashing through her mind. 'To use the popular term, we have a cash-flow problem in Urchin Limited,' Vincent was saying. 'Both the banks we have approached –'

'*I* approached,' corrected Eva.

'– both banks said much the same thing – we're over-extended.'

He was twiddling a pencil now. She remembered he'd just given up smoking. 'But we're highly successful,' she murmured. 'All my shops are thriving. You'd think somebody would be glad to lend to me.'

'Successful, yes, and your name is highly respected.'

Eva frowned. 'So where can we borrow if not from the bank?'

Vincent leaned back in his chair. 'Well, there's the mortgage institutions . . .'

'Who are they?'

'Insurance companies. They'd be prepared to lend against the security of the new building. But I can tell you now, they'll only lend seventy per cent of the total cost of buying the site and building the complex. We're talking millions here.'

Eva sighed. 'I still wouldn't be able to raise the other thirty per cent.'

'No,' agreed Vincent. 'It wouldn't make sense to tie up working capital.'

'There must be some other way, Vincent. I'm not going to let my dream die. Don't you know any rich millionaires who'd lend me money?'

'Not on that scale. What you need is a philanthropist.'

Eva brushed a fleck of dust from her blue velvet suit and stood up. 'Look, I really can't concentrate right now. Meet me again after lunch.'

He pushed the frond of hair away from his spectacles. 'I know it's a bad time but there is something else . . .'

'After lunch, Vincent.'

He sighed and got up to go. 'Very well, Mrs Finch.'

Leah climbed the stairs to her father's second-floor flat. It wasn't what she'd intended to do, but one more sleepless night at Bethany's would drive her crazy.

She rang the doorbell and waited. Moments passed, and she rang again. At last the door opened and a pretty, tousle-haired brunette in a crimson silk kimono stared at her, bleary-eyed.

'Sorry, I was still in bed,' she said with an apologetic smile. 'What time is it anyway?'

Leah stared. The girl looked to be about her own age. 'I'm sorry,' she muttered. 'I was looking for Alan Finch.'

'Yes?' said the girl. 'This is his place. He's gone to work. I'm his girlfriend. Can I give him a message?'

Leah straightened. 'Just tell him Leah called. No message.'

She turned and began running down the stairs again before the brunette could gather her sleepy wits.

Outside in the street Leah walked fast, ignoring the bustle of bodies around her. That girl must have been the Christie he had spoken of, a girl no older than herself. Leah tried to banish the mingled sense of anger and shame she felt for her father.

So, with both Mother's place and Daddy's out of the question, she had to find somewhere else to stay – but how, with so little money? Who would be prepared to wait for payment until the will was dealt with? Only someone who had no money worries . . .

A wealthy man. Someone like Clay Richards, the multi-millionaire who used to come to Mother's dinner parties in the old days. He had been so kind, so charming to a gauche fifteen-year-old. That was in the days before he beat Daddy in some business deal or other. He never came to dinner now.

His company owned a lot of rented property, Mother had said. And if he had beaten Daddy, he might just possibly feel a debt of honour somehow, some obligation to help her. It would do no harm to ask. He could only say no. Now what was that company called?

It had a Latin sound to it, she could recall. Something like Tesco. Cresco, that was it, *I grow*. Leah hurried along the street, looking for a telephone box.

Eva sat down at her desk with Vincent Galbraith after lunch.

'Right now, Vincent, where do we go from here? I'm determined to get my Calico one way or another. I want to get rid of this office and centralize everything at Venn Street. Head office and showroom, near the short take-off and landing strip – so much more convenient. I want it, Vincent, and one way or another I'm going to get it.'

'Well,' said Vincent, holding the pencil between two fingers and putting it to his lips, 'there is a third option I wanted to put to you, Mrs Finch. But this way you won't be the outright owner of Calico.'

'I won't hear of a partner or a consortium, Vincent, I told you.'

41

'Just hear me out. We could approach a developer to buy the Venn Street site –'

'What?'

'– and build the complex for us. We could tempt him by offering to be a medium term pre-let, on a lease of say, twenty-five years. On such an assurance he could borrow the money to buy and build himself.'

Eva leaned forward on her elbows. 'You mean, I should be his tenant?'

'Assured of the place for twenty-five years. It makes sense – no big capital outlay for us, and it leaves you free from all the hassle of having to find an architect, a builder, and then having to oversee the work for months, even years. You can devote your time to doing what you do now – running the business.'

Eva toyed with a silver propelling pencil. 'I see,' she said thoughtfully. 'But would this developer build just what I want, the way I visualize it, the details down to the swimming pool and Finch's restaurant and riverboat moorings and everything? It's got to have the right feel, Vincent, the right atmosphere, exactly the way I've dreamt of it, alive and exciting, not just a compromise shadow of the thing. I won't have anything less than my vision. Can you assure me of that?'

'If we find the right developer . . .'

Eva slapped the pencil down. 'Then find him, Vincent, find him.'

As he made for the door Eva turned round in her seat. 'Oh, and Vincent – maybe you should start smoking again. Next time you see Clay Richards, I don't want you to look so bloody worried. You give people the wrong idea.'

Clay Richards studied the blonde-haired girl seated on the far side of his desk. She was uncommonly pretty, far prettier than he remembered. And beneath the slim skirt and jacket he could see she had a good figure too. Like her mother, she was lively and clearly a woman of initiative to beard him so confidently on the telephone. A combination of her father's easy charm and her mother's purposeful directness – that was why she was sitting here now. He was curious to see Eva and Alan Finch's daughter now she was a woman.

'So why did you come to me, Leah?'

She crossed her legs and smiled. Clay noted how shapely the legs were. 'I remembered you when you used to come to our house. I remembered how charming you were, even to a clumsy teenager, and I felt sure you wouldn't mind my asking you for help.'

'In what way?' Whatever she was after she was halfway to getting it already.

'I need a place to stay. I know you've got property to let, and since I know you, I thought I'd pull a few strings.'

Clay was amused, but still curious. 'Couldn't your mother help? You work with her at Urchin, don't you?'

'Not any more. I resigned, and I haven't any money. But I've got an inheritance coming – it'll just take time, that's all. I'll pay all the back rent as soon as it comes if you'll trust me. I could get references.'

He chuckled. 'I know your mother. That's reference enough.' He rose and came round the desk. 'Tell you what, I'm going out for something to eat – why not come with me and we'll talk about what's available – I might be able to come up with something.'

He saw the delight that leapt into her eyes as she stood up. 'Oh, thank you. I thought I'd have a devil of a job persuading you. It's almost too easy. You're a pushover, you know that.'

He smiled and took her elbow, steering her towards the door. 'A philanthropist, that's me. And I admire people who have initiative. You'll go places, young lady.'

'I hope so,' she replied happily. 'I really do hope so.'

The brasserie was crowded as it always was at lunchtime and a knot of people waited by the bar for free tables. Clay raised a hand and a waiter hurried across to lead them through the chattering groups of customers to a side table. Clay was conscious of curious eyes turning to stare at the pretty girl as they passed. At the carvery a silver platter with a huge side of beef glistened, rosy and succulent, in the middle of a rampart of Yorkshire puddings. 'I hope you're not a vegetarian,' he remarked. Leah smiled.

'No, I'm not. And I've got an enormous appetite.' Leah finished a glass of wine and Clay poured more. By the time the waiter brought the meal Leah's face was flushed and her eyes shining.

Clay watched the way she ate, eagerly as if savouring every mouthful. She became aware of his gaze and smiled at him.

'It's good, isn't it? I was starving.'

Her evident enthusiasm was heart-warming. Clay pushed his plate aside and leaned his elbows on the table.

'Tell me, why did you leave? Your mother didn't want you to go, I'm sure.'

Leah lowered her eyes. 'I just decided it wasn't for me. I've finished with Urchin.'

'And what are you going to do?'

She shrugged and put down her knife and fork. 'Don't know. I never really thought about it. I only know I don't want to work like stink for the rest of my life like mother, no time for anything else. God knows what making money is for if not to enjoy it.'

He sensed her anger and chose his words to suit. 'I couldn't agree more.'

'I mean, there ought to be time for other things, don't you agree?'

'Yes.'

'What do you do besides work?'

He leaned back and laughed. 'You name it, I've probably done it. Everything from archery to yacht racing. And we use money for the arts too – Cresco subsidizes a theatre workshop and a concert orchestra amongst other things. Would you like coffee now?'

Clay snapped his fingers and the coffee appeared. Leah leaned her elbows on the table. 'I do hope you'll be able to find me a flat, Mr Richards. I can't tell you how much I'm looking forward to living alone.'

'Clay, please. Yes, I must say I quite enjoy being alone here in London. Well, alone but for my dog. Life wouldn't be the same without Portcullis.'

She smothered a laugh. 'Portcullis? Whoever heard of a name like that for a dog?'

'It suits him,' Clay replied seriously. 'He's noble, despite his small size. And sort of medieval too, sort of quaint. You'd like Portcullis.'

'I'm sure I would.' Leah was laughing aloud now. The wine must have been too much for her. Then suddenly he saw the light fade from her pretty face. 'I used to have a kitten I adored. She was savaged by a dog. Things like that happen on a farm, but she was my pet. Max had to put her down – he was a vet, you know.'

Clay reached out and put a hand over hers. For a moment she did not pull it away. Then she straightened, removing her hand to pick up her coffee cup. 'Mummy wanted to buy me another one, but it wouldn't have been the same. Daddy understood. He was wonderful. But it was all a long time ago.'

44

'You're very fond of your father, aren't you?'

She smiled dreamily. 'I always hoped I'd find a man like him. Don't get me wrong – he's got his faults like anyone else, but I really admire him. I could fancy a man like him, he's so attractive. Oh, that sounds awful, doesn't it?'

'No, I imagine lots of young women see their fathers as role models. Anyway, it's never wrong to love, and it's natural to be attracted to somebody older. I know I always was.'

She was leaning on her elbows, listening. 'You were?'

He nodded. 'In fact I learnt a lot from an older woman once, when I was a young man. A boy almost. I owe that lady a great deal.'

She was watching him intently, hanging on his words. Clay knew he was on the right track. 'I've always liked older men,' she murmured. 'Probably comes from mixing with my mother's friends so much. I felt at ease with them.'

'Age is all in the head. It's having the same attitudes that counts.'

'Exactly. Being on the same wavelength.' Leah put down her coffee cup and began tracing her finger in a wet patch on the surface of the table. For a moment he was able to watch her, the way her fair hair spilled forward over her cheek, the far-away look in her eyes. 'You know,' she murmured, 'I had this boyfriend once at college – smashing bloke, full of fun like my father. We could talk about anything. I thought it was so right . . .'

'What went wrong?'

She sighed. 'We went to bed together. Neither of us knew what we were doing. It was awful, so clumsy and hateful. We couldn't talk after that.'

She fell silent for a moment. Clay wanted to prolong the conversation. 'Have you slept with anyone since?'

'No. He was the first – and the last.'

'How old are you, Leah?'

'Twenty-two.'

'I'm fifty.'

He saw no change in her expression. 'Daddy's fifty.' She smiled and reached for her handbag. 'But it's all in the head, isn't it?'

Alan stared at Christie. She looked delectable in the red kimono, so carelessly fastened that the front gaped, revealing an expanse of smooth thigh, but it was her words rather than her appearance which startled him.

'Leah was here? When?'

'This morning. I was just getting up. What time is Lenny expecting us?'

'Did she leave any message? Did she say where she would be?'

'I was too fuddled to realize it was your daughter. How was I to know? She ran off before I could get any message.'

He felt keenly disappointed, but it was no use taking it out on Christie. 'It starts at two. Better get dressed.'

Alan pulled off his shoes and socks and was unzipping his trousers when Christie let her robe fall to the floor and walked past him to the bathroom. He watched the small, tight bottom swaying as she moved; pleasure and desire filled him at the sight.

He peeled off his shirt and caught sight of his reflection in the full-length mirror of the wardrobe, and once again felt a sense of regret. Where now was the lithe, muscular body he had taken for granted in his young days when he was the toast of the college rugby field? Where now the clear eyes and smooth skin? In their place he saw a fifty-year-old man with greying hair and below the spreading waistline, a definite hint of a paunch.

He turned sideways to the mirror and pulled in his stomach muscles. Whichever way he turned the lines were not pleasing. He couldn't kid himself – he was a middle-aged man who still couldn't resist burning the candle at both ends. What the hell did a girl like Christie see in a wreck like him?

Christie was beautiful, a model half the photographers in London would give their eye teeth to capture on film, and at twenty-two the same age as Leah. God forbid that Leah should ever go out with an old roué like him.

CHAPTER FOUR

The brasserie was emptying fast. Clay planned his next move while Leah kept on chatting.

'I shouldn't have laughed about Portcullis,' she was saying. 'Come to think of it, that kitten I told you about was called Saliva because she dribbled whenever she smelt fish. And I met a dog this week called Alfred.'

Clay laughed, then caught his breath and snapped his fingers. Leah looked up sharply. 'What is it?'

'I've had an idea – I do know of a flat!'

He saw her eyes gleam in anticipation. 'You do? Where? And how much?'

He glanced at his wristwatch and got up from the table. 'If we get a move on I'll just have time to show it to you before the Board meeting. Come on.'

They walked quickly along the Embankment towards Chelsea. Leah kept in step beside him. Long-legged women had always appealed to him, especially when they were also long-haired blondes. Nearing a block of flats he pointed. 'There it is.'

He saw Leah's eyes widen in amazement. 'Here? I can't afford this area.'

'Come on in first and see it. I've got the key.'

She did not question why he had it; she seemed too bewildered by the wide staircase, the suffused lighting, the stainless steel doors of the lifts and the Dalek-like control box for summoning them. She followed in silence up to the fifth floor and along the carpeted corridor.

He unlocked the door, swinging it open to reveal the room. 'Wait till you see the bedrooms,' he murmured, 'and the bathroom and kitchen.'

She walked around the room, sighing as she fingered the brocade curtains and the deep, wine-coloured velvet settee. 'It's terrific! It's right out of a Hollywood film! Oh, and look at that bathroom!'

He leaned against the door frame and watched her go through out of sight, but he could hear her exclamations of delight. Then she reappeared, ecstasy in her smile. 'I'm lost for words. It's fabulous.'

'If you like it, it's yours,' he said quietly. She turned huge eyes upon him.

'Don't be silly. It's far too opulent for me. I can't afford anything like this.'

'Can you afford a pound a week?'

Her eyes narrowed. 'A pound? That's downright ridiculous. What's the catch?'

'No catch. A pound a week. It goes with the job.'

'What job?'

'The one I'm offering you – as my personal assistant. The last one's just left. The job's yours if you want it, and the flat goes with it.'

She stood wide-eyed, perplexed. 'You must be joking.'

'Think you can handle it?'

She smiled. 'I've been my mother's PA for the last year – after her, I can satisfy anybody.'

Clay glanced at his wristwatch. 'Right. I'd better get off to my meeting now. I'll leave you to have a look around.'

She gave him a quizzical look. 'I haven't said I'll take it yet. It seems too good to be true – a pound a week for all this.'

'Suspicious little devil, aren't you? I told you – it goes with the job. Way of avoiding tax really, instead of paying a higher salary.'

'We haven't talked salary yet.'

He was standing by the door, his hand on the door knob. 'I'll meet you back here at six and we'll talk about it then. You won't be disappointed. Oh, and here's the key.'

He tossed it on the settee. Leah gave him a curious look. 'I wonder what my mother would think of me coming to work for you.'

'Her loss is my gain,' said Clay. 'See you at six.'

Eva sat in her office, biting her fingernail as she thought about Leah. Ten days since she left Scapegoat and still no news. Her hand lay on the telephone.

The buzzer sounded and Valerie's voice cut in on her thoughts. 'Mr Galbraith on the line for you, Mrs Finch.'

'Put him through. Vincent? How's it going?'

'It's all settled, Mrs Finch,' the Scottish voice said equably. 'Delaney Construction is going to put in a bid.'

'They've agreed to all my plans as they stand?'

'Just as Mr Delaney promised when you talked to him yesterday. Only a few minor changes – nothing you'd disapprove of. The main thing is, he's agreeable to do it. We're in luck.'

'So long as Clay Richards accepts his offer,' said Eva.

'So long as Cresco does,' corrected Vincent.

'Clay Richards *is* Cresco,' retorted Eva. 'He's God.'

Nathan straightened up, rubbing his aching back as he watched the new-born lamb stagger feebly to its feet, obeying the primeval instinct to find its mother's udder. The ewe lay with docile eyes under the shelter of the dry-stone wall, uttering sounds of encouragement until the lamb's mouth clenched on the teat.

Nathan smiled, then heaving the ewe up under one arm and the lamb under the other, he carried them both to the shelter of the sheep pen. All would be well now.

He looked about him in the darkening light. But for the sheep the landscape would be a wilderness of rock and scree, menacing rainclouds hanging over the hill enhancing the loneliness of the place. On the lower fields he could see new-fallen snow lying as fluffy as a lamb's wool, but up here rain had already washed it away.

Even time seemed frozen, as though the moor had been cocooned in an icicle of history. The cold wind blew into his face, seeming to sharpen the senses so that he felt he could see and feel more clearly.

A red fox stole away through a gap in the dry-stone wall. Nathan felt a surge of affection for the place. A bare moorland hillside like this meant nothing to a townsman, but those brought up in this bleak northern valley loved and respected its stark grandeur. Leah had said as much, that last day before she left.

He looked down to the farm. Scapegoat lay silent in the gloom, its back to the wind and its grey stone walls seeming to merge into the earth around it. He loved that farm with all the fervour he was capable of, but somehow it was not the same. Not since Mother and Father died. Not since Leah had left. Somehow all his grand plans for the place rang hollow without loved ones to share in it . . .

He tried to push away the sneaking desire which kept creeping over

49

him these days, the itch to go away for a while, to give himself time to think objectively, time for the wounds to heal. He could understand Leah's need.

No. He could not desert his responsibilities. He owed it to Maddie and Max to carry out their dreams. Some day, perhaps, he would go, but not yet. And if he did, he would have to come back. Scapegoat was the life-blood in his veins . . .

Leah had moved the last of her belongings by taxi from Bethany's into the Chelsea flat. In the bathroom she found a razor and toothbrush, talc and a bottle of expensive bath oil and also a thickly luxurious blue bathrobe and a towel. She packed them all together in a cardboard box and put them aside in a cupboard – she must remember to ask Clay some time how to return them to the previous tenant.

There was a particular pleasure in hanging her clothes in the mirrored wardrobes lining one wall of the main bedroom, laying out her make-up on the dressing table, and in going out on to the balcony to survey the view. From here she could just catch a glimpse of the river between the buildings.

It was only when she sat down on the huge double bed surmounted by lacy drapes that she noted something odd. The bed squelched as she moved. A water bed! In a sudden surge of delight she flung herself on hands and knees and began bouncing up and down, laughing aloud with sheer exuberance like a child who has just discovered a new toy. Then she caught sight of the bedside telephone.

Ring Mother and let her know? Or Nathan? He too would be wondering. No, on reflection it would be best to establish her new way of life, make sure of the future, and then it would be a pleasure to announce the news.

Everywhere she moved about the flat she kept discovering more delights – the cool green luxury of the marble bathroom with its impulse shower and whirlpool bath, the cappuccino coffee-maker in the kitchen, and the battery of switches alongside the bed. She stretched out full-length and began flicking them. The first brought an unseen voice.

'Porter?'

'Sorry. Just testing.'

Leah tried the other switches – a radio, a miniature TV, an alarm clock, a dimmer light and a remote control to open and close the thick, floor-length curtains. The rest of the afternoon was spent savouring the delights of the flat and arranging and re-arranging her few ornaments until she was satisfied with the effect and the place was beginning to feel like a home, with her own individual stamp on it.

She sank into the depths of the velvet settee, revelling in its luxurious feel, and looked around her with a glow of proprietorial pleasure. For the first time since she was at college she could arrange her home, and her life, the way she wanted without reference to Mother, and she was going to enjoy it to the full. Leah hugged herself in rapture – freedom at last, a new job, and all this for a pound a week!

Clay was punctual. Promptly at six o'clock the doorbell rang. 'Well?' he asked with a smile. 'Satisfied?'

'That's putting it mildly,' replied Leah.

'So you're taking the job?'

'I've moved all my things in.'

'Right. Then you start now. Dinner with me and then on to a meeting. I need you to take detailed notes.'

Days later the news arrived that Cresco International had accepted Delaney Construction Company's offer for the Venn Street site. Vincent was highly satisfied.

'You must be feeling very pleased with yourself, Mrs Finch,' he purred as he popped a mint into his mouth. 'Cresco has no idea you've outwitted them.'

'Not yet,' said Eva, but somehow the delight she should have been feeling was not there. Her anxiety about Leah was growing. Three weeks now. If only she knew where the girl was, how she was getting on . . .

Leah was taking great delight in working in Cresco's head office which was even more palatial than Urchin's. Like the flat, it was furnished with a restrained elegance which spoke of an expensive interior de-signer.

Clay's office interconnected with his secretary's on one side and Leah's on the other. He was a co-operative but demanding boss, just as Mother had been, but his manner remained always that of a boss. Any doubts which might once have flickered in her mind about his motives had soon faded.

'Stay on tonight – I want to brief you about our European offices. If you're to accompany me on my trips abroad you've got to know the set-up.'

'Fine.'

'Paris next week, Rotterdam the week after. Oh, and there's Marseilles, but you won't be going to that.'

'No?'

'No. I need you here.'

'Right.'

'Reminds me – make sure the Falconer papers are on my desk first thing in the morning when I get here.'

'OK.' It meant getting into the office almost as soon as the cleaners had left, long before anyone else, but that was part of her job. And as long as Clay found her so trustworthy, so dependable . . .

'Oh, and there's something else,' Clay added as they worked late that night. 'Would you like to come with me to a dinner on Wednesday?'

Leah smiled. 'Sounds like fun. I used to go to business dinners occasionally with Mother.'

Clay shook his head. 'Not exactly business, this one. Environmental group annual do, actually – I'm President, so they expect me, and my partner. Say you'll come.'

'I'd love to – a chance to dress up.'

'Right, that's settled,' he said with an air of satisfaction. 'Now, about the European offices . . .'

His manner throughout remained strictly businesslike. An hour later he glanced at his wristwatch. 'Better go,' he said crisply. 'Got to fetch Portcullis from the kennels.'

'Is he fully recovered now?' Leah asked.

Clay frowned. 'He's doing fine but I don't like the way he's getting attached to the kennelmaid. I'm taking him home tonight.'

Leah gathered papers together. 'I should have thought you'd be glad he was fond of someone there – makes him feel more secure.'

Clay picked up his briefcase and grunted as he made for the door. 'Portcullis is *my* dog. He loves *me*.'

At last Leah finished annotating the Falconer papers ready for the morning and pushed them into her briefcase. The kettle was almost boiling and she was looking forward to a cup of tea followed by a long, luxurious bath before bed. The television was closing down and her eyes were heavy with the desire to sleep.

In the bedroom she had just stripped off her clothes and was reaching for a robe when the doorbell rang. Leah stood motionless. Who on earth could it be at this hour of the night?

Pulling on her robe she walked through into the living room and picked up the doorphone. 'Hullo? Who is it?'

'It's me – Daniel – let me in.'

Leah frowned. 'Daniel? Daniel who?'

'Your brother, you twit. Let me in.'

'I'm sorry – you must have the wrong flat. I don't know any Daniel.'

The voice began to sound impatient. 'Cheryl – stop messing about and open the door. I'm freezing and I'm in no mood for playing games. Let me in, please.'

There was something so natural, so honest-sounding in the tone of the voice that Leah felt compelled to open the door.

'Look, I don't know who this Cheryl is, but she isn't here –' she began, and then she caught sight of the tall young man in denim jeans and a frayed jacket with a rucksack slung over one shoulder. He was staring at her, a bewildered expression in his eyes.

'Oh, I'm sorry, I was looking for my sister,' he stammered. 'Is she still out?'

'She doesn't live here – this is my flat.'

'But she was here – I've crashed out here with her before. I rang her and told her I was coming. She said it was OK.'

Over his shoulder Leah was vaguely aware of a movement at the far end of the corridor, at the top of the stairs next to the lift. Another tenant coming home . . .

She smiled at the young man. He looked like a student and his face was pinched with cold. 'I'm sorry, but she must have left as I moved in. I'm afraid I don't know any forwarding address, but the porter might be able to help.'

'Oh.' Daniel looked crestfallen. Leah felt sorry for him. 'Look, why not come in and have a cup of tea with me – we can ring down to the porter.'

'Thanks.' He came in and dropped the rucksack on the floor. His gangly height seemed to fill the small kitchen as he followed her in and watched her brew the tea. 'I'm studying at Westfield, you see,' he was explaining, 'and I often kip down with Cheryl if I can't get back. Why on earth she would move out without telling me I can't imagine.'

The hall porter had no information either. 'All I know is she left in

53

a hurry,' he told Leah. 'Told me she was off and packed her things and left same day. Week last Monday.'

Daniel looked morose. 'She must have got the sack,' he muttered between sips of tea. 'That'd explain why she's not been in touch. Doesn't want to let herself down.'

'Got the sack?'

Daniel put the cup down. 'From Cresco. Managing Director's PA. I was worried that she wouldn't be able to handle it – too much of a leap.'

'But that's my job – Clay Richards' assistant.'

'Since when?'

'Just over a week ago.'

Daniel spread his hands. 'There you are then – she got the boot. I knew it was too good to last.'

Of course, Leah reflected, the flat went with the job.

'She was so chuffed with this place, so proud of it,' Daniel was murmuring. 'Poor old Cheryl.'

Leah could sense the genuine concern in his tone. 'Look,' she said, 'if you can't get back tonight why not crash out here same as you used to? There's a spare room. Just so long as you're up and out when I go to work in the morning.'

The boy's face lost its tension. At least his immediate problem was solved; he could renew the search for his sister later. Leah settled him down, then took her bath and slept the sleep of the exhausted.

It was in the morning as she stood at the door watching Daniel's tall figure retreating down the corridor towards the lift that she became aware once again of a movement in the staircase well. A man, his face half-hidden in the shadow, moved back swiftly out of sight. Somehow Leah knew, beyond a flicker of doubt, that he had been watching. But why? And who was he?

By the time she had hurried along the corridor to the top of the stairs both Daniel and the watcher had disappeared. Slowly she retraced her steps to the flat, filled with a strange feeling of unease. And then the hall porter's words came back to her.

Cheryl left suddenly – a week last Monday. Two days before Clay had offered Leah the flat.

At the next Board meeting Leah sat taking notes. Clay was arguing the case for the acquisition of a derelict boatyard. 'You've all read my memo, gentlemen, with regard to our breaking into the highly profitable leisure and tourist industry. It's a growing market and opportunities such as this should not be ignored.'

His manner might be abrasive at times, but he seemed to inspire devotion in those who followed him. Leah could not help but be impressed by his persuasive manner and fluently unarguable logic.

'So I leave it to you, gentlemen,' he concluded. 'It's going for a song. We'll kick ourselves if we let this opportunity slip. Develop the site or buy with a view to profitable re-sale – either way we can't lose. The matter will now be put to the vote. Those in favour?'

Only one abstention. Clay had got what he wanted. The meeting over, Leah walked back to the office beside him.

'I couldn't help admiring your approach,' she commented. 'I wasn't so sure the others would go for it but they were completely won over.'

Clay turned his head to look down at her. 'Won over? My dear, they're puppets, the lot of them. I simply pull the strings.'

Leah looked puzzled. Clay smiled. 'They're all in my pocket, don't you see? What I own I like to own outright. I bought them, every one.'

She stared at him. All the men who had come to Mother's parties had been ambitious, but Clay was single-minded about it. Just like Mother . . .

'Hi, Leah – see you down at the pub later?'

It was Jeff, from Sales. Leah smiled. 'Not this lunchtime, Jeff. Maybe later this week.'

He nodded and hurried on by. Clay frowned. 'Who's that?'

'Jeff Baker – in Sales. He's been very kind.'

'See him often, do you?'

'We have coffee together sometimes, and occasionally we meet down at the pub for a snack. Tell me, you said in the meeting the Venn Street site had been sold. Who bought it, as a matter of interest?'

'Developers. Delaney Construction. Got a good figure for it too. Now let's get the Paris meeting sorted out.'

Developers. Leah's heart sank. Mother hadn't got her dream of Calico after all. Disappointment must be burning in her but, single-minded like Clay, she would find a way to fight back. She always did.

Rosary was unable to hide her concern. As she took away Eva's untouched dinner she sighed deeply.

'All that good food going to waste,' she muttered, shaking her head as she carried the tray into the kitchen, 'when half the world is dying from starvation too.'

'I'm sorry, Rosary. But I just haven't the appetite for it tonight.'

Rosary stood in the doorway, tray in hand. 'The child could be dead and buried for all we know.'

'She's all right, Rosary, I know she is. Don't fret so.'

A moment later Rosary came back and stood twirling the one long hair on her chin which she stubbornly refused to pluck. 'I wish to God that girl would ring. I been praying to every saint there is up there, so I have. The blessed martyrs are all on overtime.'

'She can take care of herself,' said Eva quietly. 'She's my daughter.'

Rosary shook her head firmly. 'Even so she could do with a bit of help. I know,' she added brightly as an idea struck her, 'I could ask Saint Anthony to intercede – he's the patron saint of lost causes. He's the fellow to sort it out.'

Satisfied she'd found the answer, Rosary marched off into the kitchen to make the coffee and have a private word with him.

Leah saw little of Clay for the next few days. Always on the move, he had taken off yet again in the helicopter to visit the site of the derelict boatyard.

So Leah was at home in the flat when the telephone rang early one evening. It was Daniel.

'Leah? Just rang to thank you for putting me up the other night. It was very kind of you.'

'No problem. Did you find your sister?'

'No. You haven't heard anything, have you?'

'Sorry. Give me a number and I'll let you know if I do.'

'I'll keep in touch. By the way, I got mugged on the way back from your place the other day. In broad daylight too.'

Leah gasped. 'Oh Daniel! Were you hurt?'

'Few bruises, that's all. But he didn't take anything. Funny that, not that I'd got anything worth pinching, but he didn't even look. Just punched me around a bit and ran off.'

'Maybe you ought to take up karate or something.'

'That's why I wish Cheryl would get in touch. Not safe for a girl in the city on her own, not with weirdos like that rapist around.'

'What rapist?'

'Didn't you see it in the papers? Some freak in London who's preying on women living alone. Twisted, if you ask me, the things he does to them. See you, Leah.'

It wasn't until Daniel had rung off that Leah remembered the watcher on the stairs . . .

CHAPTER FIVE

The Sales Manager knocked at the door of Clay's office and came in. He stood waiting silently before the desk until Clay lowered the sheet of paper he was reading.

'You wanted to see me, Mr Richards?'

Clay signalled him to be seated. 'This Baker fellow – one of yours, isn't he? What can you tell me about him?'

The Sales Manager sat foward on the edge of his seat. 'Jeff Baker? He hasn't done anything, has he?'

'How long have we had him?'

'About a year. He took over from Davis last February.'

'What's his area?'

'South West. He's doing all right.'

'References?'

'Excellent. Couldn't be better.'

'He's doing well, you say?'

'Very well. Passes target every quarter. He'll be in line for promotion before long at this rate.'

'Get rid of him.'

The Sales Manager's jaw sagged. 'Get rid of him? He's probably the best young man we've ever had –'

'You heard me – sack him at once. Find a reason. You can think of something – only make sure he's not in Cresco by the end of the week. You can go now. On your way out tell my secretary to ask Miss Finch to come in.'

'Alan? Is Leah with you? Do you know where she is?'

He could hear the urgency in Eva's voice. 'I know she's back in London. Apparently she called at the flat when I was out.'

There was a pause before she spoke, then her small, tentative voice told him better than words just how anxious she was. 'I'm worried, Alan. It's been weeks now. It's not like her.'

'You shouldn't worry so much, Eva. After all, she's not a kid who's

58

never been further than the end of the street. She's knocked about a bit.'

'I know. But I wish she'd ring.'

Compassion filled him. The vulnerability was showing behind the capable exterior she presented to the world.

'Look, what are you doing tonight?' he asked gently. 'Have you eaten?'

'No.' The voice was still small.

'Why not come round and eat at my place then? Just the two of us, steak and a bottle of plonk.'

He could hear the hesitation before she answered. 'Are you sure? No lady friend there?'

He laughed. 'Not at the moment. She's gone to a health farm for the week.'

She made an effort to lighten the tone. 'Health farm?' she said with scorn. 'You mean she's fat?'

'She's a model, silly. She needs to keep in good shape. Are you going to come?'

'I'll be there in half an hour.'

He put down the telephone and went straight into the kitchen. He remembered exactly how Eva liked her steak – medium rare, smothered in mushrooms and seasoned with just a hint of garlic.

Big Ben was booming midnight as the taxi drove up towards Chelsea. Clay leaned back against the seat and blew a cloud of cigar smoke at the 'No Smoking' sign.

'Did you enjoy the dinner, Leah? I must say you looked delightful, a real credit to me. The chairman was quite charmed by you.'

'Thanks,' said Leah. 'It's an Urchin outfit. Glad you like it. I had a lovely time.'

Clay sighed, a deep sigh of contentment. 'Still, I'm glad it's over. Been quite a week, one way and another. I'm ready for bed.'

But Leah was not prepared for his next statement. As the taxi drew up outside her flat she turned to him. 'Goodnight, Clay, and thanks again for a wonderful evening.'

He passed notes to the taxi driver and climbed out. 'Tell me over a nightcap,' he murmured. 'I'll be staying here tonight.'

'Here?' echoed Leah as the taxi slid away. 'You could ask me if it's all right first – it's my flat.'

Clay took her elbow and steered her towards the door. 'No, it's not. It's a company flat,' he said quietly. 'I often use it.'

Leah felt flustered and tried to hide her embarrassment under a veil of banter. 'You didn't tell me that was in the terms of the contract. I understood it was mine. I don't know whether –'

'There are two bedrooms,' Clay said drily as he pressed the button for the lift. 'And you have let another man stay.'

Leah stared. 'I did what? Oh – him.' Then anger began to seep through the embarrassment. 'How did you know that anyway?'

The lift doors opened and he steered her inside. 'Who was he, Leah? The man in Sales?'

'Certainly not,' she said hotly. 'It was Cheryl's brother. What about Cheryl anyway?'

'She left suddenly.' The lift stopped and he opened the door. 'Cheryl's brother, you say?'

Leah faced him squarely. 'You had someone watching me, didn't you?' Clay walked on towards the apartment. Leah hurried after him. 'Answer me, Clay – was someone watching me?'

He took a key from his pocket and opened the door, standing aside to let her enter. 'For your protection, my dear,' he murmured. 'You're important.'

She marched inside and then turned to him. 'Important? Me?'

'You're personal assistant to the chairman of Cresco International, privy to all my business. And you're precious to me, Leah. I don't want any harm to come to you.'

She turned away and began peeling off her gloves. 'Call him off, Clay – I don't want it,' she said quietly.

Clay sat down on the settee and smiled. 'About that nightcap – I'd settle for a cup of tea. And then I'm off to bed, but don't let me disturb you – stay up as long as you like. I'll be fast asleep in minutes.'

He drank the tea and then left her. An hour later Leah could hear his deep, regular breathing as she passed his door on the way to her room . . .

Three o'clock was striking. It was no use. He couldn't sleep, not with Leah lying in the next room. Clay got up off the bed and opened the door quietly.

The door handle made no sound as he moved silently into Leah's room. In the gloom he could make out the figure in the bed, and he crept closer. She was lying face down, head turned to one side and her long hair streaming out around her like a sunburst and the sheet covering only the lower half of her body. The breath caught in his throat at the sheer innocent beauty of her, a masterpiece painted in pastels. She was a masterpiece, of which he wanted to control and compose the elements. And he would.

Desire leapt in him like a fire. Already his impatient fingers were anticipating how that smooth shoulder would feel, the firm texture of her skin . . .

But not yet, he told himself fiercely, not yet. The time would come when he had all the elements composed the way he wanted them, when she would come to him willingly, loving him as unquestioningly as Portcullis did. But not yet. It was far too soon.

But he must just have a glimpse of what lay in store for him when the time was ripe. Slowly he reached out a hand, longing to caress the hollow which ran down the length of her spine, but fearing to waken her. Instead he took hold of the sheet with his fingertips and drew it slowly, carefully down, until he could see the rising curve of her bottom. Beads of perspiration broke out on his forehead, and he let the sheet fall.

Back in his own room he sat, trembling, on the edge of the bed. The blaze of desire still raged in him but he must control the urge to go back, to take her without warning. For the time being a woman's body would suffice, any woman's . . .

He put on his overcoat and went out into the night. A taxi ride away he knew Susie would still be offering comfort for those in need, and she had no objection to a client who wanted only a swift, wordless interchange . . .

Grey shafts of early morning light were sneaking in round the edges of the curtains when Alan awoke. The first thing he became aware of was the ache in his head, the muzzy heaviness which always followed too much wine, and the second was a slim arm reaching round from behind across his chest. He murmured sleepily and rolled over.

A blaze of red-gold hair streamed across the pillow. It took some seconds for him to recall that Christie's hair was not red and he screwed up his eyes to focus better. Eva. Then it all came back to him.

He hadn't meant to make love to her; that wasn't why he'd asked her to come. But over the steak and the wine, the concern for Leah and the tenderness he felt for Eva had somehow blurred into a feeling of closeness with her, the feeling they'd shared so strongly in the old days.

They'd had such passion then, for each other and for life. He could never quite remember how it had come about that their separate ambitions seemed to take over, each absorbed in building their own little empires. He'd never resented her love for Urchin, nor had she objected to the time he spent adding yet another to his chain of restaurants. Side by side they'd struggled, and somehow they seemed to slip from each other's reach. And he'd been the first to fall prey to temptation. Christie was the latest in the line of ladies who'd exasperated Eva till finally she left him.

The moment he'd touched her last night he was undone. She'd always been a woman quick to respond, a woman who delighted every bit as much as he in making love. Whatever the reason for their drifting apart, it certainly hadn't been lack of passion. Last night had proved that only too clearly.

Sensuality – that had always been Eva's strongpoint. Or did he mean sexuality? Whichever it was, making love with her had always contained some element which had been missing with all other women. It was special, a thing apart, a kind of mystical poetry.

He smiled as he remembered watching her undress. She still had the firm high breasts of a young woman. She'd smiled at him as the slip fell away, her body still slim and shapely, not thickened around the waist like most women of her age.

Desire rose in him again as he remembered. He moved the sheet gently away from the sleeping figure until Eva's naked body gleamed in the half-light. She made soft sounds of pleasure as he leaned across to kiss her . . .

Leah was revelling in her first trip in a helicopter. On the way to the seaside town Clay was trying to explain, above the noise of the engine, about the company's new interest in tourism.

'We've plans to build a marina for yacht racing, a boat repair yard, facilities for cargo handling – you name it. But that's only the start. Maybe we'll set up tourist agencies and I've an idea for a chain of Cresco Hotels.'

He sounded in ebullient mood. Leah smiled. 'This marina sounds like an expensive project,' she called.

'Not necessarily. Part of the land can be sold off for private housing development. It could almost be self-financing.'

'If the local people take to the idea.'

'That's why we're here – to sell it to them.'

Leah mused. 'Can't see that they'll object – it'll provide work for local labour and bring in the tourists. That can't be bad.'

The following afternoon the hotel booked for Clay's presentation of the scheme to the townsfolk was crowded. An orchestra was playing in the foyer as people arrived. Clay was beaming.

'You see, Cresco's benevolence to the arts pays off – we're able to bring our own orchestra with us,' he said proudly.

After the magnificent buffet Cresco had laid on, the crowd began scanning the plans pinned around the walls on hessian screens, then sat rapt as Clay's persuasive voice outlined the merits of the scheme he proposed.

'The land will be put to mixed commercial and residential use,' he told them. 'We want to provide what the public wants.'

'How do you know what the public wants?' demanded a military-looking man with a bristling white moustache in the front row. 'You can't go building marinas and things willy-nilly if it's not what the people of the town want, or need.'

'Indeed we can't,' agreed Clay. 'Which is why our plans you see around the walls are only a blueprint – the final draft will only be achieved with your suggestions and comments. We need you to help us.'

The elderly gentleman grunted. 'We don't want a repetition of what happened only five miles down the coast – was your firm responsible for that?'

'I'm happy to say it was not,' replied Clay smoothly. 'And you can rest assured that we would do nothing without your council's approval.'

The old man grunted again, apparently appeased. Clay continued. 'Our intention is to try to provide for the needs of the townspeople, and if we can't, we'll bow out gracefully.'

Murmurs in the audience showed that, having been baited with a carrot which appealed greatly, they would be hugely disappointed if he should back out. Before long they were urging him to go on with the project. Leah watched in admiration the way Clay handled them, skilfully and with the ease born of practice.

'Very well, then we must form a trust to administer the scheme. Now if you make me chairman of the trust . . .'

By teatime he was home and dry. The press were avid to interview this new benefactor. Tomorrow the headlines would be full of it. Clay Richards the philanthropist, the saviour who would give new life to the town . . .

On the homeward journey Clay was full of good humour. Leah felt proud of him.

'You won, Clay. It only needs the council to agree.'

His hand touched Leah's knee as he answered. 'It's immaterial to me either way.'

Leah was still puzzled when they alighted from the helicopter and crossed the tarmac. Clay's secretary was waiting, Portcullis on a lead beside her. The little dog began wagging its tail furiously at the sight of his master, his eyes eager and tongue flicking. Ignoring him, Clay handed over papers to his secretary and began giving a list of orders.

Leah bent and picked up the little dog. He licked her face and turned in her arms to watch his master again. Clay sent the secretary on her way and turned back to Leah. Suddenly the good humour vanished from his face.

'Stop that,' he snapped. 'Put him down – he's not a lapdog.'

Leah put the dog down and Clay marched away without a word, leaving Portcullis scurrying after him. As Leah followed she could sense the cloud of fury surrounding him. In the taxi he sat silent and unapproachable. As they drove near Venn Street Leah attempted to make conversation.

'I wonder what's happening there now?' she ventured.

Clay snorted. 'Don't know. I'm not interested in anything once I've got rid of it.'

He spoke no more until they were nearing the office. Without turning to Leah he said tersely, 'By the way, I shall be staying at the flat again tonight. See if you can find the bathrobe and towel I keep there – I couldn't find them last time.'

Conscience had been gnawing Leah for some time, but now she could bear the guilty feeling no longer. She picked up the telephone and dialled Urchin. The receptionist put her through.

'Hullo?' Mother's voice sounded as composed as always.

'Mother – it's me, Leah. I'm sorry I haven't rung before.'

She heard the catch of breath, could visualize her mother's fingers flying to her lips. 'Leah, love – are you all right?'

'I'm fine. I should have been in touch. Forgive me.'

'So long as you're all right, darling. Where are you?'

'I'm at work – in the office. I'm so sorry you didn't get that Venn Street site. Were you very disappointed?'

Eva's voice was quiet. 'I did. I pulled one over on that bastard Clay Richards. Tell me, what are you doing? You've got a job, you say?'

Leah took a deep breath. There was no way now she could reveal the truth. 'Yes, but listen – there's no privacy here – I just wanted to let you know everything's fine. I'm happy, I've got a good job and a super flat so you needn't worry. I'll fill in the details later. OK?'

'All right. Thank you for letting me know – I must admit I was worried.'

'I know. I'm sorry. Must go now, Mother. Goodbye – I miss you.'

'A meal, perhaps – one lunchtime . . .'

Leah put the 'phone down quickly.

Things were beginning to take shape at Venn Street. Eva went out of her way to drive down and see how the complex was developing. It gave her a shiver of excitement to see the skeleton of Calico taking on a recognizable shape, and an added pleasure to know that Clay Richards still did not know that he had failed to foil her dream.

The anxiety over Leah was gone. Wherever she was, she was well and happy and she'd communicate again when she was ready. A great weight had been lifted from Eva's heart and she could breathe and dream of Calico once more.

And Alan – tenderness flowed over her as she thought of him. That night had been wonderful, fierce and passionate and at the same time filled with gentleness and love. They had always had something special, she and Alan. She closed her eyes, longing to relive the moment, then sighed and shook her head. If only – but he was not to be trusted. Alan Finch would never lose his weakness for a pretty woman.

What was she like, this Christie who shared his bed now? Very young, of course – they always were – as well as pretty if she was a model. And she'd be intelligent. Curiosity filled Eva. Until now she'd never wanted to know anything about his distractions, had always been strangely numb about them, but now was different. She wanted to know more about this girl. She wanted to see her.

The board meeting was drawing to a close. Clay was handling the last item on the agenda, the boatyard site.

'Plans for adapting this site, as you know, remain incomplete owing to the arrival of a new interested party. I have pleasure therefore in informing you now, gentlemen, that negotiations for the sale are almost complete. Cresco International will emerge from it with a considerable profit . . .'

After the meeting had ended Leah walked back with him to his office. 'I know we made a good profit out of that deal, but aren't you rather disappointed?' she asked.

His eyebrows rose. 'Disappointed? Why the hell should I be?'

'You were so keen on the idea. You lost a dream.'

He gave a wry smile. 'I've made a fortune out of short-term property development deals – in and out again quick, that's my motto. Ring for my car, will you? My plane leaves at seven.'

Leah handed him his briefcase and watched him go. If he was disappointed he was hiding it well. It was inevitable in big business that he should sometimes have to make decisions he didn't really like. He had so much responsibility – so many people's lives depended on him. And he'd had to harden himself to accept occasional disappointments with grace. Power such as Clay's wasn't won easily, and it brought tremendous responsibility.

Alan lay in bed, watching Christie's back as she brushed out her long, dark hair before the dressing table mirror. She looked stunning, her hair frothing down over bare shoulders and glimpses of suntanned skin showing through the lacy panels of the black nightdress. She was humming softly to herself.

'Glad to have me back?' she asked, and he could see her teasing smile reflected in the mirror.

'Of course. It's lonely here without you.' It was hardly the reply of a passionate lover but it was hard to feign. Ever since that night with Eva . . .

'How about a drink then – a bottle in bed to celebrate?'

She turned on the stool, still smiling. More than anything in the world he wished the smiling woman was Eva. No woman would ever

66

match up to her. Not for the world would he hurt Christie with her easy, sexy warmth, but she wasn't Eva.

A drink would delay the moment; he got up and walked, naked, out into the kitchen. When he came back, bottle and glasses in hand, Christie was lying on the bed, her arms curved above her head. 'Well?' she asked softly. 'Don't I look better for the treatment?'

'You look fabulous.' He poured the wine and handed her a glass. She sat up to take it from him, sipped for a moment and then laid it aside.

'Come into bed, darling,' she said huskily. 'I've been waiting all week for this moment . . .'

He put his glass down and slithered down on the bed beside her. Her body was warm and sweet-smelling, her arms inviting. Alan felt a stab of horror; she wasn't Eva – he wasn't going to be able to make it.

Christie seemed to sense his inability and reached down to help. But it was no use. Alan closed his eyes, shutting out the vision of the lovely young girl in a sexy black nightdress, shutting out the guilt and seeing instead a naked woman with red-gold hair and searching lips, savouring in memory the unique scent of her and the wild response.

'That's good,' murmured Christie in a husky, satisfied tone. 'That's very good.'

CHAPTER SIX

Eva's opportunity to find out more about Christie came sooner than she expected. Alan rang one morning soon after she had arrived in the office.

'What are you doing for lunch today, Eva? I thought you might like to come over and eat with me at the Chelsea place.'

The Chelsea place. She could visualize it still the way it was when he'd first swaggered back into her life after college days. It was cosy then and curiously decorated; a huge china dog chewing on a clay pipe stood in the centre of the room and an ancient sewing machine was suspended from the ceiling. Alan had been so proud of his first restaurant.

But then Eva's pleasure at the warm sound of his voice was dispelled as she looked down at the appointment pad on her desk and saw the meeting arranged for noon.

'Sorry, Alan. Anyway, what about your lady friend?'

'She's gone on a shoot for the day – pictures for a magazine. Madame Tussaud's of all places. Hope they don't expect Christie to go in the Chamber of Horrors – they'll have their hands full if they do.'

'Well, I'm sorry. I'd have loved to come. I still have a soft spot for that old place.'

'Another day, perhaps? How are you fixed next week?'

She looked down at the pad. 'Away in Holland till Thursday. Sorry.'

'Never mind. Some other time.'

Eva could not help feeling a sense of regret that he did not sound disappointed. She hung on to the line, hoping he would mention the other night, that he would somehow hint that it had meant something to him. But after a moment's pause he said, 'Be seeing you then.'

And he was gone.

The meeting ended earlier than Eva expected and as she drove out from Urchin's car park a sudden whim overcame her. It would not be far out of her way to drive past Madame Tussaud's. Maybe, with luck, she could catch a glimpse of Alan's lady friend and see for herself just what the girl was like.

She parked the car at a distance and walked the rest of the way. Inside a crowd of bodies eddied around in an arc-lit area, banks of lights, cameras and jean-clad cameramen interspersed with girls administering make-up to three incredibly beautiful models – one brunette and two blondes. A small, balding man with huge spectacles watched from a bench. Eva recognized the agent and crossed to join him.

'Ben – nice to see you. These your girls?'

He nodded gloomily.

'Mind if I stay and watch?'

'Course you can. They'll be finishing any minute.'

Eva settled down on the bench beside him. 'Pretty girls,' she remarked conversationally. 'Maybe I can use them for one of my shows.'

'They're photographic models,' murmured Ben, 'but Christie sometimes does film and fashion work. She comes expensive.'

Eva leaned forward. 'Which one is Christie then?'

'Here she comes now. How's it going, kid? Hot?'

The dark-haired girl smiled, and her whole face lit up with a radiance that swept everyone around her into its brilliance. 'Not so bad,' she said, and Eva noted the husky, musical quality of her voice. 'But I'll be glad to get home and have a long hot soak all the same.'

She smiled at Eva as though ready to greet an old friend, then hesitated. 'Are you a model?' she asked.

'Me? No – why?'

She shrugged slim shoulders. 'I thought I'd seen your face somewhere – a photo, a magazine perhaps.'

'I don't think so.'

'I'm sure. I've got a good memory for faces.'

'OK, girls,' called out the photographer. 'We can call it a day. Thanks, everybody.'

Eva rose to leave. Christie touched her arm. 'Why don't you stay – we'll be going round the corner for a coffee in a moment.'

Eva looked into the girl's clear green eyes and saw what Alan must see in her. There was genuine warmth and honesty in those eyes, a total lack of dissimulation. She was lovely. So much like Leah . . .

'No thanks, I must be going.'

On the drive home she thought about Christie, about her and Alan

69

together. Christie would soon be lying in the bath, and maybe Alan would be bending over her, soaping her beautiful smooth skin. And she would turn to him with that lovely smile and he would let the sponge fall from her breasts . . .

Eva jerked the wheel of the car, narrowly missing a startled cyclist. She heard his shout of fury.

'What's up with you, missus? Are you blind or just plain stupid?'

Clay could hear the sound of running water in the bathroom the moment he let himself into the flat. He flung his overcoat over a chair and walked across to the half-open door. Leah was bending, naked, over the bath, swishing her fingers in the frothy water and a green glow from the marble reflecting on her skin.

For a moment he stood motionless, savouring the beauty of her, his nostrils filled with the fragrant scent of bath oil. Then she reached to turn off the tap and in the silence that followed she seemed to become aware of something. She turned her head and saw him.

'Oh – Clay. I didn't hear you come in.'

There was no panic, no embarrassment as she reached for the bath towel. Clay felt filled with admiration for her coolness.

'Sorry,' he muttered, and turned to go.

'Don't worry,' he heard her say. 'Pour yourself a drink – I'll be out in a moment.'

He sank on to the settee, shaking. What a fool he was, acting like a schoolboy at the unexpected sight of her. He was supposed to be a man of the world, wasn't he?

Leah came out of the bathroom. He looked up, words of apology ready on his lips. She stood smiling down at him, a pink bathrobe knotted loosely around her.

'I'm sorry,' he said quietly. 'I didn't mean –'

'I told you, don't worry about it. It's not important.'

She seated herself on the further arm of the settee. Clay itched to lean across, to rip that damn robe off her, to reveal that glorious body and bury his face between those breasts . . .

'Well?' she said. 'What about that drink?'

His hand shook as he poured the wine and handed it to her, and he wondered whether she was aware of it. When he sat down again he sat a little closer than before. She took a sip and then cocked her head to one side.

'You are an old friend, you know. I've known you since I was fifteen.'

'Old?' he murmured, trying hard to stop his stomach from turning somersaults. 'Yes, old is the operative word. The grey hairs are spreading fast.'

'Rubbish,' she chuckled. 'It's all in the head, remember. Grey hair is very distinguished, I always think. All men should have grey hair.'

He was trembling. Let her make the pace. Let her think it's her own idea.

He looked up at her and smiled. 'You're very kind. You know, if I were twenty years younger, or even ten –'

'I wouldn't have you a day younger,' she cut in, laying a finger on his lips. 'You're a very attractive man, you know that? Lots of women would go for you – even young Alison in the typing pool sighs dreamily when you go past her desk. She really fancies you.'

The bathrobe was gaping a little. As she moved he could just glimpse the inner curve of her breasts, firm and full just as Cheryl's had been; a centimetre more and a nipple might appear. Leah bent to place her glass on the table and then wriggle down onto the chair, unaware and innocent as a child.

Or was she? There was a smile in her eyes that spoke of woman the temptress. But then she was Eva Finch's daughter. More than that, she was Alan Finch's daughter too . . .

Damn that bloody student! He'd have liked to have her a virgin still, to possess her solely and utterly. He tried to make his tone sound casual. 'Sorry I made such a fuss about that man staying here – I thought it might be the young man you told me about, from college.'

Her eyebrows rose. 'Whatever made you think that?'

He shrugged. 'Maybe I'm jealous,' then, seeing her eyes widen, he added, 'Don't get me wrong – it's just that ever since that day you walked into my office I've felt protective towards you. There's something so vulnerable about you.'

Her face softened into a smile. Clay pursued his advantage. 'I felt like a father to you, I suppose, and I was jealous. That's stupid, isn't it?'

'No it isn't,' she said emphatically. 'It's very sweet. You know,' she went on, leaning forward and propping her chin on her hands, 'I've seen my father's girlfriend and she can't be a day older than me. They seem very happy.'

She reached for the glass again. From this angle he could clearly see her right breast and the small pink nipple, and started to feel light-headed.

He poured more wine. 'Was he cruel to you?'

'Who?'

'The boyfriend at college.'

'Oh no. He was nice. We were good friends, and then one night we just somehow found ourselves in bed together. He was just inexperienced, like me. Nothing happened.'

She slapped the glass down on the table. 'He was so upset, poor thing. We just pretended it hadn't happened. After that it was never the same between us.'

'And that was the only time?'

'Yes. It must be very difficult for a man the first time.'

Clay leaned across her to pour more wine, so close he could smell the sweet, intoxicating scent of her skin. 'I was lucky. I told you about the older woman, didn't I?'

She was leaning forward again, elbows on knees and fists pushed into her cheeks as she listened. He could almost visualize her in her schooldays, white cotton ankle socks and black buttoned shoes. The childlike pose inflamed him, contradicted as it was by the gaping robe . . .

'She was wonderful to me, that woman. She'd be about thirty-five and I was fifteen. It took a hell of a time before I plucked up the courage to go to her.'

'A prostitute?'

'Yes, but she was kind. She didn't make a fool of me. In fact, I rather think she took a pride in showing a young man the art of how to please a woman.'

He saw Leah's tongue flick along her lips. 'Go on,' she said.

'I'd paid for one hour and she kept me there for five. You can learn a hell of a lot in five hours. I'm still ashamed of the fact that the next time I saw her, a few weeks later, I walked right past her in the street and ignored her. I didn't know how to behave with her in the cold light of day.'

Leah gave a deep sigh. 'I ought to find a man like that.'

Clay felt his heart turn over. If he were that man, she would believe him to be so experienced, so skilled having nothing to compare him with but that bungling college youth. Nor would she expect the stallion stamina of repeated performances either.

Leah sat up. 'Have you eaten yet? I haven't, and I think the drink's getting to me on an empty stomach.'

'I don't think I'd better stay tonight.'

'Why not?'

'I might make a fool of myself.'

She rose to her feet and spoke in a quiet tone. 'You don't have to go, Clay. Please stay.'

Setting down his glass he got up and walked across to the window. His back towards her, he stood looking out into the darkness. He didn't want her to see his face; she might read the triumph there.

'You know, Leah, when I first stayed the night here, I came into your room and watched you while you were sleeping,' he said quietly. He heard her footsteps crossing the carpet towards him. 'I desperately wanted to touch you, but I didn't.'

He felt a hand on his sleeve and she laid her head against his shoulder. 'Please stay with me,' she murmured. 'Please stay.'

Clay was breathing quietly again now. Leah lay in the crook of his arm and marvelled at what had taken place. Never, never in all her days had she even begun to imagine just how wonderful it could be. Tender words and even more tender caresses, and sensations she had never dreamed existed. Part of her was eager for more.

'Well?' Clay said softly, his eyes still closed.

Leah sighed. 'You were right. It wasn't like before – it was wonderful.'

He removed his arm from under her and sat up. 'I'm glad you were a virgin still,' he said, and swung his legs out of bed.

'Was it that important, Clay? You're the only man now.'

He picked up his robe, smiling as he slipped it on. 'I'm glad. Let's keep it that way.'

As he walked into the bathroom Leah put her arms behind her head. She felt touched. He was a child despite his maturity, wanting to be the first, the only one. She could hear the sound of running water and rolled over on to her stomach to press a button on the console. The curtains slid back noiselessly, revealing a grey London sky heavy with rain.

After Clay had gone Leah sat at the table listening to the drumming of the rain on the window. She was still trying to absorb the fact that she had just been seduced.

Or had it been she who seduced Clay? It certainly hadn't been all his fault – in the event she'd been more than willing and she didn't regret it one bit. Despite her early misgivings about his motives he had never tried anything on before. It was she who'd been wilfully mischievous, leading him on, an impulse born out of curiosity and feeling so safe with him.

Be honest with yourself, Leah Finch, you know it was more than that. Clay had been Mother's friend once; now he was *her* friend, her employer, her lover, and the knowledge gave her a glow of pride. Wasn't that why she'd broken away on her own – to learn and experience for herself?

Leah looked around the room. Despite the dullness of the day colours seemed brighter and every detail of objects around her seemed thrown into sharper focus than before, as if outlined in black pencil. It seemed as though now there was an added dimension to her perceptions. She felt a surge of tenderness towards Clay, a deep sense of gratitude. She was not in love, but Clay was a wonderful lover. There had been no greed, no selfish gratification in his love-making, only an earnest desire to please, to delight. In one night she had experienced such joy as she had never known before, and it had all been his doing.

Leah sighed. Because of Clay she was a woman now in every sense, and for that she would always feel grateful. He was such a gentle, caring man . . .

The Major sat alone in a corner of the Club. The waiter lifted a questioning eyebrow but the Major waved him aside with his newspaper.

'Where the devil is that fellow?' he muttered to himself. 'Twenty minutes late already – no idea about punctuality.'

No background, no breeding, that was the problem with most of his clients. Richards was typical of the breed of ambitious upstarts infesting London these days. With money and power behind them they thought they ruled the world. Money-grubbers, jostling for prestige and power. Twenty years ago not one of them would have qualified for membership of the Club, but in these days of lowered standards . . .

The Major turned to see Clay Richards, booming out his order to the waiter as he crossed the thick pile carpet.

'Bloody traffic,' he muttered as he sat down.

'You said one o'clock,' said the Major, pulling out his pocket watch.

'I said about one,' Richards answered. 'Now, what's the score?'

The Major sighed. No social pleasantries, no savoir-faire. Still, the man paid well, very well indeed, to have his private business efficiently and discreetly handled.

'Well?' Richards demanded.

The Major took a deep breath. 'We're still having trouble with Mrs Fylde. I've done my best to charm her.'

Richards sighed in irritation. 'We've got to get them all out, you know that. Tell her she's got a week.'

The waiter brought Richards' drink and set it down on the low table. 'Can I get you something, Major?'

'A brandy and soda, please.'

When the waiter had gone the Major continued. 'I've done all I can. She's a delightful old lady – come down in the world you know, but she always offers me Earl Grey and a slice of fruit cake. Bit ga-ga these days, has a job to understand what I'm saying sometimes. Ought to be in a home if you ask me, but she's shrewd enough to stump up her savings for a decent solicitor.'

'Buy him off,' said Richards.

'Can't, old boy. Tried. He's sea-green incorruptible.'

Richards growled. 'There's no time to waste. She's got to get out, and quick. I want to get started on rebuilding Briar Court and I'm damned if I'm going to let a senile old woman get in my way.'

'She's charming, actually. Can't imagine why she wants to hang on in that crumbling old place. I warned her about those stairs – they're rotting, you know.'

Terrible shame really, fine old mansion like Briar Court being allowed to fall into squalid decay. Cresco had had it for so many years they'd probably forgotten they owned it until Richards bought it off them for a knock-down figure. Wouldn't be surprised if the scoundrel hadn't used their own money – shareholders would never know. Now it would soon be transformed. Luxury studio flats, Richards had said – tragic really, turning a beautiful old house into a barracks for chinless yuppies.

Richards was sipping his brandy thoughtfully. 'If you can't persuade her you know what to do.'

'Hennessy?'

'Whoever – just so long as she's out.'

'He's one of my best men, and they can all be trusted to obey orders . . . But you'll have to tell him what you want.'

Richards scowled. 'For Christ's sake, it's your problem – that's why I employ you to manage my affairs, isn't it.'

The Major controlled his impatience. 'It all depends what you want to pay. Hennessy operates a price list, you know.'

Richards tossed off the last of his brandy. 'For heaven's sake, whatever it costs – only get her out this week, you hear me? And no finger pointed my way. I'm going to start gutting Briar Court next month.'

The Major watched as Richards got up and walked out. He prided himself on the efficient service he provided to his clients. He felt scorn and contempt for them all – including Richards – so it gave him secret pleasure to know that he held them all in his power. He'd seen to that. It was the one thing that made the sordid business of handling their grubby little deals palatable. He had the power to destroy the whole rotten lot of them. On the day of his death the machinery would be put in motion to reveal their clandestine activities to the world. Barristers, cabinet ministers, tycoons, professors – for each and every one he had compiled a dossier the press and police alike would give their eye teeth to possess. The whole despicable bunch of them would be blown sky-high.

The last laugh would be his. Richards might think he held the world in his palm, but at heart he was still the same money-grubbing little upstart he had been all those years ago when the Major first came across him. Power had a habit of shifting unexpectedly, he would discover one day.

The Major signalled the waiter to bring another brandy. After that, he must go and find Hennessy . . .

CHAPTER SEVEN

'You really shouldn't, Clay – it's sheer extravagance.'

Leah fingered the bottles of perfume Clay had laid before her, Chanel, Yves St Laurent, Guerlain and Lancôme. 'They're lovely, Clay, but this is overkill.'

'I asked you which perfume you liked. You wouldn't tell me.'

'You spoil me.'

'I like doing it. I want to please you.'

'Well you don't need gifts to do it.'

That night he made love to Leah again. For weeks now she'd revelled in discovering yet more sensual delights, each more excruciatingly beautiful than the last. Clay was opening up for her an incredible world of sensation, and she felt affection for him deepening along with gratitude.

It always gave her pleasure to go out with him, to watch the deft way he handled people with charm and easy grace and the way they responded. Everyone seemed only too eager to please him. Life flowed smoothly for Leah, and he was a warm and witty companion, a pleasure to be with.

In the office, however, he remained Clay Richards the boss. No one, she felt sure, would have guessed at the private relationship between them. Preoccupied with papers, he called out absently as she was about to leave the office at teatime.

'Dinner tonight?'

'Great. Where?'

'Surprise. We're celebrating.'

'Fine.'

'I'll pick you up at eight.'

The kitchen door of Scapegoat Farm opened to admit a gusty blast of air and two dishevelled men. The girl at the scullery sink came out, wiping her hands on her apron.

'Oh, there you are, Nathan. I been keeping your dinner hot this hour or more.'

Nathan hung his jacket on the hook behind the door and signalled to the other man to do likewise. 'Sorry, Sandra. George'll be staying to eat.'

'No problem – casserole's big enough for two. Then I'll be off home if there's nowt else. See you in the morning.'

The girl left and the men ate with all the earnestness born of long hours of hunger and cold. George Bailey sat back at last and belched.

'Not a bad cook, that Sandra. You could do worse.'

Nathan pushed away his empty plate and eased his big body back in the chair. 'I'm not thinking of getting married for a while yet, George. Matter of fact, I'm thinking of going away for a bit, leaving the farm. Cup of tea?'

The older man's eyes widened. 'Leave Scapegoat? That's not like you, lad. You've never been away from here, 'cepting when you was a student.'

'Not leave it altogether, only for a while. I thought I might travel around for a month or so, see the world, maybe pick up a tip or two about how other folk farm. I've never been further than college.'

George took a sip of his tea and, wincing, set the cup down. 'Fancy things, them agricultural colleges. You still need old-fangled ways and folks like me when it comes to ewes dropping their lambs early.'

Nathan smiled. 'True enough, George. I don't know where I'd be without you. Which brings me to what I wanted to ask you – you knowing all there is to know about Scapegoat.'

The older man wiped his lips with the back of a horny hand. 'Aye, right enough. Many's the time I've helped out here, ever since old man Renshaw were alive and I were nobbut a lad.'

'So who better than you to take care of things while I'm gone, keep an eye on the lads? Would you do that for me?'

George rubbed his chin and took his time. 'You serious about this, Nathan?'

'I've been toying with the idea for a while. But I couldn't do it unless you agree to help.'

'What'll we do for an anchor man come Gooseberry Fair? Barnbeck's lost every flaming match since you dropped out of the rugby team – they can't be doing with losing the tug o' war against Otterley and all.'

'I'll be back, George. It's not for good.'

George grunted and picked up the teapot. 'Let's see if this tea's come to its senses yet. Aye, that's better,' he muttered, watching the flow of dark brown liquid. 'I'm supposed to be retired, you know, lad – I'm enjoying me darts matches.'

'I'd make it right, and a bit over.'

'And it'd mean early rising to get over from my place. I'm not used to that since you bought me out.'

'You could live in at Scapegoat – no gas and electric bills, Sandra coming in to cook and do the washing for you.'

George gave him a thoughtful look. 'And ironing? I hate doing the ironing since I been on me own.'

'And the ironing.'

'When was you thinking of setting off?'

'Soon. In a week or two.'

'Couldn't you make it Monday? I've a pile of shirts as high as the church steeple . . .'

'What exactly are we celebrating, Clay?' Leah asked as his car, driven by the impassive chauffeur Jim, wove its way through London's dark streets. Clay smiled.

'An old lady's made me very happy,' he said.

'What did she do – leave you some money?'

'In a manner of speaking.'

'Did you know her well?'

'Hardly at all.'

The car drew up and Clay helped Leah out. She stood on the wet pavement, staring at the railings and the glow of light from the basement. She heard Clay talking to the chauffeur.

'Don't bother waiting, Jim. We'll get a taxi back.' Then he turned to take her arm.

'This is Daddy's place,' Leah said in surprise. 'I didn't realize you were bringing me here.'

'You can rely on a good meal in a Finch's restaurant,' Clay replied smoothly. 'Come on.'

Alarm filled Leah and she resisted the pressure of his hand. 'No, I don't want to go in – he doesn't know about me working for you. He'll be furious.'

'He'll have to know sooner or later. Come on.'

Leah still hesitated. It was true he would have to learn, but she hadn't meant it to happen like this. She shook her head. 'I'm not going in, Clay. It's just looking for trouble. I've got to tell him in my own time, in my own way.'

She was turning away when Clay took a grip on her arm once more. 'Don't be silly,' he said firmly. 'He's probably not even here – he could be at any of his restaurants. Now, the table's booked, my Perrier's on ice, and I'm hungry. Are you coming in with me or not?'

She heard the controlled impatience in his tone and sighed as she followed him. With luck, like he said, her father would not be here.

Music was playing softly on a tape as they entered and Leah recognized Bix Beiderbecke. Daddy had never lost his love of jazz. Cigarette smoke lay blue across the room, flat like the branches of a cedar tree and the air was alive with murmured conversation and the tempting aroma of spice and herbs. Memories flooded back. So often she had come here as a child, laying the tables when the restaurant was closed, helping Daddy in the kitchens, spreading out textbooks and persuading him to help her with her maths homework. That was in the happy days, before Mother and he split up . . .

The head waiter glided across to meet them at the door. As Clay gave his name Leah glanced nervously around. There was no sign of her father but he could be in the kitchens, sleeves rolled up and hands deep in dough. He still loved taking a hand in the cooking now and again.

'Ah yes, your table is ready, Mr Richards,' the head waiter said in a heavily-accented voice, and then as he turned to Leah she saw his eyebrows rise. 'Good evening, Miss Finch. It is a long time since we saw you. I tell your father you are here.'

'He's here?'

'He will arrive shortly.'

Leah shivered. The evil moment of her father finding out was at least delayed, but not for long.

The waiter took her coat. Clay pulled out a chair for her in the alcove and she sat down. She felt uneasy; being in her father's restaurant with a man who had beaten him down in business felt somehow disloyal.

Clay was in expansive mood. With the main course he ordered a bottle of Château Lafite and, glasses filled, he raised his in a toast.

'To my newest venture, and to all future deals. May they all be as successful,' he murmured.

Leah sipped the wine nervously. Still her father had not appeared.

80

Behind Clay's head she watched across the tables to the door. With luck they might be able to finish the meal and leave before he came . . .

Clay wiped his lips with a napkin. 'Now, let's see what's on the dessert trolley. Waiter!'

'Not for me,' said Leah. 'I've had enough.'

It was at that moment she saw her father's tall figure enter the restaurant, on his arm the pretty, dark-haired girl she'd seen at his flat. Leah felt her stomach contract . . .

Her father's head bent to listen to the head waiter, who pointed over towards the alcove. She saw the sudden smile that sprang to her father's lips, the light in his eye. He let go of the girl's arm and came weaving between the tables towards them.

'Leah, darling – it's lovely to see you!'

He bent to kiss her and as he straightened, his hands still on her shoulders, his gaze shifted to her companion. His smile fell away and a frown immediately creased his forehead. He let go of Leah. 'What's he doing here?'

Clay smiled and sipped his drink. Leah took a deep breath. She could sense the undertow of feeling, the animosity in the air. This was all wrong.

'I'm celebrating with Clay – I work for him,' she said quietly. Her father stared.

'You work for him?'

'Don't make a scene, Daddy. Sit down, please, and have a drink with us.'

'Thanks, I'd rather stand.' He glared at Clay. 'How did this come about?' he asked roughly. Clay shrugged.

'She wanted a job – I gave her one.'

'And I love it, Daddy. I've never been happier. Please sit down.'

Alan looked back at his daughter. 'He's the last person in the world I'd want to see you with, Leah. I don't like interfering, but for God's sake – him!'

Leah could see the anger and anguish in his dark eyes and felt confused. Not for the world would she hurt him, but she owed Clay some loyalty too.

'Clay's been very good to me, Daddy, very generous.'

Suspicion leapt into his eyes. 'Good to you? Why? Why should he be generous to my daughter? There's a catch in it somewhere. Leah.'

'No – you've got it all wrong –'

'What are you up to, Richards? You've never done anything for nothing in your life. But if you harm Leah –'

'I don't think it's up to you, old man,' said Clay drily. 'The decision is Leah's. If you force her to choose –' He turned in his seat to look around. 'Now, where's that dessert trolley?'

The waiter came across with the trolley. Alan waved his arm.

'Take that away. They won't be eating dessert,' he said coldly. Waiter and trolley slid away. He looked down at Clay. 'Now, I'd be obliged if you'd leave. I don't want you here.' As Leah made to move he laid a hand on her sleeve. 'Not you, Leah – you're welcome here any time.'

Leah rose, looking up at her father with defiance. 'You leave me no choice, Daddy. If Clay leaves, so do I.'

'Not with him, darling,' Alan cried. 'You don't know him for what he is.'

The chatter in the room died away. The maître d'hôtel looked round at his other customers in evident dismay. The dark-haired girl came across the room and touched Alan's sleeve. 'What is it, darling? What's wrong?'

Leah took a deep breath. 'You choose your friends, Daddy, I choose mine. You're in no position to criticize what I do.'

'She's right,' said Clay, 'absolutely right.'

Alan scowled at him. 'What does that mean?'

'You should know,' murmured Clay. 'Remember Holly?'

Leah saw her father's face redden. 'For Christ's sake, that was years ago.'

'She was my sister. Now, how much do I owe you?'

Leah stared. 'What are you talking about? Who's Holly?'

Clay had taken out his wallet and was abstracting a credit card. Alan grabbed hold of his hand and rammed the wallet back into his chest. 'I don't want your rotten money, Richards. Get out of here – and don't you ever come back.'

The savagery in his eyes frightened Leah. Never before had she seen him so enraged, like a man gone crazy. 'Come on, Clay,' she said quietly. 'Let's go.'

Clay replaced the wallet imperturbably in his inside pocket, giving Christie an appraising glance as he did so. 'I like the look of your young lady friend, Finch,' he said equably. 'But I have to hand it to you – you always did have good taste.'

Leah was taking her coat from the waiter as she heard her father's voice, venomous with suppressed fury.

'Get out of here, Richards, and leave my daughter alone, or by God, I swear I'll get you.'

Clay was chuckling as they climbed the steps up into the street. Leah was shivering. They stood in the lamplight, waiting for a taxi and Leah seethed with mingled feelings of anger, guilt and hurt. The last thing in the world she had wanted was to hurt her father, but neither could she let him dictate her life. She looked up at Clay's impassive face, and for the first time she felt no affection in her heart. The silence around them was deepening into anger.

'You wanted this, didn't you?' she challenged.

'What?'

'A confrontation with my father. You wanted to embarrass him. That's why you brought me here.'

Clay smiled and patted her arm. 'I just felt it was about time your parents knew, that's all.'

Leah pulled her arm away, jerking her coat collar up close around her ears. 'Well, I hope you're satisfied.'

'At least it's over and done with. But I don't think your father expected you to leave with me all the same.'

The assurance in his tone irritated her and then she grew curious. 'What was all that about Holly?' she asked.

Clay held up a hand as a taxi appeared. 'She's my sister. Your father seduced her. My sister.'

The taxi drew up a few yards ahead of them. Clay followed after it and held the taxi door open. As Leah climbed in a sudden resolve came over her.

'I'm going home alone tonight, Clay,' she said quietly. 'I don't want you to come with me. Goodnight.'

She slammed the door shut and sat back. As the taxi drew away, she could see in the lamplight Clay standing, open-mouthed, on the edge of the pavement.

The whole evening had been a total disaster, Leah fumed as she let herself into the flat. She'd handled it all wrong. She should never have let Clay force her to go into the restaurant; she should not have let the sight of the girl with Daddy fill her with anger and defiance.

I have to hand it to you, Finch – you always did have good taste.

Leah flounced through the living room into the bedroom. Damn, the bed was stripped, and she remembered the bedding was still in the tumble drier. She pulled out tangled sheets, still muttering to herself.

'You idiot! You stupid idiot!'

It was her own fault. She could have avoided all this if she'd told her parents earlier. Delay was her undoing. She yanked a lurking sweatshirt out from the corner of the duvet cover and carried the pile of laundry into the bedroom.

Clay was right in saying it was high time they knew, but it was not up to him to determine when and how they learnt. He'd planned it all deliberately, she was sure, forcing a confrontation with Daddy in order to score off him. She should never have left with Clay.

Not with him, darling – you don't know him for what he is.

Leah pulled a pillowcase over a stubborn pillow and punched it into shape, trying hard to hold back the tears of frustration. She'd tried so hard not to be manipulated tonight by her father, only to let herself be manipulated by Clay, and the thought angered her.

She let go of the recalcitrant duvet which was refusing to reach into the corners of the cover and, walking back through the living room, dropped the latch on the front door. No one would come in tonight, not even if they had a key.

As she lay in the crisp, cool comfort of the vast bed, Leah debated what she should do. The best thing now would be to ring Daddy first thing in the morning and try to make her peace with him. And maybe later talk to Mother too but, knowing how she loathed Clay Richards, Leah knew it was not going to be easy.

And Clay – how was he going to behave towards her in the office tomorrow? He was a man not accustomed to slights.

'Eva? It's Alan. Yes, I know you're rushing off to work, but I just had a call from Leah.'

'Leah? Is anything wrong?'

He could hear the alarm in her tone and could not for the life of him have her worry all day. 'No. She's fine. But could we meet and talk? I'll tell you all then.'

'Yes. When? Today? I'm tied up till four.'

'Tonight, I thought. Christie's got a gaggle of her girlfriends coming and she wants me out of the way.'

84

'Would you like to come over to my place then? I'll get us something to eat.'

There was an eager tone now, almost like a young girl. Alan smiled. 'Fine. I'll be there at eight.'

As he put the telephone down Christie came out from the bedroom, her dark hair tumbled about her face and her robe buttoned all awry. She smiled sleepily and held out her arms to him.

'I want a daddy too,' she murmured. 'Cuddle me, Daddy. Tell me a bedtime story.'

'It's late, darling – I ought to be at the wholesaler's by now.'

As he pulled on his coat and made for the door Alan wondered why it was that he could find Christie's baby-talk so endearing at times, and so infuriating at others . . .

Eva sat on a settee listening intently while Alan talked. He was slumped on the opposite settee, his head thrown back against the leather, and she could watch his face, noting the hollows in his cheeks, the lines deepening about his eyes.

'So that's about it,' Alan concluded. 'The bastard scored off me – again.'

'Why didn't she tell me?' Eva asked quietly. 'I don't understand. Is she afraid of me?'

Alan shrugged. 'You know Leah – she's like you.'

'I must go to her, Alan. Where's she living?'

'I never thought to ask. But I wouldn't – let her come to you.'

For a moment there was silence in the flat. Outside Eva could hear the distant rumble of traffic. She looked up at Alan, wondering why she still felt curious about him. 'And all this about Holly – is it true?'

'Yes. She was much older than Leah, and divorced.'

'So Leah is his revenge,' murmured Eva. 'The sod.'

'He might not have tried anything on,' Alan pointed out. 'Anyway, he got his revenge when he took my restaurant.'

'Five years ago,' murmured Eva. 'That was the time of Holly, was it?'

'I was naïve. I didn't know the loan company I borrowed from was his. Not till they called in the loan and I couldn't pay.'

'That wasn't necessarily spite. He was entitled to do that and he's too big an operator to hang around waiting for small fry to pay up.'

'Gee, thanks,' muttered Alan.

Eva sat silent for a few moments. 'And you never told me all this. I thought we were friends, if nothing else.'

He sighed. 'You were engrossed in building your own empire, Eva. You were swallowed up in Urchin. No one could reach you.'

'You mean that's why I lost touch with Leah?' Eva could hear the anger in her own voice, and knew deep inside it was only a cover for the guilt she felt. Alan reached out a hand and touched hers.

'Don't feel bad, love. I was no better.'

Something in the gentleness of his tone touched off a response in her. She seized hold of his hand. 'What are we going to do, Alan? We can't just sit by and let that bastard – let him – oh, for God's sake, what are we going to do?'

Alan shook his head. 'There's not a lot we can do. Give Leah credit for some commonsense. Anyway, it's her choice.'

Eva was shaking. 'A daughter for a sister. I suppose that seems a fair enough exchange to him. I feel like charging over to his office and telling that sod what I think of him.'

'You know you can't do that.'

'But I've got to do something! I can't just sit here!'

Alan leaned forward and put his arms around her. 'That's just what we've got to do, love – sit tight and be patient.'

The note on the table from Clay's daily housekeeper was succinct.

'Mr Richards, left a snack in kitchen ready for you to heat up. Portcullis had liver for supper. Mrs Whitby.'

Clay switched on the TV so as not to miss the nine o'clock news, then waited until the pinger on the microwave oven told him his Chicken Kiev was ready. He stepped over Portcullis, who was wagging his tail and licking his lips in anticipation of supper, and placed the hot dish on a tray.

'I know you like garlic, Porty old boy, but this is for me. Just sit and be patient.'

He was carrying the tray through into the living room when the telephone rang. He set down the tray.

'Hullo? Oh, it's you, Muriel . . . Yes, everything's fine. And you? . . . Good. Look, I've just dished up my supper and the news is just starting. What? . . . No, I won't be back in Chislehurst until the weekend. Surely you can cope with the plumber on your own this time . . . Yes, about the same time as usual. Goodnight.'

He could visualize Muriel's pale face and the bony fingers fiddling in anxiety with the pearl necklace at her throat. Why did the wretched woman always expect him to deal with tradesmen when any normal wife would handle such trivial affairs without bothering a busy husband?

With a sigh Clay sat down and digested supper and news together. More political unrest in the Middle East, Government defeat in by-election, take-over bid by workers in a threatened confectionery firm . . . Portcullis sat with huge, expressive eyes at his master's feet, totally ignoring the portentous events in the world outside, intent only on procuring a morsel of garlic-flavoured chicken.

The news over, Clay flicked off the remote control switch. He set the empty plate down on the floor and Portcullis began licking it clean of the delicious sauce. That done, he looked up at Clay with a grateful doggy smile.

Clay patted his head. 'You're a good boy, Porty. Never ask questions, never ask for explanations – just do what I want, don't you?' He buried his fingers in the shaggy hair on top of Portcullis's head, digging deep into his scalp. 'Not like that naughty Leah, are you? She shouldn't have done that, should she, going off and leaving me in the street? That was very naughty, wasn't it?'

Portcullis wagged his tail eagerly. Clay reached down and, putting his hand under the dog's belly, scooped him up on to his lap. Fingers sank deep into the dog's flank and under the fur he could feel the scars. 'And we know what happens to naughty people, don't we, Porty?'

The terrier stared up at him, bewildered by his master's harsh touch on the still-tender wound. 'Yes, we know,' Clay went on softly. 'We know. Naughty people have to be punished.'

Portcullis began to whimper. The pain in his ribs hurt, but he was not accustomed to objecting. His master was gazing into space over his head. Portcullis yelped and leapt from Clay's lap then ran, whimpering, behind the settee. Clay half-turned in his seat. 'Come here, boy, come on.'

Portcullis shrank back further. Clay got down on his hands and knees to cajole. 'There now,' he said in a soft, persuasive tone. 'You know I didn't mean it. Daddy does love you. Come on out.'

Portcullis edged slowly out into view. Clay smiled. 'I'm sorry, old man. I wouldn't hurt you for the world, you know that. Blame that naughty Leah for upsetting me – come here, Porty, and give Daddy a kiss.'

*

87

Clay had been out of the office all day. There had been a telephone call to his secretary, but that was all.

'*He's lunching an American client at the Dorchester,*' Hilary told Leah, '*and then taking him down to Chelsea Harbour. He won't be coming in today.*'

Leah was disappointed. She wanted to see Clay, to talk to him. She needed his reassurance that last night's difference of opinion would not affect their relationship, at least in the office. But, she had to confess, in some strange way she was not missing him.

At least Daddy had been all right when she rang him.

'*I'm not offended, sweetheart. I must admit I was very hurt to see you walk off with him, but you had to do what you thought was right. I can't stand the man. Do me a favour, love – tell your mother. I know she feels the same way about him that I do.*'

'*I can't talk to her, Daddy. She never agrees with anything I do. She never understands.*'

'*Maybe she understands too well. You're a pair, you and your mother.*'

After work Leah stood on the pavement outside the office. As well as the headache which had been threatening all day her stomach was starting to feel queasy now – maybe she'd give supper a miss tonight, go to bed early and have a read.

A car drove past, through a puddle right in front of her, splashing her stockings and drenching her feet so that her shoes squelched as she walked. She felt thoroughly wretched as she made her way to the library. Browsing through a Dick Francis novel she might not have noticed the man at the far end of the Crime section if he hadn't sneezed so violently. Leah glanced up. He had a curious face which seemed to retreat rapidly backwards from his long, pointed nose as if in embarrassment – he looked remarkably like a whippet, she thought.

She chose a book and left. Her shoes still squelched as she walked along the rain-drenched streets towards the flat and she felt cold and miserable. It was only when she turned off the main road that she became aware of the man in the dark raincoat walking behind her and she began to feel uneasy. Could he be following her? And why?

Daniel's words came back to her. '*There's a rapist about. He preys on women who live alone – the things he does to them . . .*'

Leah began to hurry. Luckily it wasn't yet dark and she didn't have to go through an underpass. At the corner of her street Leah turned off and saw with relief that Whippet-Face carried on along the road.

She gave a wry smile. What a vivid imagination she had, getting all het-up because he used the same library and lived in the same area. The poor fellow was probably heading innocently home from a hard day in the office to tend an invalid mother, totally unaware of her libellous thoughts about him.

In the flat Leah peeled off her wet shoes and stockings and put them in the airing cupboard to dry out. Then another voice came to her. '*Do me a favour, love – ring your mother and tell her.*'

Leah gave a deep sigh. She was in no mood to argue with Mother over Clay – how could she expect her to understand that, quite apart from his kindness to her, making love with a man made him special, even if you weren't in love with him? No, she couldn't tell Mother about that. She didn't want to talk to anyone tonight. A hot cup of tea, and then bed.

She went through into the kitchen and filled the kettle. As she turned off the tap a sound caught her ear. What was that? She went back into the living room. It sounded like a sneeze outside the door. She hurried across to open it. 'Clay?'

A man in a dark raincoat was hurrying away down the corridor towards the lift. At the top of the staircase he glanced back over his shoulder before he disappeared down the steps.

With a start Leah recognized him – it was Whippet-Face. So he had been following her after all. She closed the door again quickly and locked it.

She could feel her stomach churning. She snatched up the telephone. The police sergeant listened calmly to her torrent of words.

'You did the right thing, miss. Just keep your door locked until a police officer comes round in a few minutes. But he isn't the rapist, miss – we caught him yesterday.'

Sleep was slow in coming that night, and when it did it was filled with troubled, uneasy dreams. In the morning when the alarm clock rang Leah rolled over reluctantly, and groaned.

And as soon as she got out of bed she was sick.

CHAPTER EIGHT

Nathan sat at the pavement table outside a café and, ignoring the biting wind, took a ballpoint pen from the inside pocket of his jacket. Pushing aside the empty coffee cup he turned over the picture postcard of the Eiffel Tower and wrote carefully on the back.

> Dear Eva, I'm here in Paris on the first stage of a journey to God knows where. Travelling light, going where the fancy takes me. Tried to find Leah in London to say goodbye but no luck – you were out of town and no one at Urchin could help. Give her a kiss from me when you see her. George Bailey is taking care of Scapegoat so it's in good hands. Don't worry. Be happy. Love, Nathan.

He eased back his weight on the chair, put the pen back into his pocket, then realized he was cold. A Pernod, or maybe a nip of brandy and it would be time to be on his way again. The night train for the south left in less than an hour . . .

Eva was pacing up and down her office. Her chief accountant twisted round in his chair to watch her. She was unusually edgy today, he thought, ever since she had come back late after lunch. Something about a clinic, she'd said.

'I'm not happy about Clay Richards, Vincent. He's up to no good, I can feel it in my bones,' she muttered.

Vincent re-considered carefully the facts she had outlined and could see no earthly reason for her uneasiness.

'I can't see that he stands to gain any advantage over us by employing your daughter, Mrs Finch, however secret he may have kept it.'

Eva spun round. 'Damn your shrewd Scottish brain, Vincent, I'm talking about Leah's safety, not business.'

'Oh.' Vincent pushed the sliding spectacles back up on his nose again and wished he could light a cigarette. 'I thought you were worrying that he might have found out, through Leah, that you got Calico after all. Does she know?'

'I think I might have mentioned it on the 'phone, before I knew where she was working.' Eva found it hard to concentrate, ever since she'd discovered the lump . . .

'Mr Richards wouldn't like to know you'd outwitted him.'

'No,' murmured Eva. 'He wouldn't. But Leah won't tell him. What I'm concerned about is what I ought to do for Leah.' She saw Vincent's perplexed look, the forgetful reach into his pocket for a cigarette which wasn't there. 'She's a babe in arms compared to Clay.'

'I don't see that there's very much you can do,' muttered Vincent. 'And I don't see how I can help.'

'You can't. I just needed to let off steam.'

What we've got to do, love, is just sit tight and be patient.

A week later Leah's stomach was still playing up in the mornings but was always back to normal by the time she reached the office. And the date ringed in her diary was days ago.

Doubts flickered in her head – but no, it couldn't be. She'd been taking the pill, hadn't she, ever since that first time with Clay? But when the days stretched into weeks Leah made the decision. It was no use. She would just have to put her suspicions to the test.

The colour reading was positive. Leah stood transfixed, unable to believe it. Pregnant? Could it really happen in such a swift and unconsidered way? Or could the testing kit possibly be wrong?

Clay was away in Edinburgh; Leah took the morning off. The young doctor down at the health centre with a sandy beard and pale, lizard-like eyes listened impassively, taking note of dates without comment. At the end he told Leah that a urine sample would provide the answer beyond doubt.

'When?'

'Ring in for the result first thing tomorrow.'

The next twenty-four hours were the longest Leah had known. The doctor's voice was coolly non-committal as Leah, gripping the telephone tightly between both hands, held her breath.

'Positive, Miss Finch. No doubt about it. According to my calculations your baby should be due about Christmas.'

Leah put down the 'phone, numb with disbelief. She ran a hand wonderingly over her stomach, trying to absorb the idea that a new being had taken on life and was sheltering there. But there was nothing to indicate its existence, not even the hint of a new sensation of maternal feeling. *My body is housing another being*, she kept telling herself. *What is it doing there? I didn't want it. I never even thought of it.* Somehow anger mingled with shock. *I didn't invite you in – you're an intruder, invading my body.*

It was Clay who had put it there. Strange, but she had not thought until now about Clay's part in the affair. Of course, it was his child too. A child – the thing inside her seemed nothing like a child, but it was his too.

Conceived in passion, but not out of love. No, whatever she felt for Clay it was not love. Ever since their disagreement that night at Daddy's restaurant Clay's manner had been that of the boss, not the lover. He hadn't come to the flat or taken her out, as if he'd lost interest in her as anything other than his assistant. One more good reason why the being should not go on sucking life from her body. The sooner it was gone the sooner life could return to normal and it would be as if the whole thing had never happened.

There were people who dealt with things like this, clinics which advertised in the papers. Leah rooted through the pile of newspapers stacked on the coffee table. In the personal column she found two, a clinic in the city and a nursing home in Clapham. She rang the second.

A young woman's voice answered her tentative questions smoothly. 'I'll put our brochure and an application form in the post today, Miss Finch. You should get them in the morning.'

Leah got through the day's work in the office in a haze. In the middle of the afternoon Clay's secretary came into Leah's office.

'Mr Richards rang just now from Edinburgh – he said to remind you about the Milan trip. He wants to be certain all the papers are ready.'

Leah smiled wryly to herself. If only Clay knew – but there was no reason why he should ever know.

Next morning the slim envelope arrived. For long seconds Leah stared down at the buff sheet of paper in her hand then, snatching up a pen she began filling in the boxes.

Name. Address. Date of birth. Next of kin.

Next of kin? She could not give her parents' names – Mother must never come to know of this. Nathan – they'd probably never check on it anyway.

The form completed, Leah licked the envelope, sealed it and placed it in her briefcase.

In the kitchen of Scapegoat Farm the telephone was shrilling. George Bailey, engaged in demolishing a steak and kidney pie, jerked his fork in its direction.

'Answer that, will you, Sandra lass. I can't be doing with them things.'

'Aye, all right.'

'Hello – is Nathan there?' It was a girl's voice. Sandra pursed her lips.

'No, he's not.'

'Oh.' The girl sounded disappointed. 'When will he be back?'

'I've no idea. He's gone away.'

'Gone away? Where on earth – ?'

'Your guess is as good as mine,' replied Sandra.

'Who is it?' hissed George.

'Who is it?' asked Sandra.

'It's Leah. I was thinking of coming up to see him. Never mind. I'll ring again.'

'Well?' asked George as Sandra put the 'phone down.

'It were that Leah,' she said in a self-satisfied tone. 'She wanted to come up and see Nathan. He evidently hadn't told her at any rate.'

'Eh, poor lass. She'll be fair sickened,' said George. 'They always got on right well together, them two.'

And he turned his attention back to eating the pieces of kidney he'd been saving till last.

Leah fought her way out of the crowded tube train onto the dusty platform. She could bear it no longer, the close, sweaty press of bodies and the mingled smells of beer, tobacco and mint on their breath. She needed to breathe fresh air even if it meant getting off a stop early – she could walk home across the park.

She leaned against the rail of the escalator as it rose slowly towards the surface, staring at the advertising hoardings on the wall as they passed before her. Fat fees for temps . . . elegant fashion and underwear modelled by sylph-like girls – and then the one that made her heart quicken.

'*If you want that baby, congratulations. If not, ring us.*'

The letter in her briefcase to the nursing home – she had forgotten to post it. She could do it on the way now. Leah rifled through the contents of her case. The letter was not there. Funny – she must have left it at home after all, or maybe in her office desk.

'*If you want that baby . . .*'

She didn't want the child – it would spoil her life. A spring sun glowed warmly on her back and Leah drew in deep lungfuls of cool air as she turned at the end of the park railings into the broad pathway between the flowerbeds.

Yesterday she'd been bitterly disappointed that she hadn't been able to confide in Nathan and talk the whole thing over with him. Today she was beginning to feel calmer, more able to cope with the prospect, to accept.

Ironically, the park seemed suddenly filled with children. Nannies pushed prams with chubby-faced babies and crisp, clean toddlers, cooing gentle baby-talk to their charges as they strolled. Brisk mothers marched quickly between the beds of daffodils, paying no apparent heed to their small sons with scratched knees recounting in a shriek the playground battle in school today.

Leah sat down on a park bench. The late afternoon sun was beginning to do her good as she watched the passers-by. A young woman, heavily-pregnant, hung onto her husband's arm, smiling up at him; a tiny girl staggered along in her mother's wake, clutching a threadbare teddy-bear by one ear. Her mother smiled at Leah as if to apologize, to explain that little Emma would go nowhere without the torn-eared creature, and Leah's lips curved into a smile. In her day it had been the rag doll Maddie had bought for her at the church fête and she'd never been able to part with it long enough for Maddie to wash it for the next five years.

Leah touched the toddler's blonde curls as she passed. This was how her child would look, she thought; she could see her clearly, a diminutive fair-haired child with bright eyes and boundless curiosity. Leah felt she could sense her, almost feel her babysoft skin against her own. Maddie, that was her name. '*Every death marks a rebirth.*' Leah suddenly felt content. She wanted her Maddie.

A child had been conceived, a child who had a right to life, just as much as any of these running and playing in the park in the spring sunlight. By the time she reached her flat Leah's feelings had undergone a complete sea-change. Subsconscious acceptance, hormones – whatever the reason, she knew now beyond all doubt that she could not go through with an abortion. The tiny Maddie she carried within her had as much right to life as anyone else, and Leah was going to see to it that she lived.

So now Clay would have to be told and Leah prepared herself for what he would probably say.

'*But how? I thought you were on the pill?*'

'*After the first time I was. It must have been too late.*'

'*I know a good clinic – don't worry.*'

'*No, Clay.*'

'*Don't be silly, Leah. We can't afford for this to come out. I have pull, no one need ever know.*'

Sleep eluded Leah that night as she turned the problem over in her mind, but sleeplessness only served to strengthen her resolve. No matter what Clay might say, Leah had steeled her mind; nothing on earth now would persuade her to put an end to little Maddie's life.

In the office next day Leah took the Milan papers into Clay's office. Standing in front of his desk she took a deep breath. This was it.

He was standing behind his desk, a satisfied smile spreading across his face. 'Leah, sit down. I've got some good news to tell you.'

'Clay,' Leah began tentatively, 'I've got something to tell you.'

He waved an impatient hand. 'Later. Listen. About our hotel in the Middle East – you know I needed an Arab partner before I could start up? Well, I've got one.' He jabbed a finger on the map of the world on the wall behind him. 'Here, in Dubai, at the southern end of the Persian Gulf. And I've got the hotel too, nearly completed. So now we can go ahead with our first – the first of five to start with, a really fine one to compete with the Hyatt and the Hilton.'

He sat down, beaming, awaiting Leah's reaction. She took a deep breath. 'That's great. But Clay, I have to talk to you about –'

'I've got the top hotelier in Italy to run it – Renzo Rosconi, from the Gritti Palace in Venice, no less. I'll be seeing him while I'm in Milan and soon he'll go out to Dubai and supervise the work, arrange the staff he wants and everything. Renzo is brilliant, and he knows it. Cost me a fortune to get him but he's worth it. He'll make certain everything is perfect. I'll just have to make sure he doesn't get carried away.'

'Clay – please – listen to me. I'm pregnant.'

She watched his face, the way the smile fell away and re-shaped itself into an expression of disbelief. He leaned across the desk towards her. 'Christ! Are you sure?'

Leah looked down at her lap and nodded. 'Yes. It's confirmed. The baby is due at Christmas.'

She heard his chair scrape back, sensed him come round the desk to stand by her, but she did not look up. It would be easier to say what had to be said if she avoided meeting those sharp blue eyes.

'I know what you're going to say, Clay,' she said quietly, 'but my mind's made up. I'm keeping the baby.'

His voice was low, strangled, as he spoke. 'God, Leah, you don't know what this means to me.'

'I'm sorry, Clay, but I won't have an abortion. I'll keep your name out of it if the scandal bothers you, but my mind's made up.'

'Scandal? Who the hell cares about scandal?'

No, of course not, thought Leah. How stupid of her. He was much too powerful to care about anything so trivial.

He bent down and seized her by the shoulders. 'You are certain, aren't you? There's no possibility of a mistake?'

She could see a light in his eye, a fierce gleam which made her shrink. 'No mistake, Clay. It's definite.'

He jerked her up out of the chair and hugged her close to his chest, so close the top button of his jacket dug into her cheek. 'Christ, that's wonderful!' he cried. 'After all these years, a child of my own!'

Leah was stunned. His delight was obvious, but there was a kind of manic intensity in it which she could not understand. Clay was rarely given to extremes of emotion.

He held her away from him and looked earnestly into her face. 'We must take great care of you, little one. Do you have any idea of what this means to me?'

Leah stammered. 'I can see you're pleased – I hadn't expected that.'

'Pleased? That's the understatement of the century! I thought I was going to die childless – Muriel and I couldn't have children – but now you've done it! Oh Leah, you've given me the best gift I've ever had.'

'Muriel – your wife? Is that why you separated?'

He was barely listening. 'She wanted us to adopt, but I told her. I said I didn't want anyone else's brat – I wanted my own flesh and blood or nothing. And now, my God, I've got it.'

He was standing over her, beaming down in delight. Then suddenly he reached round her and pulled her chair forward. 'Sit down, Leah –

we've got to take great care of you now. You're very precious to me. Sit down and we'll make plans.'

Leah did not argue. She was so relieved at his reaction that she was scarcely aware of what he was saying.

'I shan't tell my parents until I have to, Clay.'

'No need to tell anybody, not yet.'

'And I don't want to stay here – people will notice before long, start to talk.'

'We'll send you where no one will know.'

'Where?'

'Dubai – yes, that's it – you can work with Renzo. You can be my eyes and ears.'

By the time she left his office it was all arranged. She was to fly out to Dubai until it was time to come home. A great weight had been lifted from her mind. Now little Maddie would be safe, born in England in time for Christmas.

'I want you here then,' Clay said firmly. 'I want to be with you when the baby comes. I want to be the first to see my son.'

Sandra met old George at the farm gate just as she was wheeling her bicycle out. He scowled and gave a curt nod in answer to her greeting.

'Ironing's done and there's a piece of cod ready in the oven,' she told him. 'And that Leah rang again this aft. I told her I hadn't a clue where Nathan was. Could be in Timbuktu for all we know.'

'Lucky beggar,' growled George. 'He knew what he were about, dumping this lot on me. It's too much for a senior citizen, is this.'

'Go on,' Sandra said scornfully. 'You've got three men to help – Nathan managed well enough on his own, and he had the horses and all.'

'Help?' the old man snorted. 'You must be joking – that Wilfred's about as handy as a dose of toothache. I shall be glad when Nathan's had enough of his gallivanting and comes back home – and I hope it's well before Gooseberry Fair and harvest time.'

Sandra sighed and heaved her shopping basket onto the bicycle pannier. 'Aye, so do I, George – so do I.'

The sun was setting as Nathan paused on the cliff top and lowered his rucksack to the ground. He squatted his big body down beside it and looked out over the water.

A feeling of calm was beginning to soothe the unrest in his soul. Travelling the long, tree-lined miles of French *routes nationales* in every kind of conveyance from limousine to coal lorry had not only allowed time for the pain of his parents' death to ease, but had also given him an insight into a totally new culture, glimpses of villages and farms very different from Barnbeck and Scapegoat, and he was beginning to miss England. After a time the vista of French vineyards receding into the far distance and the exotic colours and scents of Spain had started to pall, and the gaunt mountains bordering the coast had served only to remind him of the greyness and solemnity of home. The people had been friendly enough, warm and welcoming him into their homes like a long-lost relative, and for a time he had savoured the freedom of roaming.

What was it Dad used to say, that slogan from Vienna in the pre-war days? *Freundschaft und Freiheit* – friendship and freedom. Nathan had tasted them both over the past weeks, but now foreign parts no longer held the attraction they once had.

Here, in the mountains edging on the sea, he felt at ease. The stark mountains put him in mind of Thunder Crags, high on the moor, redolent with the memory of Leah.

'*Nothing ever happens here, Nathan. It can't have changed in centuries.*'
'*That's the joy of it, Leah.*'

Leah and Barnbeck – his soul ached for them both. Soon the heat of summer would begin to make Spain unbearable, and he longed for a warm, wet English summer. In his mind's eye he could see Leah's long hair flowing in the breeze as she walked beside him down to the Gooseberry Fair . . .

The sun was dipping low now, its vivid light shimmering across the rippling water like scarlet arrows feathered with darkness. Nathan felt a void in his heart. Where was Leah, and what was she doing? He had to know. The very next village he reached he would find a telephone and book his flight home to England.

Rosary had finally rearranged what she called Eva's jungle of potted plants to her liking and was about to leave the flat to go to her night school class but she just had to have a glimpse of the evening paper before leaving. She picked up the newspaper from the table and, turning to the middle page, held it at arm's length, trying to focus on the small print.

'My stars say I've been soldiering on for quite some time but I'm due for a windfall, Mrs Finch – chance'd be a fine thing, so it would.'

Eva's voice was quiet. 'You had a rise last month, Rosary.'

The housekeeper lowered the paper and gave her a scandalized look. 'Now what in the name of heaven gave ye the idea I was hinting at anything?'

She turned her attention back to the newspaper. 'Now let's see what it says for you. Ye've a gift for the prescience, it says, whatever they may be.'

'Prescience. It means knowing beforehand, like clairvoyance.'

Rosary's pale blue eyes widened in horror. 'Ye're never a clairvoyant, are ye, Mrs Finch?'

'No, Rosary. I can't see into the future, more's the pity,' murmured Eva. *If only I could . . . that bloody lump . . .*

Rosary sighed with relief. 'Terrible sin, Father O'Leary said it was, no better than witchcraft, and we'd all go to hell if we dabbled with the likes of that.'

With a sad shake of the head Rosary resumed her scanning of the astrology column. Eva could see clearly the scar below Rosary's little finger on the left hand, a purple blemish where a sixth finger had once been.

'My mother was a pious woman, God rest her soul,' Rosary had once told Eva. 'She feared the village folk would say 'twas the mark of the devil, so she had the doctor snip it off just after I was born. Buried the finger, so she did, in my grandfather's grave, just to be on the safe side.'

The knife could still cut away evil. *A shadow could mean something or nothing, Mrs Finch. Don't worry.* Eva watched Rosary's intent expression as she cleared her throat and read aloud with lilting, soft-voiced solemnity.

'With your gift for prescience you have been assailed by doubts and anxieties over the past few months and the end of these is not yet in sight. A relative may encounter a setback and you are unable to help.'

Anxiety clutched Eva's stomach. 'Leah,' she murmured. 'I can feel it.'

'Not at all,' said Rosary. 'She's rung ye up, hasn't she? And she's coming to see ye? It could mean Mr Finch or anyone.'

'Maybe. What does it say for Leah? She's Gemini.'

Rosary squinted at the column again. 'Money worries disappear. Events this weekend will mark a major turning-point in your life.' Rosary tossed the newspaper down on the lacquered table. 'Anyway, 'tis all a load of old rubbish, so it is. I can't be soiling my soul with sinful stuff like that. I'll away to my class now, Mrs Finch, or I'll be late. Give my love to Leah when she comes.'

Eva cleared magazines from the leather settees and plumped up the cushions. 'I was so pleased when you rang, love. Come and sit down and tell me all the news.'

Leah sat stiffly on the edge of a settee, aware of her own awkwardness though Mother seemed quite at ease. 'I should have come to see you sooner,' she said quietly. 'I'm sorry.'

Eva smiled. 'No matter. I'm just glad you're here.'

She was making a big effort, Leah knew, not to ask questions, not to pry when she had always been a curious woman. Leah would dearly have liked to confide in her, tell her about the baby. But Clay's child – Mother could never come to terms with that.

'I was upset at the funeral,' she muttered.

'I know. We all were. Forget it.'

'I suppose you know I'm working for Clay Richards now?'

'Your father told me. I won't pretend I was pleased, love, but if it's what you want . . .'

'He's not the wicked creature you take him for, Mother.' Even if she could not tell the whole truth, she must at least defend the father of her coming child. 'He's really quite a caring man. He's president of a society for preserving the environment for one thing. And he's taken good care of me.'

She saw Eva open her mouth to speak, then bite her lip. Leah cocked her head to one side. 'You don't believe me?'

Eva shrugged. 'I believe you believe it. It's his motives I suspect.'

'Why?'

'If he's president of a thing like that it's got to be for a reason, to gain the sympathy of influential local people so he can get his schemes through. Clay Richards never does anything for nothing.'

Leah stood up abruptly and walked across to the window. 'Strange how the world always hates a winner. But let's not talk about him – we'll only quarrel again, and that's not why I came.'

'You're right,' agreed Eva. 'Why did you come, Leah?'

Leah could hear the tenderness in her mother's tone and allowed the stiffness in her body to melt. 'I won't be with him for much longer. I'm going away,' she said quietly.

'Away? Where?' Alarm was plain in Eva's tone.

'Dubai. In the Middle East. Supervising a new hotel they're building.'

'Who's building?'

'Cresco.'

Eva sighed. 'I might have known.' She paused for a moment and then added, 'A bit restrictive out there isn't it? Women second-class citizens? No drink?'

'That's in Saudi, Mother. Dubai is different.'

'And whose idea was this?' demanded Eva. 'Clay's?'

'He offered me the job, yes.'

'What the devil is he up to? I don't trust that man an inch.'

Leah came back to face her. 'But I do. He's a good man.'

Eva flung up her hands. 'Bollocks. You don't know him. He's the biggest con man out.'

She rose and took her daughter by the shoulders. Leah was taller by an inch, but Eva could see only the vulnerable child, the infant on her first day at school tormented by schoolyard bullies, and her heart ached to protect her.

'Leah, my baby! You're so naïve and trusting – Clay can make mincemeat out of you.'

Leah spoke quietly. 'We agreed not to quarrel. I'll be off in a couple of days. Wish me well, Mother.'

Eva felt helpless. Leah was a purposeful woman with her own quiet dignity and a kind of force-field around her it was impossible to penetrate. There just weren't the words to communicate with her. 'Leah – please – there's something wrong, I can feel it.'

Leah turned back to her and gave a tight smile. 'No, really, I'm fine. Don't worry so much, Mother. It's going to be a great adventure for me – you always used to say people should experience things.'

Eva searched her young face, uncertain still and the anxiety persisted: 'When are you leaving?'

'Saturday. I don't know my address yet but I'll be in touch.'

'Well, if you need me . . .'

Leah leaned forward and kissed her lightly on the cheek 'Thanks, but I'll be fine. I'd better be going – I've still a lot to do.'

Eva gripped her hand. 'Do me a favour, Leah. Stay the night here. Let's have one last night together.'

For a second Leah hesitated, then smiled. 'OK, I'll get a taxi back first thing in the morning.'

'And do me another favour, darling – sleep in my room so we can talk.'

It was as they were undressing for bed that Eva became aware of her daughter's gaze.

'I hope I've still got a figure like yours when I reach your age, Mother.'

Eva's breath caught in her throat. The doctor's words still rang in her head.

'A mammogram is a wise precaution for women of your age, Mrs Finch. And a shadow means little – could be just a faulty X-ray picture. You go on back for another just to be on the safe side.'

'Your father always used to say it was the most erotic thing in a woman,' she heard herself saying in a husky voice, 'to see breasts moving freely under a shirt. My mother would turn in her grave – my real mother, I mean.'

Eva could see her still, the faded little woman no older than Eva was now, but looking like a worn-out hag, unable to cope with life, let alone a child. No mother, no Maddie to confide in . . . She pushed the memory from her mind and spoke softly.

'I'll miss you, Leah. I've never spent as much time with you as I'd have liked.'

Leah sat on the bed and pulled off her tights. 'You should find something to occupy your mind, apart from business.'

'A man, you mean?'

Leah shrugged. 'Why not?

Eva gave a wry smile. 'There have been opportunities. In Rome, I remember . . . But no, there's only ever been one man in my life.'

Alan. If only I could tell Alan. He was always my best friend, but I can't tell him this . . .

'You still love Daddy, don't you?'

'Yes, but I can't live with him. I can't believe the promises.' Eva pulled a pale green satin nightdress over her head. 'I hoped for so much. You know, Leah, I kept my wedding dress in the loft at Scapegoat. Then one day I found the mice had eaten through the cardboard box, the tissue paper, the satin skirt, the lot. That was about the same time I first found out he was playing fast and loose. Ah well.'

Leah snuggled down under the bedclothes. 'Why don't you have him back? I'm sure he'd come like a shot.'

Eva slithered into bed. Why not indeed? It was heartwarming just to recall the days when they used to be everything to one another. Now even the infidelities were unimportant.

'There's never been anyone like him and there never will be,' she murmured as she switched off the bedside light. Under the cover of the sheets she ran her fingers over her left breast.

'We'll do a biopsy to be certain, Mrs Finch. In the meantime, don't worry. If there is a tumour and even if it is malignant it can be simply removed without necessarily involving a complete mastectomy.'

If the tumour is malignant – it was strange how fear sharpened the mind, making one realize how important it was to make the best use of whatever time remained, discard the trivial and concentrate on what mattered. People and relationships. *I'd have liked to lie with you just once more, Alan, to tell you just how much I have loved you, and only you.*

But could he bear to touch a woman with a missing breast? Would all the fiery magic disappear? Eva shivered. She couldn't bear him to love her out of pity. *You always loved and admired my independence and I'm damned if I'll become dependent on you now. You must keep your illusions. I want to remember the fire.*

'We always had a kind of fever for each other, you know,' Eva murmured into the darkness. 'But there we are. Let's change the subject.'

'What was all that about Venn Street?'

'I did a deal with Delaney – Clay mustn't get to know.'

'He won't hear about it from me.'

'Calico is going to be really exciting, so if you'd like to stay –'

In the darkness she heard Leah's voice cut in firmly. 'No, Mother, I'm off to Dubai, so don't try and stop me.'

Eva gave a deep sigh and turned over. Funny how the possibility of dying young could bring a kind of ancient wisdom to one's soul, but no one had yet discovered how to pass on that wisdom to a child. Youth had to make its own mistakes.

Next morning Eva stood in the doorway and watched the lithe young figure of her daughter disappearing down the corridor towards the lift.

When she was out of sight Eva leaned against the doorframe and sighed deeply. *Oh God, the time I've wasted!*

But at least the child had wanted to see her before going away, and the thought touched her. Prescience or not, her own fears faded into insignificance as the niggle of anxiety in her mind about Leah began shaping itself into an ominous cloud of fear for her child.

CHAPTER NINE

Nathan heard the sound of the telephone ringing and then Eva's voice came on the line. 'Hello?'

'Eva – it's me, Nathan.'

He heard her give a deep sigh, as if of relief. 'Nathan – how wonderful! Where are you?' It was good to hear the delight in her tone.

'Madrid. In a 'phone box right opposite Urchin.'

'What's the window look like?'

'Great. Somebody's just come out with two carrier bags.'

'Run and give her a kiss on both cheeks.'

'I'd rather not. It's a man.'

Eva chuckled. 'Are you enjoying yourself?'

Enjoying? Nathan gave a wry smile. Learning, experiencing, savouring – they would be better words for what had happened. Last night's small hotel had looked just like any other. Rather more women perhaps, and rather more coming and going than in others, but he'd suspected nothing out of the ordinary until the black-haired girl had spoken to him in the corridor.

'*Good evening, señor. You would like company, yes?*'

She was pretty, some ten years older than himself probably, and it would have been impolite to refuse. She had suggested, gently, that they took wine together in her room, that she changed into a cooler robe since the night was close, and he had felt the blood rising in his veins at the sight of her naked flesh beneath the flimsy robe. When she had snaked her arms about his neck and drawn him down on the bed beside her, he had not been unwilling.

'*You have a woman in England, perhaps, señor?*'

'*No – yes.*'

'*You have never had a woman like me. Come, señor, let us taste the wine and the love together.*'

Juanita had taught him much in the next few hours, and when he'd finally risen from the bed she had been reluctant to take the notes he offered.

'The pleasure was mine, señor. You will make your woman a fine husband and give her many children. Adios, señor.'

Nathan could tell Eva nothing of this, not yet. In the meantime he felt a mingled sense of surprise and pleasure with himself . . .

'Nathan?'

'Sorry. What were you saying?'

'Are you having a good time? Have you made any friends?'

Nathan smiled. 'One or two. How's things with you, Eva? Have you heard from Leah?'

He could hear the pause before she spoke and felt uneasy. 'She's fine. She got herself a job and a flat in London.'

His heart lifted. 'London? I'll be there tomorrow – I've just booked a flight for the morning.'

'She's going abroad tomorrow, Nathan. To Dubai.'

His heart sank again. 'Oh. Well, that's what she wanted, isn't it? To go abroad?'

Again the pause. 'Nathan, she's working for Clay Richards. I'm worried, to be honest.'

'But you say she's going abroad.'

'Still working for him. I can't explain it, but I can't help feeling something's not right.'

'I'll be home by midday. What time is she leaving?'

'Nine in the morning. I don't know what it is, but I definitely sense something's wrong.'

Urgent pips on the line told Nathan his money was running out. He made an effort to lighten the tone. 'I'm coming home anyway,' he said. 'I'm fed up of being taken for an English football yobbo by the Real Madrid supporters.'

Eva chuckled. 'See you soon, Nathan.'

'I'll ring you as soon as I land.'

'I won't be here, Nathan – I'll be away.'

And then the 'phone went dead.

It was Leah's last day at Cresco International. Her desk cleared and everything in order, she went into Clay's office. He got up from his chair and came around the desk to meet her.

'Are you all packed and ready?'

'Nearly. A few small jobs left, that's all.'

'How are you feeling?'

'Never better. Nausea all gone now.'

'Good. You check in at the airport at nine tomorrow – you've got the tickets and your passport? And are you sure you've got enough money?'

'No problem.'

He took her gently by the shoulders. 'Unfortunately I can't be there to see you off, Leah – got to go down to Kent – but promise me you'll take every care, don't take any risks. I couldn't bear anything to happen to you, especially now.'

'I promise.'

Clay's eyes crinkled at the corners as she smiled. 'I've been thinking about names.'

'Names?

'For my son. What do you think of Jonathan Seymour Richards?'

'Finch,' said Leah.

'Richards,' Clay repeated.

Leah could not help a curious feeling of flatness about his proprietorial tone. It was *her* baby.

Keen blue eyes searched hers. 'You haven't told anyone?'

'I thought it best not to, not yet.'

'I agree – keep it to ourselves for the time being.'

He glanced at his wristwatch. 'I'd better be off – I'm due down in Chislehurst in an hour. Now remember, you're booked in at the Sheraton Hotel along with Renzo – it's very comfortable and convenient. I always find you get good personal service there. Order whatever you want and put it on Cresco's account. I'll ring you there in a day or two, once you've got over the jet-lag.'

He was reaching for his briefcase when an afterthought struck him. 'Oh, by the way, I got something for you.'

He reached across the desk and jabbed the intercom. 'Hilary – bring in the little gift for Leah, will you?'

Hilary came in carrying a huge bunch of flowers – gladioli and long-stemmed red roses, fragrant freesias and carnations, lilies and gypsophila. Clay smiled as Leah took them from her. Specks of orange pollen wafted from the lilies and settled on Leah's grey jacket.

'Oh look, petal-dust,' she murmured.

'Pollen,' Clay corrected.

'Petal-dust,' she repeated quietly.

'Get it off quick,' said Hilary. 'It marks your clothes something terrible. Just look at my shirt.'

Leah reached up to kiss Clay on the cheek. 'Thank you, Clay. You're very thoughtful.'

'They're called *Enchantment*,' Hilary murmured as she turned to leave.

'What are?'

'The lilies. Look lovely, don't they, but once they've stained you it's there for life.'

Leah was on her knees in the bedroom of the flat, putting her winter clothes aside in cardboard boxes when the telephone rang. She stepped over the ready-packed suitcase to reach it.

'Hi, it's Daniel. Just wanted to let you know I found Cheryl OK.'

Leah fingered a red rose-petal amid the bunch of flowers wilting on the dressing table. 'I'm so glad. Did she say why she didn't get in touch with you?'

There was a moment's pause before he answered. 'Actually, that's why I'm ringing. She'd had to get out of your place in a hurry. Took some time to find somewhere else – that's why the delay. But what I wanted to tell you – hell, what I mean is, Cheryl wasn't very well treated by that boss of yours. He threw her out.'

Leah frowned. 'Because she wasn't up to the job, you said so yourself.'

'No. He wanted more than a personal assistant, apparently. Personal services as well. No dice, no flat. Kicked her out the same day – never gave a thought to where she'd go or anything. Selfish devil. Thought it was only fair to tell you.'

Leah swallowed hard. Somehow Daniel's news did not surprise her, but she did not want to know it. 'Thanks, but it doesn't matter now.'

'I like you, so I'd kick myself if he tried anything on with you and I'd said nothing. So watch out, Leah – he's a sod.'

'Nice of you to ring, Daniel, but I'm leaving anyway – I'm off to the Middle East in the morning.'

'Great! Wish it was me instead of Finals this summer.'

'Best of luck. Look, I've got to go, Daniel – I've just remembered I've left my pocket tape recorder in the office and I'm going to need it. Thanks for thinking of me – I do appreciate it.'

Daniel's call irritated Leah. He had meant well, she knew, but the last thing she wanted right now was to entertain doubts about Clay. Dad, Mother, Daniel – they all had cause to think badly of him, but she did not want niggling disquiet about him to start festering in her mind. Clay cared, if not for her then at least for the coming child. Everything was going to be fine, she was sure of it.

Passport, travellers' cheques, airline ticket – everything was ready but the tape recorder. Clay's desk – that's where she'd last used it, taking notes. Leah glanced at her wristwatch. Almost ten o'clock – it was lucky she still had a key.

The night porter looked up from his newspaper and nodded as Leah crossed the office foyer towards the lift. 'Evening, Miss. You going to the party too?'

'Just left something in Mr Richards' office, that's all. What party?'

He jerked his head towards the ceiling. 'The freighting lot. Sixth floor. Must be a hundred there already.'

The lift glided smoothly towards the seventh floor. As Leah approached Clay's office she took the key from her pocket and opened the door then stood, transfixed. Across the darkened room a glow of light spread over the carpeted floor from the window between Clay's office and his secretary's.

Hilary must be working late. Leah crossed to the window which was in reality a one-way mirror Clay had had installed so that he could keep an eye on everyone who came into Hilary's room, to check on strangers and avoid unwanted callers. To her surprise Leah saw Clay seated at Hilary's desk and two men standing before him.

Clay still here? At three this afternoon he'd left for somewhere in Kent. Something urgent must have cropped up to bring him back at this hour of the night. One of the men looked crisp and distinguished but the other – with a start of alarm Leah recognized him – was the whippet-faced man with a sneeze, the one who'd been following her weeks ago. What on earth was he doing here?

She stood in the darkness, conscious of the sound of muffled voices from beyond the partition but she could not make out the words. Curiosity overwhelmed her. The intercom on Clay's desk – she pressed a button and a dim red light glowed.

Clay's voice crackled over the line. 'Why the hell did you have to bring him here? What was so urgent?' he demanded. Leah saw the distinguished-looking man's lips move and heard the sound of his leisurely, cultured voice.

'He's been keeping tabs on that casino owner as you asked – now you know exactly what the fellow's up to, first-hand. You don't like things in writing.'

Clay frowned. 'OK, so you've told me. Anything else?'

'Only that girl of yours,' said the other man. 'She's done nothing out of the ordinary, seen no one but her mother. Stayed the night there.'

Leah stifled a gasp. Was it her they were talking about? Clay flung up an impatient hand.

'If that's all then you can clear off. Did anyone see you?'

'Take it easy, Mr Richards,' the cultured man said soothingly. 'I'm a professional, you know. There are hundreds of people going in and out to a party or something, and in any case we came up by the back stairs.'

'Then just get him out again without anyone seeing. You hear me – get him out.'

Leah shrank back as she heard the shuffle of chairs when the whippet-faced man moved, saw the door open and close and she stood motionless, hardly daring to breathe. Clay was still growling.

'Don't you ever do that again, you hear me, Major? I don't want to see or know anything about your men. Just get the job done, that's what I pay you for.'

'Very well,' the Major replied smoothly. 'Now, about that Briar Court job we carried out some time ago. I've paid Hennessy off.'

'So you want payment. OK, how much?'

'Two thousand.'

Leah could see Clay's jaw sag. 'How much? What the devil for? You said five hundred.'

'Two thousand,' repeated the Major. 'Hennessy made a thorough job of it.'

'You said the fee was five hundred for a broken leg.'

Leah clapped her hand to her mouth to smother the gasp. The Major's tone remained imperturbable.

'Ah, yes, but as I said Hennessy is very thorough. You did say the price was immaterial so long as you got vacant possession. Leg broken, the old lady fell downstairs and had a heart attack. Died next day.

Coroner's verdict was accidental death, of course. Pleasant old soul – she made a very good cup of tea.'

Leah's brain was reeling. Could she really believe what she was hearing? She had to get out of the office before they discovered her. Heart thumping, she slipped off her shoes and as she made cautiously towards the door she heard the Major's voice over the intercom.

'I sent a wreath, but I shall pay for that myself.'

Opening the door silently, Leah crept away down the corridor towards the lift.

'That casino chap's got to be dealt with,' Clay said, crossing to the window. 'Trying to welsh on me. Get Hennessy on to him too.'

'Limit?' asked the Major.

'Five hundred. Give the bastard a real good scare, something painful he won't forget in a hurry. He won't try it on again. And while you're at it, square things with Councillor Lewis, will you? I knew he'd get my planning application through – they couldn't preserve that village in aspic for ever. Progress has to be accepted. A thousand.'

Clay stood at the window of the office looking down on the square below, irritation still pricking him. He hoped that shifty-looking fellow had got away unnoticed. Bloody stupid thing to do, bringing him here.

The Major gave a polite cough. 'Well, if you'd like to settle up, Mr Richards, I'll be on my way while the party guests are still around. A cheque would be acceptable.'

Clay turned away from the window and reached into his pocket, then paused. A cheque drawn on Cresco's account would do just as well – after all, it was in Cresco's interests and it could easily be woven into his Milan expenses. 'One moment,' he muttered, 'I'll get the cheque book from my office.'

As soon as he entered he caught sight of the dim light glowing on the desk, and frowned. The intercom still live? And a pocket tape recorder on his desk . . .? 'Major', he called out.

The Major's voice came loud and clear over the intercom. 'What is it?'

Clay's heart sank. Someone could have been in that room while they'd been talking and maybe overheard the conversation. But how much? If they knew about the Briar Court business . . . and maybe the casino fellow . . .

He tried the door to the corridor. It was unlocked. The only other people besides himself who had a key to that office were Leah and Hilary. Whichever it was, if she knew anything she was dangerous.

And Clay's habit was always to exclude danger from his life. Hilary was dispensable, but Leah and the baby . . .

Returning to the outer office he wrote swiftly then handed over a cheque which the Major scrutinized before pocketing it. Clay seated himself in the high-backed executive chair and began swaying it gently from side to side. Then he reached out and picked up the telephone.

The night porter took his time answering. 'Porter?'

'It's Mr Richards. Have any of my staff been in tonight – my secretary, perhaps?'

'No, sir. Miss Finch did call in to collect something. She's just left. She was only upstairs a few minutes.'

'I see. Thank you.' Clay replaced the receiver and turned to the Major who was making for the door.

'I think I might have another job for you,' he remarked.

The Major turned round. 'Hennessy again?'

'No, no. It's in Dubai. I want the girl watched.'

The Major shrugged. 'No problem. We have a courier in Dubai. He can be relied upon.'

After the Major had left Clay settled himself back in his chair and, picking up the telephone again, dialled a number. A moment later he heard the timid voice on the other end of the line. 'Hullo?'

'Muriel, it's me – I can't get back home tonight after all – something's cropped up again.'

'Oh dear – the Brandons are still here.'

'Well make my excuses. Oh, and Muriel –'

'Yes, dear?'

'Tell Jackson not to forget to give Portcullis his rubber mouse when he puts him to bed. He can't settle without it.'

Leah locked herself into the flat and sat, trembling and her heart still thumping, on the edge of the velvet settee. She was still scarcely able to take in what she had just overheard. Could she possibly have misunderstood?

But she had heard with her own ears. Her first reaction had been one of fury – Clay had lied to her. Whippet-Face was still following her. And a woman had died – because of Clay.

What the devil had she got herself into? At least Clay had not discovered her, thank heaven. In any event he would not harm her while she carried his child. But who was the Major? And who was Hennessy?'

'What's in it for Clay? He never does anything for nothing – he's an unscrupulous bastard.'

Leah buried her face in her hands as she recalled her mother's words. They'd been right, Mother and Daniel, but what could she do? Go to the police? Clay was powerful and she could prove nothing.

She ran thoughtful fingers across her stomach – could she be carrying another monster like Clay? No, not little Maddie. The sooner she and the child got away from his grasp, the better.

Leah struggled to calm the tumult in her head, but there would be no sleep tonight. Her brain was dizzy with confused thoughts – she must catch that plane in the morning and maybe once she was in Dubai she'd be able to think more clearly. With luck distance would lend objectivity to her tumbling thoughts. Only one resolution was clear in her head – Clay would never lay hands on little Maddie, never.

CHAPTER TEN

Eva could not help feeling low. Even the anticipation of Calico no longer filled her with excitement. Strange. Before having the mammogram she'd hardly passed a day without visiting the site, pestering Delaney daily with questions.

'Are you sure you've remembered . . .?' she'd ask, jabbing her finger on the plans.

Delaney would smile patiently and tease her. 'After all the times you've told me, Mrs Finch, I think I could draw the plans blindfold, down to the last coat hook.'

And now somehow it had all lost its attraction. Leah was about to fly off to the other side of the world and the dreaded biopsy had still to be faced, and Eva feared to admit to herself what it might reveal. Time and again she'd found her hand sliding inside her shirt, fingering the small lump near the left nipple.

She'd been trying to push the lurking fear from her mind with petty jobs, tidying out drawers and cupboards in the flat, sorting and discarding no-longer-wanted items like a woman who knew she was going away for a long time. Old theatre programmes, tickets to Ascot, brochures from hotels in Rome and Madrid, unused bottles of perfume – everything had been thrown into the wastebin. Rosary just could not believe her eyes.

'Why, there's room to put all your things away tidy now, so there is. Are ye sure ye're all right, Mrs Finch?'

'I'm fine.'

Rosary frowned as she limped towards her. 'It's not like ye at all, and you're nothing but skin and bone these days – ye have me worried, so ye do. Will I bring you supper in now, Mrs Finch?'

'No thanks, Rosary. I'm not hungry.' Eva watched her limp away, shaking her head and her knees almost knocking together. 'What's the matter with you, Rosary? You can't walk properly.'

The housekeeper turned back and gave a thin smile. ''Tis these new tights I bought in the sales, Mrs Finch. They're crippling me, so they are.'

'Your tights?'

'They're too short, do you see?' Rosary hitched up the tweed skirt to reveal the gusset of the tights sagging between her knees.

Eva could not resist a smile. 'Why don't you throw them away? They must be dreadfully uncomfortable.'

Rosary gave her a horrified look. 'And they brand-new and never been worn before? 'Twould be a terrible crime, so it would. No, I'll wear them till they ladder, and please God it will be soon.'

After Rosary had gone Eva squatted on the living-room floor amid a pile of old cheque book stubs. Some of them dated back years – the bookshop bills from Leah's college days, the jodhpurs in young teen size, the summer camp for youngsters . . . One stub showed a brief weekend they'd spent together in the Lakes, a wonderful two days of wellingtoned walks in the rain and warm closeness.

Too little time she'd spent with the girl, and now tomorrow . . . Eva pulled her mind away from the obtrusive thought. Funny how the stubs made old memories come flooding back. Her whole life seemed to be passing before her now, reflected in those yellowing scraps of paper. She picked up a book of stubs and flicked the pages. *Finch's Restaurant, twelve pounds seven and six*. Eva sighed. That had been the time when she'd treated Alan to a birthday meal in his own restaurant in Chelsea, when it had been his first and only place and they'd been so eager for life and so much in love . . .

Eva shivered. Nostalgia gave way to a sudden impulsive desire. Tonight she needed company, even of strangers. She scrambled up from the floor and marched through to the bedroom to fetch her coat.

She recognized the sound of Charlie Parker before she even reached the bottom of the steps leading down to Finch's restaurant. The saxophone swelled as she opened the door and went in.

The air was warm and filled with the savoury scents of spice and roasting meat. So late at night most of the tables were occupied but there was one small table free against the wall.

There was no sign of Alan and disappointment welled in her. Even if she could not tell him about tomorrow, the sight of him would have been reassuring. Still, there were strangers at nearby tables; anything was better than the loneliness of the flat.

Eva leaned on her elbows and gazed around. The place had changed since the days Alan had started out here when she was opening her first Urchin shop above. There was red flocked wallpaper now and upholstered chairs in place of the old wooden ones, and the tablecloths were of the finest linen. No more plastic flowers; a single rose now decorated each table. She could recall how she and Alan used to eat spaghetti bolognaise on scrubbed deal, eagerly talking of their dreams and plans.

'Madam?'

Eva looked up at the young waiter's expressionless face. 'Oh, I haven't looked at the menu yet. Give me a moment.'

She could swear she heard a click of the tongue as he turned away. She looked at the menu card but her eyes only saw the dashing young Alan who'd stolen her heart completely. It was so disappointing he wasn't here . . .

'Ready, madam?'

'Not quite. What do you recommend tonight?'

He sighed, his eyes glazed with boredom. 'The special is langoustine.'

'And you recommend that?'

'It's not for me to say. I'll come back when you've finally decided.'

She frowned. 'I was asking your advice. All right, I'll have spaghetti bolognaise.'

The waiter lowered his order book and sighed. 'That's not on the menu, madam. Please make up your mind quickly – can't you see we're busy?'

It was on the tip of Eva's tongue to make an angry retort – but what was the point? Life was too short . . . She jabbed a finger on the card. Paella. 'I'll have paella, please.'

She could have argued. She would have once. She could have told the supercilious young man that she was Mrs Finch, since it was clear he did not know. But why waste precious time? There were more pressing things to think about. She shifted her gaze from the sad-looking middle-aged couple at the next table who never spoke a word to each other and saw a tall figure entering the restaurant door. Her heart gave a sudden leap. It was Alan.

He still had that air of filling a room with his presence, a kind of magnetism that made heads turn. Grey now he might be, but still devastatingly attractive as the women's glances showed.

His dark eyebrows rose as he caught sight of her and came across, smiling as he sat in the seat opposite. 'Eva – what a nice surprise.' There was genuine pleasure in his eyes, then he frowned. 'Anything wrong?'

He had always been quick to sense her mood. Eva gave him a bright smile. 'Not at all, Nathan's on his way home, and Leah's off to Dubai in the morning.'

'Dubai? What the hell is she going there for?'

'She's still working for Clay Richards.'

'And you're happy about that?'

Eva hesitated before answering. She leaned across the table. 'To tell the truth I'm worried, Alan. There's something funny going on, I can feel it, something to do with Clay.'

Alan was frowning, his eyes searching hers. 'If you think that, why don't you go out there and see for yourself?'

Eva avoided his gaze. 'I can't right now. I've got to go away tomorrow.' She heard him sigh as he sat back. 'No really, this is important to me, Alan. I'll go just as soon as I can. I love her.'

The young waiter came scurrying. 'I'm sorry, sir – I didn't see you come in. What would you like, sir?'

Alan waved a disinterested hand. 'I'll have whatever Mrs Finch is having. And Barry, bring a bottle of my usual wine.'

Eva saw the waiter blink, then his voice came silky-smooth. 'I had no idea, madam – I am so sorry . . .'

As he glided away Alan leaned forward. 'By the way, Fay's back in London, with her husband. After all these years.'

'You've seen her?'

'No. Someone told me.'

Eva looked across to the door leading to the kitchens. It was in that doorway she'd seen Fay that night, standing waiting for Alan while he played the piano in the dark. Alan was watching Eva closely.

'I know what you're thinking. It's all a long time ago, ancient history now. What are you planning to do tonight?'

Eva watched the fingers tracing the curve of the pepper mill and envied the other curves they must have traced over the years. She shrugged. 'Nothing special. Going home to bed.'

His hand slid across the table and touched hers. 'Why not come and stay with me?'

She felt her hand tremble under his. *Oh yes, more than anything in the world I'd like to lie with you tonight, to blot out the fear of tomorrow, but . . .*

'I can't.'

'Someone else?'

'Not for me. You've got Christie.'

'She's gone off to Barbados on a shoot, and I've got a strong suspicion she isn't coming back. End of Christie.'

Eva pulled her hand away as the waiter returned, bearing two heaped plates. Alan stared down at his, open-mouthed. 'What the devil's this?' he demanded.

'Paella, sir.'

'You know I never eat the bloody stuff.'

'But the lady, sir – she ordered paella.'

The waiter looked pleadingly at Eva. She smiled at him brightly.

'You went to a lot of trouble to help me choose it, didn't you, Barry? Do try it, Alan.'

The waiter reached to spread a napkin over her lap. 'You are too kind, madam.'

She smiled mischievously up at him. 'You're probably right.'

Alan stared down at the plate. 'I suppose I can eat the prawns,' he said moodily. 'Bring us the wine.'

Over the wine Alan's voice grew huskier. His finger was tracing the stem of her wine glass now. 'You know I think the world of you, Eva. I can't get you out of my head. Remember how it was the last time?'

How could I ever forget?

'You're the only woman for me, always have been.'

And you for me, Alan. But tomorrow still hangs over me. And yet I want you, so much, but not in Christie's bed. One last night to remember, while I'm still desirable . . .

His arms would be comfort and reassurance. Eva pushed away her half-eaten paella. 'Tell you what, why not come and stay at my place tonight then we can drive to Heathrow together in the morning to see Leah off. No promises.'

He smiled, that slow, agreeable smile of his. 'Whatever you say, Eva.'

She pushed back her chair and stood up. 'OK, let's go.'

★

Leah was standing waiting beside her suitcase for the taxi when the doorbell rang. She answered over the intercom.

'Who is it?'

A man's voice answered. 'It's me, miss. Come to take you to the airport.'

It was Jim's voice – Clay's chauffeur who'd driven her many times to meetings and restaurants with Clay. She opened the door cautiously. Jim's stocky, uniformed figure stood waiting, cap in hand.

'Car's outside, Miss Finch. I'll take your luggage down.'

'That's very good of you.'

'No bother, miss. I'm used to it.'

Leah watched as he carried the case ahead of her towards the lift. Used to it? Had he moved Cheryl's things out too? And how many others? Had he often been called upon to move out Clay's women?

Eva woke slowly, stretching her arms and yawning. Rosary was standing beside the bed, a cup of tea in her hand.

'Your bag is packed and ready like you asked,' she said primly. Eva could sense that something was wrong. The housekeeper could not contain herself. 'Mrs Finch, it is not for me to judge others,' she said sharply, slapping the tea down with a clatter on the bedside table, 'I've just seen a naked man.'

She folded thin arms across her chest and waited as Eva rubbed her eyes and sat up, staring at her. 'A man? Oh Rosary, it's not what you think – that was Mr Finch, going for a shower probably. He stayed the night.'

'Mr Finch?' Rosary's eyes gleamed. 'Mr Finch back here again? Oh, the Lord be praised!'

Eva recalled the way his long fingers had caressed her breasts last night as they sat together on the sofa.

I've always loved these breasts, Eva, perfect and lovely as a girl's . . .

'He slept in Leah's room,' Eva said quietly.

'Oh, I see.' The disappointment was plain in Rosary's tone. Eva glanced at the bedside clock.

'Oh God!' she cried. 'Alan! We've overslept! We'll never get to Heathrow in time to see Leah!'

'What time is it?' Alan's voice called back. 'Christ – we might still make it if we dash.'

★

When Leah's luggage had been checked in at the airport desk she felt in no hurry to go through the barrier. She hung on hopefully. There was just a chance Mother might turn up at the last moment . . . She sat on a bench and the chauffeur seated himself beside her, his weathered face impassive.

'I'm OK now, Jim, thanks. You can go if you like.'

He shook his head. 'Mr Richards said I was to stay till you went.'

First Whippet-Face, now Jim . . . A shabby old woman tottered unsteadily towards them and stopped in front of Leah, fixing her with a lopsided smile. 'Give us a quid for a cuppa, lady,' she whined.

Leah was reaching into her pocket when the chauffeur cut in. 'Don't give her anything, miss. She's always at it. Waste of time giving her money. She'll only buy booze.'

The old woman gave him a withering look. 'What's it to you then? Mind your own bloody business.'

'Push off,' said Jim. The old woman scowled at him and shuffled unsteadily away across the concourse towards a young couple with a toddler. Over the loudspeaker a tinny voice announced Leah's flight. She picked up her handbag and stood up.

'I'd better go – thanks for bringing me, Jim.'

The chauffeur touched the peak of his cap. 'I'll be off then, Miss. Oh, by the way, Mr Richards asked me to give you this.'

Leah stared down at the pocket tape recorder in her hand as he turned away and left. Clay must have found it last night, after she had gone.

Seconds after Leah had disappeared through the barrier Eva came running across the concourse, her scarlet coat and purple scarf flying.

'Sorry, madam – all passengers for that flight checked in and boarded,' the girl at the check-in desk told her.

Eva turned away disconsolately. She'd have liked one last glimpse of Leah before facing the day. Alan came running towards her, his face flushed.

'I just missed her.' Eva told him. 'She's gone.'

He took her arm in silence, squeezing it to his side as they made towards the exit. 'Can I drop you somewhere?' he asked as they emerged into the sunlight.

'No thanks. I told you, I've got to go away today. You go on.'

He turned to take her by the shoulders. 'We'll get together again –
soon?'

She could not bring herself to meet the probing eyes. 'Probably.
Now be off with you.'

A quick kiss, and she watched him stride away. Outside the airport
terminal she climbed into a waiting taxi and spoke to the back of the
driver's bristly neck.

'Fulham Road, please. The Royal Marsden Hospital.'

Eva lay gowned and ready for theatre. The pre-med needle had done
its job and she was beginning to feel drowsy. They brought papers for
her to sign.

'Nothing to fear, Mrs Finch. A biopsy only means removing a small
piece of breast tissue for analysis. But we need your signature just in
case we find anything we ought to treat immediately.'

Cancer, they meant. They needed her permission to remove her
breast. Eva sat up and heard the gown crackle as she signed the papers.
The porter wheeled the theatre trolley into the ward.

CHAPTER ELEVEN

Weird sights and sounds floated around Eva and she could make no sense of them. She seemed to be struggling, like a deep-sea diver, to rise above darkness and confusion to reach the surface.

Once or twice the light seemed to come close, and then recede again. Weakness overwhelmed her; she sank and then tried again. This time the light hovered and the sounds began to resolve into voices.

'Mrs Finch? Wake up, Mrs Finch. The operation's over. You're back in your own bed.'

The brightness before her shaped itself into a nurse's crisp white uniform, and above it a face smiled. 'There now – how do you feel? It's all over, and you've got a young man waiting to see you. Just a couple of minutes now, Mr Bower.'

Then it all began to come back. The biopsy, breast cancer. Eva's hand reached up to touch her breast. There was a dressing to one side of the nipple. Nathan's face appeared above her.

'Hullo, Eva. How's it going?'

'It's still there,' she murmured. 'And the lymph gland under my arm.'

Nathan seated himself. 'So why are you worrying?' His big hand came down over hers as it lay on the sheet.

'I dreaded waking up to find I had no breast.' Eva frowned. Her brain was beginning to function again. 'Nathan – how did you find me? How did you know I was here?'

'Found the hospital letter in your flat. Why didn't you tell me? But never mind that – got to get you better and home again.'

'They haven't taken my breast away, Nathan,' she said weakly. 'That's promising, isn't it?'

'Very.'

The nurse signalled and Nathan rose, his hand still on Eva's. 'You'd better get some sleep now, love. I'll come and see you again tomorrow.'

He bent and kissed her cheek, then turned away. Eva watched the large figure picking his way round the trolleys to the exit, and felt warmed. She was no longer alone. Nathan was here; now all would be well.

Renzo Rosconi, Clay's hand-picked hotel director, made it abundantly clear to Leah that he would prefer her not to interfere with his organization of Dubai's new Cresco hotel. Small and dapper, with well-oiled, thinning hair and an erect bearing which reflected his self-esteem, Renzo moved with the speed and grace of a cat. He hardly ever deigned to speak to anyone else in Mohammed al Dhin's elegant office with its mirror-glass windows.

Leah he was prepared to tolerate, provided she listened to his dictates and did not obtrude any ideas of her own. She was an obligatory adjunct to his life-long dream of setting up and running a hotel exactly the way he felt it should be run. Again and again he told Leah, dark eyes glowing and slender hands eloquent as he gestured.

'Mr Richards is a wise man – he knows that a good hotel cannot be created by a committee,' he purred in fluent English but with a marked Italian accent, 'only by one man with vision. I was trained in Zurich by Georges Rey, nephew and pupil of the great Cesar Ritz himself. For thirty years now I have been in the hotel business. No one knows better than I how a hotel should be run.'

'Like the Hyatt and the Hilton?' Leah ventured to ask.

Renzo flung up his hands. 'Pah! American glitz, all plastic and shiny chrome. Wonderful, if you like hamburgers. No, my hotel will be perfect, European and the epitome of comfort, not show. It is a beautiful building Mr Richards has bought and it is now up to me to make it perfect, to make everything run so smoothly that it will appear to run itself. I, Renzo Rosconi, who made the Gritti Palace the finest in the world, will create this masterpiece.'

He rose from his desk and crossed to stand at the window, hands behind his back. He stood looking out across the flat roofs of buildings pregnant with bellying balconies, towards the Trade Centre which dominated the skyline.

'The Desert Rally ends today,' he said quietly. 'There is to be a grand dinner tonight at the Hyatt Regency, awards presented to the winners by Sheikh Mohammed himself. I would dearly like to see how the Hyatt conducts such a grand event but the dinner is by invitation only.'

With a sigh Renzo turned away from the window. 'You have not yet seen our new hotel,' he said. 'I will ask Yussef to drive us there today.'

As Yussef escorted Renzo and Leah across the marble-tiled forecourt, Leah watched his profile, the hawk-like nose and jutting chin surrounded by the *kuffiyah*, the purple headdress he wore, secured by a double twist of black camel rope. Leah had checked in at Mohammed al Dhin's modern office every morning at eight since she'd arrived but only once had she caught sight of the stately old man, Yussef's father. His son, however, came in daily. He was extraordinarily handsome, probably in his late twenties and had the same regal manner as his father. Both men wore the traditional white Arab *dish-dash* and Leah couldn't help reflecting that it must make driving very difficult, like driving in an evening dress.

She smiled as she caught sight of the white Mercedes gleaming in the sunlight . . . 'My mother has a car just like this,' she said, then she saw the Arab girl in the back seat, young and wide-eyed behind the veil. Yussef opened the back door for Leah to sit alongside the girl. Renzo took the passenger seat beside Yussef. As he did so Leah heard him murmur a greeting in Arabic, '*Salaam al leikom.*'

'*Al leikom as salaam,*' the girl replied, and looked to Yussef.

'My sister Yasmin,' he explained briefly as he switched on the ignition. 'She too would like to see the new hotel.'

The car moved off. Leah could see Renzo's well-groomed dark head only just visible above the headrest, a clear foot lower than Yussef's. Yasmin turned away to look out of the window, and Leah lapsed into her own thoughts.

It was cool in the air-conditioned comfort of the car and she leaned back to watch the sprawling city slide by, the buildings dazzlingly white in the brilliant sunlight and throwing sharply defined shadows across the road. Cars swirled about them everywhere. Yussef drove like all Arabs, swerving from lane to lane and cutting in front of other drivers with no thought of signalling. The sound of tooting horns never ceased.

Leah felt relaxed. Life here was far less demanding than work in London had been. Renzo was staying at the Sheraton too, a magnificent hotel shaped like the prow of a ship and with cascades of water in the foyer giving the place an air of coolness and tranquillity. Even Renzo had so far found no fault with it except that it was American.

She looked at the back of his head. He was gazing out of the window, silent and clearly deep in his own thoughts of the new hotel. Leah half-closed her eyes.

From the moment she'd caught sight of Dubai from the aeroplane and its searingly white outline on the edge of the rippling blue waters of the Persian Gulf she had been enchanted. When she'd stepped out on to the tarmac she had been stunned by the heat and humidity and she'd loved it, a fairytale world, so far removed from England in a cold spring that it was not difficult to push all thoughts of Clay out of her mind. He couldn't have found out about that last night. The reality was now, here, with thousands of miles separating her from the old life; the only real considerations now were herself, her new life and her baby.

The car was speeding through wide, grass-verged roads where Indians were watering the shrubs and palm trees punctuating the roadside.

'It's amazing – so much greenery in the midst of hundreds of miles of desert,' Leah murmured.

'Imported by Sheikh Rashid,' Yussef replied. 'So is the water. We have rain only in the rainy season and it soon dries up.'

'It's so modern, as if it's just been dropped in the desert from nowhere.'

'It's all been built in the last thirty years. There was only the old mud-brick fort here before that, and wandering nomad tribes.'

Leah looked at the sumptuous villas speeding by. 'All this in thirty years,' she murmured. 'It's incredible.'

Renzo was nodding. 'Sheikh Rashid is a shrewd man with a great deal of foresight,' he said quietly. 'We have a lot in common. He encouraged foreign investment so the city grew fast. Utilizing European knowledge, but he allows no foreigners to buy property here, so it all remains in Arab hands.'

'And Dubai's so *clean*,' said Leah. 'Even the cars.'

'Because there are no cars over five years old,' Yussef told her. 'And they are all quality cars. You should see the ones in the desert rally.'

'Ah,' said Renzo, and Leah could hear the wistful tone in his voice.

'We have two tickets for the Rally Dinner tonight if you wish to use them,' Yussef went on. 'My father and I do not wish to attend.'

Renzo cast him a delighted look. 'Thank you,' he said. 'My assistant and I will be very pleased to have them.'

125

They were crossing over the handsome Maktoum bridge spanning the wide inlet from the Gulf. Along the banks of the creek small trading dhows were moored where men with headbands like pirates were loading and unloading.

Yussef pointed to a long, low building. 'That was once a palace which belonged to a wealthy Arab. It was confiscated from him and is now a riding stable.'

'Who confiscated it?'

'The Sheikh probably. He and the police deal out all justice here – we have no courts. But he has abolished our old harsh laws.'

'Like stoning and beheading? I should think so. It's barbaric.'

Yussef turned to glance at her. 'Then don't go to Saudi – they still have those laws.'

'And they cut off the hands of thieves,' said Renzo.

'I won't,' Leah said firmly. 'I'll make sure I don't.' Then she caught sight of the girl's eyes watching her, large and apprehensive.

'Doesn't your sister speak English?' she asked.

'Yes. She has had a good education. She is to marry my cousin next year.'

'But she hasn't spoken a word.'

'Because I have not given permission.' Yussef craned his head forward to peer along the sandy road. 'We are nearing the hotel now. Further along this road lies Jebel Ali. Sheikh Rashid has built a free port there. One day it will be the new Hong Kong.'

Yussef pulled the car up alongside a dusty site where Indian workers stood, sweating as they leaned on their shovels. Behind them the hotel, surrounded by scaffolding, rose white and magnificent against the deep blue of the sky. With its Moorish arches surmounting a long colonnade it looked more like the palace of a wealthy sheikh than a hotel. Before it lay a huge lake with a bridge spanning its width and dotted with fountains.

Yussef switched off the ignition and pointed. 'The fountains will be illuminated by night, the colours changing every few minutes. It will be quite a spectacle.'

'It's beautiful,' murmured Leah. 'Mr Richards chose well.'

Renzo was smiling. 'Mr Richards acquired it from the former owners when it was discovered they had Israeli connections. They were deported.'

Yussef opened the car door to get out. 'Come,' he said to Renzo and to Leah he added, 'Yasmin will stay here but you may come with us.'

Leah had already opened the car door and swung her legs out. 'I thought your sister wanted to see the hotel,' she said as she stood up.

Yussef scowled. 'She can see it well enough.'

'Can't she get out?'

He sighed. 'There are strange men here. She will stay in the car.'

Leah frowned. 'In that case, so will I.'

'As you wish.' He turned away to stride over the scrub-spattered sand towards the group of Indians. Renzo hurried after him. Leah slid back into her seat and turned to speak to the girl.

'Does he always treat you like that, Yasmin?'

The girl seemed to shrink back against the leather upholstered seat. 'I do not understand. Yussef treats me with respect.'

'You can't speak without his permission, you can't get out of the car – don't you mind?'

'Why should I mind? He is a man, and my brother. He honours me.'

'Western women wouldn't put up with that.'

The eyes behind the veil glinted. 'Our men protect us against harm. It is we who should pity you.'

Leah's eyes widened. 'Pity us? Why?'

'You western women – you are so unfortunate, but you do not realize it. You make a big noise for freedom, for equality and you do not realize you are being tricked.'

'Tricked?' Leah echoed. 'Don't you envy us our freedom?'

The girl threw up her hands in disgust. 'Freedom from what? From security? We are safe, but you western women work instead of being kept. To an Arab woman it would be a dishonour if the men of her family did not provide for her and protect her. Don't you have anyone to protect you?'

'But I want to work,' said Leah. 'I chose to.'

Yasmin gave her a pitying look. 'You have no choice. You have to work.'

Leah sat back. 'No,' she said quietly. 'I have no one.'

She saw the look of compassion which came into the girl's eyes. 'I am so sorry,' said Yasmin softly, 'I did not know.'

Leah bowed her head. There was no point in trying to explain. Yasmin clearly thought her father and brothers must be dead. The car was growing hot and close now the air-conditioning was no longer

127

running and it was a relief to see Yussef coming back, deep in discussion with Renzo.

Leah leaned her elbow on the cushioned arm rest and spoke casually. 'Tomorrow I get my rented car. I think I shall drive up here on my own then and have a look round.'

Yussef glanced back quickly at her and Leah could see the anger in his eyes. 'You will not come alone. I will come with you.'

'Oh, you don't have to – '

'I will come. It is not the custom in our country for a woman to be alone with men,' he said quietly. 'And it could be dangerous. I must insist, you will not come alone.'

'Hold on a minute, I'm English,' Leah pointed out firmly. 'I don't have to – '

Yussef cut in coldly. 'I am sure you understand. You are my father's guest and therefore my responsibility. I wish to know at all times where you are.'

Leah looked at Renzo. He was shaking his head. 'Yussef is right,' he murmured. 'When in Rome . . .'

It was useless to argue further, and Leah fell silent. Through the driving mirror she could see the eloquent eyes of the Arab girl in the back seat.

Renzo was eager to see the Ramada hotel and insisted he and Leah should go there for afternoon tea. Yussef dropped them off in the city before driving Yasmin home.

'Every hotel in Dubai I must see,' Renzo said as they crossed the forecourt. 'Every single one.'

'Bit of a busman's holiday, isn't it?' smiled Leah.

'Some people love churches. I live and breathe hotels. It is my life.'

He led the way into the foyer. 'The Ramada has the biggest stained glass window in the world,' he said enthusiastically, spreading his elegant hands as high and wide as they would go. 'This I must see for myself.'

The Ramada was impressive. The stained glass window stretched so high above Leah's head as she stood looking up at it in the Cascade restaurant that it gave her a crick in the neck.

'It's wonderful,' she murmured. 'Must be a hundred feet high.'

'Come, let us take the elevator.'

The glass-sided lift glided up fourteen floors and Renzo's dark eyes glowed as he took in the full length of the window at close quarters. Afterwards they descended to the coffee lounge.

It was quiet during the heat of the afternoon. They sat at a corner table and Leah watched as other customers began coming in, Europeans and Arabs served by Filipino waitresses. One tall, distinguished Arab was followed by the tiny, slender figure of a woman shrouded and veiled in black. She seated herself demurely on a couch against the wall while her husband strode across to a centre table.

Leah watched while the Arab seated himself with slow dignity, then arranged the folds of his white *dish-dash* with care. The swarthy face beneath the purple-banded headdress wore a severe expression as he studied the menu then gave his order to the Filipino girl waiting attentively by his side. Renzo was studying the waitress closely. When she disappeared the Arab raised a hand and pointed to the empty chair opposite his own. At once the black-shrouded figure against the wall leapt to her feet and came scurrying across to sit where he had pointed, her eyes downcast.

'These tables are two centimetres too high for comfort,' Renzo remarked. 'I would have the legs shaved.'

Leah leaned on her elbows. 'You know a lot about the Middle East, Mr Rosconi – have you worked out here?'

He smiled. 'You may call me Renzo. I work in all the best hotels in Europe, under the best masters, but never here. But I am thorough. I read much, I ask questions. I do my homework well.'

Leah looked back at the Arab girl. She seemed no more than fourteen years old, Leah thought, though it was hard to tell when nothing but her eyes could be seen through the slit in the black veil covering her face. How on earth would she drink her coffee when it came, if strict Islam forbade a woman to reveal her face to strangers?

Renzo was absorbed in critically inspecting a table knife while he sipped. He put down his cup and looked across to the door.

'The door makes a clumping sound,' he commented. 'In my hotel it will be silent.'

Leah saw the waitress return to the Arab's table with two glasses of milk and pastries. The veiled girl waited until her husband began to drink, then took up her own glass. Would she unfasten the veil now and let it fall? Leah watched, fascinated, as gold bracelets on a slim arm rattled as the girl took hold of the lower edge of the veil and lifted it, and the glass disappeared underneath.

Leah turned back to murmur a comment to Renzo. He was no longer at the table. Then she caught sight of his dapper little figure in the corner, peering earnestly behind a screen. In a moment he came gliding back.

'It's a small office, with telex and fax,' he reported. 'I thought it might be a servery of some kind.'

The Arab was rising now, going to pay his bill. He made his stately way across to the deak, laid coins before the woman, and turned to go, leaving the veiled girl still sitting at the table, her dark eyes following his every move. The moment her husband vanished through the door into the street she leapt up and hurried out after him.

Unquestioning and in blind subservience, thought Leah. That's just the kind of wife for Clay. Funny, but she'd hardly given him a thought during the last week. England seemed another world. Clay – and the baby. Under the table Leah ran a hand over her stomach. There was no feeling of being pregnant, nothing.

'What a beautiful waitress,' said Renzo. 'But why do they put her in such a terrible uniform? Overalls like that should never leave the kitchen.'

Leah smiled. 'She's lovely, so slim – and so are the Arabs.'

'Ramadan has just ended,' Renzo said briefly. 'Fasting for a whole month. Bad time for business in a restaurant.'

'And I was thinking about that girl who's just gone out. If that's an Arab woman's lot, running after her man like a pet spaniel, then I'm damn glad I'm a westerner.'

'Napkins,' said Renzo. 'Remind me to change my order for napkins. Ours must be the best quality in Dubai.'

He took out a notebook from his pocket and a pen, and began writing. Leah leaned across and twisted her head to read. 'What's that?'

Renzo licked his lips. 'Just names. Cosima. She worked for me in Venice and I will have her for my head housekeeper. And the names of the men I want for my chief cashier, my manager and assistant manager, and my maître d'hôtel. All from the finest hotels in Europe. These I will have or no one.'

I must watch Renzo doesn't get carried away. Leah frowned. 'Won't that be very expensive?'

Renzo beamed proudly as he stowed pen and notebook away. 'Mr Richards has ordered the very best in the world for Cresco and the best he will have – he knows that costs money. Ah yes, the restaurant manager – I know the very man.' Renzo took out his pen and notebook again.

When the telephone rang in her hotel room that evening Leah was unprepared. Clay's voice startled her. 'How are you, Leah? Enjoying yourself?'

It was strange to hear him again, thousands of miles away in London yet as clear as if he were only in the next room, so close it made her shiver. 'I'm fine,' she answered. 'It's great. We're going to the Dubai Desert Rally Dinner tonight.'

'Good. The heat isn't too much for you, is it?'

'No, I've grown used to it.'

'You are taking things easy, aren't you?'

His voice was full of concern. He couldn't know what she'd overheard. 'I don't have much choice,' she answered cautiously. 'Renzo doesn't leave a lot for me to do. The job's a sinecure really.'

'Rubbish – I told you. You're my eyes and ears, reporting back to me. What could be more important than that? Anyway, I'm glad you're OK. I wouldn't want any harm to come to you or the child. I could hire a nurse to look after you.'

'Oh now really, that's not necessary. I'm fine.'

'A nanny later then, after he's born. My son must have every advantage I can give him.'

His son. Leah felt her heart hardening. The child was all-important; she was only a carrier, a means to an end. It was ironic, hearing the tenderness in Clay's tone after what she had overheard . . .

'I'll fly out to see you soon, to make certain all's well with you. I'll let you know when I can make time.'

He rang off. Leah gave a deep sigh and muttered into the mouthpiece. 'Do whatever you bloody well like, Clay Richards, but you're not going to get my baby. She's mine.'

CHAPTER TWELVE

Renzo was excited as they entered the hotel through the maze of the Galleria mall with its shops and ice-rink.

'An ice-rink, and so huge, in the middle of the desert,' he breathed. 'Unbelievable.'

The crystal ballroom was magnificent, lofty and elegant with glittering chandeliers. Hundreds of people, westerners and Arabs, seethed around the tables searching for their places. In one corner a giant screen displayed a video recording of the rally, cars scorching through the dunes of the desert, throwing up spumes of sand behind them. Renzo sat before the array of Arabian delicacies, soaking up every detail with glistening eyes. Leah watched the other occupants of the table; four stewardesses from the Emirates airline accompanied by their publicity officer, a dour young Scot, two Arabs and a young tousle-haired European who never took his eyes off Leah. She avoided his gaze by studying the uniform of the stewardess opposite, a cream suit and small red hat with a white scarf pinned to one side and flicked back over the other shoulder. Leah bent towards Renzo.

'I like the outfit, don't you? A bit more attractive than British Airways.'

Renzo looked and frowned. 'Exotic perhaps, but not very practical. How would you like that trailing in your soup?'

Leah was listening to the young man talking to the Arab seated next to her and it was evident they were co-drivers in the rally. He had a nice, crumpled sort of face, amiable and bright-eyed. Renzo was chattering away happily.

'I am so grateful Mr Richards gave me the chance of a lifetime, to create my own hotel. I do not listen to Yussef. I know exactly what I want. Marble floors we shall have in the elevators, the same marble as in the foyer. No noise. The pageboys will carry cards as in the old days to page my clients.'

Leah held up a hand. 'Listen,' she said. 'They've just announced we're to help ourselves from the buffet.'

As she rose to go, Renzo turned to the airline hostess and began talking animatedly to her. Leah made her way to the buffet table and picked up a plate. Then she became aware of the Arab standing beside her. It was the rally-driver from her table and he was eyeing her openly as she helped herself from the exotic array of dishes.

'Your golden hair matches exactly your golden blouse,' he commented quietly, his gaze travelling down her body. Leah pretended not to hear.

He was not deterred. 'I would like to buy a villa for you,' he purred and, seeing no reaction, added, 'and a business of your own.'

'No thank you,' said Leah firmly.

She speared a morsel of spiced meat and moved on. Black eyes gleamed and he moved closer.

'I only wish to please you, nothing more. A hundred camels?'

At that moment a voice cut in. 'You cannot make gifts to the lady, Hassan,' the voice said coolly. 'I don't think her husband would approve.'

It was the tousle-haired young man from her table. Leah could only stare. She was grateful for his intervention, but either he had mistaken her or was making a noble gesture.

The gleam in the Arab's eyes faded and was replaced by a look of embarrassment. 'I am so sorry,' he murmured. 'I hope you will forgive me.'

The young man smiled. 'Now let's get our food.' He reached behind Leah for a plate and began filling it. 'I haven't seen you around,' he said amiably. 'You must be new to Dubai.'

'Thank you,' said Leah. 'I'm grateful.'

'No problem. Any time. You haven't got a husband, have you?'

She smiled. 'No.'

'Good. I'm Patrick Lynch.'

'Leah Finch.'

They both began juggling plates and cutlery to try and shake hands, then Patrick laughed, and the atmosphere between them was at once one of ease.

'You know, you can't blame Hassan for trying,' said Patrick, licking a fingertip.

'You know him well?'

'I'm his co-driver. We drive a Porsche. I'll make a champion out of him yet.'

By the time Leah returned to the table she found that Patrick had changed places with Hassan and was now sitting next to her. Renzo had still not released the airline hostess.

'Mini-fridges? No, no, signorina, there will be no mini-fridges in my hotel bedrooms. They are a confession of poor service, I always say. Personal room service, that is the answer, knowing each guest by name and all his preferences. I will make certain my staff make notes of everything, how many spoons of sugar in the coffee, everything. If a gentleman guest regularly orders Soave, the next time he comes he will find the Soave already in the icebucket.'

The stewardess tried to hide a yawn with a smile.

Patrick leaned forward. 'What hotel is this?' he asked.

Renzo drew himself erect. 'The new Cresco Hotel,' he answered with pride. 'It will have a reputation for warmth and friendliness. There will be no impersonality in my hotel.'

'The Cresco?' repeated Patrick. 'That's the one they moved in on when the owners got deported, isn't it?'

Renzo leaned forward eagerly, 'Mr Richards, yes. But it is very good for me. It is hard to find someone else who has the same vision as I, and harder still to find someone with vision and money. Mr Richards offered me the hotel and a free hand. It is a good arrangement.'

The stewardess had escaped to the buffet. Patrick wagged his fork at Renzo. 'You'll have a job to beat the hotels we've already got here – they're fabulous. Can't be faulted.'

Renzo leaned across Leah and, taking hold of Patrick's fork, steadied it in mid-wave. 'Hmm,' he said quietly. 'I'd ask the waiter for another fork if I were you. This one has missed the dishwasher.'

When the dinner had ended the Awards ceremony began. One after another the winners of various sections of the Desert Rally went forward to receive their prizes. Leah watched as Patrick and Hassan went up to the platform to receive a trophy from Sheikh Mohammed, to the sound of rapturous applause from the other contenders.

'Congratulations,' she said as Patrick sat down again, laying the silver trophy and a cheque on the table.

He grinned sheepishly. 'It's only a minor prize, not the biggie, but the Sheikh is very generous.' He leaned his elbows on the table conversationally. 'How about coming out for a drink with me one evening to celebrate? I'll show you the sights.'

'Thanks. I'd love to.'

'Give me your 'phone number.'

'I'm staying at the Sheraton.'

'I'll give you a ring.'

And he did. By the end of the week Leah felt thoroughly at home. And all because of Patrick . . .

This afternoon, while the offices were closed during the heat of the day, she was to meet him in the George and Dragon bar in the Ambassadors Hotel. It was a curious bar, looking as if it had been lifted straight out of an English village pub. The air was cool even if noisy, and the barman, shirt-sleeved and with dark patches of sweat showing on the back of his shirt, was polishing glasses. Leah smiled, reflecting how Renzo would probably insist on a regular change of shirt every hour if it were his staff. Renzo has the right idea.

The young expatriates gathered here were sun-tanned, lively and enthusiastic. Patrick had evidently not yet arrived, and she felt disappointed. He might not be extraordinarily handsome but he had a lazy, agreeable air about him which was likeable and the whole party seemed to come to life when he was around. She glanced towards the doors of the bar.

'Bloody Ramadan,' someone behind her grumbled. 'Whole place was dead. Couldn't get a meal anywhere. Can't think why every man jack of them starves to death for so long.'

'Except for the kids and pregnant mums,' another voice cut in.

Leah shuddered. She'd almost forgotten the baby. At that moment she saw Patrick coming in.

His face lit up as he saw her. 'Well, seen everything in Dubai now?' he asked as he eased himself on to the stool next to hers and nodded to the barman.

'I was going to drive down to Kameera, to the fishing sheds. I got stopped by the police on my way.'

He nodded. 'White woman, alone, driving a car. Arab women don't drive.'

'And I got my bottom pinched in the al Ghurair.'

Patrick laughed. 'I warned you about the Indian markets. You wouldn't be told.'

'I quite enjoyed it.'

135

'You'd enjoy the gold *souk*, I'll take you there or wherever your heart desires.' He was looking into her eyes, talking to her alone; the others didn't exist for the moment.

'Sounds great.' Anywhere with Patrick would be great.

'And don't forget the beach party tomorrow night.'

Leah's fingers touched her stomach. 'I don't think I want to swim.'

He threw back his head and laughed. He was really very attractive, thought Leah, with that easy, warm smile which reminded her of her father. 'Swim? In the Creek? You must be joking. I'll pick you up at nine,' he said.

Late at night the beach party at the ski-club was still in full swing. Leah sat on the soft white sand, feeling it still warm through her thin cotton skirt. All afternoon she'd watched Patrick and the other young men ski-ing behind the powerboat. He had a good body, hard-muscled and bronzed.

He was dressed again now in jeans and T-shirt, sprawling on the sand beside her, his young face both illuminated and heavily shadowed by the blaze of the camp fire. Someone called out to them to come and join them.

Patrick rolled over. 'We're talking,' he shouted.

'You're always talking,' the voice complained. 'Come and be sociable.'

Patrick rolled back, leaning on his elbow. Above the splashing of the waves Leah could hear the squeals and laughter. 'Who are they?' she asked.

'Who? Them? Failures and misfits mostly. Look at David over there, fifty if he's a day and chatting up a seventeen-year-old. Came out here because of two failed marriages. And Pete, and Babs – they've all left problems behind, or so they hope.'

Me too, she thought. Patrick went on. 'I'm not criticizing. I'm no better myself. I ducked out on a perfectly good job – accountant, would you believe? Got a bit of a travel agency now and pick up whatever's going.'

'What kind of thing?'

He shrugged and grinned. 'Anything. I'd do a bit of smuggling if it came along. If I could think of a foolproof way of smuggling gold out of Dubai I'd make a fortune. What were you saying about this Yussef?'

Leah picked up a handful of sand and watched it trickle through her fingers. 'He's a funny bloke,' she said. 'Conscientious but bossy – not

136

easy to talk to. And I don't like the way they stifle their women.'

'Not all of them. You should meet the Lebanese girl up at the radio station. She's savage. She sacked a friend of mine last month.'

Patrick's finger was touching her arm. 'Come on, let's have a drink,' he said. 'We can slip away and the others won't even notice.'

He scrambled to his feet, brushed the sand from his jeans and took her arm, leading her away across the beach towards the road. He took her arm in a quietly proprietorial way which pleased her. And at the same time it puzzled her. Was it natural for a woman who was pregnant to feel excited like this?

The Range Rover was unlocked. There was no need to lock anything in Dubai. No one ever stole. As they drove back into the city centre Patrick pointed up to an office block. 'You wanted to know where I work – it's up there, fourth floor.'

Leah looked up at the windows, trying to visualize Patrick at work. She knew only that he was in travel.

'We deal with the wealthier Arabs. They don't want to be bothered with detail – they tell me what they want and leave the rest up to me. They pay well for service.'

'Damn!' exclaimed Leah, slapping her arm. 'Mosquito.'

Patrick grinned. 'It's not the mosquito you kill you need to worry about – it's the hundred that come to its funeral. Here's Thatcher's.'

He parked the Range Rover and guided Leah inside the Dubai Marina hotel. Thatcher's Bar, with its mahogany counter and tankards and beer pumps, could have been in a London side street. They sat at a small, beer-splashed table. A waiter in white jacket and red bow tie came across and wiped it clean. Renzo would have approved of him, thought Leah.

'Good evening, sir, madam. What can I get you?'

Patrick ordered wine for her and orange juice for himself. He never drank alcohol, she noted. When the waiter had left Patrick leaned his elbows on the table and gazed into Leah's eyes. The clear, probing blueness embarrassed her.

'You've told me about Yussef, now what about your boss?' he enquired.

'Who – Renzo? He's quaint, but I love his enthusiasm.'

'No – the English one. The one who sent you out here.'

Leah looked down at the table. 'He's all right. Shrewd. Single-minded.'

'But you don't like him a lot.'

'To be honest, no.'

'Snap. I don't care much for mine either, but I know when I'm on to a good thing. What's wrong with – what's his name?'

'Clay. I just don't feel he's to be trusted.'

'In what way?'

He was probing too deeply, but the temptation to talk to a friendly face . . . 'I think he uses people – and the company too. I think he could be using it to his own ends.'

'Sounds normal. How exactly?'

Leah shrugged. 'Using the firm's reputation, maybe its funds. Perhaps as a screen for something else.'

'You have any proof?'

'Instinct, I suppose. I couldn't help shivering when you said the original owners of Cresco Hotel got deported. Renzo told me someone put the word about that they had Israeli connections.'

'And you think it might have been your Clay?'

Leah bit her lip. 'I've said too much already.'

Patrick pulled his chair round closer to hers. 'OK, let's talk about what we'll do tomorrow. How about the revolving restaurant at the top of the Hyatt?'

As they left the bar he slid an arm about her shoulders, and again Leah felt a tremble of excitement. Would he try to kiss her tonight when they reached her hotel? No, she must not think it – not now.

Back at the Sheraton Leah stepped quickly out of his car. 'Goodnight, Patrick, and thanks for a lovely evening.'

From the hotel steps she watched him drive away, and felt curiously reluctant to let him go.

In her hotel bedroom Leah undressed and went through into the apartment's large, airy bathroom to take a shower. Clear, soft water cascaded on her skin, warm from the cold tap. So much water, here in the desert . . .

Stepping out onto the cool tiles she dried herself down and wandered back into the bedroom, the towel draped around her. The telephone rang. It was Renzo.

'Ah, you are back,' he said briskly. 'I want you to make notes for Mr Richards. Come up to my room?'

Leah smiled to herself as she dressed. To Renzo in his enthusiasm

138

it did not matter whether it was day or night. Picking up the tape recorder from the bedside table, Leah went up to Renzo's room. He let her in and leapt straight into business.

'Make notes of these points,' he said tersely. 'All linen in our hotel will be hand-laundered, by our own laundresses. Sheets will be changed daily – crisp, newly-ironed sheets will please our clients and they will last longer.'

He stopped, rubbing a thoughtful hand on his chin. 'Did I ever tell you of the client I once had in Madrid? New sheets he wanted every day. I told him we have clean sheets every day. Then he told me he meant *new* sheets, straight from the shop. Some clients are difficult.'

The misty look left his dark eyes and he turned back to Leah. 'Ah yes, we shall employ our own electricians, tell Mr Richards, and two furniture polishers, two plumbers and two upholsterers. Have you got all that?'

'Just a minute,' said Leah. 'I'll put it on tape. Let's just see where I am.'

She switched on the tape. The sound which issued from the machine made her sit bolt upright. It was Clay's cold, clear voice.

'Remember you are my eyes and ears. Eyes and ears only, remember. You have no mouth.'

Leah felt a flicker of alarm. Renzo's jaw fell open. 'Eyes and ears?' he repeated softly, then in a louder voice, 'Eyes and ears? You have been sent to spy on me! On me, Renzo Rosconi? Get out, get out of here this instant! I will have no spies in my hotel!'

Almost in tears he snatched up the recorder, shoved it into Leah's hands and pushed her out of the room, heedless of her protests. Leah stood in the corridor, bewildered, her mind a confusion of anger and dismay. Did Clay know after all what she had overheard that night?

Anger came uppermost. Renzo must be made to believe she was no spy. Leah banged on his door. Eventually he opened it. 'Well?' he demanded.

Leah pushed open the door and marched in, then turned to Renzo. He had taken off his trousers and was wearing only a pair of bright yellow boxer shorts. Leah was not deterred. 'Look here,' she said firmly. 'I did not come to spy on you at all. I'm as anxious as you are to make this hotel work.'

'I heard Mr Richards' voice – eyes and ears, he said,' Renzo said darkly. 'What else could he mean?'

'And did you hear me agree?'

The admission came slowly. 'No.'

'Well then. Don't jump to conclusions so fast, Mr Rosconi, or you'll have me thinking you're paranoid.'

Renzo drew himself up to his full five-foot-four. 'I am Renzo Rosconi, the best hotelier in Europe,' he said proudly.

'Then prove it,' said Leah. 'About that list – two each of plumbers, electricians, upholsterers and furniture polishers, wasn't it?'

Renzo's eyes grew bright. 'You remember – and we need four laundresses too.'

'Six,' said Leah firmly. 'A hundred and eighty beds changed daily – at least six.'

CHAPTER THIRTEEN

Mohammed al Dhin was paying one of his rare visits to his Dubai office. The old man summoned Leah to his room.

'Miss Finch, I do not wish you to corrupt my daughter with your western ideas. In future if you and she should meet, I would prefer you not to speak to her.'

Leah's cheeks flushed. 'Why, what did she tell you?'

He waved an imperious hand and turned away towards the window. 'You will not question me, Miss Finch. As a matter of fact it was my son who told me – as a dutiful daughter she told him everything and I am displeased. I shall inform your employer.'

Leah left the office angrily. So Yussef was reporting back on her, was he? Anger crystallized into determination. She would work all the harder now to ensure Renzo got exactly what he wanted.

As a dutiful daughter . . . Leah wondered why the words made her feel a prickle of guilt.

She awoke feeling odd, ill at ease and almost nauseous. Whether it was because she was pregnant or whether it was because of Clay's message on the tape, she did not know.

He must know she had overheard the conversation that night, otherwise why should he remind her not to open her mouth? But even so, she was not unduly alarmed. After all, she was carrying the child he so desperately wanted.

Or maybe the nausea could be due to the mosquito bite. There was a pronounced lump on her arm which itched furiously. Maybe she should get something for it before it turned septic. The health centre – she'd call and see a doctor today.

As she drove up to the health centre a loud, high-pitched wailing began to fill the air, the same sound which woke her from sleep at six every morning, the sound of the *muezzin* calling the Muslim faithful to prayer. Not a man these days, Patrick had told her, but a tape recording played over a loudspeaker. Once, he told her, two young Britons had substituted a tape of George Michael which had wailed all over Dubai one morning; they had swiftly been deported.

Leah looked across at the mosque. Hundreds of pairs of shoes lay on the hot, dusty pavement outside the door. Yussef would be at prayer now. It was curious to think of the haughty Yussef on his knees.

The doctor was a well-built Dutch woman, cheerful and confident, who wore a gold charm bracelet which jangled as she took hold of Leah's arm. 'Mosquito bite? Let me see.'

She asked a lot of questions and finally wrote a prescription. 'I think this will take care of it,' she said as she handed over the piece of paper. As Leah made to go she added thoughtfully, 'Are you pregnant?'

'No,' said Leah quickly. 'Why do you ask?'

The doctor shrugged. 'I just wondered. A single girl who is found to be pregnant cannot stay in Dubai.'

As Leah emerged into the sunlight again, feeling its heat strike her head, she felt angry with herself. Why had she lied? The words had sprung from her lips before she could think. But she had the feeling that the doctor hadn't been fooled for a moment.

Leah felt a sudden urge to talk to her mother, to tell her the truth.

The car pulled up in Venn Street and Clay Richards stepped out. The complex was rapidly taking shape and it looked interesting. He found Delaney in the site office.

Clay kept his voice coolly under control. 'I hear Eva Finch has got the lease on the complex for the next twenty-five years,' he said. 'Is it true?'

The builder straightened and flicked dust from the sleeve of his tailored suit. 'That's right. She had all the plans drawn up, right down to the finest detail. It made it worth while for me.'

This was Leah's doing, Clay fumed inwardly. She'd betrayed him to her mother; how else could Eva have known how to outwit him? This little bitch Leah wasn't as naïve as she'd seemed after all. She'd have to be punished.

'I'll offer you a higher rent for the complex, Delaney.'

The builder shook his head, frowning. 'I can't, Mr Richards – it's well on the way. It's gone too far down the line now.'

'I'll make it worth your while. Finish the job and I'll buy you out.'

Delaney looked up, eyebrows raised. 'Buy me out? Do you know how long it's taken me to build this firm up? I started out with just a small garage, and today –'

'I don't think your shareholders will turn down what I'm prepared to offer. Think about it.'

'How much?'

'A figure that'll make your eyes stand out. Agreed?'

The builder's eyes glinted. 'What'll I tell Mrs Finch?'

'Nothing. She'll pay rent to Delaney Construction just the same – she doesn't need to know it has a new owner.'

If Leah was quiet that evening Patrick did not seem to notice as he stocked up at the Indian supermarket. It seemed to stock everything, from Indian and English branded foods to clothes and cheap costume jewellery. When Patrick had finished filling his basket a young Indian packed everything into a cardboard box.

'We deliver it for you?' he asked. 'You give us the address.'

Patrick shook his head. 'Take it to my car.'

Back at the Golden Sands apartment block a beautiful Arab girl in western dress was coming out of the lift. She smiled at Patrick. '*Salaam al leikom*, Mr Patrick. You like to come to my house and I tell your fortune for you again soon?'

He gave her a roguish smile. 'Soon, Kara, I'm still waiting for the fortune you promised me last time.'

The girl shook her head, her long black hair swinging loosely about her shoulders. 'If it is in the stars, Golden Shadow, then it will come, and *inshallah* you will live to enjoy it.'

'*Inshallah*,' replied Patrick as they got into the lift. 'We'll come and see you tomorrow, how's that?'

'Who's that?' asked Leah as the lift glided upwards.

'Kara – she's Hassan's sister.'

It was the first time Leah had been to Patrick's apartment. It was large and comfortably furnished with substantial American furniture, colonial-style, with brass trims on every piece. For the first time Leah realized that there were no fireplaces in Dubai; no focal point to a room.

She helped Patrick put the groceries away. 'That girl called you Golden Shadow,' she remarked. 'Why?'

'I had a blonde beard once as well as blonde hair.'

'Can she really see into the future?'

143

Patrick set down a packet of sugar and turned to take Leah by the shoulders. 'Look, what's troubling you, Leah? I can feel something's up. Is it Renzo or because Yussef told tales on you?'

She could hear the genuine concern in his tone and was tempted. 'No, I get on fine with Renzo now – I really like him. It's other things that are bothering me, Patrick – things I've kept to myself for far too long. I'm going to get in touch with my mother and tell her all about it.'

'You can tell me,' Patrick said seriously. 'I'd like to help if I can.'

His touch was warm, reassuring, but she turned away. 'I know. Thanks, but I want to tell Mother first. I've drafted the fax I'm going to send her. I want her to come out here so we can have a long talk. I'm going to tell her everything. I think it's the right thing to do.'

Clay Richards was a contented man. When he emptied his head of business for the day he would lie in bed and dream his dream of the future. It was becoming his favourite occupation these days; it had completely replaced the needs of the flesh. Even Muriel had stopped trying to interest him, wearing her best perfume in bed and that damn flimsy silk nightie he'd once bought her in Paris. It had been a welcome relief to him not to have to gratify her eager embrace, followed by grateful, lumpish submissiveness.

Since Leah had gone he'd touched no other woman – she had become holy in his mind, deified as the mother of his son, and she would not be replaced. It made little difference that his idol had turned out to have feet of clay. Some small punishment – that would ensure she'd never do it again.

His son. He could see the boy now, holding his father's hand on his first day at school, bringing him his cricket bat to oil and proudly displaying his end-of-term school reports. Captaining the team and speaking from the platform on Speech Day with all the confidence of Head Boy. Then on to Oxford, winning a Blue for cricket and maybe rowing . . .

Clay made a quick calculation. By the time the boy graduated he himself would be just turned seventy. Not too old – he could hang on to the reins till the boy was ready to take over Cresco. Cresco – Clay Richards Enterprises – perhaps it would be as well to name the boy Charles. It had a regal sound to it. Charles Richards Enterprises. He needed Charles to take over the empire it had taken years to amass.

Not all at once, of course. He'd start him off in one of the minor companies – Keypoint, perhaps, the professional and executive appointment register which had proved so profitable. The boy could get a taste of each of the companies in turn till he was ripe. And when he took over, Clay could retire, content that there would be family continuity and he had worked all his life to good purpose. It would be a handsome inheritance. Clay had every reason to feel content.

Alone in her hotel room Leah re-read the message she had drafted. Its contents were too revealing to say over the telephone to Mother – you never knew who might be listening. She would send it directly to Mother's office where she alone would read it – but where from? In the office Yussef or Renzo could see it. The hotel office – that would be safer. That way no one else would be any the wiser.

The bright-eyed little Filipino girl in the hotel office was willing enough. 'I'll send it at once for you, don't worry.'

'I'll do it,' said Leah. 'I don't want to trouble you.'

The girl waved a slim hand and smiled. 'No trouble, Miss Finch. Leave it with me – I have three others to send out. I'll do it in a minute, so it will be no inconvenience at all.'

Gratefully Leah slipped her a ten-dirham note and left.

Nathan could barely see Eva's face in the subdued lighting of her flat, but she was talking with animation now, all the weakness in her voice gone.

'I should get the full results any day now, but I'm not worried any more,' she was saying. 'My only fear was that I'd wake up with only one breast.'

Nathan listened. Maybe now she was strong enough to hear what he had to tell her. He leaned forward, elbows on knees. 'Eva – I had a letter when I got back to Scapegoat,' he began.

She looked up, frowning. She'd always been quick to detect a nuance in the voice. 'Letter? Who from? Leah?'

'From a clinic in London. They wanted to contact her. It seems she'd quoted me as next of kin.'

'You? Not me – or Alan?' Her eyes widened. 'What clinic?'

He could hear the alarm in her tone and reached out a hand to touch hers. 'They wanted to know if Leah still wanted the booking with them. I tried to find out what she was going for, but they wouldn't tell me anything.'

Despite the gloom he could see Eva had gone pale. 'Go on – tell me,' she said quietly.

'I went to see them today. In the end they told me it was for a termination of pregnancy. She never showed up.'

For a moment Eva sat, white-faced and silent. At last he heard her muttering under her breath. 'Clay Richards,' she murmured. 'I knew it. The sod. He's responsible for this. I knew there was something, I could sense it that last night. She was so strange. Oh, for Christ's sake, why didn't she tell me?'

She buried her face in her hands for a few moments, then looked up. 'What's she doing in Dubai, Nathan? Is she still pregnant? Is she going to put herself in the hands of some butcher? Oh for God's sake, Nathan, I've got to get in touch with her!'

'We don't know where she's staying,' said Nathan. 'She hasn't let us know.'

Eva seized hold of his hand. 'But we can't leave it at that! Alone, and pregnant – what are we going to do?'

Nathan stood up, huge and broad against the Chinese lacquered screen, looking down at her with an expression she'd never seen before. 'Clay Richards,' he muttered, 'I'll kill him. I'll find the bastard wherever he is and break his bloody neck.'

His face wore a venomous expression Eva had never seen before. She reached up a hand to pull him down beside her. 'No love, not yet,' she said, flicking away a tear. 'First we must make sure Leah's safe. Later we'll find Clay and get our revenge. Go and tell Alan, tell him to put his brains in steep and see what he can come up with. In the meantime I'm going out to Dubai.'

Nathan was still not appeased. 'If he's done this to Leah,' he growled, 'I'll tear the bastard limb from limb.' Then, catching sight of Eva's pale face, he touched her cheek. 'But what about the biopsy results? You can't go –'

'Bugger the biopsy,' snapped Eva. 'I'll settle things up at the office and catch the first plane out.'

The Major sat watching Clay Richards' face, suffused by the whisky as they sat together in a discreet corner of the Club. He was in expansive mood this evening, for some reason in unaccountably good humour.

'So the warehouse was completely burned down?' Clay enquired.

'Gutted,' replied the Major.

Clay shook his head. 'Such a pity. I shall claim on the insurance of course.'

'Which is more than Williams can do. He wasn't insured, did you know that?'

'Very short-sighted of him – all his capital tied up in stock. He'll go bankrupt now, of course.'

'Ruined,' agreed the Major. 'But you'll have a valuable site vacant.'

'Why, so I will,' said Clay, raising his eyebrows. 'So I will. And Williams can start again. Strange how setbacks can often be turned to advantage. I had a showroom once – the bank wouldn't lend me any more on it, so I sold the lease and with the money I kitted out the reps in Jags and expensive suits. Believe in your own self-image and so will the customer.'

The Major set down his drink. 'Did it work? Can you sell a product without a showroom?'

Clay beamed. 'When it's car phones you're selling? Wouldn't you be impressed if a well-turned out rep took you out to his Jag to demonstrate? Four Jags, four mobile showrooms. Of course it worked.'

For a few moments the two men fell silent. The Major sipped his brandy and soda and thought yet again how deeply he loathed Richards. And he wasn't alone. Clay seemed to read his thoughts, and smiled.

'There are few people who could harm me, Major,' he said softly. 'The art of good management is concealment.'

Yes, thought the Major grimly, you've covered your tracks well. But for one thing. It was almost a pleasure to break the news. 'I have one piece of information for you – your fears about the girl have been confirmed,' he said mildly. 'I had a message from my courier in Dubai today.'

He could have sworn the fellow blanched. 'What message?'

'My man intercepted a fax meant for her mother. She mentions both me and Hennessy.'

Clay seemed to collapse against the back of his chair. 'So she did overhear. Damn!'

'What do you want me to do? My man will obey orders without question.'

Clay looked up from under his brows. 'Anything?'

147

The Major laughed. 'You can do anything with money. Even Arabs can be bought.'

'Will he kill?'

'Of course.'

'A woman?'

'Whatever he's ordered to do.'

Clay sighed. 'I'll let you know. Goodnight, Major.'

The Major watched him go. This was the first time he'd seen the fellow hesitate in a decision. Maybe he wouldn't have made such a good officer after all.

CHAPTER FOURTEEN

Back at home in Chislehurst Clay paced up and down the library which was his pride and joy, lined from floor to ceiling with expensive hand-tooled volumes. Muriel was not allowed to touch them. Every book had been carefully aligned, never to be taken down and read or the effect would be ruined. Portcullis was scampering around his master's heels, but Clay ignored him. He needed time to think. Muriel wore a worried expression as she came in carrying a cup and saucer.

'I brought your coffee in here, dear – you left the table so suddenly. Is something the matter? You hardly ate a thing.'

'Be quiet, Muriel, I'm thinking,' her husband growled. Muriel put down the cup and slunk away to her drawing room, her own private retreat where Clay never entered and she could read *The Lady* in peace without being mocked.

A debate was raging in Clay's head. He had a decision to make, and it was far tougher than any business decision had ever been. Leave emotion out, man, marshal the facts. Leah had let him down. If Eva had read the fax . . . oh my God! But on the other hand he wanted the child. Could he risk keeping Leah alive long enough for his son to be born?

Maybe the child could be born first, and then . . . It could be made to look like a death in childbirth. Clay stopped at the big mahogany desk where a chocolate biscuit still lay on the leather-inlaid surface. He picked it up.

'Portcullis!'

The little dog came bounding, his expression eager and tail wagging. Clay bent to stroke his head.

'You wouldn't let me down, would you, Porty old boy? You'd know better than to do a silly thing like that. What am I going to do, eh?'

He sank down on the leather chesterfield, breaking the biscuit into fragments between thick fingers. The only safe solution would be to dispose of Leah now, before irreparable harm was done. Thank heaven the fax to Eva Finch had been intercepted – she'd have loved the chance to hold him to ransom. Baby or not, Leah had to be rendered harmless. Oh God, life was cruel! He'd longed so much for that son!

With the back of his hand he brushed away the tear trembling on his eyelid. At any rate Leah had served to prove one thing – he could father a child. It had been Muriel's fault after all. And if he could father one . . . There were always other girls.

He became aware of the chocolate melting in his fingertips and looked around for Portcullis but he was no longer there. He must have gone into the drawing room. Clay walked across to the door and looked through the crack.

Portcullis was standing on his hind legs, reaching up his forepaws over Muriel's stomach and trying to lick her hand. Muriel was trying to push him down gently.

'No, no, boy, don't make a fuss of me,' she whispered urgently, 'or we'll both be in trouble. Get down, there's a good boy. Go back to your master, please.'

Fury seared in his heart. Clay stood away from the door. 'Porty!'

The dog came running. Clay bent to feed morsels of biscuit into the eager mouth, murmuring as he did so. 'I heard what happened in there, old man. I'm afraid we're going to have to use the strap again, aren't we? Can't have you being disloyal, can we?'

Portcullis wagged his tail, eyes gleaming happily as he waited for the next sweet mouthful.

Patrick was away but Leah found her time filled with Renzo's demands. Together they worked late at the office and by the time Renzo pronounced himself satisfied and put his papers away the sun had set.

'You are a very thorough young lady,' he told Leah with a smile. 'With such attention to detail one day you will make a good hotel manager. Perhaps I shall employ you.'

Leah smiled. She was pleased – Renzo's enthusiasm for the business was infectious and she was learning fast. She was enjoying working with him far more than she would ever have dreamed possible. 'It's my mother's training,' she replied. 'She's a stickler for detail.'

Renzo nodded approval. 'I have seen her shops all over Europe – she has an eye for business.'

'Too right,' said Leah. 'It's her life.'

So why hadn't she answered the fax, wondered Leah as she walked back to the Sheraton. All day she'd half-expected the office telephone to ring – she had given the numbers both there and at the hotel.

Maybe she should ring her mother, just to ask if she'd received the message and if she would be coming. But if Mother was away, possibly even out of the country when the fax arrived . . .

Be patient, Leah, she told herself. She'll be in touch. She's never let anyone down in her life.

It was as she was nearing the hotel that Leah again noticed the young Arab. He'd been loitering outside the office when she emerged. She remembered observing how thick-bodied he was, a distinct paunch beginning to burgeon under his narrowly-cut *dish-dash* despite his youth. If he'd been slim like most young Arabs she'd never have singled him out from all the other rich youths who hung around in the city streets at night, laughing and joking on the pavement or leaning against their luxurious, gleaming cars.

Now here he was outside the Sheraton. He turned away as she climbed the steps into the hotel so that his face was obscured in the darkness.

The next day was Friday, the Muslim holy day when all offices were closed, and as Leah set off to meet Patrick she saw the Arab was still outside – could it be coincidence, or was he following her?

'I think I'm being followed. There's this Arab,' she told Patrick over coffee. He smiled.

'He's got a crush on you. Blonde European girl –'

'I'm serious. I really think he's tailing me.'

'But why would anyone want to do that? It's crazy.'

'It happened in England.'

Patrick leaned his elbows on the table, his expression sober. 'Are you in any sort of trouble, Leah? I'd like to know – maybe I could help in some way.'

'Not that I know of.' Lying again, she thought. *A single girl who is found to be pregnant in Dubai* . . .

'Well, it could be Yussef,' said Patrick. 'He said he wanted to know what you were doing at all times.'

'If it is, I'll tell him he can damn well put a stop to it.'

After they'd finished coffee they walked along the Creek to the jetty. Crowds of people, chattering and jostling, were waiting for a dhow to take them across to the other bank. They were mostly Indians, but a few were Arab women, all heavily veiled and occasionally an older woman wearing the traditional leather mask. Leah was watching the seething mass of bodies streaming towards and over the rocking dhow, thinking how Mother would admire and adapt the exotic Indian saris, vibrant in the sunlight, when suddenly she caught sight of the Arab with a bellying *dish-dash*.

She clutched Patrick's arm. 'That's him! That's the man I told you about!'

Patrick held up a hand to screen his eyes from the sun. 'Where? Which one?'

She'd lost him. He'd melted away into the crowd. 'He can't be far away – he was here only a second ago.'

Patrick took her arm. 'Come on. The sun's a bit too much. Let's go and look for some ice cream.'

She was still looking back as he drew her away but the Arab was nowhere to be seen. But he wasn't just a figment of her imagination, brought on by sunstroke. Even if Patrick didn't believe her, the fellow was real and he was following her, she was sure of it.

They were walking down a side street now, away from the busy quayside. 'There's a short cut down here,' said Patrick. 'It'll save us walking all the way round.'

As they turned into the alley Leah started. The Arab was face-to-face with them, only inches away. 'Oh my God, it's him,' she breathed.

At once Patrick leapt on him and Leah saw the two men crash to the ground.

The alley was deserted, the air silent but for the sound of two bodies flailing on the sandy earth. Patrick's blue jeans and the man's white *dish-dash* seemed knotted into one. Leah could hear grunts as fists met flesh, but it was difficult to see what was happening.

The bodies rolled over and over. Leah saw Patrick straddling the Arab, his face contorted as he pounded with all his strength. With a huge effort the Arab threw him off and again their bodies tangled on the ground. Leah watched, mesmerized, hearing their gasps and grunts. Then suddenly the *mêlée* resolved itself into one still figure and the other rising to his feet. It was Patrick, a trickle of blood running from his lip. He scrambled up, wiping his mouth with the back of his hand, then stood looking down at the prostrate figure on the ground.

The Arab rolled over and tried to get up but he was clearly too weak. He was kneeling, his hands on the ground in front of him and his face wore a bewildered expression. The white of his *dish-dash* was spattered and streaked with crimson and blood was seeping from his mouth and nose. Patrick gave him a shove with his foot and the Arab fell against the wall and lay still, unable to rise.

Patrick rubbed his hands on his jeans. 'There, I don't think he'll bother you again,' he said quietly. 'Let's go.'

He was still breathing deeply as they walked away, leaving the crumpled body in the alley. Leah had the strange, surreal feeling that it had all been a dream, but a dream of sudden and frightening violence. She looked up at Patrick, his lips set tightly.

'Ought we to leave him like that? He's bleeding.'

Patrick gave a deep sigh. 'You don't know the police out here – we could be slapped in jail for weeks while they sort it out. Forget it.'

'We should have asked him why he was following me.'

'You don't know what he might have done to you if I hadn't been here. He could have had a knife.'

That was true, and she was grateful. And yet he might only have been tailing her. After all, Clay had had her followed once before. Could it be Clay's doing now? He had the power, and the money, and he had warned her . . .

Patrick drew her arm through his and squeezed it close to his side. 'When in doubt – lash out. That's what I was taught. I'm just glad I was there, Leah – I couldn't bear anything to happen to you. Not yet, you've only just come into my life.'

It was a wonderful day of warmth and closeness, and that evening as they drank wine in Patrick's flat Leah was reluctant to part from him. A Lionel Ritchie tape played softly in the background and they were sitting together on the settee holding hands when Patrick murmured close in her ear.

'Don't go, Leah. Stay here for the night.'

Leah withdrew her hand from his. 'Patrick, I'd love to – but I can't.'

'No strings attached, I promise. You can have the bed and I'll sleep here on the settee. I just want you to stay.'

Leah hesitated. She wanted to be with him, but nothing more. She was carrying another man's child, and still she was attracted to Patrick. She smiled at the hopeful look in his eyes.

'I'll stay.'

She saw the happy smile which lit up his face and felt wistful. If only she knew what was going to happen. Leaving Dubai before her pregnancy became obvious, giving birth to little Maddie – and then what? 'Isn't it a pity we can't look into the future?' she murmured. 'Would Kara tell me my fortune, do you think?'

Patrick's tone was tender as he spoke softly into her hair. 'I know your future already, Leah. It's here, with me. I'll take care of you.'

He honoured his word. It was late when she finally left him, spreading a sheet on the settee, and in the small hours of the morning when she got up to go to the toilet she peeped into the living area. Patrick was lying naked and curled on his side, sleeping like a baby.

Leah smiled, filled with affection for him, and went back to bed.

Next morning she wasted no time in tackling Yussef. She headed for his office full of determination.

She knocked at his door and, not waiting for an answer, marched in. Yussef looked up in surprise.

'I did not send for you, Miss Finch.'

'No, but I want to see you. Are you having me followed?'

He laid aside his papers, taking his time. 'Yes.'

'Why, for heaven's sake?'

'For your own safety.'

'Well stop it. I don't want it. And anyway, he's no good at it.'

Yussef's eyebrows rose. 'No?'

'No. I saw him outside the office, at the Sheraton and again at the quayside – everywhere. He's so bad, in fact, that he got a pasting for his pains.'

'Yes, I know.'

'Patrick taught him a lesson he won't forget.'

'Perhaps too severe a lesson, Miss Finch.'

'I suggest you get rid of him.'

'Someone did that for me. Have you seen today's paper?'

He pushed a newspaper across the desk to her. Leah could see only a page full of Arabic symbols. 'I don't read Arabic,' she said.

'I'll tell you the gist of it. This morning a man's body was found in the Creek. He had been beaten and stabbed. It was your man, Miss Finch.'

She stared, open-mouthed. 'Your man, you mean. You set him on to me.'

'My man saw it all. You never saw my man – he could hide himself in the desert unnoticed. But he saw everything.'

154

Leah was confused. Two men following her? And the paunchy one was dead? Why? And who killed him?

'Yussef was eyeing her soberly. 'I think somebody wishes you harm, Miss Finch. That is why I must keep an eye on you. You are my responsibility.'

'But this man – the one who is dead –'

'Nothing to do with me, Miss Finch – your friend Patrick did a thorough job.'

Leah stared at him, horrified. 'Patrick didn't kill him – if your man saw everything he must have told you that.'

'He saw the fight. He followed you when you left. Who else would kill him but your Patrick?'

'It wasn't Patrick! He couldn't have – he never left the flat.'

'And you would know, wouldn't you, Miss Finch? You were there all night.'

Leah picked up the telephone in her office to warn Patrick. He'd been showering and dressing when she left his apartment and he might still be there. She must warn him that he might be under suspicion of murder. At that moment Renzo came into her office, shaking his head gloomily.

'What is this I hear? Spending all night in a young man's apartment? I would not have believed this of you,' he said, with all the sadness and disappointment of a personal betrayal. 'If the authorities come to hear of this –'

'Renzo,' Leah interrupted as she replaced the telephone, 'it's my business.'

'It will mean instant deportation for you. I agree with Yussef. Why did you not think of your career? How can you hope to run a hotel of your own one day –'

'Renzo, please, I've got to get in touch with somebody. It's urgent.'

He sighed. 'I beg you, from now on think of your good name and be careful. A good reputation cannot be bought.'

The moment he'd gone she picked up the telephone and dialled Patrick's number at the Golden Sands. No one answered.

Clay drove miserably up the drive towards the house. It was no use staying at the office – he just couldn't concentrate. Muriel would be surprised because he hadn't thought to ring and warn her he'd be home tonight.

The trees overhanging the long drive were in full leaf now and normally the sight of them and the impressive house at the top afforded him great pride but today they evoked no feeling in him at all. Even the prospect of Portcullis' eager greeting left him unmoved. Poor old Porty. He would give the dog a special treat tonight to make up for the beating.

Clay was swinging the car around the curve in the drive when the flash of white in the undergrowth caught his eye. He pulled up the car and wound down the window.

'Porty, here boy – come on.'

The white patch did not move. Clay switched off the ignition and climbed out of the car.

'Portcullis – come here.'

He'd never failed to respond to a peremptory tone before. Clay stepped off the gravel on to the grass and moved towards the glimpse of white between the bushes.

'Porty?' He was curious now. It couldn't be the dog; unresponsive as it was, it must be a piece of paper he'd mistaken for the dog. But as Clay brushed the branches of a bush aside to bend down, the breath caught in his throat. It was Portcullis, and he was lying on his side with his throat ripped out.

Clay stared for a moment, then let out a groan as he knelt, taking in the full horror of the dog's injuries. Portcullis lay in a pool of his own blood, gashes round his face and paws showing only too well how the little fellow had fought for his life before the end came. Clay stroked the shaggy head. There was nothing more he could do – the dog was dead. The only creature he'd ever trusted . . .

He sank back on his haunches and gave a cry of anguish, making no effort to stem the tears. Then he slid his hands under the limp body and lifted it gently, and turned towards the house.

Muriel must have heard him come in for she same hurrying out into the oak-panelled hall, smoothing out her skirt as she walked towards him. 'Hullo, dear – I wasn't expecting you.'

She stopped suddenly at the sight of the dog in his arms. Her fingers fluttered to her lips and then she turned large, fearful eyes to her husband's face.

Clay's voice was small, choked. 'How did he get out?'

156

'I don't know. Perhaps when the fish-van came . . .'

He shook his head and she could see the tears glistening in his eyes. 'Christ almighty, woman,' he croaked, 'how did you let that happen? He's my dog, for God's sake. Is there no one I can trust?'

'Poor thing,' Muriel said in a weak voice, looking closely at the corpse and shuddering. 'What do you think happened?'

'Bloody Kersey-Brown's Rottweiler,' muttered Clay. 'He's been slavering at the gate for weeks to get at Porty. Well, he won't live long enough to see his supper tonight, by God he won't. I'll speak to you later.'

He brushed past his wife, carrying the little dog through into his library. He swept the papers off his desk then laid Portcullis on a velvet cushion which he placed in the centre. For a time he sat at his desk, gently stroking the dog's matted flank. Tears were blurring his vision when, with a deep-drawn sigh, he picked up the telephone and dialled. He heard the man's voice answer.

'Major? Richards here. About Dubai – I've decided. The final touch. You know what to do.'

The receiver replaced, Clay lay his head on the desk alongside Portcullis' body and wept like a child.

CHAPTER FIFTEEN

Leah rang both Patrick's office and the Golden Sands without success. He wasn't at home and, according to his secretary, hadn't yet arrived at work. Before she left him this morning he'd been almost ready to leave. Where on earth could he be?

The next thought made Leah's heart sink – if Yussef told the police what he knew, there was little she could do to help Patrick. She must try to find him, to warn him of what they suspected. She put her head round Renzo's door.

'Just going out for a while, Renzo.'

She was crossing the road to the waterfront car park when a sudden shout behind her made her turn. It was Patrick, running along the pavement towards her.

'Hi,' he said with a wide smile. 'I thought it was you – I'd know those legs anywhere. Leave the car – let's walk along the quayside.'

Relief flooded over her as he took her arm. 'I've been trying for ages to get hold of you. Where were you?'

Patrick looked completely relaxed and at ease with the world. 'I'm flattered,' he said. 'I was having coffee with Hassan. Look at that – they're loading armchairs onto that dhow.'

Leah ignored the men heaving furniture up the gangplank and spoke in low, urgent tones. 'Listen, we've got to talk. You know that Arab you had a fight with, the one who was following me? He's been found dead in the Creek. Yussef thinks you did it.'

'What?' Patrick's smile faded and his bronzed face grew serious. He let go of her arm and she could see the mark were his lip had been cut. 'You're joking.'

'I wish I was. Yussef was having me followed all right, but by another man, not that one.'

Patrick looked bewildered. 'This is ridiculous. First you say I'm suspected of murder, then that you were being followed by two men – I must be dreaming all this. Your Yussef is up the creek.'

'Listen, Patrick. He says his man saw the fight.'

'But the fellow was alive when I left him – you saw that.'

'He also saw us go to your flat. Yussef believes you went back and knifed him and chucked him in the Creek.'

'What the devil for?' said Patrick. 'Why on earth should I do a stupid thing like that? You don't think I did it, do you?'

'Don't be silly. I told him you didn't do it. But even so, what if he tells the police?'

Patrick took hold of her arm again and began walking. 'I wouldn't stand a snowball's chance in hell if he does – I'd land up in a police cell till I'm proved innocent.'

'I can give evidence for you. I'll tell them you couldn't have done it – you were with me all night.'

Patrick shook his head. 'A woman's word carries no weight here – especially an immoral woman. Sorry, but that's how they'll see you.'

'What else can we do?'

Patrick sighed deeply. 'I guess I'd better stay out of sight for a while till it blows over.'

Leah frowned. 'Won't that make you look guilty, running away?'

'I've told you, it means jail if I stick around.'

'All right, but they'll be sure to check your English friends and all the usual expatriate places.'

'So it would be best to get away.'

Leah stopped and looked up at him. 'We're assuming Yussef will tell – he might not.'

Patrick shook his head. 'Of course he'll tell. The man's an Arab, and so was the dead man. It wouldn't have mattered if he'd been Indian or Filipino.'

'I'll ask him what he means to do, soon as I get back.'

'Wait till I get out of the way. I'll fetch what I need from the flat then go up to Hatta Fort, to Hassan's. He's loyal. He'll help me.'

'Shall I come with you?'

'No, you stay here and let me know what you find out.'

'Shall I drive you there? They could be looking out for your car.'

He smiled and touched her cheek. 'Anyone would think you'd done this kind of thing before. No, it's OK. The Range Rover's in the car park and the police aren't around. You can follow later if you like. Ring me tonight.'

★

159

Eva stood near the flight desk in the busy concourse of Charles de Gaulle airport. In front of her a pretty French woman with two small, impeccably-dressed children, was looking bewildered.

'But my husband is expecting me,' she was saying in French. The Emirates airline girl spread her hands.

'I'm very sorry, Madame, but the flight for Dubai has had to be postponed,' she explained in fluent French. 'A technical fault, you understand.'

It really was exasperating, thought Eva. She wanted so much to get to Leah quickly. And not only was the flight delayed but it seemed the plane was to touch down en route for refuelling at Nicosia and Kuwait, so she wouldn't reach Dubai until tomorrow evening.

Ah well, she thought philosophically, she could take the opportunity to pay an unexpected visit to her Paris shop. The elegant, efficient Madame Villeneuve wouldn't be in the least perturbed.

Yussef's expression was severely unsmiling when Leah put her question to him that afternoon.

'Have you told the police what you told me?'

He shook his head. 'I shall not tell the police,' he said slowly, and added, 'but justice will nevertheless be done. The dead man was an Arab – a thief and of no account, it is true – but he was an Arab. We deal with such matters ourselves, in our own way.'

Leah swallowed hard. 'What do you mean? Who is *we*?'

Yussef smiled, a wry, humourless smile. 'Word flies in Dubai like the desert sand in a *shamal*. Soon all the Arab community will hear of this outrage.'

'It wasn't Patrick – I told you. You've got to believe me!'

Yussef turned away, murmuring to himself. 'If a mad dog kills a goat he may acquire a taste for goat's flesh, and that we cannot allow.'

'Why won't you listen to me? It couldn't have been Patrick – he was with me, you know that!'

'You would do well to take care, Miss Finch. Those who keep company with mad dogs may well fall under the same shadow. Revenge will be swift.'

Leah telephoned Patrick that evening from her hotel room. He sighed deeply. 'That's it, then. I can't come back to Dubai. I'll have to get out.'

'Where to? They'll be watching at the airport.'

'I've got money and my passport. I'll go over the mountains into Oman.'

'I'll come up to Hassan's tomorrow. Wait for me.'

'Just make sure that fellow isn't still following you then. They're probably hoping you'll lead them to me.'

'Don't worry. I'll think of something.'

It wasn't going to be easy; Yussef had said his man could hide himself in the desert. Sitting in a busy hotel restaurant that evening surrounded by Arabs, Leah looked around her. Which one of them was Yussef's man? It could be any one of the customers. She turned her attention to the waiters. She studied their faces. What a dismal, unsmiling bunch they were! Now when she came to run *her* place, she'd make sure . . . Heavens, what was she thinking of? She was becoming as bad as Renzo.

The air in the hotel bedroom was suffocatingly close. The air-conditioning must have gone faulty, and with a night temperature of around eighty it was going to be unbearably hot and sticky in bed. She tossed and turned, conceiving and rejecting plans to elude the man, and at last she got up and went through into the bathroom. It was soothing to press bare soles on the cool tiles. By morning she had it clear in her mind just what she would do.

Straight after breakfast she took her car to the service garage and left it there.

The Arab bent to give a few coins to the Indian shoeshine boy as the girl passed him to climb into a taxi. He waved down the next cab and followed her.

She got out at the gold *souk* and walked along the street, peering into all the shop windows. It was easy to keep his distance as he followed; that glorious golden hair shone like a beacon so that she was easy to pick out in the crowded street.

She was behaving like any European tourist, calling in at one or two of the shops. She made a couple of purchases – in a little Indian clothes shop and in a jeweller's. After that she sat in a hotel and drank coffee.

His taxi followed hers at a distance back to the Sheraton as the midday sun emptied the streets. He watched her go up on the escalator, carry her shopping across the foyer and take the lift up to her room. No doubt she would take a nap now, as many Europeans did during the afternoon, but he must remain on guard just in case she went out again. At least the air in the Sheraton foyer was cool and soothing with its cascading fountain, and he could sit against the wall on one of the many settees dotted around the area and watch the escalator, the only way in and out of the high-level foyer.

There were few people about in the heat of the afternoon. An American couple in jazzy shirts and shorts sipped coffee at a table; the Arab averted his eyes quickly from the woman's exposed legs, then involuntarily returned to them in fascinated distaste. Behind her a tall, blonde man, probably Norwegian, was changing money at the desk. The Arab glanced at his watch. With luck he should be able to relax soon – in half an hour Ali was due to relieve him.

The curtains drawn against the sun, Leah quickly unpacked her purchases in the bedroom and changed into the Arab robe and headdress. It took a little time to adjust the veil so that it looked authentic, and she surveyed herself in the full-length mirror critically.

With only her eyes visible, not even her mother would recognize her now. She slipped the sandals on her feet. One detail more to perfect the image of a well-off Arab woman – Leah took out the three gold bracelets from another bag and slid them on her arm. Watching herself in the mirror, she practised walking with the smooth, effortless glide she had seen so often here in Dubai, a grace born of confidence and self-assurance.

Kohl pencil gave her eyes the dark, slumberous look she needed. Leah surveyed herself once more. He was around somewhere, she knew it. Though she had not seen him, she had been aware of a presence, a shadow which never left her. Let him not notice the Arab woman leaving the hotel. And please God, let no one speak to her in Arabic in the next half-hour!

The Arab was growing restless. Half an hour had passed and still Ali had not appeared. Nor had the girl. She must be sleeping. This could be a long wait. He turned his attention back to the brassy-voiced American woman in the shorts. She seemed to be haranguing her husband over something, waving her arms so that her breasts jostled under the jazzy shirt, and he wondered why her husband did not silence her.

Ten minutes later the lift door opened and a woman came out, an Arab lady of some standing judging by her jewellery. She moved with all the grace and suppleness of a cat, smooth and elegant as she glided across the foyer towards the escalator. As she passed the jewellery shops the blonde-haired fellow noticed her too, and his lascivious expression showed his interest. He smiled and nodded to the woman, but she only tossed her head and walked on by.

The American woman let out a screech. She was pointing to something in the jeweller's window and dragging her husband inside.

The Arab gave a thin smile. Arab women knew how to behave. This gracious lady could teach the American harpie a thing or two. He watched appreciatively the slender figure of the woman as she reached the escalator, stepped onto it, and sank gracefully out of sight.

Leah stood on the narrow pavement outside the Sheraton, swathed in the dark robe and veil, and lifted a hand to signal the taxi. Despite the blistering sun it was surprisingly cool inside the voluminous folds of the robe. The car drew up before her. And no one else was outside the hotel. The problem now was how to do the customary bartering with the Arab driver without revealing her ignorance.

'Ramada,' she said briefly, and watched his face. His gaze travelled up and down her, taking in the gold bangles and the bag she carried before he answered.

'Five dirhams?' She nodded and stepped into the back seat. Thank heaven she'd learnt how to count up to five in Arabic. As the car drew away she watched the hotel through the back window. No one emerged; no one appeared to be following her.

At the front entrance of the Ramada hotel she paid off the driver and went inside. The turbaned commissionaire inclined his head as he opened the door for her. Leah glided straight across the foyer to the Ladies.

Five minutes later she emerged, dressed now in jeans and shirt and carrying the bag containing the robe and bracelets. She waited for a moment to make certain the foyer was momentarily empty, then crossed quickly to the entrance. This time the commissionaire did not open the door for her.

Another taxi ride to the service garage, and as she unlocked her own car Leah looked about her. Not a soul was in sight. Switching on the ignition she eased the car down the ramp and headed out of the city. The road to Hatta Fort was a long, clear highway across the desert and through her driving mirror she could see no cars behind her, only an aeroplane circling to land. She could breathe again now – with luck she had thrown her follower off the scent at last.

Eva stepped off the aeroplane in Dubai and the heat and humidity made the air so thick it clogged her throat. After passing through Customs she took a taxi into the city.

She found Cresco's office without difficulty and marched straight in. Dropping her suitcase on the floor she spoke to the smiling Filipino girl behind the desk.

'I am sorry, Miss Leah is not here today. You may speak with Mr Rosconi if you wish.'

Eva debated. She was more likely to learn what she wanted from a more senior person. 'Very well.'

The girl lifted the telephone. 'A lady here to see you, Mr Rosconi.' Replacing the receiver she added to Eva, 'Please take a seat.'

Eva sat down on the leather-covered settee under the shade of a huge potted plant. A moment later a small, neat man in a grey suit hurried in, a worried expression on his swarthy face. As he caught sight of Eva the frown faded.

'You are the lady who wishes to see me?'

Eva rose and held out her hand. 'Mr Rosconi? I'm Eva Finch, Leah's mother. I've flown out from England to see her. Can you tell me where I can find her?'

The little man's face broke into a beam. 'Signora Finch? I am delighted to meet you. I have seen your beautiful Urchin shops in every capital in Europe.' He pumped her arm up and down vigorously. 'Leah is not here today. Sometimes the heat bothers her a little. I fancy she will be still in the hotel – the Sheraton. It is not far – shall I accompany you there?'

He bent to pick up Eva's suitcase. 'If anyone calls, I am out,' he announced to the girl, then taking Eva's arm he led her out into the street. 'Come, we shall walk – it is only a minute away.'

By the time they reached the Sheraton Eva had learnt that Leah was his assistant and that she was a good, capable girl who learnt fast.

'She tells me that you trained her well,' Rosconi said proudly. 'She will be an asset to a good hotel one day. Ah, here we are.'

'Don't bother to come in,' said Eva. 'I don't want to detain a busy man. Thank you for your help.'

He seemed disappointed, reluctant to leave her, but finally he went.

Eva stepped inside, eager to meet Leah again and to get out of her clothes which by now were sticking to her back. A cool shower would be sheer heaven . . .

During the one-hundred kilometre drive along the dusty road to Hatta Fort Leah met only one car coming in the opposite direction, and an abstracted camel whose mind was clearly on other matters. He was at one moment well clear of the road, and at the next he was ambling on to the tarmac just ahead of her, staring at her out of huge, liquid eyes. Leah slammed on the brakes, coming to a halt just inches away from him.

The camel blinked, looked slowly around at the expanse of sand dunes stretching for miles in every direction, then lumbered away again across the desert. Leah exhaled a deep sigh of relief as she started off again. It was a mercy she had not hit him. Here camels were not only revered, like sacred cows in India, but also highly dangerous; if a motorist hit one, knocking it off-balance, its weight would crush both car and occupants.

In the distance now she could see the outline of the mountains, rising black and majestic out of the gold of the sand. Soon she would reach the road veering off left towards Hatta Fort. As the car swung round the corner towards the village the smooth surface of the highway gave way to a gravel road pitted with a series of vicious humps. Ahead she could see where the track billowed like an orange ribbon over the hill, falling steeply to cross wet *wadi* beds . . .

A flock of goats suddenly appeared on the road and Leah was obliged to slow down to let them pass. No one seemed to be with them; a long-maned billy-goat led the group, strutting proudly with his beard jutting before him. As Leah waited she noticed the brightly-painted iron doors of the houses decorated with motifs of Arabic coffee pots. A curly-haired child watched from a doorway, one finger in his mouth.

The last goat gone, she drove on, past gardens carefully planted with shrubs and trees surrounding the lush villas of the rich. Before long she found the entrance to Hassan's villa and as she drove up the curving drive she saw Kara emerging from under the archway.

The girl came across to meet her as Leah pulled up and got out. Her pretty face wore a troubled expression. 'Mr Patrick is unhappy,' she said. 'The heavens do not look kindly on him. There is a black omen of death in the stars. I fear for him.'

'No need,' said Leah. 'He can take care of himself. Where is he?'

The girl pointed towards the garden. 'By the pool with my grandfather but be careful, my grandfather does not know of Patrick's trouble. He is old and sick.'

'Don't worry,' said Leah. 'I won't breathe a word.'

As the girls neared the pool Leah could see Patrick lying on the grass beside an old man seated on the bench. He appeared almost to shrink inside his white *dish-dash* and seemed wizened and fragile. But as they approached he held up a hand to shield his eyes from the bright sun.

'Grandfather, this is Mr Patrick's friend, Miss Leah,' Kara said softly. The withered face creased into a smile.

'You are welcome here, Miss Leah. Like Kara, you make a beautiful sight for the failing eyes of an old man.'

Leah smiled and looked at Patrick. His eyes were shadowed as though he had slept little. 'Are you OK?' she asked.

He gave a wry smile. 'Blooming,' he said.

The old man murmured some words in Arabic to Kara, who nodded and went towards the house. 'Such a long journey you have made across the desert,' he said to Leah in his thin, cracked voice. 'You will appreciate a glass of iced lemon, I am sure. Did you see any accidents along the road today? So often there are head-on crashes on that road.'

'Why, no. The road was deserted. I only met one car.'

The old man's eyes were misting as he dipped back into memory. 'So different from the days when I was a boy. Then the little camel always gave way to the big camel.'

Patrick got up stiffly and held out a hand to Leah. 'Come and have a look at Hassan's stallion,' he said. 'Excuse us, we'll be back in a minute.'

He began walking towards the stables. Leah followed, noting that he was limping. The old man watched them go, smiling and nodding and waving a thin brown hand. Once they'd gone through the archway into the stable courtyard Patrick turned to Leah and seized her arm.

'Are you sure you weren't followed?' he demanded.

'I went through the most elaborate exercise you ever saw. No, I wasn't followed, I'm sure of it.'

'OK.' He let go of her arm and began limping towards one of the stables. 'Let's have a look at that bloody horse.'

'Why do you say that? And why aren't you walking properly?'

Patrick opened the top half of the stable door. The glossy black head of the stallion peered over it. 'He did it,' muttered Patrick. 'I tried to ride him.'

Leah rubbed the stallion's nose and he whinnied in pleasure. Patrick shook his head. 'Just look at that,' he murmured. 'And the brute tried to bite me when I touched him.' He leaned against the wall, taking the weight off his right leg. 'Shamal, they call him. Sandstorm. Seems pretty appropriate after what he tried to do to me today, bucking and rearing like he was in a rodeo.'

'You probably tried to mount too fast. You have to win his confidence first.'

Patrick rubbed a thoughtful hand down his shin. 'Well, anyway, he's put paid to this leg for a day or two. I won't be able to get to Oman just yet.' He looked up at Leah and his sunny smile returned. 'Unless you'd like to drive me.'

She took hold of his arm. 'Of course I would.'

'And stay with me?'

She hesitated, not knowing just what he meant. 'Well – there's my job –'

'It's only a sinecure – you said so yourself.'

'Not any more. I've got really wrapped up in this hotel business. But I'll drive you wherever you want to go.'

'We'll go in a day or so – we mustn't appear rude – and by the way, not a word to them about what happened. Kara and Hassan only know I'm in trouble, nothing more.'

Leah hugged his arm against her body. 'Patrick, you can trust me with your life. Now we'd better get back and join the others.'

Eva found the hotel manager very obliging. 'Miss Finch should return before long. I know she would wish her mother to take full advantage of her room. Please make yourself comfortable, Mrs Finch. Shall I order something to be sent up to you? Tea, perhaps?'

She took a cool, refreshing shower and put on Leah's silky blue robe which she found lying behind the bathroom door. It was a pleasure to open the wardrobe and see Leah's familiar clothes hanging there. Somehow it made her feel closer to her already.

She wandered around the room, picking up a bedside book and flicking over the pages. As she put it down she noticed the sheet of paper with Leah's handwriting on it. Her own name leapt at her from the sheet. She picked it up and scanned the words.

'Oh my God!'

Her face turned pale as she sank down on the bed.

CHAPTER SIXTEEN

Still holding the sheet of paper in her hand Eva waited for the familiar dialling tone. Then Nathan's voice came on the line.

'Hello?'

'Nathan – it's Eva. Listen, I want you to do something for me.'

'Go ahead. What is it?'

She looked down at the paper. 'I've found this letter – meant for me, but Leah never posted it. No, hang on a minute, it's a fax. She must have faxed me, but I never got it.'

'Where is Leah? Isn't she with you?'

'Not yet. She's out. But listen, Nathan. The fax says she knows now what a bastard Clay is, apologizes for doubting me, and says she overheard some terrible things before she left. Seems there's someone called the Major and a man named Hennessy involved – they carry out Clay's dirty work.'

She heard Nathan's gasp. 'Does Clay know about this?'

'I don't know. I haven't seen her yet. But in the meantime I want you to do some background foraging. I want you or Alan to go and see an old friend of mine – he might be able to give us something on Clay.'

'Give me his name. I'll see to it.'

'OK, I'll give him a ring to warn him.'

'Reg? Is that you? Thank heaven. It's me, Eva.'

'Eva Finch. My Gawd, blast from the past you are. How's it going, girl?'

'I've had the very devil of a job finding you.'

Reg Fowler chuckled. 'Ah well, we don't advertise my line of business, darling, not in the 'phone book anyway. Sex shops aren't all that popular round here, more's the pity. Now, what can I do for you, sweetheart?'

'Reg, I need your help. You've still got your contacts in the under-world, haven't you?'

Reg scowled. 'Now hold on a minute – watch what you're saying,

Eva. I run a regular business, books kept proper and all. You can't go saying things like that.'

'Listen, Reg, I need help and you're the man who can help me. I remember what you did for me in the old days.'

He laughed. 'Ah well, I always did have a soft spot for a pretty girl. What you wanting, sweetheart? Need somebody light-fingered, do you?'

'No,' Eva answered tentatively. 'It's a person –'

'Somebody bothering you? Listen, darling, just you let me know who he is. I'll soon sort him out.'

'I can't talk, Reg – I'm out in the Middle East. I want you to talk to my stepbrother. He'll come and see you, tell you everything. Give him all the help you can, Reg, it's important to me.'

'You betcha, kid. You can always rely on Reg Fowler.'

The family were all seated on the floor – grandfather, Hassan, Kara and their two English guests. Between them on the thick-pile Persian carpet lay silver dishes containing the remains of their meal.

Patrick turned to Leah. 'Tell you what, tomorrow I'll take you into the desert. It's fabulous.'

'The desert,' said Grandfather in a reedy voice, 'is best left to the Bedouins.'

Kara reached for the silver jug and poured more of the yoghourt and water mixture into Leah's glass. 'It is unwise to venture alone into the desert. You should have another car with you. If one car should break down, you could die.'

'Camels very rarely break down,' said Grandfather.

'I'm not altogether a stranger,' said Patrick. 'I've been *wadi*-bashing and I've driven out loads of times with Hassan, practising for the rally.'

'But always in twos,' Hassan pointed out. 'Kara is right. My servants will follow you.'

'Thanks,' said Leah. 'I heard you have to keep clear of camel-spiders because they sneak up on you while you're asleep and spray some sort of anaesthetic over you and then eat the flesh. A man in Dubai told me his friend woke up with half his leg gone.'

Hassan was exchanging a smile with his sister when there was the sound of a telephone bell and he rose to go. Kara turned to Leah.

'The camel-spider looks vicious, big as a tarantula, but its bite is harmless. Your friend was having you on, as you say. Even so, I would advise you to take care.'

'We won't be stopping,' Patrick assured her. 'We'll be very careful.'

The old man was shaking his head. 'Always the young are foolhardy,' he muttered. 'By the time wisdom sits on their brow, they are too old to benefit by it.'

Hassan came back into the room. Instead of squatting down again with the group he remained standing. Patrick looked up at him. 'What is it, Hassan? What's up?'

'You are no longer welcome in my house,' Hassan said quietly. 'You must leave first thing in the morning.'

Leah saw Patrick's mouth open and then close again. 'You've heard,' he said at last. Hassan nodded. 'You can't believe I did it, surely?'

Hassan shrugged. 'I cannot be involved one way or the other. I have not told them you are here. You must leave at dawn.'

'OK,' said Patrick. 'If that's what you want.'

The old man stared at his grandson in bewilderment. 'This is no way to treat honoured guests,' he said. 'It is not the teaching of the Koran.'

Kara bent her head. 'If Hassan commands, then he has his reasons, Grandfather.'

Hassan was looking at Patrick with a strange expression which Leah could not understand. It could have been pity, or distaste, or disbelief . . .

His dark eyes turned to Leah. 'You are welcome to stay as long as you wish. But Patrick must be gone by dawn. Now I bid you all goodnight.'

He turned and left the room abruptly. Kara took her grandfather's arm and they followed. Leah heard Patrick sigh. 'Ah well, the end of a beautiful friendship,' he murmured. 'Funny lot, these Arabs. Unpredictable. You never can tell which way the wind blows with them.'

Leah caught up with Hassan at the foot of the stairs.

'Hassan, please. You must believe him – he didn't do anything. It's all a terrible mistake. He needs his friends now – don't let him down.'

There was deep sadness in Hassan's eyes. 'He does not know the meaning of friendship. He was never a friend to me.'

'That's not true, I'm sure it isn't!'

'Why else should he lie to me – about your husband?'

'That was to protect me. He meant well.'

'You would have been safer with me. As my sister's friend, I would have honoured you.'

Leah sighed. 'I shall leave in the morning with Patrick. His leg is still bad – I will drive him, if you'll let me leave my car here for a while.'

'Of course,' said Hassan. 'Come back whenever you wish. You will always be welcome here.'

In the back room of a fish and chip shop in a grimy side street Nathan sat waiting for Reg Fowler to show up. He was half an hour late already. Nathan looked down at the remains of greasy chips and soggy batter on his plate and wondered how long it would be before the vociferous woman proprietor would complain that he was taking too long over his meal.

The door opened, admitting a breath of grease-free air and a thick-set, balding man in shirt sleeves with tattoos all the way up his arms.

'You Mr Bower?'

Nathan nodded.

'Thought so.' The man eased his weight onto the bench opposite. 'I'm Reg. Sorry to bring you to a dump like this but I gotta be careful.'

'Eva thinks you can help us,' said Nathan. 'We need to know –'

'Eva got trouble?' Reg pulled out a crumpled pack of cigarettes from his shirt pocket and withdrew one. 'If so, you've come to the right bloke.'

'Sort of. Her daughter's on to something about a man who's done Eva down. A ruthless man. Name of Clay Richards.'

'Sorry, mate. Never heard of him.'

'He owns Cresco.'

'Ah, now I've heard of *them*. They own Pierrepoint, who own Holloway Holdings, and they own a bloody great chain of sex shops. Thirty-seven of 'em, and they want my four.'

Nathan stared in amazement.

'They'll get 'em in the end,' Reg went on. 'They always get what they want. But I'll make 'em sweat a bit first, put the price up.'

'Have you heard of someone called the Major then?'

Reg lit the cigarette and then shook the match till it died. 'Sorry, mate,' he mumbled. 'I can't tackle him – he's out of my league.'

172

'But there must be something you can tell me,' Nathan protested. 'Eva was so sure.'

Reg shook his head firmly. 'More than my life's worth, mate. He's one of your big boys, far bigger than I can handle. He'd have Hennessy turn me into sausage meat before I could say Jack Robinson. Sorry, mate.'

He was rising to go. Nathan laid a hand tightly over his. 'Just give me something to go on – who's Hennessy?'

Reg hesitated. 'Well, for Eva . . . Hennessy's in the elimination game, takes on dirty work for this fellow you call the Major. Don't know his real name – everybody knows him as the Major. He's a middleman, gets jobs done for his clients, for a fat fee of course, and they never gets to know who done what. No names, no pack-drill, see?'

'And where can I find him?'

Reg pulled his hand free. 'Wouldn't know, mate. But you could try Bernard – he used to drive him.'

'Where can I find Bernard?'

'Down the Concorde Club. He's bouncer there.'

'Thanks, Reg. I'll take it from there.'

Reg frowned. 'Here – you don't want to go tangling with the likes of the Major. He's trouble, and I mean big trouble.'

'I can handle myself,' replied Nathan.

Reg eyed him up and down. 'We're talking guns here, mate. You make a bloody big target.'

Reg's cigarette had burnt down to his browned fingertips. He leaned across the table and stubbed it out on the plate among Nathan's uneaten chips. 'See you then, mate,' he said cheerily. 'Don't let the bastards grind you down.'

Eva was worried. Leah had not come back to the Sheraton all night. In the morning she rang Leah's office.

'No, she has not come in yet,' the Filipino girl reported. 'Only Mr Rosconi and Mr Yussef are here.'

'Who's the boss?' asked Eva. 'The head man.'

'Mr Mohammed, but he is in England. Mr Yussef is his son.'

'Then tell Mr Yussef I'm on my way to see him,' Eva said curtly. 'I'll be there in ten minutes.'

★

'Where is my daughter?' Eva demanded. The regal-looking Arab, impressive in flowing robe and headdress, gave her a cool stare.

'I do not know where she is, Mrs Finch. She has not contacted us.'

'She hasn't been back all night – she could have come to harm. For heaven's sake, don't you feel any sense of responsibility? One of your employees could be lying injured somewhere. Aren't you interested in what's happened to her?'

His dark eyes gleamed. 'Oh yes, I am interested, Mrs Finch. I would very much like to know where she is. For her own safety I have had a man keeping an eye on her since she came here.'

'Ah – so you do know something?'

'Only that she gave my man the slip yesterday afternoon.'

'In that case perhaps we should go to the police.'

'Unwise, Mrs Finch. They would only charge her with immorality.'

Eva's jaw dropped. 'Immorality? Leah?'

'By her own admission she spent the night with a young man in his apartment. Such immorality is a punishable offence in our country.'

Eva bit her lip. Leah, pregnant, sleeping with a young man? It seemed unlikely, but maybe the young man . . .

'Where can I find this man?'

'You won't. He has committed a murder. He disappeared yesterday, and so did your daughter.'

Eva felt a chill of fear. Leah gone – with a murderer? Oh my God! What the devil was happening to her now?

By dawn the Land Rover was packed and ready to go. There was still a chill in the air as Leah climbed into the driving seat and Patrick eased himself gingerly into the passenger seat beside her.

He said nothing as she drove along the bumpy gravel track till it joined the main highway. 'Good road this,' he remarked. 'Follows the ancient caravan route across the mountains to Oman. I wonder how many other people have fled this way before us.'

She felt his arm slide along the back of her seat. Funny, she thought, but for some reason she could not pin down, she had a strange, uneasy feeling.

It wasn't regret – she wouldn't for the world let Patrick down when he needed help, unjustly accused as he was. But it was a feeling that she ought not to be here, but in Dubai.

A magnificent silver car appeared in her driving mirror, catching up

174

with speed. As it passed them Leah caught sight of an Arab at the wheel and heard the blast of pop music . . .

'Look at that,' breathed Patrick. 'A Mercedes 560 SEL. Beautiful.'

The car had vanished already, veiled by the cloud of sand rising in its wake. Patrick gazed out over the sea of sand dunes stretching to the black mountains of Oman.

She glanced at him. 'Are you sure you're doing the right thing – running away, I mean?'

'I'm not running away – I haven't done anything. You do believe that, don't you?'

'Of course I do.'

'So what else can I do? I can't go to the police, Yussef is planning to get me – what else is there?'

Leah sighed. 'So I might not be seeing you again for some time.' She glanced at his averted face. 'I won't say a word about you when I got back, I promise.'

'I know that. You told me I could trust you with my life.'

Strange, thought Leah – was it really only yesterday? And all the time she'd been wrapped up in Patrick she'd forgotten her own plight. The baby, possible deportation or worse, imprisonment till the child was born. No, she thought fiercely, I must think of Maddie. I will not have her born in prison.

Patrick was still gazing out of the window, humming softly to himself and drumming his fingertips on the back of her seat. He turned to her.

'There's one thing I'd like to do before I go – I said I'd take you into the desert. Let me just show you a taste of it – it's the most fantastic experience.'

Leah's heart leapt. 'I'd love it – but Hassan said –'

'We'll only go a little way off the road, just far enough to see how vast and empty it feels.'

'All right then, if you think you've got time.'

He smiled. 'I might not be seeing you again for quite a while, remember.'

Leah swung the wheel round, feeling the firm surface of the road under the tyres give way to unresisting soft sand. Patrick smiled. 'You're going to remember this,' he said. 'Till the end of your days.'

★

The Concorde nightclub appeared to be a narrow doorway with peeling paint in a shabby London side street. Nathan stood across the road watching as a couple of youths approached.

From the dimly-lit interior a squat, broad figure with a lop-sided bow tie under a double chin appeared.

'What you want?' Nathan heard him growl. The youths made some inaudible reply. 'Not in here you ain't,' the man rumbled. 'Clear off or I'll help you with my boot.'

One of the youths tried to brush past him. Nathan saw the big fist reach out and grab him by the scruff of the neck. 'You heard me,' the bouncer growled. 'On your way.'

He hurled the youth towards the pavement edge. The other youth took his friend's arm and hurried him away. The bouncer turned back to the door, brushing imaginary dirt off his hands and grinning.

Nathan strolled across the road. The bouncer paused till he came near. 'How'd you like to throw me out, Bernard?' Nathan enquired mildly.

The bouncer looked at Nathan's huge shoulders. 'I'd think twice about it,' he muttered.

Nathan smiled. 'Let's not have any hassle then. Tell me where I can find the Major.'

Bernard eyed him suspiciously. 'Who wants to know?'

Nathan reached out one thick arm to seize his shirt front and lifted him until he teetered like a ballerina on points. 'I do.'

Bernard's voice was squeaky. 'How would I know?'

Nathan still held him aloft. 'You used to drive him, didn't you?'

'Well yeah, but that was ages ago.' Bernard's face was turning purple.

'So where did you drop him off? And I want the truth, mind. You don't want me to come back, do you?'

With a huge effort the bouncer managed to croak. 'Try Clark's club. Dexter Street.'

'Thank you, Bernard,' said Nathan amiably, setting him down again. The bouncer took a deep, gasping breath. 'It's been a pleasure,' he croaked.

Nathan nodded. 'I'd better find him or I'll be back,' he murmured.

Bernard brushed himself down and straightened his tie. As Nathan turned to go a spotty-faced youth ducked behind him and tried to dash inside the club. Bernard stretched out an arm and grabbed hold of him. 'Here, where do you think you're going? I told you – go on, bugger off.'

And he threw the lad into the gutter.

It was two-thirty in the morning when Bernard took his supper break. He sat in the corner of what the management called the rest room, eating a ham sandwich and racking his brain to remember what it was he'd wanted to do. Ah yes, he'd written it on the back of his wrist.

He rolled back his cuff. There, among the black hairs, he could just make it out. M-A-G-E-R. Major. That's right – he wanted to tell the Major something. What was it now? Oh yes, that ugly great brute who'd come asking after him. He was up to no good, that bruiser. The Major ought to be told.

It must be nearly two years now since the Major had given him the sack – yes, two years come September. He might be pleased that Bernard had the foresight to warn him. Pleased enough to give him his old job back, maybe. It was a damn sight better paid than bouncing for Carney. Mean devil he was.

The management, Carney called himself. *The management wishes to inform the staff . . . the management forbids smoking anywhere on the premises other than the rest room.*

The management. Bernard grinned. One seedy little Irishman – he wasn't a patch on the Major. He stuffed the last of the sandwich into his mouth and lumbered along the corridor to the telephone booth.

Maisie was in there again, giggling down the 'phone to her boyfriend. She did that every night. Bernard sat on the rickety bench to wait.

It used to be good working for the Major, though he wasn't always easy to please.

'Bernard, you oaf, what were you thinking of . . .'

'When I said park right by the front door, I didn't mean on the lawn, you idiot . . .'

'Bernard, you're absolutely useless. Thick as two short planks. I need men with intelligence – somehow nature seems to have overlooked you in the brains queue.'

Bernard growled as he remembered. *'You cretin, Bernard. If you'd been in my regiment you wouldn't have lasted five minutes . . .'*

In the end the Major had thrown him out of his private army. It hadn't been easy finding a new job; he'd been lucky really, getting this one with Carney. And at least Carney didn't sneer at him. Who the hell did the Major think he was, making a fool of him, time and time again?

Maisie came out of the telephone booth. 'It's all yours,' she sang as she minced away down the corridor. Bernard went in and shoved a coin in a slot. Nothing happened. He took it out and shoved it in the other slot.

He dialled a number, muttering to himself. 'I could beat that fellow into a pulp if I wanted. With one hand tied behind my back.'

He could hear the 'phone ringing at the other end now. He picked his teeth with the corner of a membership card while the ringing went on. 'Come on, answer the bloody thing,' he muttered. 'What the hell are you doing? I'm trying to do you a favour and you can't even be bothered . . .'

As the ringing went on he grew irritable. 'Too thick to be any use, am I? Not as stupid as you think, Mr High and Mighty Major. Who the devil do you think you are?'

The ringing stopped. A curt voice spoke. 'Yes?'

'Bugger you,' said Bernard. 'You can look after your sodding self.'

And he slammed the 'phone down and marched out.

CHAPTER SEVENTEEN

Rosary was enjoying having a man to look after while Eva was away. She fussed over him like a mother hen with a chick.

'There's more casserole if ye've room for it, Mr Bower, so there is. And a big chunk of apple pie with cream for afters. I'll serve it up for ye now if ye'll be after putting that telephone down and coming back to the table.'

'Rosary, I've got an important call to make. Hello, Alan? It's Nathan. I'm at Eva's place.'

Rosary sighed and went back to the kitchen. She could hear Nathan talking about a place called Clark's club. So he'd be going out again soon.

'You're a member? Well that's great – can you take me along as a guest? . . . Are you still paid up? Yes? Right . . . Where and when? . . . OK, see you then.'

Nathan and Alan walked up to the imposing front door of Clark's.

'I haven't been here in ages,' Alan was saying. 'I've only been two or three times altogether. Once I found out Richards was a member . . .'

The doorman saluted as he opened the door. 'Evening, Mr Finch.'

Alan stared at him in surprise. 'You remember me?'

'Of course, sir. Never forget a face, sir.'

Nathan leapt in. 'Then you'd remember the Major, of course?'

The doorman looked him up and down warily. 'I don't think you're a member, sir. I'd remember you.'

'He's a guest – my brother-in-law,' said Alan.

The doorman nodded. 'In that case, which Major are you referring to, sir? We have three to my knowledge – Major Farrington-Jones, Major Bellamy –'

'You've proved your point,' Alan cut in. 'I'll sign my guest in now.'

★

The beautiful woman with the glorious red hair was pacing up and down Mohammed al Dhin's office. He watched her with interest.

She stopped and placed her hands on his desk. 'Look, your son tells me that Leah has been keeping company with a young man who might be a murderer, and they both vanished yesterday. The police either didn't understand me or they didn't want to know. Surely there's something we can do?'

Mohammed shrugged. 'Ours is a vast country, Mrs Finch. It is like trying to find one flea on a camel's back.'

'I know, and I just don't understand your customs. Our police would have acted immediately when I reported her missing. She could be in terrible danger – her safety must be your concern. You are answerable to her employer as well as to me.'

'Not so,' said Mohammed quietly. 'I reported what has happened to Mr Richards only today and he washed his hands of her.'

He saw her eyes gleam. 'Richards washed his hands of her? How very convenient. Did he tell you she might be carrying his child?'

Mohammed was too wily to show surprise. 'He talked only of a new dockland development he has acquired and asked if I was interested.'

'Dockland?' she echoed. 'Where?'

He shrugged. 'On the Thames. A shopping complex.'

She gave him a sharp look. 'What was it called? It wasn't Venn Street, was it?'

'That sounds familiar. But what has this to do with your daughter?'

She had stopped pacing and was staring out of the window over the sun-baked roofs. 'He's bought up my site and he doesn't care if Leah's vanished,' he heard her murmur, then turning back to him she said, 'Venn Street is mine, Mr al Dhin, for my Calico complex. Richards has cheated me before and now he's done it again over my daughter. Don't you see, she's an embarrassment to him – he wants her out of the way. You've got to help me find her.'

Mohammed raised a hand. 'Do not concern yourself, Mrs Finch. The young man will be taken care of. Your daughter will be returned to you.'

She looked down at him, her eyes clear as a *wadi* pool after the rains. 'Can you be sure of that? I'm helpless. I want to believe you.'

'*Inshallah*, Mrs Finch. If Allah is willing.'

★

Alan and Nathan sat in a corner of the Clark's elegant lounge, Alan against the wall and Nathan opposite him. Suddenly Nathan saw Alan stiffen.

'It's him,' Alan muttered. 'Richards – he's just come in. Don't turn round.'

Nathan sat motionless and watched Alan's face. He saw the dislike written there change to interest. 'He's standing over that chap with a moustache,' Alan muttered. 'Talking quietly. Slipped a paper to him – possibly a cheque. Now he's heading for the door.'

Nathan did not turn until Alan's expression showed that Richards had gone. Then he glanced over his shoulder. 'Grey hair, navy blazer, by the window?' he asked.

'That's the one,' said Alan. 'Looks the military type, doesn't he? For two pins I'd grab the devil now –'

'No,' said Nathan firmly. 'Leave him to me. You'd be recognized.'

'What'll you do?'

'Follow him when he leaves. You go home and wait.'

It was ten minutes after Alan had left the club when the man moved to go. Nathan walked out casually just behind him. As he emerged into the street the doorman nodded.

'Goodnight, Mr Bower.'

'Goodnight. Which way did the Major go?'

The doorman pointed. 'That way, sir. Glad you found him.'

He was fifty yards away, nearing the corner of the main road. Nathan sauntered along, hoping his quarry would not call a taxi. As Nathan turned the corner he saw the man striding away ahead.

A taxi passed him. The Major turned and held up a hand. The taxi slowed and stopped, and the Major got in. As the cab pulled away again Nathan turned to look behind him. Two more taxis were coming, and he flagged down the first.

'Where to, mate?' the driver asked.

'Wherever my friend's going – he's in that cab.'

For the next ten minutes London seemed to become a maze of streets, winding and weaving and turning back on themselves till Nathan was dizzy. At last the Major's taxi pulled up.

'Go past him,' Nathan ordered the driver. 'A hundred yards or so. How much?'

'Four pounds sixty. Here, you a private dick or something?'

Nathan put a fiver in his outstretched hand. 'Something like that. Thanks.'

He looked back along the street. The Major's taxi was doing a U-turn, but of the Major there was no sign. Nathan looked up at the houses. They were tall, Victorian houses, neat and cared for, just the kind of place a retired military man might choose. He hurried back to the spot where the Major had alighted, but there was no sign of a light in a hallway, nothing to mark where he might have gone.

Nathan hung around across the road, hoping for some clue, a light being switched on or milk bottles being put out. Nothing happened. Nathan slumped against the railings, wishing there was some way he could shrink and make his bulk less obtrusive.

A dog came loping down the street towards him, a thin, bedraggled-looking mongrel with more than a touch of border collie in his blood. He gave Nathan a cursory glance in passing, lifted his leg against the railings, then ambled off down a passageway. Nathan watched him go. Poor devil. It could do with the space and freedom of Scapegoat. It was no place for a dog here, with the freedom only to roam and to starve.

An hour later he was forced to admit he'd lost the Major. He could have kicked himself for his carelessness. After all the trouble Alan had taken . . .

He was almost ready to admit defeat when a door opened. A man walked down the path towards the gate. It was not the Major, but a shorter man in a raincoat.

He clicked open the gate and emerged on to the footpath but then, instead of walking away, he came straight across the road. By the light of the street lamp Nathan could see the casual step, the amiable smile on his face.

'Evening,' said the stranger, sticking a cigarette into the corner of the smile. Nathan watched the hand dip into the pocket for a lighter.

A second later the street lamp glinted on metal in his hand and Nathan saw with a start that the lighter was a gun.

'We're not going to make a fuss, are we?' The man jerked the gun in the direction of the house. Nathan considered. The man was some six inches shorter than he, but it would be foolish to argue with a gun. He crossed the road, conscious of the man walking close behind. A figure appeared in the doorway. It was the Major.

'Bring him inside,' he said curtly. Nathan let the man hustle him into the dimly-lit hallway.

'Well, well,' said the Major coolly. 'What have we here? I don't think I know you.'

'No reason why you should,' muttered Nathan. 'Tell your man to put that gun away.'

'Not yet,' said the Major. 'Come inside.'

He led the way into the living room. Nathan followed, the man close behind. Once inside, the Major turned.

'You were following me. I'd like to know why.'

'Get rid of the gun,' said Nathan. 'I don't like it.'

The Major seated himself on the sofa, indicating the armchairs opposite, then nodded to the man, who put the gun in his pocket. 'Don't forget,' said the Major, 'we all know where it is.'

Nathan hitched up his trousers, bent his knees and leaned forward, as if to lower his bulk into the chair. He was learning fast. The man, still rolling the unlit cigarette between his lips, sat down quickly, unaware of Nathan's fist curling round the leg of his chair.

Nathan straightened sharply, jerking the armchair over on its back, then swung round and pushed it hard against the wall. The man lay almost upside-down but uncurled himself quickly, a bent cigarette still between his lips as he blinked in surprise and his hand went for his pocket. Nathan reached over and, clamping one hand over the man's face, seized the hand in the pocket so firmly that the man yelped.

'I wouldn't pull the trigger now if I were you,' said Nathan. 'You might blow your balls off.'

The Major sat, stupefied, watching as Nathan withdrew the man's hand and pulled away the gun. Coolly he opened it, tipped out the bullets, pocketed them, and threw the gun across the floor. It slithered out of sight under the sideboard.

'Well,' said Nathan, 'we all know where it is now.' The Major took a deep breath and composed his face. The man scrambled to his feet, awaiting an order. The Major flicked a finger towards the door. 'I'll speak to you later,' he murmured, and the man shuffled out. Nathan smiled.

'Now, what were we talking about?' he asked mildly. 'I was asking why you were following me tonight. You must have had a reason.'

'Oh yes,' said Nathan. 'I had a reason. I heard you could use a good man.'

'Who told you that?'

Nathan cocked his head. 'A man called Hennessy?' he said.

The Major's gaze travelled up and down Nathan's body. 'You're lying,' he said quietly. 'Has somebody sent you here?'

'Why should they?'

The Major shrugged. 'To try and frighten me, perhaps?'

Nathan was thinking fast. The paper which had changed hands in the club . . . 'Did you get paid tonight?' he asked.

He could swear the man's face tensed. 'Why do you ask?'

Nathan touched him lightly on the cheek with the back of his fist. 'Don't answer a question with a question. Did you?'

'No.'

'And don't you wonder why?'

He saw the quizzical look in the Major's eyes, the suspicion and then the blink. 'Are you saying there's some kind of double dealing going on?' he asked.

Nathan shrugged big shoulders. 'What do you think? Where do you think I got the name Hennessy from?'

The Major frowned. 'If we're talking of the same man, he wouldn't do that. He needs me.'

'Does he? You know too much. You could be a danger to him.'

The Major laughed softly. 'I'd be a damn sight more dangerous dead. He doesn't know that – perhaps you'd like to tell him.'

Nathan was beginning to enjoy the game. He didn't understand all of what was being said, but he could see he'd got the Major rattled. 'Why should I?' he said. 'Let him worry.'

The Major came close, peering at him curiously. 'What's your game?' he asked quietly. 'Are you playing on both sides? Have you got a grudge against him?'

'Hasn't everybody?'

'Hmm,' said the Major. 'Let's have a drink.'

The gathering heat of morning had now dispelled the fresh coolness of dawn and the distant black mountains shimmered in a heat haze. The Land Rover drove on across the desert, a flurry of sand flying from its wheels.

At first it was just a series of rippling dunes like an English beach, but gradually the dunes became higher and steeper. Leah glanced at Patrick.

'Shall I drive between the dunes? Go round?'

He shook his head. 'Drive straight at them and whatever you do

184

don't veer off a straight course halfway up or we'll turn over. Go on. You're doing fine.'

Leah did as she was told, aiming straight and driving fast, and felt exhilarated each time they reached the brow of yet another mountainous dune. Each time there was a plateau of even surface before the next perilous descent, and from the plateau she could see the desert stretching on for mile after undulating mile into interminable distance. The dunes were like sculpted mountains, each curved like a sickle. It was a scene of impressive beauty and symmetry, and the sense of isolation was just as Patrick had predicted.

Suddenly Patrick pointed towards the mountains on their left. 'Look, there's that Mercedes again.'

The silver Mercedes was moving fast along the plain below the foothills, a Range Rover hard at its heels.

'What are they doing out here?' Leah asked.

Patrick reached for the binoculars on the dashboard. 'Hawking,' he said. 'The other man's got a hooded falcon. They must have spotted some prey – a curlew or a bustard probably.'

He seized Leah's arm, his eyes gleaming with excitement. 'Stop here on the top – let's watch the hunt.'

Leah stopped and switched off the engine. Patrick handed her the binoculars and she could see the falconer driving the Range-Rover with his right hand and holding the falcon on his left wrist. She trained the binoculars on the sheikh in the Mercedes. He was holding a pair of binoculars in one hand as he drove, and they were trained on her.

Quickly Leah lowered the glasses. The two cars were speeding forward along the red scrub-spattered sand. Suddenly one of the cars hooted its horn. Patrick took the binoculars.

'Look!' he cried. 'They've scared a curlew off the ground – see it up there?'

Leah could see it, a black-winged bird rising steeply into the cloudless azure sky. She looked down again at the cars, and saw the driver of the Range Rover reach out a gauntletted arm to release the falcon.

She heard Patrick's quick intake of breath as the bird circled and then soared. 'A peregrine falcon,' he murmured. 'The curlew hasn't got a chance.'

Leah shaded her eyes against the bright sun. The falcon had soared so high that she could no longer see it in the heavens, only the curlew flying desperately away. Then suddenly she saw it, a speck swooping down swiftly, growing into a huge black shape with menacing talons outspread. Leah held her breath. The paths of the two birds coincided, and the hawk soared away again, the curlew held fast between its talons.

'Poor thing,' Leah breathed.

Patrick shrugged as he laid the binoculars down on the dashboard. 'Survival of the fittest – that's nature.'

The Mercedes and the Range-Rover were speeding away now in search of the prize. Patrick nudged Leah's arm. 'Change over for a bit,' he said. 'I love driving in the sand.'

Leah climbed out of the driving seat and went round while he slid across. She could see the light in his eyes as he slipped into gear and set off.

'What about your leg?' she asked.

He laughed. 'Funny how you can forget discomfort when you're doing something you enjoy. Hassan and I used to spend hours . . .'

His voice died away. Leah touched his arm. 'I'm sorry about Hassan. One day I'm sure he'll believe you.'

He wasn't listening. He was staring at the high barchan ahead, so high it seemed to curve over on itself at the top like an ocean wave. Leah held her breath as Patrick put his foot down to the floor and raced at it.

Nearing the top the Land Rover seemed to lose its momentum and hover, and for a split second Leah felt they were going to turn turtle. Then, with a mighty effort, the Land Rover crept over the lip onto safe ground. Patrick was beaming. He raced on across the plateau to fly down the further slope at such a speed that Leah could not understand why they did not somersault forward, but already Patrick was racing at the next barchan. Once again it took all his skill to reach the safety of the ridge.

Leah gave a deep sigh. 'You drive well,' she muttered.

He turned to smile at her. 'You ain't seen nothing yet.'

There was something in the way he spoke the words that made Leah shiver. 'Don't you think we've gone far enough? We ought to be getting back to the road.'

Patrick gave her a quick glance. 'Sure?'

'It's been exciting – I know what you mean about the immensity of the place. I feel utterly lost. We ought to go back now.'

186

'OK, I'll head round and circle back.'

Obligingly he swung the Land Rover around. As he did so a rucksack fell off the back seat, thudding against his. Leah leaned across to pick it up.

'Don't bother,' said Patrick. 'I'll do it later.'

But Leah had already heaved it back onto the seat. A small book still lay on the floor. As she retrieved it she recognized the photograph of Patrick. It was his passport.

She scrutinized the photo. 'Not a very flattering picture,' she remarked. 'How long ago was it taken?'

But even as she spoke she caught sight of the name. Andrew Timothy Gilchrist. She looked up at Patrick in surprise. He shrugged.

'My firm takes good care of us. Extra passport in case of trouble.'

'Trouble?'

'You never know in the Middle East – sudden political upheaval, anything.'

It was a reasonable explanation, but Leah could not help wondering why she still remained uneasy. She ought to be in Dubai. Mother could be there . . .

'We'd better get you to Oman and me back to Dubai,' she said quietly. 'My mother should have answered my fax by now. I did try to ring her to make sure she got it – I rang her at home and at the office before I left.'

'No go?'

'No.'

He was driving the Land Rover up and down ridges but she had the curious feeling that they were only moving in circles, not retracing the route back to the road at all.

She looked over her shoulder. The mountains of Oman still loomed black and distant to their left.

'Patrick – we're going the wrong way. The mountains should be to our right now.' She looked at him enquiringly. His face was set and unsmiling. 'Patrick?'

He didn't appear to hear. Leah took hold of his sleeve. 'Patrick – do you hear me? We're going the wrong way. You've got to turn the car around. Patrick!'

He shook off her hand. 'I know exactly what I'm doing,' he said quietly. 'Just shut up and keep quiet.'

Leah began to feel alarmed. 'What is it? This isn't like you. What's happening?'

'I'm obeying orders,' he replied calmly. 'And my orders are very clear. I'm to ditch you in the desert.'

CHAPTER EIGHTEEN

The Major sat at his ease in his own living room with a brandy and soda before him; the stranger who'd laid out one of his best men was sipping a tonic water.

'How did you find me?' the Major was saying.

'Easy,' said Nathan. 'I saw Richards pass a paper to you in Clark's.'

'The Judas touch?' said the Major. 'Did you really think I would believe your story about being sent to deal with me? I saw you in the club, of course. Even from a back view you're a man not easily forgotten and you're not very good at concealing yourself when it comes to tailing, are you?'

The stranger shrugged thick shoulders. 'OK. I wanted to talk to you. I wanted to know what a professional killer was like.'

The Major smiled. 'My soldiering days are over. I'm retired now.'

The stranger shook his head. 'You're a professional still. Word is, you're the best there is.'

The Major sipped his brandy thoughtfully. Either the fellow was looking for work with him or he was trouble. 'What's your name?' he asked.

'Martin Black.'

The Major considered. It was unlikely to be his real name and he had a vaguely northern accent. 'Where were you born?'

'In Clark's, tonight.'

The Major smiled. 'Where do you live?'

'A hotel.'

'Where do you work?'

'I'm self-employed.'

The Major leaned forward and spoke quietly. 'You could have killed one of my men tonight. Have you ever killed before?'

'What do you think?'

The Major paused. There was control along with strength in the big fellow. 'I think you have,' he murmured. He had to tread warily – the man could be a policeman although he did not seem it. He set down his drink and got to his feet.

'It's getting late,' he said. 'If you'll forgive me . . .'

The big man rose too, towering inches above the Major. 'You wanted to know who I work for,' he said quietly. 'I look after Clay Richards' girlfriend since he doesn't seem to be doing it any more. I came here to make sure she's OK.'

'I know nothing of his lady friends,' said the Major. 'His private life is no concern of mine.'

The big man was barring his way to the door. 'Richards has been making use of Leah and I want you to know that if anyone harms a hair of her head – '

'I don't know who you're talking about,' the Major interrupted sharply.

'Oh yes you do,' said the stranger. 'Leah Finch. I know about you and Richards and Hennessy. Let me tell you that if anything happens to her, I'll personally tear you limb from limb, and enjoy doing it. I don't like sewer rats.'

'Now look here,' said the Major icily. A huge fist grabbed hold of his lapel.

'No, you look here,' the voice murmured gently. 'I have no time for well-bred phrases masking the dirty jobs you get up to – or rather, get others to do for you.'

The Major felt a shiver of alarm. He was out of condition, no match for this ox of a man. 'So see to it that she comes to no harm,' the stranger went on. 'I'll be waiting and watching.'

The Major paled. By now Patrick had probably dealt with the girl. He glared at the stranger. 'What makes you think I can influence events in Dubai?' he asked coldly.

A thin smile spread on the big man's lips as he let go of the Major's jacket. 'Did I mention Dubai?' he said softly. 'And in case you're thinking of setting one of your boys on me again, be warned that the police will know just where to look.'

The Major rubbed his throat where his tie had been pulled tight by the stranger's grip. If the fellow left here he would talk. If only he could reach the drawer of his desk where his service revolver lay . . .

'So I'll be on my way now.' The voice went on evenly as the stranger moved towards the door. The Major crossed casually towards the desk.

As he pulled the top drawer open the settee suddenly seemed to leap at him, trapping his fingers as it slammed the drawer shut.

He looked up and saw the stranger's smile. 'You don't get me that easily,' the big man said. 'I'm not an old lady you can trip on the stairs.'

So he did know something – he wasn't bluffing. The stranger was eyeing him coldly.

'I can kill too, you know,' the big man said, spreading huge hands. 'But I don't need a gun. I've got these.'

Nursing throbbing fingers the Major watched from the window as the stranger strode away down the street. He could still feel the strength of those hands on his throat. The fellow might be built like a bull but he did not lack intelligence. With his undamaged hand the Major reached for the telephone.

But although he left it ringing for ten minutes, there was no answer from Patrick.

From a small hotel in Bayswater Nathan rang Alan.

'I didn't want to go back to Eva's place, or yours – he might be having me followed.'

'I'm glad you rang,' said Alan. 'Eva's just 'phoned from Dubai. Leah's gone missing.' A silence followed. 'Nathan? Are you still there?'

'Yes. I'll go straight back to the Major now.'

'What the devil do you hope to achieve by doing that? You've already threatened him. Best to lie low for a bit now. He's lethal. Reg warned you.'

'I've got to keep an eye on him, Alan.'

'And he thinks you're a killer.'

'I am.'

'What the hell are you talking about? You've never killed in your life.'

'I have. I'm a devil with chickens and pigs.'

'Give me the address and I'll keep an eye on him. He won't recognize me. You stay out of sight.'

Eva stood resolutely in front of Rosconi's desk.

'Now look here, Mr Rosconi, you work with my daughter every day, so you must know something about what she does – where she goes with this Patrick fellow, who his friends are – something which might help me find her.'

Renzo Rosconi's hands fluttered in denial. 'I know nothing of this Patrick, Signora Finch, only that he is a rally driver. Crazy about a Porsche, so crazy he spends much time with Hassan.'

'Hassan? Where will I find him?'

The telephone on the desk rang. Eva could see the apprehension which sprang into Rosconi's dark eyes as he picked it up. 'Hello? Yes, speaking.'

Eva laid a hand over his. 'Where?' she repeated. Rosconi covered the mouthpiece.

'Hatta – the girl in reception will tell you.' As Eva turned to go he spoke again into the mouthpiece. 'Yes, Mr Richards, everything is going well.'

Eva turned back at once. 'Give me that,' she snapped, snatching the telephone from his hand. 'Clay? It's Eva. What the devil have you done to my daughter? You're a filthy, rotten bastard, messing up her life. I knew you were a sod, but this is too much.'

There was a few seconds' pause before he answered. 'You had your chance in Rome, Eva, my love, but you turned me down. Can you blame a man if he finds a beautiful woman's lovely daughter exciting?'

'You didn't have to take her to bed, for God's sake. She's half your age.'

'Pity you didn't tell your husband that. Alan knows better than anyone what a man needs to warm his bed on a cold winter's night.'

Eva's cheeks burned. 'What Alan does is none of your business.'

'It is if it's my sister he's seducing.'

Eva was aware of Rosconi's eyes watching her, wide in disbelief. 'Listen,' she muttered angrily, 'Leah's gone missing. If anything happens to her it'll be your fault and I'll get even with you, Clay, I swear I will, if it's the last thing I do.'

She heard him laugh. 'My dear, don't you realize? There's nothing you can do. I can take Leah, Venn Street, whatever I want. I hold all the cards.'

Eva slammed the 'phone down and turned to Rosconi. 'Where can I hire a car?' she demanded. 'I've got urgent business to see to.'

The heat of the noonday sun blazed mercilessly down on the roof of the Land Rover. Patrick switched off the engine. Leah sat aghast.

'Ditch me? Out here? Is this some kind of game, Patrick? Because if so, I don't think it's very funny.'

He shook his head. 'No game, Leah. I'm in deadly earnest.'

'By why, for God's sake? It's you who's in trouble – I'm trying to help you.'

He shrugged. 'I was ordered to do away with you and I need the money.'

Leah felt her cheeks grow hot. 'This is ridiculous! Why would anyone want to harm me? And you of all people – I thought we were friends?'

Patrick shrugged. 'I just obey orders. I was told to get to know you and keep an eye on you at first, then the day before yesterday he said I was to wipe you out.'

She stared, unable to believe what he was saying. 'Who said?'

'My boss.

'What boss? Who is he?'

'Makes no odds. He's acting for a client.'

Leah's bewilderment erupted into angry protest. 'You mean you met me on purpose? Wait a minute – that Arab who was following me –'

'I set him on to watch you while I was away.'

'But you had a fight with him.'

Patrick gave a wry smile. 'Had to – I didn't know whether he was about to speak – he might have given the game away.'

'And then he got killed.' Sick fear was clutching at Leah's stomach and she felt her heart contract. 'That wasn't you – was it?'

'Of course.'

'Oh my God! Why?'

'He might have told what he knew when you were reported missing.'

Leah was frightened now as well as bewildered. If Patrick had killed already . . . She needed time to assimilate what was happening, time to think.

'This client – you must know why he wants me out of the way?'

'You're a danger to him.'

Fear clutched Leah's heart. Danger to him – could it be Clay Richards? Despite the baby? Patrick was looking at his wristwatch.

'I've got to get a move on. Are you going to get out under your own steam or do I have to make you?'

'Is it worth a lot of money to you, Patrick?'

He sighed. 'Don't try to top the offer – it's more than my life's worth. And stop wasting my time – come on, get out.'

Leah looked him directly in the eyes. 'Can you really just ditch me here, in all this heat, with snakes and scorpions and everything? Don't you feel anything for me?'

He spread his hands. 'You're a nice kid, but I've a job to do. Without food or water you won't last more than twenty-four hours at the most. Sorry, but that's the way it's got to be.'

He was willing to sacrifice her to slow but certain death – Patrick, whom she'd liked and trusted all these weeks, whom she'd wanted to kiss and hold her. Leah's disbelief gave way to anger.

'Do you know I'm pregnant?' she said coldly.

He sighed. 'It makes no difference to me. Get out.'

Leah gritted her teeth. 'Make me.'

'OK, if that's the way you want it.' He slid out of the driving seat and began to walk round to her side. Leah seized her opportunity, slithering across into the driving seat and reaching down for the ignition. The key wasn't in the lock. Through the windscreen she could see Patrick, shaking his head.

She sat, head bowed, as he came back to her. 'Do you think I'd be that stupid?' he snapped. 'Come on.'

He grabbed hold of her arm and pulled her sharply. Leah tried to wrench free. Her shoulder bag fell, spilling its contents on the ground, and then as he dragged her out she fell face-down on to the hot sand.

He was about to step past her into the Land Rover as she sat up, gritty sand between her teeth and grabbed hold of his ankle. Turning, he snatched hold of her ponytail with one hand, jerked her head back, and with his free hand he slapped her hard across the face. Her sunglasses flew off as the blow took her breath away and she was forced to let go of his leg.

He leapt into the driving seat and bent to put the ignition key in the lock. Leah scrambled to her feet and clawed at his hand. Patrick swore and rammed the key into her face. As she stumbled back she heard the key scrape into the lock and the engine sprang into life.

'Patrick! Don't leave me, for heaven's sake!'

She could see his set face as he swung the vehicle around, making the sand spurt under the wheels. It was a cruel, determined face, so unrecognizable that it made her shiver. Clambering to her feet she ran after him, trying to find a handhold to scramble in, but he pushed her off and drove away fast, leaving her sprawling on the sand.

'Patrick! For God's sake, come back!'

On her knees she watched the Land Rover climb the barchan and vanish over the ridge, then heard the sound of its engine dying away in the distance.

'Bastard!' she shouted after him. 'Rotten bastard!'

She retrieved the fallen shoulder bag and its contents and brushed the sand off her sunglasses, then stumbled to the edge of the ridge to look about her. She could see nothing but dune after dune, and the mark of the Land Rover's tyres. No breeze blew, not a puff of cloud marred the intense blue of the sky. The silence was terrifying.

And the heat. The sun scorched down on her head and the air in her lungs felt thick and strong, seeming to clog the nostrils. She would give anything to exchange it for the sweet, pure air of summer in Barnbeck. But she must keep going and try to find her bearings. If she could spot the outline of the Oman mountains and keep them to her right, she would go in the direction of the main highway again. She could follow the tyre tracks Patrick had left. She wasn't done for yet.

The sun scorched the back of her neck. Leah pulled her ponytail loose and let her hair fall about her shoulders. She began to descend the steep dune, slithering and sliding to the bottom. Following the tyre tracks in the soft, loose sand was like walking in mud. The next barchan loomed before her, its near concave curve making it impossible to reach the summit however hard she struggled. There was no alternative but to go round and pick up the track again on the other side.

But if she stayed in the valleys between the ridges she would never spot the mountains. If only there was some patch of shade from the sun's rays, somewhere to shelter until the heat of the afternoon cooled to evening. Night came swiftly here in the Gulf, bringing with it more dangers. She must try to find her bearings before nightfall.

She looked at her wristwatch. Quarter to three. There was a way of using a watch as a compass but she had no idea how it worked. Oman was more or less due east, so if she travelled in the opposite direction to the sun's path . . .

She looked up. The sun seemed to be more or less overhead. The tyre tracks in the sand were growing fainter, and as she stumbled round the next ridge she could not pick them up on the far side. Leah drew the back of her hand across her forehead, wiping away the perspiration which was trickling down her face, making the sunglasses slip down her nose. If only she could have a drink. She tried to push from her mind the image of the cool, clear waters of the river Garth bubbling down through Barnbeck on its way to the sea. God, she was thirsty!

Every step grew heavier as she stumbled on, trying again to climb a ridge only to slither down again when she reached halfway. Her vision seemed to be blurring too, or maybe it was just the blinding glare of the sun on the unrelieved acres of sand. The immensity and loneliness of the place was frightening – you could scream your lungs out here, and no one would ever hear.

Leah pushed the thought away and trudged on.

With relief Eva drew up at last in the driveway of Hassan's house. The drive to Hatta had proved further than she had expected and her anxiety as well as the heat and dizzying miles of blank desert had given her a pounding headache.

The young Arab received her with dignified hospitality, offering iced lemon tea and a deep sofa to rest on. 'I regret my grandfather is indisposed and cannot come down to meet you,' he was saying, 'but my sister will be here in a moment.'

Eva leaned forward. 'It's you I wanted to see. You know Patrick Lynch, don't you? Have you any idea where I can find him?'

Hassan's eyes gave nothing away. 'Why do you wish to find him?'

The door opened and a beautiful Arab girl entered as Eva answered. 'My daughter is missing and I think she's with him – she could be in danger.'

Hassan held out a hand to the girl, who came to him. 'My sister, Kara. Kara, this is Leah's mother.'

The girl bowed her head and smiled. She looked to be about Leah's age, Eva noted as Hassan spoke again. 'We have not seen Patrick for some time,' he said. 'He does not drive with me any more.'

'And my daughter – have you seen Leah?'

Eva saw the quick exchange of glances between brother and sister. 'I should not worry unduly, Mrs Finch,' Hassan said quietly. 'Go back to Dubai. Your daughter will be safe, I am certain. You must be patient. I can tell you no more.'

It was no use. She could sense the conspiracy between them. Whatever they might know, they would not tell. Eva picked up her handbag.

'You know more than you're telling me,' she observed quietly. 'Well, just remember that if anything happens to my daughter it will be your fault. You will never forget it.'

It was as she was leaving the villa that some sudden urge made her look back. Brother and sister had disappeared into the house again and an Indian servant was making his way to an archway. Eva threw her handbag into the car and followed him.

The archway led into a cool stable yard, deep in shadow. The servant had opened the door of one of the stables and disappeared inside but Eva's attention was arrested by the dusty, open-topped sports car parked in the shade. She made her way across to it, curious that it should be so dirty in a household clearly dedicated to perfection. It must have made a journey only very recently.

As she stood beside it the servant emerged from the stable leading a nervous black stallion. The man's dark eyes surveyed her with curiosity and he muttered a few words she could not understand. Behind her Eva heard footsteps and turned to see Kara.

'He is apologizing for the car,' Kara explained. 'He will clean it later.'

Eva looked down again at the sports car. Despite its dustiness the interior was impeccably tidy, not a cigarette end or a discarded sweet wrapper to be seen. As if to deter would-be smokers a spray of imitation flowers bloomed from the ashtray and Eva felt her heart leap. Leah had always done the same thing with her car in London – she could never bear cigarette smoke in her car.

Eva looked accusingly at Kara. 'She's here, isn't she? Leah is in the house.'

Kara's eyes were clear as a child's. 'I assure you, she is not. Nor is Golden Shadow. They are not here.'

The servant led the horse out under the archway. Eva looked down again at the car. Tape cassettes lay neatly stacked on the ledge below the glove compartment, alongside a lipstick and an unopened tube of sweets. Eva leaned over and snatched them up.

'Violet cachous,' she muttered angrily. 'Leah had a passion for them. Don't tell me she isn't here – I know she is!'

Beyond the archway Eva could see Hassan mounting the stallion. Kara shook her dark head. 'No, madame, not any more. She was here, but she is gone.'

'Where? Was she with him?'

The girl looked back over her shoulder and then sighed. 'I should not tell you this, but I understand your concern. She was to drive Mr Patrick to the Oman border so do not worry. She will return soon.'

'Oman?' echoed Eva. 'How long ago? How long should it take?'

'They left at dawn.'

197

'But it's mid-afternoon now – shouldn't she be back?'

The girl touched her arm. 'Hassan will see that everything is all right. Trust him.'

Eva folded her arms resolutely. 'If she's coming back here, then I'll wait. I'm not going back to Dubai until I see my daughter.'

Hours seemed to have passed and Leah was exhausted. Her bare arms were already blistering from sunburn, her tongue was clinging to the roof of her mouth with thirst and she was beginning to feel desperate. Without water she could collapse soon from dehydration. With no tracks now to guide her she could be stumbling around in circles for all she knew. Or she could be near the road and not know it. Panic seized her and she tried to make herself concentrate. What was it she'd read somewhere recently? In the *Gulf Times*, something about people found dead in their car – yes, that was it, only half a mile away from the highway. Mother and father and two small children. Hidden between the dunes they never saw how close they were to safety, and passing motorists couldn't see them. Poor parents, forced to watch their children die – or was it the little ones who'd survived long enough to see their parents die? Leah shivered and tried again to concentrate. Weeks had passed, the paper said, before a helicopter pilot had spotted them. What a terrible tragedy, she remembered thinking, and shivered again.

Think of other things. Her vision was going peculiar. From the top of the ridge she could see a lake below. Silly, she thought, there couldn't be a lake here. It was a cliché in every old film from *Beau Geste* to Abbott and Costello for a pool to appear to the beleaguered desert traveller. Even so, Leah hurried down the slope, slipping and sliding as the sand gave way beneath her feet. But the lake was only a vast stretch of yet more sand shimmering in the heat. Her heart sank. Would she ever find her way back to safety? She'd give anything to see something that was alive, even the old bearded billy-goat leading his herd again.

If only she could spot the mountains. Stopping on the next ridge, she shaded her eyes against the sun and stared into the distance. Her breath caught in her throat – were those mountains she could see? Or were they just another mirage?

With a sudden spurt of newfound energy she hurried down the slope and scrambled to the next rise. Still she could see them. Then she turned around. There they were again – and again over there. These were no mountains, only a figment of wishful imagination. Leah sank to the ground.

She was weak and tired and hopelessness was beginning to seep through her. She felt tiny, as insignificant as a grain of sand in the desert and was tempted to stay there and rest, but she mustn't give in.

'*Come on, now, Leah, you can do it. Don't be silly now, you know you can if you try.*'

She could hear her teacher's voice, back in the infant schoolroom in Barnbeck. Miss Lyman had no time for weaklings. '*Come on, dear, try again. You'll do it in the end.*'

Yes, thought Leah with renewed determination as she staggered to her feet. I can do it, if only for little Maddie's sake. Maddie, she could see her now, a baby growing into a toddler, excited and enthusiastic about everything from birthday parties to beach picnics. She could see waves breaking on the shore in the bucket-and-spade days of her own youth.

'*Come on, Leah, let's build a sand castle and you can put this paper flag on the top.*' Mother's voice was eager and full of love. '*There, isn't it wonderful? Now let's fill the moat with water.*' No, she must not think of water. Think of now and what she must do. Think of scorpions and snakes.

'People are frightened of the big black scorpions,' Patrick had once said. 'But it's the smaller, pale-coloured ones that'll kill you. The others are harmless by comparison.'

And there were the snakes. Someone else had told her that the bite of a sandviper was fatal, and that they lay just under the surface of the sand with only their eyes and nostrils showing. You didn't see one till you trod on it. Leah looked down at her feet scuffing up the sand and shivered. Death could be only inches away . . .

CHAPTER NINETEEN

By the time the sun began to dip towards the western horizon Leah was scarcely aware of anything but shifting sand sucking at her feet and her tongue so swollen it seemed to fill her parched mouth.

It was as if she had been stumbling through this sticky world for days; her shirt, which had been clinging wetly to her back with sweat, had now dried out. Her skin could no longer perspire. Her brain too seemed numbed. She'd forgotten what she'd been searching for, the mountains and the road.

She tried to struggle up the next slope, her brain so bemused that she was unaware that every ridge was growing less steep than the one before. It seemed as if she had been alone in a vast, terrifying waste of endless sand since time began, trapped in a void of ominous silence. On the edge of eternity.

She felt desperately alone, sick with fatigue. Her legs were giving way beneath her, and as she stumbled onto level ground she sank down, exhausted.

For a long time she lay there, head resting on outstretched arms. Inches from her nose she could see the winding trail left by a snake, and tried feebly to struggle to her feet. It was no use. Her strength had gone and she could only lie, helpless, dazzled by the sun.

Bitterness and despair brought tears to her eyes. She knew she was dying and felt cheated. In death one ought to be able to grasp some essential truth, see some glimpse of the meaning of life – but there was nothing, only a sense of failure, of being cut off from life before having the chance to make something of it.

What might she have done, given the chance? She'd have loved and cared for her child, and run a hotel of her own, so well that Renzo would have been proud of her. And she'd have made sure Mother knew just how much she loved her, more than words could ever say. And Daddy too. And Nathan, dear, gentle, protective Nathan. She'd have enjoyed helping him with the horses at Scapegoat – he deserved no less.

She lay, eyes closed, floating in the total silence of the desert, all emotion draining away. A thin sound penetrated the fog in her brain, a faint, shrill sound like the cry of a bird. Leah opened her eyes. Below, in the hollow, she could see Barnbeck, bathed in summer sunshine.

Phantom figures seemed to move down there. You fool, Leah told herself, you're delirious, and then she gave a start of surprise – there was Mother, beaming as she led Clay by the arm among the trees. He was smiling kindly at Leah. She felt her cheeks redden with embarrassment and pleasure. The trees behind him looked familiar – yes, it was the wood in Barnbeck, cloaking the side of the valley down to the river.

The Garth looked cool and inviting. Clay was swimming now under the trees. She could hear him calling.

'*Come on, Maddie, it's not too deep – come on in.*'

From out of the woods a little child came stumbling, running into the shallow waters by the river bank and on towards Clay who held out his arms to her. Leah felt her stomach contract.

'*No, no,*' she cried. '*Don't let him touch you, darling – stay away from him!*'

She was in the water now, swimming with all her strength to reach the child, but the current was too strong, sucking her relentlessly back and edging her ever further from little Maddie. Behind her she could hear Mother's voice, urging her on.

'*Keep going, darling, I'm with you.*'

Clay's hands were on the child now. Leah cried out in fear. On the far bank she could see a car coming along the road, a Land Rover with Patrick at the wheel, and he was laughing. Fury mingled with fear. She fought all the harder against the current, but knew that she was losing the battle.

What was that? A horse high on the hill, a rider unaware. It was Nathan! Leah cried out, but he did not hear.

Clay's hands were on little Maddie's throat and he was pushing her under. Leah could hear the little one's cries and gurgles as the river water began filling her lungs . . .

When Maddie finally sank from sight there was a smile of triumph on Clay's face, and on the further bank Patrick was still laughing. Mother sobbed, and Leah felt her heart would break. She clutched her stomach and wept. I'm sorry, Maddie, I tried, I truly tried . . .

But as she wept a sudden realization came to her. She was

hallucinating. Little Maddie wasn't dead – she was still safe and warm inside her. For her sake she must fight to live. Leah rolled over to look down again on Barnbeck.

The river gleamed as it flowed on its way past Thorpe Gill. The big house lay silent in decaying elegance. What a terrible shame it had been allowed to die, its former splendour forgotten. For someone with the money it would make an ideal country hotel. Hotel! Of course, the very place! Little Maddie and her own hotel in Barnbeck. Who could want a more perfect dream?

Again a sliver of sound filtered through the heat-soaked air as Leah looked down from the edge of the ridge. Then something caught her eye – a dark shape spreading in the hollow. As she fought to focus dazzled eyes on it she made out the outline of a vehicle. It was Patrick's green Land Rover, but now it lay overturned on its side against the slope.

Leah blinked her eyes repeatedly. The mansion, the river and wood faded, but the green vehicle remained. Could it possibly be real? Or was she being fooled by delirium and futile hope yet again?

If it was real, there was water in a plastic can. Leah rolled her aching body over the edge and let herself roll and slither down the slope as she had done so often before, but this time she came to rest only halfway down.

The green of the Land Rover still glowed, and the promise of water. Thick tongue licked against cracked lips and, summoning up the last shreds of her strength, she dragged herself slowly on hands and knees towards it, half-expecting it to vanish. She crawled close to it and laid a tentative hand on its metalwork, then drew it sharply away with a cry. It was red-hot and had seared the tips of her fingers.

Water. Again she was licking her lips in anticipation as she crawled into the shade behind the Land Rover and pulled at the rear door. Thank God – the water-carrier lay within reach, half-hidden under a blanket. Please God it wasn't empty. She pulled it to her. No, it was still half full!

The liquid ran warm and musty down her throat but to Leah it tasted like manna as she sucked like a starving baby at its mother's breast. She could feel its life-giving coolness spreading throughout her body, and tears of joy trickled from her eyes. All heaven was here . . .

She opened her eyes again to find herself lying on the sand, the water-carrier beside her. In a haze she sat up slowly, realizing she must have passed out. It was then she saw the figure lying on the farther side of the Land Rover, sprawled face-down, his legs trapped under the roof. It was Patrick, and his eyes were closed.

Was he sleeping, or dead? She bent over him. He was still breathing. As she watched his eyes flickered open and he groaned. She could see the sand crusting his eyebrows and lips, the half-closed eyes blurred with pain.

'For Christ's sake, help me!'

Leah bit back the angry reply which sprang to her lips. She loathed him and could not bring herself to speak.

Patrick's face contorted. 'My legs – get them out – snake.'

'Snake? Where?' She looked about and saw the trail weaving around the Land Rover then ending abruptly several feet away. So close – while she slept. Patrick groaned.

'Sandviper – no time to lose – need serum!'

Then she saw it, the neat puncture, almost imperceptible just above the wristwatch on his sunburnt arm. The thing must have come up out of the sand and attacked him. It could have been her.

But she had been spared. Newfound energy surged in her. She wanted to live, she was going to live! She sat back on her haunches and looked at Patrick. His legs were firmly trapped under the roof. She began trying to scoop the sand away from around them, but as fast as she made a hollow the loose sand filled it in again.

'Help me,' Patrick moaned. 'I don't want to die.'

Leah's lips tightened. 'Neither did I, you bastard.'

Patrick's eyes were wide now in terror. 'Hospital,' he pleaded. 'Get me to hospital.'

'Shut up, I'm thinking.'

'I could die!'

'So what? I don't really care. I'm only going to help because if I don't, I'll only have to live with myself later.'

'Not much time,' he whimpered. 'Must get serum.'

'Stop whining. I'll do what I can. Is there a jack in the Land Rover?'

Totally oblivious now of the pain of the sunburn blisters coming up on her face, Leah pulled out the jack and looked for something to place beneath it to give it leverage on the shifting sand. She found shovels, various tools and what looked like a roll-up aluminium ladder, but nothing which would serve as a strong base.

'Arabs,' Patrick whispered. 'Bloody Arabs.'

'Belt up,' snapped Leah, 'or I'll put you out of your misery with this jack. How the devil am I going to get this damn thing upright? If the Egyptians could build thumping great pyramids on this stuff, surely there must be a way.'

'Bloody Arabs,' she heard Patrick whine.

'What the devil are you on about? There isn't an Arab within miles. We'll have to cope on our own.'

'They got me. I'd have made it but for bloody Arabs.'

Leah came round to stare at him in the gathering dusk. 'What are you bleating about? It wasn't Arabs who made you overturn. You're delirious.'

Bleared eyes were closing. His voice came faint and low. 'Snake,' he muttered. 'Snake.'

He gave a violent shiver. He looked desperately ill. Leah snatched up the shovel and began digging away around his legs, but still could make no progress against the persistent sand. She grew angry with the jack as she turned it round, wondering how to use it. Finding the right way, she edged it under the near side of the bonnet to try and raise the weight off Patrick's legs, but again to no avail.

'Oh for heaven's sake, what am I to do?' She'd spoken the words aloud without realizing. She looked across at Patrick. 'Well?'

He made no answer. She looked at him more closely. There was a strange look about his face; she bent low and listened. He didn't seem to be breathing. She slid a hand inside his shirt and felt her own heart leap. There was no beat; Patrick was dead.

He couldn't be dead – he'd been moaning only moments ago. She refused to believe it. A strange feeling of unreality came over her. Her brain told her he was dead but her heart wanted to scream denial. There was a strange compulsion to cry, and at the same time to laugh with relief because she was still alive.

She squatted on her haunches beside his dead body, still unable to believe the enormity of it. The gap between life and death was so minute, and at the same time so horrendously final.

No tears came, but his face was growing dim. She realized that the sun had gone down and darkness was thickening about her. She stood up, shivering. It was growing cold.

She pulled the blanket out of the van and draped it over Patrick's head, then crawled inside and made herself as comfortable as possible in the tilted angle. No point trying to find her way in the dark. Might as well sleep and recoup her strength for morning.

But sleep eluded her. Pangs of hunger gnawed at her stomach and as the night wore on it grew colder and colder. Leah shivered in her thin shirt. The only blanket lay out there, covering Patrick. In the end, shivering violently, she crept out to fetch it and in the darkness she felt for his head and covered it with sand.

Eva could not sleep. She was listening for Hassan's return and as soon as she heard his step she hurried out into the hallway of the villa. She searched his impassive face apprehensively. 'Well?'

'There is no sign of them on the road to Oman,' he said. 'I shall go in search again at first light.'

'Not on the road?' said Eva anxiously. 'Then they must be in the desert – how on earth will they survive the desert at night?'

Hassan shook his head. 'Unless a *shamal* blows up and covers the Land Rover, Patrick will know what to do. There is nothing we can do until daylight.'

Kara appeared at the doorway. Eva saw Hassan raise one eyebrow almost imperceptibly in question, then she turned away and he made to follow her out of the room. Eva seized his elbow.

'I'm coming with you,' she said firmly. 'I want to look for my daughter myself.'

Hassan bowed his head as he disengaged his arm. 'Very well,' he said quietly. 'At first light.'

He disappeared into a private room and Eva loitered. Some sixth sense warned her that something was afoot. She could hear voices murmuring in Hassan's room and crept closer, putting her ear to the wood panelling to listen. Men's voices murmured, but the words were in a language she could not understand. Then a chair scraped, and she hurried away to the stairs.

From the top of the staircase she saw three men emerge, their faces indistinguishable in the folds of their *kuffiyahs*. Hassan ushered them out of the door then turning around he caught sight of Eva.

'Patrick is dead,' he said in an emotionless voice.

Eva caught her breath. 'And Leah?'

'Please Allah your daughter will still be alive.'

There was something odd about his tone. Eva grew suspicious. 'Those men – what did they want? How do you know Patrick is dead?'

Hassan gave a deep sigh. 'If he is not, then he will surely be so by morning. The serpent deals with its own kind in its own way.'

In the morning Leah awoke stiff and painfully sore and still ravenously hungry. She gulped down the small amount of water still mercifully left in the plastic carrier then, trying hard to push from her mind the thought of the corpse outside, she reached for Patrick's rucksack. Maybe she'd find something to eat in there.

She tipped out the contents. Clothes, shoes, papers, a tube of mints, and a roll of thick cloth containing something very heavy, far too heavy to be food. She opened the packet of mints and put one in her mouth. At least the saliva flowed again.

There was a coil of rope under the rucksack. Leah eyed it thoughtfully. Maybe, if she had enough strength, she could make use of it to try to pull the van upright. Better check first whether the ignition worked. It did.

She put another mint in her mouth and turned the papers over, then frowned. Yesterday she had seen a passport with Patrick's photograph in it and a false name. Here was yet another, bearing the name John Hazeldine. She picked up another. It was an Irish passport with his own name, and yet another was an American passport for a Henry Wilbur Trelinski. Every one of them bore Patrick's picture.

What the devil could he have been up to? She flicked over the pages of a small notebook but the handwriting in it was microscopic. She pushed it into her pocket. Right now it was more important to get the van upright while she felt she still had some energy and before the full heat of day made it impossible.

It was useless tying the rope to the roof and pulling from the side furthest from the slope. Panting and aching she sat down on the sand and considered. Maybe if she tied it to the far side of the roof and tried pulling again from this side . . . She watched in fascination as the blisters on her leg started to burst and dribble. If only she could attract attention.

What did the heroes of the old films do in situations like this? Indians made smoke signals – yes, there was a spare can of petrol in the van! Now if there was something to set fire to . . .

It took some effort to unscrew the spare tyre from the rear door then, trying to ignore the pain which seemed to burn all over her body, she dragged it well clear of the Land Rover and lay it flat on its side. The can of petrol was heavier than it looked, but she managed at last to pour it carefully into the tyre rim. Mercifully the cigar lighter still worked, and she dropped it into the tyre and leapt back.

Instantly flames soared into the air. With luck the tyre, its rubber already softened by the heat, would catch fire quickly.

Leah clambered up the slope and stepped over Patrick's body. As she did so she saw his hands, risen clear of the sand and clenched into fists. She shivered. Had this happened after he died, muscle-contraction perhaps, or had he clenched them in his death agony, while she sat unaware in the van? The thought made her shudder, but she tied the rope securely to the roof and went down again to the lower side.

Come on, damn you, come upright, she swore under her breath as she heaved with all her might. I don't want to be stuck in this god-forsaken desert to die like Patrick!

Black smoke began to curl upwards from the fire. Leah gathered all her energy for one last attempt, then heaved, the rope cutting deep into her shoulder as she pulled. Her hands were bleeding, her lips swollen and her strength giving out. Then all at once as she gave a mighty final heave, a hideous pain ripped through her guts like a sabre. She screamed out in agony, clutched at her stomach and fell, unconscious, on the hot sand . . .

Eva peered through the dust-bleared windscreen of Hassan's Range Rover, still desperately hoping for some object to break the monotony of one sand dune after another. A figure, a girl walking alone but safe . . .

For three hours now Hassan had been driving, three of his servants following behind in a Land Rover. Eva could see by his grim expression that as every quarter-hour ticked by, hope of finding Leah alive was growing more and more faint.

'How do you know we're going in the right direction?' she challenged Hassan. 'This bloody desert goes on for ever.'

'The Land Rover was seen in this area,' Hassan answered briefly. 'She cannot be far away.'

Eva bit her lip and fell silent. How the devil he could tell one area from another in this eternity of sand seemed impossible, but he had been brought up here. She would just have to trust that he knew what he was doing . . .

It was growing unbearably hot. Please God the child had water to keep her going. She wouldn't die easily, not Leah. Not without a hell of a fight.

Then suddenly, as if conjured up by hope, something materialized in front of the Range-Rover, a tall, dark line on the horizon.

'Look!' cried Eva. 'Smoke – a signal!'

Hassan swung the wheel round and drove towards it. Within moments they could see it, a raging fire with a great black plume of smoke soaring skywards. Just beyond a large dark shape began to appear. It was a green Land Rover lying on its side.

'That's it!' cried Eva. 'That's Patrick's!'

'Yes.' Hassan slowed and stopped. Eva began to scramble out.

'Aren't you coming?'

'No. Patrick has been dealt with. Your daughter isn't there.'

Eva's hopes fell. 'Let's go and have a look.'

'Because he was once my friend I do not wish to see him dead. If he should still be alive, I cannot save him.'

'Please yourself,' snapped Eva. 'I'm going to take a look. If that swine's harmed my Leah I want to see what the bastard looks like.' Eva stumbled away through the shifting sand towards the Land Rover . . .

Through a searing mist of pain Leah opened her eyes to see a blinding midday sun overhead. She moaned and rolled her head to one side. Fancy, or maybe it was sheer pain, was making her mind play tricks on her again, for there was a black cloud and out of it a woman running towards her across the sand.

Not just a woman – Mother. And behind her a dark, looming shape. It was Thorpe Gill, wasn't it? It must be a mirage again, a dying vision of Barnbeck and all she held dear. She held out her arms to Mother . . .

CHAPTER TWENTY

In a cool, air-conditioned ward of Maktoum Hospital, Eva sat by Leah's bed. Leah leaned back against the pillows, thinking admiringly how striking her mother looked, cool and elegant in a pale green dress with red-gold hair piled high.

It had been reassuring to have her close during the haze of pain. Every time she'd opened her eyes Mother had been there and not once had she spoken a word of reproach. In her silence Leah recognized with gratitude the depth of her love.

At the same time Eva was reflecting how much better her daughter was looking, despite the reddened skin and scabs on her face where horrific blisters had gathered and burst. Only last week she'd been lying desperately weak and ill, drips in her arms and losing blood at a terrible rate. Only a hair's-breadth away from death. Thank God she was young and strong. Though still weak, she looked a picture of health now compared to that awful day . . .

'The client must have been Clay, in spite of the baby,' Leah murmured.

Eva nodded. 'It was. I found the Major's name in that notebook. Patrick was working for him.'

'But why? Clay wanted a son so much.'

'You're dangerous – you overheard too much. Clay hates a weak link in his chain.'

Leah leaned forward and hugged her knees. 'I wonder if he knows I'm still alive, if word's got back to him. If it has –'

Eva gripped her hand. 'We've got to get you away from here, just as soon as you're well enough.'

'Where? Back home? Have you told Nathan and Daddy?'

Eva nodded. 'They were saddened, of course, about the baby, but so long as you're OK . . .'

'Little Maddie,' murmured Leah. 'I did so much want that baby.'

Eva gripped her hand tightly. 'It was a boy, Leah.'

'I know. I was rather looking forward to sending Clay a telegram.

I'd have said "Congratulations, it's a bastard, like you." ' Leah gave a thin smile. 'Patrick must have bribed that girl in the hotel office to get hold of the fax I was sending you.'

Suddenly she sat bolt upright in the high bed, staring over her mother's head towards the door. 'Here comes Renzo,' she muttered. 'Not a word about Clay – or the baby.'

The dapper little figure in a neat grey suit hurried towards the bed, an expression of anxious concern on his dark-featured face. He laid a bunch of wilting flowers on the end of the bed and came to inspect Leah's face closely. Clicking his tongue he touched a finger to her cheek and, satisfied that his assistant was alive, he shook his head.

'Such an ordeal, to be stranded so long in the desert,' he moaned, wringing his slender hands. 'You are so brave, little Leah – never would I go out there, not for a hundred million lire. You might have perished, and a great hotelier of the future would have been lost to the world.'

He rolled his eyes at the enormity of the thought. Leah smiled. 'Thank you, Renzo. I'm fine now. But there's something I must tell you – I shall be leaving Dubai.'

'Oh no! This is too much! It is more than flesh and blood can bear!' Renzo wailed. 'First Mr Richards, now you.'

'What about Richards?' Eva cut in.

Renzo threw up his hands. 'Always he promised me I may pick my own staff, my own people from wherever I choose. Now he tells me I must have this Mr Bryant from Acapulco to be the supplies manager, he calls him. And Mr Bryant must have his own suite on the top floor of the hotel. What kind of hotel is this to be, I ask myself, where an under-manager occupies his own suite? A man I do not know, a man I do not hand-pick? And now, on top of this, you tell me you will leave me, little Leah, the only person I can trust, who understands what a good hotel needs. What am I to do? The world is falling down about my ears!'

Tears were filling his dark eyes and Leah was touched. 'I'm sorry, Renzo, but I tell you this, when I run my own place one day, I'll tell everyone I owe it all to you – you taught me to love the business.'

She could swear he blushed with pleasure, but then she caught sight of her mother's expression, thoughtful and far-away.

'Acapulco,' Eva murmured as Renzo made his farewells. The

moment he'd gone she turned to Leah. 'Where else was Clay setting up Cresco hotels? Acapulco?'

'And Bangkok, San Francisco and Zurich, to start with.'

Eva rubbed her chin. 'And Dubai. Interesting.' She leaned over and patted her daughter's hand. 'I'm going to get you back home and into hiding as quickly as possible where Clay can't find you.'

'Hiding be blowed,' said Leah. 'I want to get on with my life – run my own hotel. And I'm going to find some way to get even with Mr Bloody Richards. Book the tickets as soon as you like.'

Eva's tone was tentative. 'Are you sure you're ready? You were delirious for days and you've lost a lot of blood.'

Leah jutted her chin. 'I'm fine, honestly. I want to get back and teach him a lesson. Then get my plans moving.'

Eva smiled. 'You're really serious about this hotel idea, aren't you?'

'You bet. I'm not going to let Clay Richards foul up my life.'

'That's my girl,' said Eva proudly. 'And I'm with you all the way. We'll bring him down, by God we will. He won't know what's hit him.'

At visiting time that evening Kara came to see Leah, her dark eyes liquid with unshed tears.

'All day the police have been at the villa, asking Hassan questions about Golden Shadow,' she said sadly. 'It gives him much grief to speak of his dead friend.'

'Why, what do they say?'

Kara shrugged. 'They found many passports, and asked if Hassan knew anything of his business. Poor Patrick. I warned him it was in the cards that he might not live to enjoy his wealth. The cards knew he was a man with two faces.'

'Was he wealthy?'

'Hassan says they found gold in the Land Rover, much gold. He was not to know that a sandviper would end his days so swiftly.'

Leah watched the girl's bent shoulders as she walked away down the ward. Clearly Kara did not suspect that the bite of the sandviper might not have been an accident. Mother did.

'Hassan knew he would be dead or dying. He said he couldn't save him if he was still alive. Could be some kind of Arab ritual vengeance, don't you think, an eye for an eye?'

That was it. Somehow they'd known that Patrick had killed the Arab whose body was found floating in the Creek. They'd seen to it that justice was carried out. Now it was Clay Richards' turn.

The Major was uneasy as he waited for Richards in the little park surrounded by railings in a London square. It was one place where they could be assured of privacy.

This time the Major was not looking forward to the interview. Patrick hadn't yet rung him to report mission accomplished. Repeated calls to his apartment and his office had failed to get any reply, no matter what hour of day the Major had tried. Something must be wrong. And any minute now Richards would be demanding a report and he was a man not accustomed to waiting, and even less to failure.

The Major reproved himself sharply – failure was not a word in his vocabulary either. He put on a smile as he strolled around the herbaceous borders with Richards.

'Don't worry – Patrick's very reliable,' he said smoothly.

'Aren't you concerned that you haven't heard from him?' Richards' tone was equable enough. The Major measured his step to match his companion's and shrugged.

'He did say he had to go to Oman – spot of bother, I understand – but he'll see to it. He's never let me down yet. The problem will be disposed of, I assure you.'

Richards stopped and turned to face him. 'I had a call from Rosconi. The problem is arriving back in England at midnight tomorrow.'

The Major felt his stomach turn over. 'You mean – the girl?'

'Rosconi was delighted she'd survived the desert. Just make certain you do not fail in the next attempt.'

Richards turned away and headed towards the gate. 'Her mother's with her,' he added quietly. 'She probably knows too much now. An accident, Major, both of them. No police asking questions.'

They reached the gate and the Major stopped. 'Her mother? How many others in her family might she have told?'

Richards' tone was irritable. 'How would *I* know?'

'This could grow – it could get out of hand.'

Richards wasn't listening. As he strode away down the street the Major heard him add, 'Rosconi said her companion died in the desert. Snakebite. I think maybe you need a new courier.'

Stunned, the Major watched the tall, erect figure disappear round the corner of the square and bit his lip reflectively. He couldn't afford another failure. Maybe it was time to call in the top brass.

Hennessy sat on a bench in the airport terminal, a neat, inconspicuous figure reading the *Evening Standard*. Over the loudspeaker a woman's nasal voice announced the arrival of the flight from Paris. Hennessy looked at his wristwatch. Midnight – it was dead on time.

He folded his newspaper meticulously and tucked it under his arm before rising from the bench and making his way towards the barrier.

He was to look for a twenty-two-year-old blonde accompanied by her redhead mother. The girl might well be showing the signs of recent severe sunburn. He didn't question why they were to be eradicated or what they had done. It wasn't important. His job was simply to carry out the Major's orders. He never questioned anything – that was why he was still in business. No emotion necessary. Fifty-one now. Within the year he could retire to his little place in Norfolk with the greenhouse, grow chrysanths and photograph wildfowl like he'd always wanted. And buy the white Mercedes. Not long now . . .

He stood unobtrusively among all the others waiting by the barrier for relatives and friends. In dribs and drabs the passengers started to appear, two Arabs followed by a group of youngsters, evidently French students, an English family of holidaymakers keeping a wary distance from a nun. One by one they were claimed with eager cries or silent embraces. Then a gap – and then a good-looking redhead holding the arm of a young blonde. The blonde's face was patchily red and the bridge of her nose still scabbed. This was undoubtedly the hit. All he had to do now was follow them until the right moment came. There was a time and a place for everything, including death.

A movement caught Hennessy's eye. A young man, head and shoulders taller than the rest, pushed his way to the front of the crowd. Something was familiar about him – big, burly, built like a wrestler – the description the Major had given of the Martin Black he was to look out for. This was surely him.

Hennessy watched as Black strode forward and engulfed the blonde in his arms. The red-headed mother stood watching with a smile. Well, well . . . This was a turn-up for the book. The Major had been so impressed by Black, having him followed and checked all this time.

Hennessy would have shot him at the outset but the Major wouldn't listen. Now the fellow was likely to prove troublesome.

At last Nathan held Leah at arm's length. 'You all right?' he asked gruffly.

Leah nodded dumbly. Eva could see the tears in her eyes. 'Right,' said Eva as Nathan steered them towards the exit. 'Where to? Not my place.'

'Alan's – he's waiting for us.'

As they drove through London's rain-dark streets towards Chelsea, Eva could see that her daughter was clearly moved. She was looking out into the darkness, watching in silence the reflection of lamplight on wet pavements. She was happy to be home again in England.

Alan's restuarant had closed for the night but he was waiting eagerly for them. As they reached the bottom of the basement steps he hurried to the door to meet them. Eva saw his dark eyes cloud as he surveyed their daughter's ravaged face closely before folding her in his arms. He reached out and drew Eva into the embrace, silently holding the two women close. Nathan stood on the bottom step, raindrops clinging to his hair.

'I'm starving,' he grumbled. 'What's to eat?'

Laughing, they broke the embrace and went inside to sit down at a centre table, the four of them alone in a pool of candlelight. Eva watched her husband as he served out spaghetti bolognaise from a large bowl. His thoughtful eyes and the way he inclined his head made her heart quicken, just as it had in those far-off days. Then it had been just Alan and herself who'd sat like this, here in this same room, planning a golden future . . .

She jerked her mind back to the conversation. Alan and Leah were talking of her future plans.

'A hotel – and I know just the place. Thorpe Gill.'

'Thorpe Gill? But it's almost derelict,' said Alan.

'Run down,' said Nathan. 'It needs a bit spending on it.'

'Which means I could get it cheap,' said Leah.

Eva watched the candlelit faces of the three people she loved most in the world. There they sat, talking in animated voices about the future, momentarily forgetful of the immediate problem. Just like schoolkids, she thought, planning the summer holidays while determinedly ignoring the end-of-term exams. She was loath to break into their good humour, but reality had to be faced. 'You won't have much of a future unless we get this business sorted out,' she said. 'Clay will be looking for you. Does he know your home's in Barnbeck?'

'Not from me. I only talked of Yorkshire.'

The solution seemed obvious; Leah should hide at Scapegoat with Nathan. Eva was reluctant to let her out of her sight yet. Nathan cleared his throat.

'I've got business to finish in London.'

'Right,' said Alan. 'Leah can stay here at the restaurant. I've got a couple of rooms for when I'm working late.'

'The second place Clay will look, after my flat,' said Eva.

'Just for tonight,' said Alan. 'What about you, Eva?'

Eva seemed far away, in a reverie. 'I think we should tell the police what we know about Richards.'

'They aren't going to pay much attention, Mother,' argued Leah. 'No witnesses, no proof.'

Eva was looking up at Alan. 'Do you still have policemen among your customers, Alan – someone I could talk to, off the record? Just for advice?'

Alan considered as he stacked up the empty plates. 'There's the commander – he's something in Scotland Yard. Not a bad idea. I'll get in touch with him tomorrow.'

Leah was looking pale and tired. Alan pushed back his chair and stood up. 'Time to sleep. Coming, Leah?'

Nathan took car keys out of his pocket as they stood up. Eva looked at Alan, reluctant to leave. 'I'll stay here,' she said.

She saw Nathan's eyebrows rise. There was a hint of a smile in Alan's dark eyes. 'I'm not leaving Leah tonight,' she said defensively, 'not after coming this far.'

Leah smiled. After Nathan had gone Eva watched her daughter prepare for bed and once she was safely under the duvet she closed the door quietly. Alan was still in the kitchen. Eva leaned against the counter watching him.

'She's very keen on this hotel idea,' he remarked as he dried his hands.

'It must be in the blood. She gets it from you.'

'Wherever she gets it from, I'm glad. We mustn't stand in her way.'

'You mean me. I won't. If she's found what she wants, I'll back her.'

He put his arm around Eva's shoulders and led her from the kitchen.

'Maybe we could help her out financially,' he murmured. 'It would be great to see old Thorpe Gill restored to its former glory.'

She looked up at him, anxiety plain in her eyes. 'I can't think seriously yet about that, Alan. I'm still worried sick about Clay – he's up to something big, I'm sure he is, and I'm worried what he might do to Leah. I've got this feeling –'

Alan's tone was pensive. 'I remember that night you were convinced you saw someone looking in at us.' He nodded towards the window by the basement steps. 'Remember?'

She looked at the window, and shivered. 'I was right, if you recall.' She shivered again. He pulled her closer.

'I'm glad you're staying the night.'

'So am I.'

It was as Alan was leading her into the bedroom that Eva gave another convulsive shudder. Alan looked at her questioningly, a hint of a frown on his face. She shook her head.

'Look, I know it sounds stupid,' she said, crossing to the window and drawing back the curtain, 'but I've got that same queer feeling again. I feel somebody is watching us, out there in the dark.'

Turning, she saw Alan had peeled off his shirt and was coming to her with outstretched arms. Just like so many times in the past she let him enfold her and buried her face in the warmth of his chest.

Commander Oxshott sat next day in Alan's office, legs neatly crossed and plucking gently at the crease of his trousers, listening intently to Eva's account. Leah sat watching his face.

'Well?' said Eva. 'Is there anything you can do?'

'We've no evidence,' added Leah, 'but we could try to get some.'

The Commander shook his head. 'No. Leave that to us. We've been interested in your Mr Richards for some time, but he's a shrewd customer. He takes care to leave no tracks.'

'So what can we do?'

'Nothing – yet.'

'But he damn nearly killed my daughter – and he's killed before. You can't just do nothing,' cried Eva. 'For heaven's sake, what have we got a police force for?'

The Commander leaned across Alan's desk and took a sheet of paper and a pen and began to write. 'As your daughter rightly remarked, Mrs Finch, there is little evidence we can usefully put forward to prosecute. But we'll keep an eye on him. In the meantime,' he paused to fold the sheet of paper, 'I would strongly recommend that you and your daughter go home to Yorkshire. And if you should hear anything or have any bother,' he paused again to hand the sheet of paper to Eva, 'just ring this number. It'll come directly through to me.'

Eva accompanied him to the door. Leah held up a hand. 'Just one other thing – the hotels.'

'Ah yes,' said Eva. 'I don't know if it's significant, but Richards is opening five hotels all at once in five different continents. So far apart, it can hardly be commercially viable – but if I know Clay Richards, there must be a reason.'

Leah saw the gleam of interest in the Commander's eyes. 'Really?' he said, taking out his notebook again. 'Tell me where they are?'

After he had gone Eva turned to her daughter. 'I wonder,' she said thoughtfully, 'Acapulco and San Francisco, Bangkok and Zurich. What's Dubai famous for?'

'Oil – and gold.'

'Hmm. I wonder what Clay's up to. Whatever it is, it's got to be something big. If only we could get a look at his personal file.'

'No chance. He keeps it under lock and key in the office.'

Bryant was leaning over the parapet of his balcony to survey the lie of the land. From this vantage point he had an excellent view of the main road out of Dubai and also the sweep of the Creek. The bulldozers were all gone now and only the paraphernalia of plasterers and electricians still spattered the ground in front of the hotel. Very soon now it would all be ready to start business.

It was too hot out here; he turned back into the cool of the bedroom and kicked off his shoes. As he pulled his sweat-soaked shirt out from his trousers and flapped it around his thin body, the telephone rang. He picked it up.

'Bryant? How's it going? On schedule?'

He recognized Richards' aggressive tone. 'Yep.'

'Any problems?'

'Only Rosconi. He's fussing round like an old woman.'

'Forget him. When can we start moving stuff down the line?'

'I'm going to need another month. I've got to tie up the supplier then get over to Switzerland.'

'Made sure the compartment's foolproof?'

Bryant took a cheroot out of a packet and reached into his pocket for a lighter. 'The priest-hole? I've got my builders in now – that's what Rosconi's fussing about.'

'You're sure he doesn't suspect anything? It's got to be completely undetectable.'

Bryant lit the cheroot and inhaled deeply. He lifted the 'phone from the table and, pulling the length of cable clear from the legs, walked through into the adjoining bathroom. 'Safe as houses. Leads off the bathroom, behind a one-way mirror.'

'Big enough?'

'Of course. I know my job. I've been doing it long enough.'

He heard Richards' impatient sigh. 'When are you expecting the first – ah – first cleric?'

Bryant frowned. 'The what? Ah, priest, yes. Everything will be ready in a month.'

The voice at the other end was sharp. 'Three weeks.'

Bryant bit the end of his cheroot. The tooth with the loose filling he'd been meaning to have seen to shrieked with pain. He clutched the side of his face. 'If I say a month I mean a month,' he snapped. 'I've stayed alive in this business because I plan in detail. I know exactly what I'm doing – all I need from you is your money.'

He heard Richards slam down the 'phone. Stupid, interfering idiot. He wasn't used to anyone arguing with him. He'd have to learn patience if he was going to succeed at this game.

Bryant kicked at the full-length mirror on the bathroom wall with his socked foot, sending the mirror-door flying inwards. Inside, in a dark, windowless cell of a room, he could see the bunk bed, a toilet and sink and the telephone with a red light indicator. It wasn't the Cresco's finest suite, but it was adequate for a man on a short stay with a valuable package.

Clay Richards poured himself a whisky and soda. His palms were sweating. What the devil had he got himself into? He'd never handled anything as big as this before. This was one time when he couldn't mastermind what was going on – he had to hand over to those who knew the trade inside out. But Bryant wasn't an easy man to deal with; experts, it seemed, weren't all as biddable as Rosconi.

His palms were still clammy as he downed the last of the whisky.

He was playing for damned high stakes this time; he couldn't afford to lose.

But give it time. Inside twelve months he'd know all there was to know about this game, and then he'd show them.

CHAPTER TWENTY-ONE

It had not been a good day for the Major and now Hennessy was on the line. He was making it even worse.

'They were met at the airport by that Martin Black you were on about. Foolish of you, Major.'

He didn't need to be told. Intelligence had already discovered for him that the Black character fitted exactly the description of one Nathan Bower, half-brother to the girl's mother. He told Hennessy.

'So he too needs to be eliminated,' Hennessy's cold voice stated calmly.

'Oh for heaven's sake,' said the Major testily, 'we're not in the wholesale business.'

'There's no other way. He's got to go,' said Hennessy firmly.

The Major clicked his tongue. 'We can't start wars. We lose wars. We're snipers, picking people off one by one.'

'Then here's another one for you,' Hennessy remarked drily. 'They've talked to a Scotland Yard man.'

The Major's jaw sagged. 'You're sure?'

'I saw him go into the restaurant while it was closed. Stayed an hour.'

'What the devil do we do now? Wipe out the whole damn police force?'

'If it comes to that. I'll start with the family. All at one go, that's the neatest way. Would be more satisfying to pick them off one by one, but you can't have everything. Pity.'

'How will you deal with them all at once?'

Hennessy's tone was reflective. 'That needs thought. It could be a bomb thrown into the restaurant –'

'God, no – that could kill many others!'

'– which would be put down to terrorists,' Hennessy went on imperturbably. 'It's the only place I'm likely to find all of them together.'

There was a sick feeling at the pit of the Major's stomach as he hung up the telephone and re-dialled. Matters were getting out of hand, and so was Hennessy. He had a strange feeling that this was the beginning of the end, that the palmy days of captaining his own highly efficient and successful mercenary force could be coming to an end. And if it did, it would bring everything to light. The whole catalogue of crimes he'd master-minded along with clients like Richards. After his death it wouldn't matter – in fact it was inevitable once his papers at the solicitor's office were read, but to happen now . . . He was still shuddering when he heard someone lift the 'phone at the other end.

'Richards speaking.'

He could take no pleasure in telling Richards about what had happened. His client was clearly displeased.

'And I fear Hennessy is getting out of hand,' he wound up miserably. 'He seems to have got the blood lust.'

'My God, I thought I could trust you to pick the right man. Can't you reprimand him, punish him or something?'

'He's not listening to reason any more.'

'You've got to bring him back into line. If he goes around killing all and sundry we'll all end up in the soup.'

'It's no good, Richards. I can't stop him. He's out of control.'

Vincent Galbraith sat on the opposite side of Eva's desk, watching her expression as he talked. She didn't appear to be paying as much attention as usual; her trip out to Dubai must have been very distracting.

'So I've had to go through the contract for the lease in fine detail with Cresco's solicitor,' he wound up, pushing the stray lock of hair away from his spectacles.

'Lease? Why, what's wrong?'

'Nothing really. I think your friend Mr Richards is just trying to make life difficult. The contract was finalized before he bought out the company so there's little he can do.'

'That's right, that's his ploy,' said Eva. 'Well, he'll soon find out people can make life equally difficult for him.'

The telephone on Eva's desk rang. 'Mother? Nathan's agreed to leave whatever it was he was going to do and drive us north tomorrow.'

'Good. I'll come up with you for a day or two.'

'But there's something I want to do first – meet me for lunch, will you? I've got an idea.'

'I'm not so sure this is a good idea after all,' Eva muttered as she drove down the street where Cresco's headquarters stood. 'It could be damn dangerous if Clay were to come back to the office – you know he sometimes does at night.'

'Not tonight,' said Leah. 'It's his club night. And since I've still got a key it strikes me as a damn good idea to try and get at that file. You're only jealous because you didn't think of it yourself.'

Eva changed down the gear and slowed to a halt. 'Well OK, but I'm coming in with you.'

'Dope – I need you outside to keep watch. Look – you can see the night porter from here through the glass. If he leaves his desk and follows me, rush in and ring his bell. That'll get him off my back.'

'But how will I know you're OK? Suppose Clay's up there after all?'

'He won't be. Anyway, if I'm not out in fifteen minutes, go and get help.'

Eva sighed as she watched her daughter climb out of the car and run across the road and into the porticoed building. Through the enormous plate-glass windows she saw her cross the foyer towards the lifts.

'Evening, Arthur.'

The night porter pulled off his spectacles and looked up from his newspaper. 'Miss Finch – what are you doing here? You're not on my authorized list.'

Leah swung round with a smile. ''Course not – I've been out in Dubai, haven't I, running the office there? Anyway, I shan't be a couple of minutes. I only need one or two things.'

The porter looked dubious. 'I'm sorry, Miss Finch –'

Leah frowned. 'Look here, are you prepared to tell Mr Richards you wouldn't let me in?'

Arthur gave a deep sigh. 'Sign the book then.'

Leah did so, conscious of his stare at her blemished face. 'Sunburn,' she said briefly as she straightened. 'Mad dogs and Englishmen . . .'

Arthur returned to his *Evening Standard*. Leah breathed a sigh of relief as the lift carried her up to the floor where she found Clay's office mercifully in darkness. She unlocked the door and went in, closing it softly behind her.

The middle drawer of his desk was where he kept private files. It was locked, and she no longer had the key. However hard she tugged or prised with a steel letter-opener, the drawer would not budge.

There must be some way. She looked about for a tool to break in, and then she saw it – the half-size silver hammer resplendent on its oak stand on the polished surface of Clay's desk. She hardly glanced

222

at the inscription. *Presented to Clay Richards on the occasion of laying the final brick of Cresco Sunset Home.* She had only a fleeting memory of him tapping the last brick into place, the admiring faces of local dignitaries, as she crawled under the desk and began attacking the underside of the drawer.

She could feel her heart pounding as the hammer crashed home and the wood began to splinter. It was impossible to do the job silently. Any minute now someone could hear and come to investigate. Speed – she must get those papers and get out of here as quickly as she could.

At last, with a crash the bottom fell out of the drawer, sending papers flying to the floor. Leah scooped them together – no time to go through them – and reached for her bag. Damn – too small to hold them. A briefcase, there on the chair. That would do perfectly.

Seizing it she tipped the contents out on the floor – make-up, a hairbrush, a half-eaten sandwich, a pair of tights, a pack of condoms and a glossy women's magazine. They said a lot about Clay's new assistant. Leah began sifting out the papers from among the wood fragments and pushing them into the briefcase.

Eva watched impatiently from the car. She ought to be up there with Leah instead of just sitting here, doing nothing. At least the night porter was still deeply engrossed in his newspaper so Leah had time to get what she wanted.

A double-decker bus drew up, cutting off her view. Eva drummed her fingertips impatiently on the steering wheel. When the bus pulled away the porter was gone.

She leapt out of the car and ran across the road, heedless of an alarmed motorist's frantic hooting on his horn and the squeal of his brakes as he swerved, swearing, to a halt.

Leah was still under the desk scooping up papers, most of them covered with figures, into the briefcase when the office door suddenly opened and her heart leapt. Arthur stood there, blinking and scratching his head with the pencil he always kept ready behind his ear for his daily crossword. From where he stood he could see only Leah's head, not the shattered fragments of the drawer.

'What's going on?'

Leah scrambled up. 'I dropped my handbag – everything fell out.'

'Oh, let me help you.' He was crossing the carpet towards her and

Leah felt panic rising. He must see her handbag, sitting there complete on Clay's desk. A shrill sound cut into the silence.

'Dammit,' muttered Arthur. 'Me bleeper – somebody's downstairs. Now who the hell can that be . . .?'

To Leah's relief he went away, still muttering to himself. All the papers now safely stowed in the briefcase, Leah composed herself to make an exit.

Arthur was licking the pencil, eyes gleaming as he prepared to enter the answer to the clue which had been eluding him all evening. 'Everything OK, Arthur?' asked Leah as she breezed past him.

'Fine,' he nodded, 'only some dozy American woman here a minute ago. Smashing looking she was, but thick as two short planks. Kept insisting this was the American Club. Wanted to know where the party was.'

'They're all the same,' Leah called over her shoulder. 'See you, Arthur.'

'Got what you wanted, Miss?'

'I think so. Goodnight.'

Early next morning Nathan was at the wheel of Eva's car as they sped northwards up the motorway. Leah sat alone in the back seat, feeling a sense of relief gradually easing the tension in her body as London slipped further and further behind them. Clay's fury when he discovered his personal papers gone would make his thirst for revenge unquenchable. He would not rest until he had recovered them and punished the thief.

Nathan was quiet. Mother was talking to fill the silence. 'I'm glad you agreed to leave that unfinished business, Nathan. I think I can guess what it was – and it can wait. Ah, let's stop at the Blue Boar for a cup of coffee and then I'll drive for a while.'

Hennessy drew up in the car park of the service station and switched off the engine. He watched the three figures disappear inside and took out a flask of coffee from the glove compartment. Easing the neck of the blue-grey sweater he was wearing he took a swig from the plastic cup. He was ready for a break. There was serious work ahead, but not yet. They'd stop again before they reached Yorkshire. This time it would be coffee – next time they'd eat. That would give him the chance he needed. He could be patient until then . . .

224

A couple of hours later Hennessy's patience was rewarded. The girl, her mother and the Black fellow went into the service station and from the doorway Hennessy watched them fill their trays. Good – this was the opportunity he'd waited for.

He checked his road map. Within the next eight miles there were three exits. Hennessy refolded the map and put it away. Then he took the device carefully from his own car and walked across to the white Mercedes he'd been following since leaving Chelsea early this morning. It was locked. He could open a car door within seconds – a Mercedes took a little longer.

In the restaurant Leah could find little appetite for the liver and bacon. Excitement and apprehension filled her. She was anxious to be home again in Scapegoat.

Mother was eating chicken casserole with relish. Nathan appeared to be eating slowly but had already nearly finished. Leah looked down at the liver and bacon on her plate and smiled apologetically at Nathan.

'I'm sorry – I can't eat. No appetite, I'm afraid.'

Nathan smiled. 'Don't apologize. I'm just going to fetch my cigarettes – I've left them in the car.'

Eva looked up. 'Since when have you started smoking again?'

'Since this business began. Won't be a minute.'

Nathan sauntered out into the sunlight, then stopped in surprise. The bonnet of Eva's car was raised, and he could see a man's trousered legs, his head concealed by the bonnet. He hurried across the tarmac.

'Here – what are you doing?'

The man's face emerged, a thin, dispassionate face with pockmarks. As he straightened Nathan saw the RAC patrol uniform sweater and trousers.

'I saw smoke coming from under your bonnet, sir. I decided I ought to have a look.'

'How did you open it?' Nathan demanded, but the man was bending again over the engine.

'See here what I found.' Nathan stepped forward. As he lowered his height to duck under the bonnet the little man stood up. 'I'll go round the other side,' he said.

Some sixth sense warned Nathan, but too late. All he was aware of was a sudden, head-splitting explosion when the bonnet crashed down on the back of his head, driving his face into the engine.

A heavy weight lay across his neck. Nathan heaved the bonnet up and through the crack he saw the man's feet running.

He rubbed his face. Blood was seeping from a cut on his cheek. The bastard – he'd been trying to steal Eva's car. Nathan felt anger beginning to burn in him. He turned round and saw the man jump into a beige Sierra.

Nathan started to run towards it. The car leapt into life and sped away. A toddler scrambled out of a car just as his young mother had parked. The Sierra swerved past him and tore on. The mother screamed.

Nathan could catch glimpses of the car as it tore round the back of the car park and then it disappeared towards the slip road. The mother had snatched up the child and was hugging him close, slapping his legs and crying. Nathan wove his way down to her through the ranks of cars.

'It's all right, love,' he soothed. 'The little chap's fine.'

The woman looked up at him, her pretty face tear-stained. 'You're hurt,' she said, 'your face . . .'

Before Nathan could answer an almighty explosion shattered the sunlit peace of the afternoon. Nathan felt the force of the blast hurl him off his feet and throw him to the ground, his bulk spread over the woman and child. For a moment he lay, gasping and winded.

He staggered to his feet and pulled the woman up. She and the child were unhurt.

'Christ Almighty,' she moaned. 'Look!'

Nathan stared in disbelief. Cars lay twisted and mangled everywhere; of Eva's car nothing remained but a heap of blazing junk. From somewhere a woman's voice was crying out in pain. Nathan ran back towards the restaurant.

'Leah! Eva! For Christ's sake, Leah!'

A mile away from the service station Hennessy was speeding up the northbound fast lane. Suddenly it came, the sound he'd been expecting, a reverberating boom like a distant bomb.

Death and damnation. His plan had misfired. What on earth had provoked that hulking great oaf to come out just when he did? Just two minutes more and the timing device would have been set, timed

226

to go off when they were all on the road again. Now he'd failed to accomplish his mission. And worse than that, if Black was still alive he could give the police a description of him.

Hell. Still he had planned for every eventuality. He'd have to dump the Sierra and get another car in Worksop. And then he'd keep an ear to the radio for a newsflash.

The Commander looked down at the file bulging with sheets of paper which had just been shoved in his hand, then looked up again at Alan enquiringly.

'How did you come by these?'

Alan shrugged. 'Does it matter, so long as they give you the information you need?'

The Commander's eyes narrowed. 'Did you steal these from Richards?'

'What makes you ask that? Has he reported them stolen?'

'No.'

'Then just have a look at them. I can't make head or tail of them – just a mass of figures – but maybe your boffins will. You could be thanking me yet, Commander.'

The Major lay on his bed, trying to take his usual after-dinner doze. But sleep wouldn't come. What the devil could he do now? With his chief assassin gone crazy, matters had got totally out of hand.

That report on the radio about a bomb at a service station on the motorway – was it just a coincidence that Hennessy had talked of bombs? And what had the fellow's last words to the Major been? *'If I don't get them at the restaurant, Major, I'll get them in the car.'*

The evening newspapers had been full of it, the dozen people killed or maimed, none of them yet named, and the pictures of the mangled wreckage of cars, but not one had suggested that it could be put down to the IRA. The police were in possession of certain evidence, they said, but at the moment they were not prepared to give a statement.

It must be Hennessy. He seemed to be getting obsessed with the idea of wholesale murder. The wretch was probably revelling in the gory detail right now.

Police investigation would be sure to be thorough – Hennessy couldn't hope to get away with it. And it wasn't only himself he'd bring down with this crazy attack. Richards was right; his judgement of the man had been at fault, and he'd always prided himself on his ability to assess the qualities of a good soldier.

And what if Hennessy had failed, and the girl and her mother still lived? She knew too much before – if she'd survived a bomb attack she'd be sure to tell the police her life had already been threatened and by whom. If she was dead, well and good. If not, the police could be knocking at his door any second.

The clock in the hall struck the hour. The Major rolled off the bed and switched on the television for the news.

There it was – service station disaster. The Major sat on the edge of the bed and watched the scenes of devastation. *Five dead, nine seriously injured . . . A man is now helping police with their enquiries. His name has not been revealed.*

Hennessy. The Major's head sank between his hands. The newscaster's voice went on. *'Those listed as dead are . . .'* The Major lifted his head, waiting for the names. Finch and Bower, he prayed. But there was no Finch or Bower. His head sank back into his hands.

The shame of exposure was inevitable. It would mean photographs in the press of himself amid the Cabinet ministers and bishops, the peers and judges also brought low. And if he died it would all be revealed by the papers he'd left in the solicitor's hands. Those papers had been his insurance policy. Who knew just when an unscrupulous client like Richards might take it into his head to eliminate all danger? Death held no fear for the Major, but he'd been determined that if he had to go suddenly then all the upstarts and hypocrites were damn well going to go down with him. Violent death or peaceful, Laverick could be trusted to see to it that those papers reached the press and police the moment the Major ceased to be.

Either way he couldn't face it. No, that was the one sure thing in his life – he didn't want to be there.

The Major got up off the bed and opened the wardrobe, taking out his best dress uniform and hanging it on the doorknob. He brushed it down carefully, inch by inch, then did a sharp about-turn and marched through into the bathroom to take a long, thorough shower and shave.

Nathan was growing impatient. For hours now they'd been questioned about the man in the RAC uniform and he could see Leah was growing wan and tired. The service station was still alive with activity; police

228

officers in uniform and plain clothes were everywhere, as well as men he took to be from the bomb squad.

There was a well-spoken man they said was from Scotland Yard. He was very civil and kept them informed. He told Nathan they'd circulated the description of the man he called Hennessy. The car registration number proved useless – within an hour of the explosion they'd found it abandoned – in Worksop.

'But we're contacting all the hire-car agencies – we'll come up with something,' the senior man said confidently. 'Now let's see about getting you home.'

'Get me a hire car – we can go on our own,' said Nathan.

'Not when there's already been two attacks on the young lady's life,' said the Scotland Yard man. 'We'll give you an escort, just to be on the safe side.'

Nathan sat in tight-lipped silence as the police car took them home to Barnbeck. More than anything he wanted to be on the road, finding Hennessy. It meant wringing it out of the Major, but he couldn't leave Eva and Leah, not now.

His face was grim as the tarmac miles sped by under the wheels of the police car. Leah's head was leaning against his shoulder, her hair tickling his cheek alongside the Elastoplast, and he thought she was asleep. Eva sat wide-awake and voluble on his other side.

'If it was the Major's doing, I'd like to get my hands round that bastard's throat,' she was muttering to herself.

'Hennessy,' murmured Nathan. 'It would be Hennessy. I'll kill that devil when I find him.'

Eva nodded, gazing out of the window over the dark moors. 'That's just what Alan said. I rang him, just to let him know we're OK.'

Silence fell again until the police car pulled up at the gates of Scapegoat Farm. Leah was half-asleep as Nathan accompanied her indoors. As they went into the living room he could hear Eva's voice behind him, down at the gate, saying goodnight to the policemen. Leah sank onto the settee, yawning.

By the time Eva came in Leah was already asleep. Eva smiled. 'The local police are going to keep an eye on the place,' she whispered to Nathan. 'The others have gone.'

She went on into the kitchen and Nathan heard her switch the kettle on. He stood looking down at Leah. She looked so peaceful, so vulnerable, her face as innocent as a child's in sleep. Slowly, as gently as he could, he dropped a delicate kiss on her nose. In her sleep she smiled, and he felt as if his heart would burst with the sheer beauty of her. And to think that that devil Richards wanted to destroy such beauty . . . As he stared out of the window into the night, fury and raging helplessness burned in Nathan's soul.

Night was falling as Alan drove in search of the Major's house. From him he'd find out where to lay hands on Hennessy. It might be difficult to make him speak, but speak he damn well would before he had done with him.

It was Hennessy's doing, that massacre near Worksop today. Innocent people killed and maimed because of a bastard like him. And he'd have killed his lovely Leah and Eva too. The thought made him feel sick.

It was dark and the suburban side street deserted when Alan pulled up at last outside the Major's house. He jumped out of the car and hurried up the path to the front door, ringing the bell repeatedly. No one answered.

He walked across the flowerbed and was standing knee high in antirrhinums, trying to peer in at the window, when he saw the lace curtains next door twitching. Then the door opened a crack and a woman's cultured voice spoke through the darkness.

'He is in – I heard the most frightful bang a minute or two ago. Sounded like furniture falling over to me. Dreadful noise.'

Right. If he was in, Alan was going to see him – he hadn't come this far to be thwarted now. He rang the bell several more times while the neighbour retreated to her vantage point behind the lace curtains to watch. Still no sound from within. Alan stood back, flexing his shoulder muscles. He could do with Nathan's help right now. Then an inconsequential thought crossed his mind, and he tried the handle on the door. It turned and opened.

The house was in total darkness. Not a light glimmered in the hallway, the parlour, or the kitchen. Alan thrust open the door of the remaining ground floor room and stepped in. His foot slithered on something wet and slimy.

He snapped on the light switch, and then wished he hadn't. The door, the walls and the carpeted floor were all spattered with a gleaming crimson substance; one patch of it slid silently down the wall to the skirting board as he stared, mesmerized. And lying across the desk sprawled a khaki-uniformed figure with the back of his head completely blown away. Blood was still seeping from the gaping hole, rippling down over the revolver before him.

Alan had never seen anything quite so dead as the Major. Picking his way carefully across the carpet he reached over, retching, for the telephone on the desk.

CHAPTER TWENTY-TWO

Hennessy was alone on the station. He sat in the photo booth, the curtains drawn, sifting through the wallets in his case.

There were five wallets in all, each one containing a passport, a cheque book, a cheque card and a driving licence, and each one bearing a different name. Like the bundle of banknotes, they formed an integral part of his stock-in-trade, just as indispensable as his weapons.

He opened the first wallet and inspected the driving licence. John McMahon – no, he'd used that one to hire the second car. And the Faversham cheque book and card he'd used at the hotel last night. He must keep throwing the police off the scent.

Through a gap in the curtains he could see an elderly woman with a little girl in a Brownie uniform coming this way. She paused outside the booth, digging deep into her handbag.

'Won't take a minute, love, only Granny needs some new snaps – for me bus pass, you know.'

Hennessy pushed all but one of the wallets back into his case, glanced at his wristwatch and came out. The woman didn't even look at him as she brushed past him and eased herself into the cubicle.

'There was no suicide note,' the Commander told Alan, 'just a note-book. There was an H in it, no name, just H and a telephone number. If it's traced to Hennessy . . .'

'Let me know when you find out.'

'Leave him to us, Alan. We'll deal with him.'

'He's mad, he's bloody dangerous and he's still on the loose,' Alan protested. 'No one is safe –'

'We're on his track. We found the car he hired in Worksop abandoned near Wakefield.'

'Wakefield? That's too damn near Barnbeck for comfort.'

'We'll get him, Alan.'

'And Richards – anything happened about those papers?'

The Commander shook his head. 'Not a lot.' He glanced up and added quietly, 'Look, I didn't tell you this if anyone asks, but those figures – they're the numbers of companies registered at Company House – a meat packaging company, a garment manufacturer and a cement company, among others.'

Alan frowned. 'So what does that tell you?'

The Commander shrugged. 'He's up to something. They could be covering other activities but we have no evidence. We just have to bide our time and hope he plays into our hands.'

Alan considered. 'You think the Cresco hotels could be a cover for something else then?'

'They could be – drugs perhaps. We're watching his house, seeing who calls, just waiting for him to make a false move.'

A neatly inconsequential little man followed the breezy salesman out of the office and across the yard to where a newly-cleaned Mercedes gleamed in the sunlight.

'There's your driving licence and receipt, Mr Hennessy. Lucky we had the Merc in since you say you'd set your heart on one for your trip.'

Hennessy's step faltered. 'Oh – it's blue. I really wanted a white one.'

The young man spread his hands. 'Sorry, Mr Hennessy. This is all we have. Let me show you the controls.'

He slid into the seat and began his spiel. Hennessy sat listening patiently. 'Here's the headlight switch, and this is the bonnet release.'

'Yes,' said Hennessy. 'I know where the bonnet release is.'

The young man smiled. 'Well, I think that's all. Here's the keys, sir, and there's a full tank. Have a good trip, Mr Hennessy. Bon voyage, as they say.'

The salesman watched the car as it glided away down the street and then went back into the office. Funny how little men with nothing about them always went for the big cars . . .

Leah was enjoying the feeling of being home again, walking around the farm, rubbing the horses' muzzles, breathing in the scent of leather and hay. It gave her particular pleasure to stand by the ancient dry-stone wall surrounding the farm, fingering its rough texture as she looked out over the fields. There was comfort, reassurance in the solid permanence of it.

The local policeman pacing the lane beyond the wall nodded a greeting. 'Evening, Miss Finch.'

She leaned her elbows on the wall. A real pretty lass she was, thought the policeman, only a year or so older than his own daughter.

'You know what,' she said softly, 'more than anything I'd like to ride up on the moor. Feel the clean wind in my face –'

'Nay,' he interrupted, 'we'll have none of that. You'll have to stay in. I'm not a mounted policeman, you know.'

He gave an awkward smile. 'Best if you stay here where I can keep an eye on you,' he added. 'You can rest easy in your bed. Nobody'll get past me.'

'I don't know,' she said with a frown, 'this chap's not the sort to brazen it out and walk through the gate. He's a professional killer, a sniper really.'

He watched her go into the house and waited until the lights came on. Dusk was beginning to creep across the fields, giving the distant trees a vaporous, ghostly quality.

Sniper, the girl had said. A marksman who stalked his victim unseen and then killed with a single shot. He felt a prickle run up the back of his neck under his helmet.

'You're out of your depth here, George Brooks,' he muttered to himself, 'way out of your depth.'

Hennessy sat in the Mercedes across the road from the corner shop, watching through the window the small, bespectacled shopkeeper as he served a young man with a packet of cigarettes.

It must be nearing closing time, even for a shop of this kind which stayed open all hours to catch the evening trade. He could see the shopkeeper turning to glance at the clock on the wall behind the counter.

The young man hurried out, lit up a cigarette on the pavement with all the earnest intensity of a confirmed smoker who's been deprived for an hour, and set off down the street. No one else was about. Hennessy waited until the smoker had turned the corner and vanished.

It was time. He slid the car gently into the alleyway alongside the shop and parked it round by the back door, then walked around to the front.

The little shopkeeper was standing on a stepladder, reaching down stock from the top shelf. Hennessy closed the door behind him, dropped the latch and turned the 'Closed' sign around to face the street.

The little man clambered down. 'Can I help you? I was just about to shut.'

'Actually, I'm trying to find this address,' said Hennessy. He laid a small piece of paper on the counter. The shopkeeper bent to peer myopically at the small handwriting.

Hennessy reached out, took hold of the balding head with both hands at the base of his skull, and pulled hard with a sideways wrench. He heard the click, and then the grunt, and the shopkeeper fell silently across the counter. Hennessy gave him a push, and the body slid down out of sight.

It took only a few minutes to open the back door, switch off the lights, then drag the limp figure out to the car and bundle it into the boot.

The Mercedes purred through the darkness of the moor, its headlights picking out the verge edging the unlit winding road. Hennessy leaned back on his seat, driving with luxurious ease.

It was a beautiful car, the Mercedes he'd wanted all his life, but in his profession it had been necessary always to have anonymous cars. The girl's mother had had one. It had been heartbreaking for him to blow it up, sheer sacrilege.

And now, for the first time, he was driving one – but not for long. Desire had to be sacrificed to expediency, but his day would come. Soon now, very soon, he'd be able to retire and buy his own Mercedes. Once this job was done and he'd reported back to the Major, maybe . . .

Here was the spot he'd picked. Behind him and ahead he could see for miles, and not a light glimmered in the darkness. Nothing but moors and rocks and the steep cliff edge to the left of the road. With careful precision Hennessy accelerated, veered off course, then slammed on the brakes so as to come to an abrupt halt two feet short of the sheer drop into the valley below. On the tarmac behind him lay a long, erratic black trail of tyre-rubber.

He switched off the engine and got out. From the boot he pulled out the body of the little shopkeeper and the grip containing the bundle of his own clothes, then meticulously stripped and re-dressed the body. Bodies were always difficult, unco-operative in these circumstances. Hennessy was sweating by the time he laced up the shoes.

Breathing heavily, he placed the body carefully in the driver's seat.

235

The spectacles – they must go. Hennessy pocketed them, making a mental note to dispose of them along with the clothes later. Then, to make certain of a fitting funeral pyre for such a noble car, he loosened the petrol cap and placed the timed explosive in the glove compartment. Then he released the handbrake and pushed the car over the edge.

The place was isolated, which was why he'd chosen it. He could hear metal splintering on rocks jutting like bared teeth from the undergrowth as the car plunged headlong. The noise was deafening. Then suddenly there was an ear-splitting explosion. Hennessy peered over the edge and saw the fierce, crimson blaze illuminating the rocks below.

There was a glisten in his eyes as he turned away. Twice now in his life he had committed this heinous crime. But the next Mercedes he'd treasure till he died.

Clay Richards flew into Heathrow late that night, highly satisfied with the last three days in Zurich. Business with the bank had all been neatly tied up, as well as a promising arrangement with the voluptuous German widow who'd been staying at the same hotel. Frieda had good taste, a kind of understated sexuality which delighted him, and a charming disinterest in commitment. He stepped off the plane feeling good with the world.

Jim was waiting with the car. 'I want to call at the office on the way home,' Clay told him. The chauffeur evinced no surprise. He'd served his master for too many years.

But he did notice things. Mr Richards had been silent and uncommunicative from the airport up to town, but it had been a satisfied silence. Not like the heavy gloom surrounding him after he came out of the office at nearly midnight. He never spoke a word all the way to Chislehurst.

Jim dropped the boss off at his front door and sighed as he parked the Bentley in the huge garage alongside the Porsche. The way Mr Richards had stomped off into the house showed this was definitely not the moment to ask him about time off for his niece's wedding. He should have done it in the rosy glow just after they left the airport.

'Dead? Are you sure, Commander?'

Eva and Leah stopped talking abruptly. The tone in Nathan's voice showed shock as well as disbelief.

'Who?' asked Eva.

236

'Burned-out car? Where? . . . Tonight? . . . Are you certain it was Hennessy?'

The women held still, both watching and listening.

'Well if the body was so charred . . .' Nathan was saying. 'Oh, I see. It's a relief, I must say. Thank you for letting us know so quickly, Commander.'

'Was it him?' Leah demanded as Nathan sat down.

'No doubt about it. He hired the car this afternoon.'

Eva breathed a sigh of relief. The tension in the farmhouse kitchen eased and the flames in the hearth began to dance again. The women sat silent for a few moments, digesting the news. 'Well, George Brooks can go home now,' said Eva. 'He doesn't need to stand out there all night. I'll go and tell him.'

After she'd gone, Leah looked up. 'It doesn't end there, you know, Nathan. Clay isn't the kind of man to give up yet.'

'No,' said Nathan. 'Look, I'm going to leave you and Eva here for a bit – you'll be OK now. I won't be long.'

'Where are you going?'

He stood, blocking out the firelight with his breadth. 'To see to unfinished business. I'll be back tomorrow.'

'But why tonight, for God's sake?'

'It'll all be in the papers in the morning. It's got to be tonight.'

Leah rose to her feet. 'Don't do anything silly, Nathan, please. We need you.'

He squeezed her arm as he passed her on the way to the door. 'I'll do what has to be done.'

Clay Richards was not finding it easy to sleep. And it wasn't only that damned puppy squealing down in the kitchen. Muriel had meant well, he supposed, but nothing could take the place of Portcullis.

It was the disappearance of those papers from his office desk. Whoever had broken their way into that drawer had known what they were after. And they obviously weren't interested in them for his welfare. Who the devil could it be? The temporary night porter had been no use at all.

Few people knew about them. Fewer still knew their significance. But it was a curious coincidence that it should happen just as he was about to put the new venture into operation. Bryant should be receiving the first consignment any day now. Maybe he should contact the Major for a report on what had been happening while he'd been away – that might shed some light on the mystery.

He was halfway down the staircase, still barefoot so as not to disturb Muriel, when he recalled the Major's outburst, a year or so ago. *'Just so long as you never ask me to get involved in drugs, Richards. If there's one thing I find too despicable for words, it's peddling drugs. Wouldn't touch them with a barge-pole.'*

It couldn't have been the Major who stole the papers, surely? There'd never been any love lost between the two of them but they needed each other. And the fellow knew nothing of the drugs operation, not a breath.

Clay went into his study and switched on the lamp over the desk as he sat down. Thank heaven the blessed dog seemed to have worn itself out at last and gone to sleep. The house lay as quiet as a tomb. Clay leaned back in the leather executive chair and took a deep breath, trying to still the anxiety and ease the discomfort of his indigestion.

Gradually he became aware that his bare feet felt chilly. A breeze – he swung the chair round. The curtains were billowing gently. He stiffened and felt the hairs on his neck start to prickle.

'Who's there? Come out,' he rapped. If only he hadn't swung away from the desk he could have reached for his gun. The curtain lifted and a huge presence stood outlined against the night sky.

'Who the hell are you?' demanded Clay. The giant stepped inside and let the curtain fall behind him. By the lamplight Clay could see him now, a young, well-muscled fellow with black hair and piercing eyes. He stood immobile, watching Clay with a kind of resolution which Clay recognized. 'Well?' he snapped. 'What do you want here? Who are you?'

His voice came low and clear. 'Hennessy.'

Clay felt his heart turn over. Hennessy – the killer without a conscience. Wait a minute – the Major . . . 'What are you doing here? You've no business coming here.'

'I came to report.'

'You're supposed to report to the Major, you fool, not me.'

'I can't. He's dead. He's shot himself. So I have to report to you.'

Clay felt his blood run cold. The Major dead . . . Uneasiness stirred in him again. Things were going badly wrong. He must stay cool, get rid of the fellow . . . 'What have you got to report?'

'They're dead, all three of them.'

The Finch family. Clay raised incredulous eyes. 'All three? You sure?'

The huge figure stood, arms at his side, totally relaxed. 'I cut the petrol pipe. The car crashed in the fast lane of the M1. It burst into flames. They hadn't a chance. They were all dead before the ambulance got there.'

Clay leaned back in his chair. 'Thank God for that,' he muttered. 'You're a man after my own heart. Come and sit down, have a drink.'

The girl and her mother disposed of, and that stepbrother – Clay was beginning to feel better in spite of the stolen papers. He opened the drinks cabinet.

'Whisky? Dash of soda with it?'

The big man hadn't shifted. Still he stood by the open window, dark eyes watching his every move. Clay filled two glasses and took a sip from his own. He was beginning to feel almost genial.

He held out a glass. 'What are you planning to do next, Hennessy?'

'I've got one other commission to carry out.' He made no attempt to take the glass. Clay looked up at him, curious.

'Another? Who is it?'

The young man's tone of voice didn't change as he answered. 'You.'

In his office at Scotland Yard the Commander yawned and reached for the whisky bottle in the drawer of his desk. Without warning the door opened and he shoved it hastily back again. Lambert came in from the ops room.

'Just had a call from the surveillance car down in Chislehurst, sir. Fellow just gone into Richards' house through the french window.'

The Commander looked up sharply. 'At this hour of the night? Anyone we know?'

'No, sir. This fellow's different, big as a barn door, they say.'

The Commander started up from his chair. 'Christ! Nathan Bower! I hope to God – look, tell them to forget orders, go in there and get him out. If he hasn't harmed anybody, treat him with respect, but get him out.'

Clay felt the sweat burst out of his palms and the whisky slopped over out of the glass. 'God Almighty,' he said with an attempt at a laugh. 'You frightened the shit out of me for a moment – I almost believed you.'

239

'No joke, Richards – you're the hit.'

'But who? And why?'

The stranger only stood looking at him in silence. Clay's mind was racing. Who could possibly have hired Hennessy? The same person who stole the papers? No, it didn't make sense. He tried to keep his voice level as he set down the glasses on the desk.

'Look, whoever it is, I'll pay you double. Work for me, I'll give you whatever you want. I'll make it well worth your while.'

The young man took a deep breath. 'Money isn't the important thing, Mr Richards,' he said quietly. 'It's a matter of professional pride – but then, you wouldn't know anything about that, would you?'

He stood there, towering above Richards, his great physique making Clay feel diminutive. He stood between Clay and his gun, leaving him helpless. The fellow could break his neck with one twist of those huge hands. His eyes, his stance – everything about him radiated venom and contempt. Clay stared, impotent, fear curdling his blood.

'Look here,' he said wildly, 'I'm a rich man. I've spent a lifetime getting money together – just tell me what you want – anything – and I'll see you get it.'

'No.'

'My wife – she needs me – she's helpless without me! And others are dependent on me too – my family, my employees . . .'

The voice came sombre out of the gloom. 'It's too late, Richards.'

Clay could feel the bullet already, burning into his heart. Or the cold slither of a knife between his ribs. He flung himself on the chair, burying his face in the leather so he wouldn't see . . .

A sudden sound cut through the silence, footsteps crunching outside, and then the curtains parted. Two uniformed police officers stood framed in the french window.

'Is everything all right, Mr Richards? We saw the open window . . .'

Clay felt a leap of relieved delight. He sprang up from the chair. 'Oh, thank God! Officer, this man was trying to kill me!'

The officer's eyebrows rose. 'Really? Is this true, sir?'

He looked at Nathan, who shook his head.

'It is!' cried Clay. 'He's a professional killer – he's already killed three people! His name's Hennessy.'

The second officer shook his head. 'I don't think so, sir. If I'm not mistaken this is Nathan Bower. Isn't that so, sir?'

The intruder's eyes never left Clay as he nodded. Nathan Bower –

Eva Finch's stepbrother – oh, my god, what had he said to the fellow? And if he'd been lying, were the girl and her mother really dead or not? Clay felt dizzy. The first police officer cleared his throat.

'Would you like to file a complaint, Mr Richards?'

Clay shook his head miserably. The officer turned to Bower. 'If you're ready to leave, Mr Bower, we'd like to have a little talk with you.'

Clay slumped into the chair at his desk as the three men made for the french window again. In the doorway one of the police officers turned.

'By the way, I don't know whether there's any connection, sir, but there was a Mr Hennessy found dead in a burnt-out car earlier tonight. Looks like he'd blown himself up. A man with a rather nasty reputation, we understand.'

Clay buried his face in his outstretched arms. In the kitchen the puppy began crying miserably again.

CHAPTER TWENTY-THREE

Hennessy found the Public Library without difficulty. He knew it was a pretty sure bet in a northern industrial town to be a large building in the town centre, second in size only to the Town Hall.

He scoured every one of the newspapers, but he found nothing more about the body in the car, even in the small columns. So far, it seemed, he was safe.

But it was still early days and it would be foolish to assume too much. Soon, with luck, he could go and settle in Norfolk, but not yet. The locals there knew him as a recently retired stockbroker's clerk who'd bought the cottage by the lake and that he spent frequent weekends there.

And when he did settle they'd keep a respectful distance, leaving him alone in a corner of the village pub to drink his half-pint in peace. They had more interesting things to do than listen to the insignificant little Fred Killingley who only ever talked about birds and chrysanthemums. Killingley – the pseudonym had appealed to his sense of humour.

But before he could go, there was one job outstanding. It would be his swansong, and he wanted to quit with a hundred per cent record. He didn't have to do it; no one was paying him any more; now it was simply a matter of pride.

Eva walked briskly into her office in Urchin and slapped her briefcase down on the desk. It was good to be back to normality after the nightmare of the past weeks.

She lifted her nose and sniffed. Stale tobacco – that could only mean Vincent Galbraith had been in, and that he'd begun smoking again. Trouble? Whatever it was, she could face it now. She took the letter out of her briefcase and read it once more, just for the reassurance of it.

'Dear Mrs Finch, Following the recent biopsy examination of your left

breast . . .' Her eye travelled on to the next paragraph. '*We are now able to inform you that there is no evidence of any serious disease . . .*'

Relief surged in her. She'd put it all out of her mind out in Dubai, but to find the problem gone . . . She could face anything now. She rang through for Vincent to come in.

'Any news I ought to know about? Anything urgent?'

'Nothing desperate,' said the Scotsman in his dour, laconic way. 'No more news about Calico. Mr Richards seems to have gone to earth somewhere.'

Eva smiled grimly. This was no time to start telling her chief accountant about the depths of Richards' depravity. 'It doesn't matter, Vincent. Whoever is landlord, I won't let him affect the way I run Calico whatever he does. It's mine.'

Within half an hour Alan rang. 'I'm glad you're back – I'd like to see you.'

'I'm only here to sort out a couple of things. I'm off back to Barnbeck tomorrow. Leah's on her own now except for Sandra, and she's no company – she's moody because Nathan's gone again. Anyway Leah's anxious to see what we can do about Thorpe Gill. She's determined to have it.'

'Then let's talk about it. How about dinner tonight?'

'I'd love to.'

'My place?'

No, just you and me, she thought. No ghosts of Christie. 'Make it mine. You bring the steaks.'

She felt light-hearted. Alan, wine, firelight, closeness – just like the old days. If only it could last forever. It was time for peace, for stability . . .

'By the way,' Alan added, 'the papers from Richards' desk – the Commander says the Fraud Squad are very interested.'

'Good. We didn't waste our time then.'

'He's still digging for that vital piece of information he needs to pin something big on him.'

'I wish I knew where the hell to look – we'd get it for him, Leah and me.'

She heard his soft chuckle. 'You're fantastic, know that, Eva?'

'What the hell are you talking about?'

There was a gentle tenderness in his voice which delighted her. 'It's the hardest thing in the world to let your children go. I'm proud of you, love. See you at eight.'

'Alan –' She paused, uncertain how to say it, then added quietly, 'Bring your toothbrush.'

Muriel Richards tapped timidly at the door of her own library. In her other arm she clutched the puppy, its wet nose reaching up to her face in gratitude. She held it as a kind of barrier between herself and the possible onslaught of words.

'What is it?' she heard her husband say. She opened the door, just a few inches.

'Can't I get you something to eat, dear? You've hardly eaten a thing in the last week.'

His voice came low and unusually quietly from where he sat in the corner of the leather chesterfield. 'No.'

Encouraged, she went on, 'It isn't healthy, you know, Clay, staying in here all this time. Six days now. And you aren't washing and shaving properly.'

'Go away.'

'At least let me bring you some fresh clothes –'

'The newspaper – just bring me the evening paper. Then leave me alone.' He reached forward and snapped on the television.

'I'll go and see if it's come.' With a sigh Muriel put the puppy down and went on to the hallway. He wasn't making 'phone calls either these days. It was so unnatural, so unlike him. She could almost wish he'd start being his old sarcastic self – at least she would feel life was something like normal again.

The paper wasn't on the mat. She was reluctant to tell him, but when she did peep round the door of the library she smiled. The television was still on but Clay had fallen fast asleep, his head lolling back against the leather and, by his side, its nose buried under his sleeve, the puppy was sleeping too.

Muriel crept across the carpet, lowered the volume gradually on the television until it was silent, then switched it off. He did not move, thank heaven.

Clay awoke feeling refreshed and alert. The library clock showed five to eleven. The evening paper lay neatly folded beside him, and under it a small damp patch was spreading. He picked up the paper and read.

Nothing. He was beginning to feel he could breathe again. All this time now and nothing had been said to expose him. The Major and Hennessy were dead, but if the Finch women were going to harm him surely someone would have come knocking at the door?

Silence augured well. Clay stood up and stretched his arms above his head. It was time to stop skulking like an animal too frightened to come out of his lair. Time to make discreet enquiries about what was happening in Dubai. Cresco – I grow. Time to eat, to recharge the batteries.

'Muriel!' He crossed to the door and wrenched it open. 'Muriel! Where the devil are you?'

A fine September morning lay mistily over Barnbeck as Leah and Eva pushed open the rusting wrought-iron gates of Thorpe Gill and walked the length of the grass-grown drive towards the old house. Broken windows watched their approach with the vacant stare of a blind man.

Leah stood at the top of the flight of steps leading up to the front door, screening her eyes against the morning sun with one hand.

'I can't see Scapegoat from here – those trees are in the way – but it'll be nice to know it's there, and Nathan too.'

Eva turned to look across the lake. 'Isn't it lovely?' she breathed. 'But terribly overgrown and neglected.'

'I know there's a lot of work, but I've got plans for that lake – make a feature of it, boats and lighting – just imagine this façade floodlit. And people can ride from Nathan's stables. I want to make all my guests feel as if they're living a gracious life of luxury, like a country squire in the old days.'

'The way the Westerley-Kents used to in their heyday?'

'I don't really remember them, it was so long ago. I want to make Thorpe Gill the perfect hotel, a place people want to come back to again and again. I've learnt a lot from Renzo, but thinking about it I've realized there's a hell of a lot of questions I'd still like to ask him.'

'Then list them and ring him up. Nothing simpler,' said Eva.

'I'm going to. I've got the list ready.'

Eva laughed. 'I should have known. Come on, let's see if we can climb in the window. We'll see what state the place is in.'

Leah climbed in a ground floor window and sat on the sill. 'What about you, Mother? You and Daddy?'

'How do you mean?'

'Don't play naïve with me. Daddy rang – he told me about the other night. Any chance you and he might get back together?'

Eva nudged a stone with her toe. 'Maybe. Wait and see.'

Leah smiled as she stepped off the sill into the shadowy room. She stared around her as Eva scrambled in.

'Heavens, just look at that fireplace,' she exclaimed. 'Fantastic!'

'Hell!' said Eva.

'What's up?'

'My jeans – caught them on a bit of broken glass. Sorry, Leah. They're yours again.'

Nathan let himself into Eva's flat and picked up the newspaper lying on the mat. In the living room he could hear the hum of a vacuum cleaner and a shrill voice singing.

'Spring cleaning?' asked Nathan as he wandered through and then he stopped in amazement. Chairs were piled on the velvet settees, all the chinoiserie was gone, and the crystal chandelier lay on the floor.

Rosary straightened up, rubbing her aching back. 'Ye should have seen the state of this place yesterday,' she said philosophically. 'Like a tribe of monkeys had been let loose.'

She bustled out to the kitchen and he could hear her shifting plants out of the sink. 'Come on now, little fellow, ye can have another drink in a moment,' she soothed. He smiled and, pushing aside a heap of cushions, he sat down on a stool next to the supine chandelier. Then he shook out the newspaper and turned to the front page.

Suddenly he sat bolt upright. The headline screamed out at him.

Missing Shopkeeper Found Murdered

Swiftly he scanned the story. A body found last week in a burnt-out car had now been identified by the dentures as that of a missing shopkeeper and not that of the man they had previously believed. Nathan's breath caught in his throat. God, Hennessy was still alive – and the women were alone at Scapegoat!

Flinging the paper aside he ran from the room.

Hennessy was breathing heavily by the time he reached the crest of the hill. In this exposed terrain it would have drawn attention to drive any closer, and it had been a long walk across the moor.

Below him a valley spread along the bank of a river and a cluster of cottages circled an old grey church; that must be Barnbeck, the village

246

on his map, and that farm halfway down the slope must be Scapegoat.
A thin plume of smoke spiralled from the chimney – they were there.

There was only one tree on the hillside, a thick-bodied oak about a
hundred yards from the farm. That was all he needed. He fingered his
gun lovingly and gave a deep sigh of satisfaction. Not long now . . .

In the kitchen of the farm Sandra had just finished washing and drying
the dishes from lunch. She stood in the kitchen doorway, wiping her
hands down her wide hips and watching Eva who was frowning as she
threaded a needle.

'Is there owt else you want me to do before I go?'

'No, thanks, Sandra. Will you be back to do dinner tonight?'

'Aye – how many for?'

'Just Leah and me – Nathan won't be back yet a while.'

The girl's face fell. 'Oh. Well, I don't know how much longer I can
keep coming, only me dad needs me. It was all right when it was a
man who needed seeing to, them not being able to cook for themselves,
like!'

Eva looked up from her sewing. 'It's OK, Sandra. If you want to
pack it in –'

The girl looked surprised. 'I thought you'd be mad at me.'

'Why should I? You've been invaluable to Nathan and to old George,
and I know they're grateful to you.'

Sandra shifted awkwardly from one foot to the other. 'Could I have
me money then? Only Nathan kept forgetting . . .'

Down in the stables Leah was saddling up the half-schooled filly. The
horse was restive, pawing the ground and snorting when she touched
her, but Leah persevered gently.

'Come on, girl, you need exercise. You haven't been on the moor
for days. Come on, my lovely, I won't harm you.'

Gradually her soothing words calmed the filly. Leah was humming
to herself as she tightened the girth . . .

Crouched behind the old oak tree Hennessy waited and watched.
Patience was finally rewarded when he saw the door open and a woman's
figure emerge. Blonde – it was the daughter. He took careful aim, and
fired.

She sank to the cobblestones without a sound. Hennessy kept the gun pointed. The mother should come running now if she was there. One more shot . . .

Eva heard the door closing behind Sandra as she took the pair of jeans upstairs. She had just reached the top step when the crack rang out, and she stiffened. It was not the sound of a farmer shooting rabbits. This one meant business. Dropping the jeans she ran to her bedroom window, overlooking the yard.

Her hand flew to her lips and she gasped. A blonde figure lay huddled on the cobblestones – Sandra! She saw the figure move, the arms twitch, and the girl struggled to rise.

Eva was turning, about to run down to her, when a movement caught her eye. Up there, on the moor, a man's figure detached itself from the shadow of the oak, and he held a gun. He was moving down the hill towards the farm. Leah was out there somewhere, maybe riding up on the moor, but she too would have been alerted by the sound.

A gun. Somewhere downstairs was Nathan's double-barrelled shotgun. Eva ran headlong down the stairs.

For a second Leah was mesmerized by the sound of the gunshot and the filly reared. Leah held fast to the reins till she quietened, then turned to look out.

Through the open door she could see Sandra lying slumped on the ground. What the devil had happened? She let go of the horse. Sandra was struggling to get up and Leah could see a splash of crimson on her chest.

She was about to run out when another shot shattered the quiet peace of the sunlit farmyard, and Leah drew back.

Sandra fell again into an untidy, crumpled heap, and this time she lay still. Leah froze. Whoever it was out there, he meant business. And Mother was alone in the farmhouse.

Her first instincts were to run to Sandra though it was clearly too late, and then to run back into the farm. But whoever he was, he could be waiting for just that . . .

As she hesitated in the shadow of the doorway she heard footsteps approaching, the steps of a man on the cobblestones. And then she saw him, small and balding with a gun in his hand.

Turning back to the filly she murmured words in her ear. 'Come on now, none of your nonsense, I need you.' The filly made no objection as she mounted silently and eased the horse across towards the door, the sound of its hooves deadened by the hay.

He came close and, bending over Sandra's body, he rolled it over. Leah heard him mutter.

'Shit!'

As he looked up she saw the thin, cruel, pock-marked face, and dug her heels into the horse's flanks. The filly reared, and charged . . .

Eva was panting as she tore open the door of the cupboard. The shotgun was there – and cartridges. She broke the gun open and loaded both barrels. Rushing to the door she yanked it open and raised the gun, ready to take aim.

And then she lowered it again, staring in horror. In the stable doorway she could see Leah, mounted, and she was crouching in the saddle as the horse charged out, bearing straight down on the gunman.

He lifted the gun. Eva saw the barrel levelled at her daughter, and she let fly. The force of the recoil made the shotgun jerk upwards in her hands, and she swore. The man staggered backwards with the blast but was unhurt, just as Leah reached him. The horse's shoulder caught him mid-chest and he fell.

The impetus of the charge carried Leah to the far side of the farmyard. Eva saw her turn, ready to race back. The man was rolling over, reaching for his fallen gun and Eva knew it was for Leah. Oblivious, Leah was crouching in the saddle, ready to charge again.

'No!' screamed Eva, and ran at the man with shotgun upraised. Six feet from him she heard the sound of her own shot, saw the fear in his pale eyes before his face suddenly seemed to collapse into a mass of raw flesh. Without a sound he fell backwards, blood spurting from his head and chest.

Leah dismounted and led the horse across. Overwhelmed, the two women stared down in silence at the lifeless body.

'It must be Hennessy,' said Leah at last. 'Poor Sandra.'

'I missed first shot,' murmured Eva.

Leah put her arm around her shoulder. 'But not the second time. You go and 'phone the police. I'll get something to cover them with.'

Eva looked up at her. 'Are you sure?'

'Yes. Go on.'

Leah watched her mother walk slowly to the house, then led the filly into the stable. She took a horse blanket from the peg and went out to kneel by Sandra's body. For a moment she held the girl's hand, feeling the callouses of hard work on her palms.

A life hardly begun. Tears pricked Leah's eyes. She covered Sandra's body gently with the blanket, then walked into the house without looking back at Hennessy. A solitary rook swooped down and perched on the guttering of the stable roof to keep vigil on the uncovered corpse.

Clay Richards beamed. 'Right, thanks, Hilary. You seem to have handled things very well. You can go now.'

The secretary looked surprised, but took her opportunity and left. Clay got up from his desk and crossed to the window.

He was feeling quite perky today, quite his old self again. From here he could see his reflection in the ornate gilt mirror on the far wall – the image of a successful man, bright-eyed and confident, with a taut body and a spring in his step.

And why not? News had arrived that the first consignment had reached Bryant in Dubai safely, so the first stage of the new venture had been safely tested and found watertight. If the rest of the chain worked as smoothly . . .

He could almost hug himself in delight. It wasn't that he needed the money – he could make that hand-over-fist with his legitimate business: it was the excitement he revelled in, the thrill of flouting the law. Laws were only made for ordinary men.

And of the other business, not a word. After so long now it was unlikely there would be any kickback. He stood looking out over the city roofs, beaming. He could afford to smile. In fact, there was little he could not afford now.

Looking out over the same expanse of city roofline only a mile away Ernest Laverick stood at his office window. Inwardly he was regretting having to exchange the heat of lazy Provençal sunshine for a misty autumn in London, but after a month away the office was in need of his attention.

He turned to his secretary who was sitting waiting, straight-backed with pad in hand. 'Right, Miss Forshaw, what've we got? Mrs Laycock's divorce settled?'

'All but the absolute,' Miss Forshaw replied. 'She wants us to apply for it as soon as possible.'

'Have you seen to it?'

'Yes. And Mr Downes wants another letter sent – it's that dog again.'

'Oh, Christ!' Laverick sighed. 'Still, it's the Mr Downeses of this world who keep me in business. Anything else?'

Miss Forshaw consulted her notepad. 'Oh yes, the Major's dead. Shot himself, apparently. Can't think why – he can't have been short of cash, surely.'

The solicitor sighed. 'Who knows why people do things. It's something I stopped speculating over years ago.' After a moment's thought he added, 'Hang on, I've got some papers of his somewhere.'

'To be opened only after his death,' said Miss Forshaw, rising from her chair. 'They're in the filing cabinet. I'll get them for you.'

'No, I'll do it. Fetch me some coffee while I look.'

The moment she'd gone in a flurry of black barathea and leaving a whisper of Chanel No. 5, Laverick opened one of the oak filing cabinets against the wall and began flicking through the folders. He could recall clearly the Major ordering that the envelope should only be opened after his death.

A will, of course, thought Laverick, possibly naming himself as executor. And the Major was a gentleman of the old school – not many of his kind left nowadays – and he would certainly remember that it was customary to leave some kind of consideration for the executor's time and trouble. It could be more remunerative than Mr Downes' perpetual letters.

Ah, here it was. Laverick carried the sealed envelope across to his desk and sat down. It was rather bulky for a will. Taking up a tortoiseshell paperknife he slit the envelope open with all the solemnity due to the recently deceased. Unfolding the sheets of paper he began to read.

After a page his eyes were bulging. 'My God,' he muttered, and turned swiftly to the next sheet, scarcely able to believe what he was reading. Rycroft, the Shadow Chancellor? Seldon, the bishop? And tycoons and businessmen he'd only ever read about in *The Times*.

And Clay Richards, head of Cresco – why, he'd met the man once himself – a beaming, genial fellow opening that home for the elderly last year down in Sidcup. Where did the catalogue end?

Laverick read and re-read the closely-typed pages, savouring every word and feeling a mounting sense of excitement. Murders, extortion, assassination – the Major involved in all this? He'd talked to the

251

courteous softly-spoken man himself – he sat across from him at this very desk.

Still, he'd always thought there was something strange about the Major. But whatever else he was, the man had been thorough; his instructions were not only to contact Scotland Yard but he'd also given the name of the Commander and the telephone number.

When he had laid aside the final sheet Laverick lifted the telephone with a trembling hand.

CHAPTER TWENTY-FOUR

Alan was still sleeping when Eva awoke. She stretched her arms lazily and smiled at the tousled head beside her on the pillow, recalling the wonderful, intoxicating events of the night. She felt fulfilled and supremely happy.

One memory of the night stood out crystal-clear, those long fingers caressing her left breast while his mouth nuzzled her ear.

'Such beautiful breasts, my darling, just like a young girl's.'

He hadn't noticed the tiny scar. He need never know – no one would. Eva slid quietly out of bed and he did not move. She was reaching for her robe when the bedroom door opened. Rosary stood there, cup and saucer in hand.

'Are ye ready for your tea now, Mrs –'

Her pale eyes moved quickly from Eva's naked body to the man's head half-buried in the pillow and Eva saw her thin frame stiffen. 'Mother of God,' she muttered. Eva pulled on her robe.

'It's all right, Rosary. It's Mr Finch.'

The pale eyes glowed suddenly and Rosary moved forward to the bed, the tea slopping over into the saucer. 'Mr Finch! May the holy saints be praised! I never thought to see the day. Mr Finch, would ye like a cup of tea?'

Alan rolled over and struggled to sit up, rubbing his eyes with clenched fists. Rosary thrust the cup into his hand and began pulling the pillows from under him, punching and rearranging them behind his back. Alan muttered thanks.

'Away with ye – no need for thanks,' rattled Rosary, beaming fondly at him. 'Will ye be eating breakfast with us, Mr Finch? A nice kipper, maybe, or a poached egg?'

Alan gave her a bleary-eyed smile and glanced across at Eva. 'No thanks, Rosary. Tea's all I need.'

And sleep, thought Eva. He had precious little last night. 'We'll have kippers, Rosary,' she said firmly, 'and eggs. I'm as hungry as a hunter. And from today Mr Finch and I will be taking breakfast regularly.'

Rosary was still beaming as she made her way to the door. Eva cleared her throat.

'Rosary?'

The housekeeper turned. 'Yes, Mrs Finch?'

'Could I have a cup of tea too?'

But when Rosary came back she found the bedroom door firmly locked. She shrugged. 'So what harm?' she murmured as she carried the tray back to the kitchen. 'Me kippers'll not spoil for keeping hot a while longer.'

All was well with the world once more. Above the rattle of the coffee-grinder her thin, clear voice rose in a joyful rendering of a folksong learnt long ago.

> '*He moved away from me as we moved through the fair*
> *And fondly I watched him move here and move there*
> *Then he laid his hand on me, and this he did say,*
> *It will not be long, love, till our wedding day.*'

From the train window Nathan watched the landscape roll by, feeling a sense of excitement mounting as verdant fields began to give way to the bleaker scenery of Yorkshire and home. It was good to be going back.

The train pulled in at last at Barnbeck's little station. The guard tipped his cap as he took Nathan's ticket. 'Nice to see you home, lad. Just in time for Gooseberry Fair and the tug o' war. Don't know how we'd have gone on without you.'

'I'll be there, Jim, don't you fret.'

He climbed the lane uphill with long, eager strides. He couldn't wait to see Scapegoat, nestling in the hollow in the hillside, brooding and still, with a kind of dogged patience just as it had done for centuries. Down there in the meadows lay Thorpe Gill, beautiful and serene, but Scapegoat had something special; it was his heritage.

And Leah's too. Lovely, adventurous Leah. She'd grown and changed over these last months, but she was still the idol of his dreams. Leah at his side in Scapegoat – what more could any man wish? But at least she would be close by, fulfilling her own dream . . .

He reached the gate of the farm and, pausing for a moment before going in, rested a hand on its familiar rough wood. And then suddenly, as if the thought of her had somehow conjured her up out of his imaginings, he caught sight of her, high on the moor.

She was riding his filly, her long hair streaming out behind her in the wind, unaware that he was watching. He smiled. She belonged to this place every bit as much as he, and somehow he had the feeling that this time she would stay. He was content.